CW00552679

ISBN: 9781731038012

Imprint: Independently published

BLACK MATTER

PARKER

1

The medical centre made Tommy feel anxious, fearful, yet excited. These emotions flowed through his veins at the idea of a new generation medical implant designed to increase the wellbeing of mankind. The reception area of the medical centre was pure white with shiny white floor tiles and white leather sofas, and a sweet perfume filled the air. He walked precariously towards a large white reception desk, becoming increasingly nervous, but he was then greeted by a calming, beautiful woman with long dark hair, piercing green eyes and a smile that almost left him speechless – he almost forgot for a moment why he was there.

'H, hi, I'm here for my IPEA procedure,' he said with a stutter, mesmerised by her beauty.

'No problem, sir. Please confirm your name and date of birth?' Her voice was soft and clear with precise pronunciation.

'Tommy McGregor, tenth of November nineteen eighty-eight'.

'Thank you, Mr McGregor. Please take a seat.' Using her hand, she gestured him towards the waiting area.

'Thank you, err...' He looked at her name tag on her prominent chest. 'Katrina,' he said, feeling almost proud of himself, expressed by a slight smile from the corner of his mouth.
Tommy turned and sat himself on a white leather sofa that squeaked as he sat, then glanced around the area. The place was huge, and the ceiling must have been at least twenty feet high, which echoed voices and shone bright interchanging coloured LED lighting, which filled the large open space. There was a TV screen hung on the wall, which played an advert he recognised for the IPEA.

I.P.E.A
Intra-body Profiling Examination Application
The IPEA was developed by a professor called Tammy Bezuidenhout from Germany. She created a microscopic implant that attaches itself to the central nervous system. A neurological smart injection directly into the brain collects data from every single cell in the body and transfers this information back to the implant. It then communicates this data to an Android or Apple OS via Bluetooth technology. This information is analysed by the application and provides the user with anything they need to know about their body – A breakthrough in medical science.
Authorised by –
Medicines and Healthcare Products Regulatory Agency

After a short wait, Tommy heard his name being called; 'Tommy McGregor, please?'
He looked round and saw a tall man, about twenty-five years old, who he assumed was a doctor, standing holding a clipboard - he looked very formal.
'Yeah, that's me,' he announced, holding up his hand like a twelve-year-old in school. He then stood to greet the man.
'Nice to meet you. Please Mr McGregor, follow me,' said the man, ushering Tommy towards a large and endless corridor.
Footsteps echoed from the doctor's shoes hitting the white floor tiles. There were a series of doors which led to the

unknown. Tommy's anxiety came back, causing questions to run through his mind - *What if something goes wrong? What if it damages my brain? What if I have an allergic reaction?*

After a minute of walking, the doctor stopped at a door. The sign displayed 'X19', which didn't mean anything to Tommy, but he proceeded to follow the doctor into the room.

The room was large; the back wall had black glass from floor to ceiling and the wall to the left was full of computer equipment, like something you'd see at the bridge of the *Enterprise*. In the centre of the room was a large white chair, like the type you would find in a dentist's surgery, with a large device above it integrated into the ceiling, which looked very precarious.

'Please, Mr McGregor, take a seat and make yourself comfortable. You're going to be here a while.'

Tommy simply nodded and sat down in the chair. He looked up at the contraption that was embedded into the ceiling, wondering what on earth it was. It looked like a network of cameras or something, and God knows what else. Still feeling anxious, he turned to speak to the doctor.

'What's that?' he asked, pointing with his finger trembling.

'I'm not a doctor, Mr McGregor. I'm a medical technologist. My job is to ensure this procedure goes smoothly and to abolish any problems that might occur. You have been made aware of the risks, haven't you, sir?'

'Well, yeah sort of, but I'm not worried about them!' his voice wobbled again – he was clearly nervous.

'It's important that you understand the risks and side effects of the ECoG binding compound.'

'I know, I know,' sweat beaded on his forehead.

'Look, Mr McGregor, if your body rejects this binding compound, it can affect your central nervous system, which can cause blindness, loss of hearing and smell, and can obstruct your ability to walk or manoeuvre properly, all of which are irreversible. However, studies have shown the odds of rejection are one in sixty-seven million so there's more chance of winning the lottery than your body rejecting the compound, but it's still very important you are aware of the risks before signing the wavier.'

He then handed him a leaflet containing all the information. Tommy skimmed through quickly and then returned it.

'Yeah, it's all good. I'm happy to proceed,' he said with a non-convincing smile.

'Ok, well empty your pockets, remove any electrical items you may have, and the surgeon will be in shortly to answer any further questions.'

'Great, how long will this take?' Tommy asked, thinking, *he could have asked me to empty my pockets before I sat down.*

'It takes 48 hours all in all. You will be asleep in an induced coma for nearly all of it, as we need the brain and all other organs functioning at the lowest possible level. It's a bit like restarting a computer after an upgrade of software.'

He looked at Tommy with frustration, 'IF, Mr McGregor, you had read all the information, you would know'. Tommy returned an ignorant smile.

There was about a ten-minute wait before the surgeon walked in. He was tall, grey and very skinny, and he was wearing a long white coat – his shoes were shiny to military standard.

'Mr McGregor, welcome to our facility. My name is Dr Bowen. I'll be by your side along with my technician, Mr Ellis.' His voice was deep, and he was very well-spoken.

'Dr Bowen, one question; will this hurt?' Tommy asked, with a gaze like a rabbit in headlights. 'I'm not a- wimp or anything, I'm just wondering,' Tommy then shrugged his shoulders to hide his concerns.

Dr Bowen smiled, 'We get asked that a lot, Mr McGregor. I'd be lying if I said there'd be no discomfort, but you shouldn't

6

experience any considerable amount of pain. The most you'd experience is a headache and a slight soreness around the new implant - all being well.'

Dr Bowen handed Tommy a clipboard. It contained a twelve-page document explaining all the ins and outs of the procedure, which Tommy needed to confirm that he accepted the risks and side effects. Dr Bowen was then required to examine Tommy and to complete a review of Tommy's medical records, to ensure he was of sound mind before proceeding with the procedure. After forty-five minutes, Dr Bowen was ready to begin.

'Ok Tommy, I would like you to take this robe, go behind the screen over there and return with nothing on but the robe.'

The robe was a classic standard green medical robe with the print *"IPEA tm X19"* displayed on the back in bold black letters. It smelled medical with a strong smell of Dettol.

Tommy went behind the screen, stripped down to his birthday suit and couldn't help noticing that his little man had shrivelled to the size of a peanut. *Must be the fear*, he thought to himself, whilst placing the robe over his head and tying it off at the back.

He then walked back to the chair. The floor felt cold beneath his bare feet. *All this bloody money and they can't even provide slippers.*

'Please, Mr McGregor, sit and relax. Our technical nurse will be along shortly to put an IV drip in your arm, hook you up to this little machine here,' the surgeon tapped it with his long bony fingers, 'so we can keep an eye on what's going on inside you.'

Tommy didn't say anything, he just sat right back in the chair, shook off his arms and took a nice deep breath. Dr Bowen then reclined the chair back so that Tommy was now completely horizontal. Tommy closed his eyes, trying to relax. Mixed emotions flowed through him; nerves, excitement, apprehension – he'd never been under before.

The door opened and in walked the technical nurse, dressed in a long white coat, flat shoes, with her blonde hair tied back and, like the receptionist, she had a massive smile on her face with a beautiful set of teeth. *It was like they only recruited a certain type of woman - hot!*

'Mr McGregor, my name is Billie. I need you to lift up your robe, so I can put in this catheter. Is that ok?' She was holding up a thin plastic tube in a gloved hand.

Tommy nodded and closed his eyes. Lifting up his robe, he felt an uncomfortable burning sensation for a few moments and a strong urge to pee.

'All done, sir! Now, I need to place this on your finger and these pads on your head.'

Tommy felt extremely anxious at this stage, wondering what was to come?

Billie gently put a line into Tommy's arm. It was just a scratch, but Tommy hated needles and felt a little -queasy for a moment. He was quickly distracted by her smile; she smelled so good, and her skin was fresh and clear. He couldn't help but fancy her, even though he had a girlfriend, Taylor, at home, who had no idea where he was.

Dr Bowen then caught Tommy's attention as he started to explain the procedure.

'So, Tommy, we need to put you into a deep state of unconsciousness by using a barbiturate drug, which will put you into a temporary barb coma. This is to protect your brain whilst we administer the ECoG compound.' He smiled at Tommy, 'Relax, we've done this a thousand times.'

Tommy gave a nervous grin, and Dr Bowen proceeded to administer anaesthesia whilst telling Tommy to count to ten.

'One, two, three...' Tommy's eyes felt heavy and they slowly closed. He tried to fight it, tried to keep his eyes open, they were too heavy, then moments later he was in total anaesthesia.

As he slowly regained a form of consciousness from the induced coma, he experienced a moment of panic. He could only hear but was unable to move. His instant thought was that he would be trapped in his sub-conscious mind for eternity. He could hear voices around him talking but the words were all muffled. He could feel the temperature of the room and the sweat that had accumulated in the small of his back as he lay in the medical bed. He felt uncomfortable, as there was a need to scratch an irritating itch, that tormented him for what felt like hours with no ability to relieve the torment. He felt compelled to shout out for someone, to remind them he was there, so they could reassure him that everything was ok. But, no muscle would even twitch, apart from his heart, that pounded like a prisoner on the door to their cell. His breathing was slow and controlled, and he could hear the air whistling through the tubes that were working as a conduit from his lungs to the outside world.

Why? he thought to himself, *why did I do this? I knew the risks involved, and I still went through with it. What a waste. Taylor is going to go insane! If this is my life, I hope it ends sooner rather than later.*

The negativity of his thoughts snowballed. This increased his heart rate, which he could simultaneously hear with the beeping and pulsing on a machine that was nearby. He could cry with no tears or any sign of physical emotion. On the inside he was screaming with fear.

There was a lot of muffled talking, then a sudden sharp pain that provided a sense of coldness, which quickly spread up his left arm and around his shoulder. There was a slight twitch in his fingers and his toes, and he could then move his jaw, which ached like he'd just done ten rounds with David Haye. He was able to open his eyes. His vision began to come back with a blur, as though there was glue spread across his eyeballs. He was able to rub them, which created images of a well-dressed doctor looking over him.

'He's coming round; keep the oxygen going. There we go, Mr McGregor. How are you feeling?'

Dr Bowen's voice was almost robotic; clear with perfect pronunciation.

'Like shit, excuse my French,' said Tommy. His voice was husky, his mouth was bone dry, and he gasped for water.

'Well, that's expected, Mr McGregor. You've been in a coma for two days.'

He stood up straight and folded his arms with a comforting smile on his face.

'The procedure went exceptionally well, although your blood pressure dropped significantly, so we'll need to keep you in for a few days just to make sure.'

'Well, it didn't go exceptionally well then! I've got to go home! What day is it?' Tommy became agitated.

Dr Bowen was taken aback with the attitude he was receiving from Tommy.

'It's Monday the eighth of January two thousand and eighteen, Mr McGregor. We would like to keep you in under observation - you've had an IPEA implantation along with a neurological smart injection. This can have an impact on your central nervous system. It's extremely important we monitor you for a few days.'

His voice was stern. Dr Bowen made it clear that Tommy was going nowhere.

'I understand that! The four-hour interrogation made sure I was aware of everything to be expected prior to the procedure, but I've got to go. My girlfriend has no idea where I am, and you don't know what she's like!' Tommy sat up with a long grunt - there was aggression in his movements.

His girlfriend, Taylor, was not of complete sound mind, which caused Tommy anxiety and made him on edge. He knew she would instantly think Tommy was with another girl, rather than in a medical centre having an intrusive procedure carried out. He had lied to her though; he told her he was on a training course with work. He didn't want her to know about this procedure, knowing full well she'd be against it – like any caring partner.

Tommy was a well-built man, standing at five foot eleven inches tall. He was handsome with big brown eyes and short dark hair.

He burst through the front door to his apartment at 0030 hours on the Wednesday morning. He was relieved to finally be back home in his apartment, which he shared with his "beloved" Taylor.

'Taylor, you in?' he asked, as he briskly searched the apartment, but no one was home. He then pulled out his mobile and gave her a call.

Surprisingly, after one ring, she answered – it was as though she had been waiting for his call.

'Where the fuck have you been?' said Taylor. She was angry and needed answers.

'Told you, babe, I had to go away on a training course for work. I just got home now. I'm knackered. Where are you?' His voice wobbled, he was never a good liar.

'Bull!' she shouted. 'You've been with that girl from the gym, Emily! Do not fucking lie to me, Tommy McGregor!'

He could almost feel her screaming breath through the phone as she yelled at him.

'Ok, chill…' He was confused by her allegations. *Emily?* 'I've told you, I've been on a training course with work. I told you weeks ago. We even said goodbye to each other on Wednesday morning last week as I left.'

He was very confused how she came to the conclusion he was with another woman - he did know of an Emily, but certainly wasn't with her.

'Yeah, I know, it was all bullshit. It's a bit of a coincidence that when you're away, she's away too.' Taylor paused. 'I checked!' There was a little shame in her tone.

'What do you mean, *you checked*?' Tommy was completely bedazzled. Yeah, he was lying, but not about that.

'Her Facebook... said she was looking forward to a secret escape with a lover, with a shit load of winking emojis, on the same day you went away?'

'Ahh, right... ok, so Mystic Meg worked it all out from that, bravo!' He hung up before Taylor had a chance to say anything else.

Taylor was a very insecure twenty-two-year-old. She was petit, brunette and cute, but God she had the worst fiery attitude. There was a huge chip permanently on her shoulder, as though she thought the world owed her something. That aside, Taylor was extremely intelligent and worked for a top computer firm as an assistant, but her employers could see huge potential.

Tommy and Taylor had been together for two years and had moved in together after six months. Being thirty himself, Tommy always thought Taylor was a little too young for him, along with her irrational behaviour and the constant jumping to conclusions – she actually drove him mad.

It had crossed his mind many times about leaving her, but when she was happy and things were great, they had a lot of fun together. Whenever they were going through a dodgy moment and Tommy was thinking about leaving her, he held on to those moments with the hope that one day, when she actually grew up, things would change – Tommy didn't give up on things easily.

He sat back on his sofa and went through his phone to find the IPEA app recently installed. The screen loaded to various options, including: Brain Health, Internal Organs, Blood Levels etc... He clicked on "Brain Health", which was highlighted in red to notify that there was an issue.

High Cortisol levels detected: Learn to minimize your physical reaction to stress by consciously breathing from your diaphragm. A few minutes of diaphragmatic breathing will lower levels of cortisol and stimulate the parasympathetic nervous system to induce a state of calm.

Tommy read this and thought, it was a bit extreme, as he didn't feel that bad. Then he remembered something that was said during the *"intense* pre-interrogation":

"A lot goes on inside your body you are unaware of. The idea of the IPEA is to highlight things that are unknown to you and to assist in you living a longer, healthier life by taking action when required."

Tommy followed the guidance and could see after a few minutes that his Cortisol levels were slowly decreasing along with his blood pressure. *This is some pretty clever stuff!* he thought to himself and continued to relax for a few more moments.

He then checked other features. The app stated that he was over-tired and that he needed to drink at least 1.3 litres of water to avoid dehydration after he's had an eight-hour sleep.

Feeling tired, he went into the kitchen, downed a pint of slightly warm tap water and filled another glass to take to bed. He got undressed to his pants and looked at himself in the mirror, flexing his biceps, abs, shoulders and chest all at the same time in a crab-like pose. He felt a little weak, but still admired his hard-earned physique.

He laid in bed in the dark. The light from outside shone through the small gaps in the blinds to his bedroom with dust flickering in the beams. He could hear the sound of a few cars passing by. He felt somewhat blessed to be home in his own bed, but still held onto a little anger towards Taylor, although he felt calmer. He thought about how this IPEA was going to assist him in a healthy lifestyle; how it was going to tell him when he was over-tired, eating enough of the right foods, drinking enough and doing everything possible to enhance his health and wellbeing, especially reducing stress. He had saved for a long time to have this done and was hoping to see a vast improvement in looks, health and mental soundness.

It's easy to be led at times and to fall into a "change your life" sales pitch; be happier, slimmer, richer... live forever, there must be ramifications for interfering with nature. The effects of technology in this world will have a negative impact on us some day, the terrifying thing is... the future is now!

2

There was a sudden cold, wet, intense feeling as ice cold water was splashed into Tommy's face, that awoke him from a sound sleep. He opened his eyes to find Taylor had come home, still pissed off and still convinced Tommy had been away with that girl from the gym - Emily. When Taylor had an idea or a scenario in her head, she convinced herself it was real, it had happened, was happening or was going to happen. She was insanely insecure and so quick to react on emotions rather than think things through logically.

'Fuck sake, babe!' shouted Tommy, holding his t-shirt over his face to wipe off the water.

'Go on, tell me the truth for once in your life?' There was a visibly blue pulsating vein throbbing in Taylor's temple as the insecurity raged inside her body, convinced that Tommy had cheated on her. It was then that he could clearly see he had to be honest with her, so he went for it.

'Okay, okay, I went for minor surgery; had that new diagnostic thing we saw on TV installed! I'm sorry I lied to you. I knew you'd be against it, but I wanted it done for me!' His honesty came with a self-refreshing feeling – a slight exhilaration.

'What?' she frowned so hard her eyebrows met in the middle, but that frown quickly faded, displaying an immediate sense of calm.

'You know, babe? Remember, that thing we saw the other week on TV? Where you have a smart injection that reads your insides and tells you what's going on inside your body.'

'Oh, so you haven't been with that Emily?' she took a step back. Once again, her assumptions were wrong and she looked confused.

'No babe, I've been to the place where they carry out the medical procedure.' He showed her some bruising that had formed where the drip line had been inserted.

'Wait!' there was a pause whilst the cogs in her brain turned and worked out what he was talking about. 'That thing that cost a shit load of money?' she asked, her face slowly turning a purplish red.

'Yes, but what I spend my money on is up to me.' This was something Tommy always felt defensive about, the subject of money. He'd always felt he should never need to ask if he could spend his hard-earned cash.

'T, we could have gone on a nice holiday or something?' Taylor moaned.

'We will babe, I just wanted to invest in my health.'

'You mean use it for vanity reasons, to get the attention of other girls?'

'No babe, for fuck sake, get that shit out of your head.' He stood up from the bed pressing both hands on his chest. 'For me, to make me feel better,' there was a pause, 'about me.'

Taylor sighed and jumped onto the bed giving another sigh of relief that this Emily wasn't in the picture. She felt silly for spending the last four days obsessing and stressing over nothing.

She couldn't help or control these feelings; it was something she just needed to try to deal with.

'Well, if you can afford 5k, I'm sure you have some money to treat me tonight! Why don't we go out?' Taylor kissed Tommy's cheek and slowly tickled his chest in an attempt to seduce him into agreement.

'I think you need to apologise first for pouring water over me!' Tommy pushed her hand away. 'You need to stop all this nonsense, all this jumping to conclusions, the paranoia, and start trusting me. I love you and only want you. This has to stop for fuck sake, you are pushing me away!' Tommy tried to keep his tone sympathetic, but Taylor's brain didn't work that way, and she went straight on the defensive.

'What?' exclaimed Taylor, her face changing once again. 'So, you're going off me because I love you so much?'

'Eh? No babe, I'm not saying that, but this behaviour is too much. I don't want to argue with you every single day. I don't want to have to watch what I'm saying or be on edge every time my phone beeps, because you think it's a girl!'

'I know, T! God!' she said through her teeth, displaying an element of frustration. 'I'm sorry, I do try, and I promise I'll try harder. You know I've had a tough history with boys.' Her eyes started to fill with tears. Tommy couldn't help but fall for her tears; it broke his heart seeing her upset.

'I know you have sweetheart, but just remember, I'm not those boys, I'm me,' he held up two thumbs and gave a big cheesy grin in an attempt to lighten the mood.

'I know, T. You do treat me right. You really are the best boyfriend I've ever had!' They cuddled with a slight awkwardness, so Taylor pulled herself right into him to make it feel real. 'And... sorry for throwing water over you. I'll make it up to you tonight!' She gave Tommy a wink as a cheeky gesture and kissed him passionately.

They both laid there for a few moments and absorbed the conversation and the lightened mood. Tommy noticed a little blue notification light flickering on his phone. He looked at the preview and saw that it was just the IPEA telling him his stress levels were elevated once again, so he carried out the breathing technique.

After an hour of chatting and cuddling, Tommy left the room to take a shower. With Taylor being the hyper-insecure girl she was, she took this as an opportunity to install a ghost app she had been working on "unofficially" at work onto Tommy's phone, which would enable her to mirror everything on his phone on to her own phone, so she would be able to monitor what he was up to. The app took a while to install. She heard the shower shut off. Knowing Tommy wouldn't take long to dry himself off, she only had a few seconds to spare, and the app was only fifty percent installed.

She became impatient. 'Come on,' she shouted quietly through her teeth, her heart rate beating hard in her chest followed by a hot flush that cursed her body momentarily – sixty percent complete. 'Come on!' the words seethed through her teeth.

The bathroom door opened, she panicked and tossed his phone under the bed in the hope that he wouldn't try to look for it straight away.

She had designed the application, so it would work in the background and was completely undetectable to the user. Tommy would be completely oblivious to its presence and would just continue to use his phone as he always had.

'Who you talking to?' Tommy asked. There was a white towel wrapped around his waist showing his well-defined physique.

'No one, T. Just gonna make a coffee. Want one?'

'Please!'

Taylor went to make the coffee, opened her phone and could see that the ghost app had installed properly. Now she could access Tommy's phone from hers. She took a quick look through his messages. This was to firstly check that the app was working, but also to see what activity had been taking place on his phone.

Tommy walked into the kitchen as Taylor was snooping. She quickly locked her phone, which looked highly suspicious to Tommy – something Taylor would have gone ballistic over.

'What you up to?' He gave a partial frown.

'Nothing! I was on my phone, and now I'm not. Problem?' Her attitude had started once again.

'Not a problem you being on your phone, but a problem that you quickly locked it as I walked in. You know what they say?' he smiled and turned, walking back out of the kitchen.

Taylor made chase, confused by Tommy's comment. 'And... what is that supposed to mean?'

'You know,' he smiled at her sarcastically, 'those that are paranoid about their partner cheating are the ones who normally have something to hide.' He smiled again, feeling as though he had the upper hand.

He walked into the bedroom and started to get dressed. Taylor stomped after him. 'What the fuck is that supposed to mean?'

'Just saying, babe. You are constantly on at me, assuming, accusing, making sly little comments that I'm cheating, when I don't do anything to give you that impression.' He sat on the bed. 'I'm literally sick to my back teeth of all this bullshit hassle from you, and the moment you actually look a little bit suspicious by quickly locking your phone as I walk into a room, YOU start to lose your head! Feeling a little defensive, are we?'

Taylor became frantic, waving her arms around, screaming at Tommy and getting up into his face. She was in a state of rage; a side of her that Tommy hated. Looking at her, you wouldn't even guess she had the temper she did.

This was now his time to leave the apartment and give the girl some space to cool off. Tommy wondered what state the place would be in when he returned, knowing there was a nine out of ten chance she would trash it.

He got into his seventeen-plate silver five series, turned the engine over and sat there thinking about how everything was and how this girl was causing so much stress and aggravation in his life. 'Bitch!' he shouted, punching the steering wheel of the car.

He put the car into reverse, abruptly drove out of his parking bay and sped off down the road, tyres screeching as they tried to grip the tarmac.

Taylor, on the other hand, was on the bed, tears streaming down her pretty cheeks. She actually felt a lot calmer than expected, but was annoyed with herself.

She knew where her issues lay, but she just couldn't come to terms with her past.

It went back to about four years ago, when she had been around seventeen years old. There was this man she had met online and she had been massively attracted to him. His name was Mick. Taylor had fallen crazy in-love with this man. He was twenty years her senior, well put together and carried himself well. He was well-off and made his money as a car dealer, which meant he always drove around in nice cars. This had been impressive to Taylor, and was something to show off to her friends about.

He did look after her for a while, but she had found out he was already married and had a daughter of a similar age to her, so had been living a double life, which had caused big concerns. Taylor hadn't been able to bring herself to do anything about it.

She was so in love with him, she couldn't leave, so had continued with their relationship as they had been.

After a while, Taylor had found it increasingly difficult to accept that he was still sleeping with his wife and her at the same time, so she had tried to call it off with threats of telling his wife. Mick wasn't the kind of person to piss off and didn't take to the threats very well, so this had caused things to become nasty.

Shortly after the threats, came a night from hell for Taylor. She had refused to have sex with him until he left his wife. His male ego couldn't accept the rejection, and he had become aggressive and had repeatedly raped her, humiliated her and beat her unconscious.

He had kept her locked in his "secretly rented flat" – his little love nest - for two days. When she was finally able to leave, she was scared to death of him. As soon as she got home, her mother had taken one look at her and had burst into tears. Taylor had confessed all, so her mum had taken her to hospital and had called the police. Mick had been arrested for that incident and charged with a prison sentence of a measly thirty-two months. This did, however, have a catastrophic effect on his wife and teenage daughter, which had caused Mick to hang himself in his prison cell one night. Taylor had never been the same again.

Tommy, with the greatest respect, didn't know this. All Taylor had told him was that Mick had cheated on her, so now she found it hard to trust anyone. There's always a reason why someone acts the way they do. Taylor couldn't stop herself falling for Tommy, had let her guard down, and now she felt ridiculously vulnerable. She knew he'd never beat her or physically harm her, but she had this dreaded gut-wrenching feeling in the pit of her stomach that all blokes were the same and that he would cheat on her. This had turned into a crazy obsession that had progressively got worse over time, and she couldn't let go. Her insecurities controlled her life, which had put tremendous strain on hers and Tommy's relationship.

So, she had designed and installed the ghost app onto Tommy's phone to reassure herself that he wasn't cheating and that she could trust him. By keeping tabs on him, it meant her mind was at ease. This was her way of dealing with her mental health issues.

Tommy pulled up in his car on a cliff edge near a beach on the south coast of Wales. He sat there staring out over the Bristol Channel. He'd been driving around for most of the day and had ended up here watching the darkness engulf the sea in front of him. As the sun set, the oranges and pinks collided, creating a beautiful scene that words couldn't describe. He sat there in a daze thinking about how his future would look if he was to stay with Taylor. *Will it always be this way? Or is there someone else out there for me?* he wondered. *She's a good girl, but is deeply insecure and damaged, and it's pushing me away.*

Tommy had had a good life so far, and now, at the age of 30, he was ready to get married and settle down, start a family, enjoy life and watch his future "non-existent" children grow. He knew Taylor loved him and he knew she would marry him in a heartbeat, but he had serious doubts as to whether she was right for him or if she was ready for such a commitment.

Tommy had grown up in the country with his mum, dad and sister. He had been well looked after, was well-educated, had worked his way up the ladder in the corporate world to management and was now earning a fairly decent income. He was proud of himself and his achievements. He had never been in trouble with the police and had always had steady girlfriends, who were always younger, always cute, petite, and overall just nice girls. Most of his previous relationships had just fizzled out to nothing with pleasant memories and no real dramas.

However, Taylor was pushing him, testing him and driving him to the point of no return, and when he was done he was done.

He reached into his pocket to grab his phone, expecting thousands of missed calls, but it wasn't there. He must have left it back at the apartment. He'd been gone for hours. He then panicked, knowing Taylor would be going out of her mind, and he became worried about how she would be feeling. He started to stress himself and drove home erratically.

On the drive back home, he said out loud, 'This isn't normal; relationships shouldn't be like this. I need to end it, and I need to do it tonight!' He repeated those words over and over out loud, as if he had to convince himself that this was it and he had to leave her.

When Tommy pulled up outside the apartment, he briefly looked around and noticed all the lights were off and the area was dead silent. There was a light breeze in the air and the smell of the summer night flowed into his nostrils. He had a moment of calm, then a sudden surge of adrenaline pulsed deep in his stomach at the thought of ending it with Taylor. He was worried and anxious about how she would take it. Part of him hoped she wouldn't be home, just so the whole process could be prolonged, just for a little bit longer.

'Deep breaths,' he said out loud. He looked up and could see a figure staring down at him from the apartment above his. All the lights were off, which generated a spooky silhouette. He waved at his neighbour and gave a little smile, but his neighbour simply turned and disappeared back into the darkness of his flat.

'Freak!' said Tommy. That guy always gave him the creeps. He would always stare, would never say much, but strangely always tried to intercept his post. He would then knock on Tommy's door and say that the postman had left it for him. He would hand the post to Tommy and then strangely walk away.

Tommy shook himself in preparation and entered the apartment block. He slowly made his way up the stairs to his first-floor apartment and pressed his ear to the door to try and sense any movement - there was nothing.

He opened the door slowly and turned on the hallway light. The door to his left led into the bedroom and he peered in. No one was in there and the place was strangely how he had left it. He expected it to be trashed, as it had happened so many times before.

Tommy slowly moved down the corridor which opened into the lounge area. In the darkness laid a figure on the couch.

'Babe,' he said in a soft tone, 'you ok?'

Taylor stirred and opened her eyes. Tommy took a step back and turned on the lights. Taylor covered her face as the light burned her eyes and rubbed at them. Tommy could clearly see a blood-stained tea towel wrapped around her arm and hurried towards her.

'What have you done to yourself, babe?' He was angry but upset at the same time.

'I thought I lost you forever, T. I'm sorry about everything, I really am. Please don't leave me. I can't live without you.' She burst into tears.

Tommy wrapped his arms around her and squeezed her. She sobbed into his shoulder and he could feel her shaking dramatically.

'My phone smashed too,' she said, sobbing.

'You mean you smashed it?'

'Ok, I did, but I was so angry, T. Not with you, but with myself!' she continued to cry.

Tommy pulled away from her. 'Let me see,' he said, as he gently pulled her arm towards him to unwrap the towel. He then started to cry gently. 'Babe, you are so silly.' Luckily, it wasn't a deep cut and more of a cry for help.

'Look T, I need to tell you something,' Taylor announced. 'I need you to understand me. I need you to have an understanding of why I am the way I am with you, as we can't carry on like this.'

Tommy sat back. 'Okay, I'm all ears, babe.'

Tommy was confused. He had never seen her like this, and he knew something was up. He had a gut feeling that she had been with someone else and was thinking of the worst thing possible. However, he couldn't have been any further from the truth.

'Let me say what I have to say before you say anything back?' Taylor said.

'Of course, just tell me?' He sat back, folding his arms ready to listen, looking at her in the eye, trying to second guess what she was about to say.

Taylor went through her entire ordeal in detail about Mick and everything he had done to her. She finished, wrapped her arms around Tommy and sobbed.

Tommy held her tight and cried with her. He closed his eyes and thought to himself, *All this time, and the poor girl was suffering, keeping this from me. No boyfriend wants to hear that, but at least she has told me.* He held her shoulders and looked her deep in the eyes.

'Sweetheart, I understand why you kept this to yourself, and I now understand why you've been the way you have. I'm so sorry you had to go through that with him, I really am, and I'm so proud of you for opening up to me.'

He found it hard to hold back and cried again, thinking about how terrified she must have been. He really did care about her and felt guilty for having armed himself for a breakup. Everything started to make sense to him now; why she had been so quiet and closed-off for the first few months of dating; why it had taken months before they had slept together; and why she behaved so erratically during arguments. The poor girl must have been on the back foot from the offset.

Things felt more relaxed around the place for both of them. Taylor was a lot calmer and Tommy just fell in-love with her all over again. The arguments literally stopped the night she confided in him.

Taylor's mind was clear. She'd had some counselling, which helped her no end, and everything was as it should be.

After another couple of weeks, things were better than ever for them both. Taylor gained a promotion at work running her own contract. It was only a small contract, but her career was definitely going in the right direction.

Tommy was still doing well, keeping track of his health using his IPEA, and had signed himself up to compete in a bodybuilding competition in the "Beach Body" category. Taylor was very supportive, helped prepare all his meals and gave him the motivation he needed when he was feeling down and struggling with his intense training regime.

It was a Saturday night and the pair decided it'd be nice to go out for a meal, especially as Tommy could have a "cheat meal" - a meal outside of his normal diet routine. The weather was now cold, so they wrapped up and made their way to the car. As they walked down the stairs in their block, their neighbour from the flat above was passing.

'Hey,' said Tommy with a nod, but the guy just kept walking.

'Oi! You ignorant prick!' Taylor shouted. She just couldn't help herself.

'Babe! Don't!' said Tommy, and he put his arm across her front.

'No! He can't just ignore you!' She turned back to the neighbour. 'Oi! Do you have a problem?' her voice was raised and anger was pouring like venom from a snake.

The neighbour then stopped on the stairs and slowly turned around, a magnified insincere smile stretched across the width of his face. It was clear this guy didn't give a shit.

'No problem, love.' The neighbour's lips barely moved as he spoke, and his voice was fairly high pitched for a thirty-something-year-old.

'So, why did you ignore my boyfriend? He was only being friendly.' Taylor was still angry, and she stared intensely into his eyes, which he reciprocated.

'I did, did I?' He raised his eyebrows, then stepped forward in his dirty white trainers that squeaked as he moved down a step. He had a long camo anorak on with the hood up. His eyes were deep. There was something not quite right.

'Come on, let's go!' said Tommy, gently turning Taylor around and ushering her towards the bottom of the stairs and out the door. They never looked back, but if they had, they would have seen that the guy didn't move until they were out of the building.

'Fucking freak!' said Taylor.

'I know, he's a strange one, so please just ignore him from now on. Don't start kicking off, especially when I'm not around. Anyway, fuck him! Let's have a nice night!' said Tommy.

They jumped into the car and made their way to The Bay to find a good place to eat. They decided to eat at a nice all-you-can eat Chinese restaurant. Tommy wanted to make the most of his cheat meal and was not going to hold back at all. He piled on the Chinese chicken curry, chips, duck wraps, chicken satay, bloody everything he could possibly get his hands on. He then moved onto the desert and just kept filling up.

'You ok, babe?' he said, sitting opposite Taylor. She had a sad look on her face.

'Yeah, T. Sorry, was just thinking.' She looked down at the table.

'Come on, babe, spit it out.' Tommy flicked some cream from a cake across the table that landed straight in her hair. She looked up and smiled at him.

'Prick!' she exclaimed in a jokey kind of way.

'Come on, babe. Why do you look so sad?'

'I'm not sad, T. I'm feeling overwhelmed.' Taylor paused and took a breath. 'Over the last few weeks since I told you about you-know-what, things have just been amazing. I've got this hot, sexy man who loves me more than anything in the world, my job is going great, I'm so happy, you make me happy.' She smiled with a tear running down her left cheek and another running down her right side a little further behind.

'That's so lovely to hear, babe.' Tommy leant forward and with both of his thumbs he gently brushed away her tears and then held her face. 'I fucking love you so much!'

Intense passion filled them both and they started to passionately kiss each other over the table, not caring about others trying to eat their meals. They pulled away from each other with a mischievous giggle and Taylor had to wipe a little saliva from her mouth.

'I love you too,' she replied, smiling from ear to ear.

'Now, can I finish my dessert?' Tommy said.

'Crack on!' She wiped the cream from her hair and threw it back at Tommy. They both giggled and laughed.

They finished up their desserts, settled the bill and quickly walked to the car to get out of the cold winter evening. In the car they were both smiling, not saying a word, yet fully content and comfortable with the silence.

When they got into their flat, Tommy felt all bloated and lethargic. He checked his IPEA on his phone. It showed that he had consumed over six thousand calories during the day and his sugar and insulin levels had increased. The app recommended that he should drink a litre of water over the next few hours and that he should fast for the next sixteen hours.

He laid on the bed. His belly was painful, almost stretching and ready to burst.

'Babe!' he groaned. Taylor was in the kitchen.

'Yeah, T?' she shouted back.

'Can you bring me a pint of water, please. I'm dying,' he said, followed by a groan. 'And... try not to throw it over me.' This had now become a running joke.

'Yeah!'

'Make sure you run the tap until the water is cold, please. You know I'm funny about drinking tap water.'

'Yeah, coming!' Taylor shouted, as she walked through to the bedroom. 'Here you go.' She went to hand Tommy the glass, only to find that the cheeky sod had instantly fallen asleep.

'Well... I'm not getting any tonight,' Taylor huffed. She went into the bathroom, took off her makeup, brushed her teeth and climbed into bed next to her bloated, sweaty boyfriend. She kissed him on the cheek, turned off the light and closed her eyes with a fruitful smile on her face. 'What a lovely evening,' she whispered to herself – *she had finally found that happiness... For now!*

3

It was a cold, crisp winter's morning with the sun gleefully shining through the blinds in the bedroom. Taylor smiled and turned to Tommy, instantly realising he wasn't there. Thinking nothing of it, she climbed out of bed and put on her dressing gown to try and protect herself from the cold air in the room.

She walked through the hallway into the lounge. Tommy wasn't there either. She silently walked around the flat checking every room – there was nothing.

'Where is he?' she said out loud to herself. She went back into the bedroom and picked up her phone, pulled out the charger and checked - no messages. This did cause her a little concern, as this was out of character for Tommy. She decided to give him a call.

'Yeah babe?' he sounded breathless.

'Where are you, T?' Taylor asked, her voice low with concern.

'Sorry, babe. I just nipped out for a brisk walk to try and do a little fasted cardio, especially after last night's extravaganza. I didn't want to wake you, you looked so peaceful.'

Taylor breathed a sigh of relief. 'Ok, T. Had me worried for a moment then. You could have at least left me a note or text?' Her tone was calm. *At least I know where he is now*, she thought to herself.

'I did, on the kettle. Thought that would have been the first place you went to, you coffee addict.'

Taylor walked into the kitchen and there it was; a cute little scribble.

"Sexy girl - I've gone for a walk - no need to worry. See you soon - love ya xxx"

'So I see. Now get home, I miss you!' She blew a kiss down the phone and hung up.

Tommy got home about twenty minutes later and the first thing he did was check his IPEA, hoping to see that last night's binge hadn't had much of an effect on him – with regard to his body fat levels.

The IPEA basically told Tommy that he had high sodium levels, he had twelve percent water retention and no gain in body fat. He was happy with this. *Good to know you can't get fat in a day*, he thought to himself.

After Tommy had finished reviewing the analysis of last night's binge, he decided he was going to train in the gym today, as he felt full of carbs and energy. He walked into the lounge and gave Taylor a big kiss on the lips.

'Your lips are cold?' Taylor said.

'Yeah, it's freezing out there,' he said as he jumped onto the sofa, cuddling up to her – she loved lots of attention.

Whist they laid there cuddled up on the sofa, they could hear the freak upstairs moving things around. Normally they didn't hear anything from him, so this was unusual.

'Wonder what he's doing?' said Tommy.

'I'll get out my crystal ball, shall I, and home in on the freak?' They both laughed together.

'Ha, yeah, if only, ey? Why don't you get this week's Lotto numbers too, whilst you're at it?' Tommy leant forward and gave Taylor another kiss on the lips. 'I'm going to nip to the gym later, do you fancy joining me?' He smiled at her, already knowing her answer.

'Nah, but...' Taylor then slowly rubbed her hand up his thigh towards his man bits.

Tommy declined the offer by pushing her hand away.

'What's wrong?' Taylor asked, having felt a moment of rejection. This wasn't like Tommy at all. She normally had him on tap.

'Sorry, babe. I'm just not feeling it. I still feel all bloated and unsexy.'

'It's okay, babe. We don't have to.' Taylor hated the rejection. A little insecurity started to haunt her slightly, which she tried to ignore and turn her thoughts around. *He's not always going to be in the mood for it. If I felt unsexy, I certainly wouldn't,* she thought to herself, which made her feel better.

'I'm sorry, babe. It's not you at all, I promise.' Tommy kissed her on the cheek to give her reassurance. 'Maybe later, yeah?'

'Don't force yourself!' Taylor snapped, regretting her words, then back tracking. 'What I mean is, it's ok to not be in the mood. I understand.'

Tommy leaned in and kissed her again. 'I'm gonna take a shower and have a shave to freshen up. I'll see you in a bit.' He walked off into the bathroom to take his shower.

Whilst showering, Tommy had an intense headache, making his head feel freezing cold and heavy, a bit like the feeling of brain freeze. He crouched down in the shower and held his head, hoping the pain would go away, but it grew stronger and stronger. He then got up off the floor of the shower; the headache had gone, and he felt fine. *That was weird,* he thought to himself.

An hour had passed. Tommy went back into the lounge, where Taylor was watching some girly wives of Cheshire, or whatever, on the tele.

'You ok, T? Took your time, didn't you?'

'I was only ten minutes, babe?' Tommy was confused. He checked the time. 'Strange, I only thought I was in there for a few moments?'

'Maybe you got carried away with yourself?' Taylor winked at him, implying he had been having a little "alone time".

'No, I didn't do that, honestly. I did have an horrendous headache though. I then got up off the shower floor. I think I may have passed out?'

Taylor looked concerned. 'You ok? There's painkillers in the cupboard. Do you want me to get you some?' She stood and began rubbing the back of his head.

'I've got a bit of a lump on the back of my head, I think I must have passed out, babe.'

'Well sit down, I'll get you some water.' Taylor offered.

Tommy sat down, rubbing the back of his head, feeling confused. He had lost fifty minutes somewhere, and it felt strange.

'Right, what are we doing today?' Taylor jumped with excitement, prancing around like an hyper-active school kid in an attempt to get Tommy's mind off his headache.

'I'm training, babe.' Tommy didn't even look at Taylor when he spoke, and his tone was a little off.

'T!' She gave him a little playful kick to the knee.

'What?' Tommy snapped at her for the first time since she could remember.

'What's wrong?' Taylor asked. 'Why are you being moody all of a sudden? This isn't like you!'

'I'm not! I told you earlier, I'm training today.' Again, Tommy snapped, but this time his tone was even more off balance. 'It's important for me to stay focused on my goal.'

'Yeah, but you're not training all day, are you? Let's go out for some lunch and go and watch a film?

You can train after,' Taylor said gleefully, trying hard to not mirror his mood.

'As if I'm going to feel like training after lunch and a film - idiot.' Tommy stood and walked towards the bedroom, brushing past Taylor and giving her a little nudge with his shoulder.

'What the fuck was that, T?' Taylor could feel anger building up from inside her stomach. *What's wrong with him. Who the fuck does he think he is?* She was fighting her anger, trying her utmost to not retaliate and wind him up even more. 'Come on, give me a smile!'

'Babe, seriously, just fuck off! I'm off down the gym. If you want to go and do something, then call one of you friends and stop bugging me!' By this point, Tommy had put on his gym kit and was ready to leave.

'Who do you think you are talking to?' Taylor snapped. 'Why is it ok for you to talk to me like that? Who are you... really?' She was totally shocked at his behaviour. 'You know I don't have many friends, T. That was a low blow.'

'Not my problem. Why don't you give your old, dead friend Mick a call! I'm sure he'd be happy to hear from you!' Tommy instantly regretted his words; words he couldn't take back; words he knew Taylor would hold on to and that would play with her mind.

'You evil fucking bastard!' Taylor shoved her hand into his shoulder.

Tommy fell backwards, and his headache came back, this time with a vengeance. He knelt down, trying to take the pain, then he stood. He looked different. His face had changed and the muscles in his face were all relaxed.

Taylor looked at him concerned. 'Are you ok?'

Tommy didn't say a word. He clenched his fist and slammed it straight into her face. Her body buckled as she fell to the floor whimpering. He stood over her, glaring, not saying anything. He was still, like a statue, then he snapped out of it with a shake of his head.

Blood ran from Taylor's eye, which was already beginning to swell. Tommy just stood there staring at her in disbelief.

'What has just happened?' Tommy asked. 'Why are you on the floor? Shit, you're bleeding!' He was confused and his voice was broken.

Taylor groaned and managed to stand, holding her eye, trying to catch the blood at the same time, but some had already trickled onto her clothing.

'This will be the last time you ever see me, I swear on my life, Tommy McGregor! You are a fucking horrible, nasty person! I never ever thought you would ever lay a hand on me – how naive must I be?' Taylor glared at Tommy, focusing directly into his eyes.

'Taylor, I have no idea what happened. I blacked out, honestly.' Tommy placed his palms together as a plea for her to believe him.

'Funny, that's what Mick said after he raped and beat the living shit out of me! If you ever make contact with me again, I will call the police. Now, fuck off down your precious gym!' Taylor finally burst into tears.

Unspeakable hurt boiled in her heart. She knew she had to leave him. She would never forgive or forget. She'd never ever seen Tommy like that ever. Even when they were going through their really bad patch, he had never spoken to her like that and had never given any tiny indication that he would be violent towards her. Taylor sat on the sofa and sobbed her broken heart out, hurt by the vicious words, hurt and wounded physically and mentally. Her soul had been broken once again.

Tommy drove towards the gym to give her space. He felt utterly confused. *I blacked out, I know I did?* He couldn't focus. When he parked up outside the gym, he sent Taylor a WhatsApp message;

"Babe, I'm so sorry. I do not know what happened, nor can I explain it. I love you so much. I'll give you some space. Please don't do anything rash xxx"

Tommy watched the message. The first two ticks appeared, confirming the message had been delivered. He continued to wait until they turned blue – an indication the message has been read. Within a few minutes they turned blue, and Taylor simultaneously went offline again. Clearly, she didn't want to talk - and who would blame her.

The gym was liked by many, but to Tommy it was like a playground for adults. It was his place for escapism, somewhere to clear his mind and to also feel good about himself. He scanned the gym to see if any of his mates were around, but the place was pretty dead, as expected for a Sunday. He did, however, notice Emily. *The girl Taylor was once convinced he was sleeping with.*

She clocked him and gave him a smile – he'd never spoken to her before, they'd just exchanged the odd flirtatious smile once in a while. Tommy knew she fancied him, but he only appreciated her looks. He'd never cheat on Taylor.

Emily then came over. There was a slight dance in her step. Tommy was a little surprised. *Didn't realise she was this forward,* he thought to himself.

'Been here long, Hun?' Emily said.

Tommy looked her up and down but felt uncomfortable with the approach.

'No, just got here. You ok?' he asked, trying to be polite. Emily ignored his question and asked, 'What happened to your hand?' It was slightly swollen and purple from hitting Taylor.

'Ah, I punched a wall. It's nothing.' Tommy looked at his watch. 'I need to get on. Nice to see you.'

'Wait, would you like to train together?' Emily gave a slight grin. She clearly loved herself.

Tommy tilted his head to the side and made an awkward facial expression. 'Ahh, I can't. I've got to get on, sorry. Maybe another time, yeah?' He tried to walk off, but she interrupted him again.

'When?' she asked.

'When?' Tommy pulled a confused expression.

'You said we can train another time. When would you like to?' Emily asked again. *Christ she's full on. Get the hint girl. I don't want to train with you,* he thought, rather than saying it out loud.

'Yeah, I'm not sure. I'll let you know!' Again, Tommy attempted to walk away.

'Do you want my number then?' she asked.

'Errm, it's ok, thanks. We'll catch up next time we bump into one another.' Tommy then managed to walk off, leaving her confused by what had just happened – probably because no one had ever rejected her before. She was used to guys falling at her feet.

Tommy's workout was a good one, considering the emotional trauma he'd endured due to hitting Taylor, which he still had no recollection of. He looked at his hand, which was deep red and swollen. It hurt. He rubbed it and reality hit him. *It was real. It really did happen. Why don't I remember?* He became upset, trying hard to not cry, holding in his emotions, but it was too much.

He briskly walked from the gym into the changing rooms and sat in a toilet cubicle behind a locked door, then he let it all out.

He kept checking his phone, but there was nothing – Taylor hadn't got back to him. *She's gone, I've lost her.*

Tommy shook himself off and washed his face to try and disguise his upset, then walked back out into the main gym area. Emily clocked him and walked over. She could see he had been upset.

'What's wrong, hun?' she rubbed her hand on his shoulder, but he instinctively pulled away.

'Don't!' Tommy said.

'Is it because you've split up with Taylor?' Emily asked.

Tommy looked at her, astounded. 'Excuse me?' He frowned hard, and his face went slightly red. *What the fuck!* he thought.

'Taylor, she's left you, hasn't she?' Emily gave a smarmy smile with a look of gratification.

'No! She hasn't left me! What business is it of yours anyway?'

'None, I just know,' Emily said.

'Know what?'

'Everything, Tommy McGregor.'

All of a sudden, the pretty girl who Tommy appreciated for being hot-looking became ugly from a personality point of view.

'How do you even know my name, or Taylor's for that matter?' Tommy asked.

'I just do, but... when you've finished, we're going to need to shower. I'm going to use the staff showers today, as it's only Jake on duty.' She turned the flirting back on.

Jake was the brother of the gym owner. He was about 30 years old and so laid back he was pretty much dead. Emily wanted to use this opportunity to sneak Tommy into the showers where they wouldn't be disturbed.

'No, I shower at home, and don't change the subject!' Tommy exclaimed.

'Well, Tommy, I'll be up there in the next forty-five minutes. If you want to join me, you know where to find me.' She winked, turned like she was all innocent, as though butter wouldn't melt, and strutted off, moving -her body in a way that Tommy couldn't look away, even though he didn't like her.

All of a sudden, his headache came back. This time he could hear an awful ringing in his ears. It was deafeningly loud – horrendous. He held his head, pushing at his temples, then he just stood up straight with no emotion, breathing gently – he was still, like a statue; a little freaky.

Tommy walked over to Jake at the desk. 'Can I have a bottle of cherry egg whites and a bowl of porridge with a cup of almond milk, please?' His speech was slightly slurred.

'No probs, mate. Good session?' asked Jake. Tommy just grunted.

'What's your problem, mate?'

'Nothing,' Tommy said, as he walked off with his order and sat down. His movements were slow and he was a little wobbly on his feet, but he managed to sit on a chair before he fell over.

Once Tommy had finished his food, he stood and walked up the flight of stairs leading to the changing rooms. He walked straight into the staff changing area, glancing behind just before he entered to see if anyone was watching. He was moving differently, with a slight stagger, and his knees buckled once or twice, but he managed to not fall.

The room was steamy. Tommy staggered through. Emily heard him and exposed herself from behind the shower curtain. Tommy just glared at her. She stepped towards him, and he placed his hand on her breast. He showed no emotion.

'Are you fucking numb or something?' Emily asked. Tommy just continued to stare at her. 'Ok, now you're freaking me out.' She grabbed her towel and pulled it around herself to cover up.

Tommy then snapped out of his daze. 'What are you doing?' he asked. Confusion, anxiety and a dose of fear coursed through his body. He had no idea how he had got to where he was.

'I told you to meet me in here, but you've gone all freaky on me. I've changed my mind,' Emily said.

'About what?' he asked, literally having no idea what had just happened.

'About us, you know, getting down to it,' she winked – this girl just could not help herself.

'I'm not interested in you, sorry.' Tommy walked out of the shower room and headed towards his car.

He had a moment of rage. He felt like he had cheated on Taylor, even though he hadn't. He felt like a bad person; first he had punched Taylor, then he had been in the shower room with a hot, naked girl, *what next, why?* He screamed at the top of his lungs, punching his steering wheel in rapid succession.

When he eventually calmed down, he could see Emily standing in front of his car, gobsmacked by his actions. She walked over to the driver's side window, which he simultaneously wound down.

'You're not all there, mate,' Emily said, as sweat ran down Tommy's face from the stress. 'Remember, I know you, Tommy McGregor. You could have had this.' She ran her hands down the side of her body.

'Yeah, and I didn't want it! Fuck off, you slag!' Tommy wound up the window and she punched the glass followed by a big ball of phlegm – lovely.

'Classy girl!' Tommy shouted through the window and held up both thumbs in a sarcastic manner.

Emily hated this and started to hit the window again, shouting something, but Tommy couldn't make out what it was. He sat there, letting her get on with it, as she shouted all sorts of abuse and gave offensive gestures. *God she really can't handle rejection this one.* He smiled at her and gave a little wave, which infuriated her even more. She then gave up and walked off – probably feeling a little silly.

Tommy checked his phone. There was still nothing from Taylor, just a bunch of notifications from his IPEA, which at this point he didn't care about. He started the engine and drove back home.

When he parked up, the freak from upstairs was standing outside smoking a fag. Tommy got out of his car and politely said, 'Alright!'

'I know what you did,' the freak replied in his high-pitched voice. His eyes were just glued to Tommy's.

'You know what?' Tommy asked.

'Everything!' He then walked off past Tommy and through the carpark.

'Freak!' Tommy shouted. He didn't think too much of what he had said and made his way into the apartment block.

Tommy took a deep breath and walked into the apartment. He felt anxiety. There was pressure applied to his chest, causing him to struggle for breath. He was scared about what he might find. He walked into the lounge, and Taylor was nowhere to be seen. He checked all over, but she was gone. Some of her clothes had gone, her toothbrush and toiletries, even the toothpaste.

'Could have left me some bloody toothpaste,' Tommy said to himself.

He pulled his phone from his pocket and gave Taylor a call, which was rejected after two rings, making it clear she didn't want to talk. He tried again, and the same thing happened, so he sent her a WhatsApp message, only to find she had blocked him. He sat on the floor in the hallway and said to himself, 'Shit, what have I done?' He put his hands over his face and sobbed – his world was starting to crumble.

Some time had passed, and Tommy was still sitting on the floor. He pulled himself together and made himself a cup of coffee. The battery on his phone had died due to the fact that he had been staring at it for so long, just waiting for Taylor to make contact with him. He decided to go to her mum's house to try to explain.

There was hesitation before he knocked on Taylors mums door. *Do I really want to do this?* He had to. He owed Taylor and her family an apology. He used the brass door knocker, flicking it twice. It didn't take long for Taylor's mum to answer. As soon as she saw him, she lunged towards him, almost falling, but managed to steady herself.

'You've got some nerve coming around here! You're not welcome! You're lucky Taylor's dad's not alive; he would have killed you for hitting her!'

Tommy pleaded with her, 'I'm so, so sorry! It wasn't meant to happen! I don't remember it!'

'That doesn't make it ok now, does it, you vile, disgusting human being! You're lucky I haven't called the police. It's only because Taylor begged me not to that I didn't. Now clear off!' Taylor's mum shouted whilst thrusting her hand at Tommy, which caused him to flinch. 'Yeah, you flinch! God, I could swing for you!' She slammed the door behind her. Guilt twisted inside of Tommy for what he had done.

Back outside of his apartment, Tommy pulled out a packet of fags – he didn't normally smoke, but he needed something to calm himself, and that was all he could think of. He sparked up and looked up to the sky. There was a beautiful mixture of orange and pinks. An aeroplane caught his eye, with a long contrail stretched for miles. Tommy wished he was on that plane, imagining where it was going. *Lucky people going about their lives,* he thought.

Tommy finished his fag and flicked it across the path. He looked up, and the freak was standing in front of him, staring. He was surrounded by his strange aura, which caused Tommy's hairs to stand on end.

'What mate?' asked Tommy. 'Why are you so weird?' The freak looked at him. 'Can't you fucking speak? What do you want?'

'Nothing, Tommy,' the freak answered and went to walk past. Tommy stepped to the side to block his path.

'Look, right, stop all this bullshit nonsense!' Tommy said. 'You don't need to stare at us. Just walk past, understand?'

'Us?'

'Yes, me and Taylor!'

'There is no Taylor now, is there, after what happened?' announced the freak.

'What do you know about that?' Tommy could feel his cheeks glowing red as the anger rose inside him. He repeated his words again, 'I said, what the fuck do you know about that?' Tommy stepped forward, so close that their noses were almost touching.

'Everything, my friend. Now move!'

Tommy let the freak past. *What's going on?* he asked himself.

He lit up another fag. He couldn't take the stress. Things were really getting to him. He tugged hard on the fag and drew it deep into his lungs. He then heard a voice.

'Didn't know a fitness fanatic such as yourself smoked?'

He looked over. It was Emily. 'What the fuck do you want? If you've come round here to cause more drama, then don't bother. I've had a shit arse day as it is!' Tommy exclaimed.

'I came round to apologise for my behaviour. I'm truly embarrassed and ashamed of myself,' Emily said.

'Forget it; I have.' Tommy had a don't-give-a-shit attitude.

'Can we start over?' Emily gave him a cute smile. Presumably it had always worked for her.

'Start what?' Tommy asked.

'Just being friends. Look, right, I reacted the way I did, because I've liked you for so long. I hated you rejecting me. I felt ugly.'

'I'm sorry I made you feel that way. If it was another time, when my life wasn't so fucked, then yeah, but I'm not in a good place at the moment.' Tommy dropped his head down, showing signs or adversity.

'Sometimes, Tommy, we all need a friend. Look, why don't we go up to your apartment and have a hot drink and a chat?' Emily rubbed his arm.

This time Tommy accepted the comfort from her gesture and nodded.

'Nice place you have here,' said Emily, as they walked into the kitchen. 'Do you own it?'

'I do, yeah. Bought it a few years back. Sugar?'

'No thanks.'

Tommy finished making the tea, and they sat on the sofa together. Emily had that look about her. She was very pretty and petite. Tommy was hugely attracted to her. She leaned forwards and he just couldn't help but kiss her, which turned into passion. The mugs of tea went flying. He picked her up and carried her to the bedroom.

The next morning, Tommy woke up to find Emily laid next to him, which made him feel surprisingly good. *Maybe she's right, sometimes we do just need a friend.* He watched her sleep. Her skin was perfect without makeup. Her platinum blonde hair spread across the pillow and her breathing was gentle. She was wearing one of his work shirts that looked really sexy on her. He felt like a creep just watching her sleep, but it gave him comfort. He leaned forward and kissed her, causing her to stir and wake up.

'Morning beautiful,' Tommy said as she opened her eyes and looked at him.

Emily smiled at him and sat up. She leaned forwards and gave him a closed-mouth kiss.

'Morning breath,' she said as she covered her mouth, and they both laughed – no one likes morning breath.

4

Three days had passed, and Tommy had had Emily over every night - they couldn't get enough of one another. They were in a whirlwind of passion - one little look and they were all over each other.

His working week was a struggle. He'd been under a lot of stress with work, and his boss had been on his case for various reports he hadn't managed to finish. There had been no training all week in the gym and he hadn't been eating properly, which had caused the IPEA to inundate Tommy with alerts and notifications. He had ended up muting the alerts to enable him to focus on work and to get himself back on track with things.

It was Friday night and Tommy just sat staring at the TV screen, not taking in what was on show. His mind was going around and around and his stress levels were through the roof. His job had peaks and troughs; for weeks on end it could be quiet and then all of a sudden, he would be inundated.

Whist sitting there, another one of his insane headaches came from nowhere. His eyes rolled back in his head and he fell off the sofa and onto the floor. He convulsed for a few seconds, but then settled quickly into a state of calm.

Moments later, he stood up and felt a strong urge to strip down naked. He walked over to the full-length mirror and stared at himself whilst taking off each item of clothing at a time. There was no emotion from Tommy, just a long stare at himself deep into the mirror. His mind was clear, but his body had urges. He walked towards the front door, opening it slowly with no concern that he was completely naked.

He stood outside his apartment block, naked from head to toe. It was freezing cold and windy, but he didn't react to the coldness of the night – it was as though he had no sense of feeling. He turned and looked up at the freak's window and could see him staring down with a deep smile. Tommy was thoughtless, he turned away with no emotion and slowly walked off towards The Bay, where there were clubs, bars and restaurants.

Passers-by stared at Tommy. One couple walked past, and the woman couldn't help but admire his display, resulting in her partner covering her eyes then turning her away. Tommy was still emotionless. He looked like he was in a zombie-like-state, as though he was in a trance. People probably assumed he was on Spice or some other dodgy drug.

When Tommy reached The Bay, there were two police officers jogging towards him and one had his handcuffs at the ready. Tommy suddenly snapped out of his trance, coming back to life. He could feel his nakedness and the cold struck his body, causing all of his muscles to tense up and forcing him into a shiver. The coppers doubled their pace towards him. Tommy's survival instinct kicked in, he turned and began to run for his life back towards his apartment.

His bare feet pounded the pavement. The police made chase and were gaining very fast. Tommy became breathless quickly, but still ran as fast as he could. Drivers passing by in their cars tooted their horns. Tommy was in shock. He couldn't work out what was happening. *Is this just a bad fucking dream?* He lost his momentum and fell to the floor, admitting defeat – he couldn't carry on.

A second later, one of the officers jumped on him, pushing him face down to the floor. He handcuffed Tommy and read him his rights. Tommy didn't say a word as he laid there waiting for his transportation to arrive. Seeing a meat wagon pull up and mount the pavement gave Tommy relief – the humiliation and vulnerability he was feeling would soon be gone and he could not wait to get in the back of that van.

A small crowd had gathered around the arrest, watching in excitement to see what would happen next. The officers kindly put a foil blanket around Tommy to warm him up and to protect his modesty. As he was being escorted into the van, he caught a glimpse of the freak standing in the crowd. He had a long smile on his face and just stared deeply into Tommy's eyes. It was as though he was enjoying the drama. He held up his thumbs sarcastically as Tommy disappeared into the back of the van.

Tommy's mind was mystified as he rocked from side to side in the back of the meat wagon. He just couldn't work out what had happened and why he had been walking around the streets naked. It was as though he had been sleep walking, or in a trance, and strangely had no recollection of it, no memory whatsoever.

He was checked in at the police desk and a few disguised sniggers could be heard – who could blame them. The standard process was carried out; DNA swabs, finger prints and mug shots. Then Tommy was taken to a cell where they handed him a pair of joggers and a jumper, then shut the cell door. The locking mechanism to the door could be heard distinctly, and the sound went through Tommy. He was trapped. He had never been arrested before. He felt scared but tried to reassure himself. *It's a life experience, just character building.*

Then one of the coppers opened the hatch. 'You're here for the night, fella. Sleep off whatever it is you have taken, and we will see you in the morning.'

Tommy didn't look up and didn't even respond – *yeah, yeah, whatever.*

He laid there all night, wide awake, staring up at the dull grey, gloss ceiling. His mind drifted and his chest felt a little tight from anxiety. The cell was cold and grey. Tommy laid on an inch-thick mattress with no blanket. He could hear others in their cells; some were shouting, and others were just banging, effing and jeffing - probably pissheads after a night out.

Tommy then heard a strange voice in his head, *'Tommy!'* This caused him to sit up quickly, looking around his cell. It was empty. There was no one there. *You're just overtired. It's nothing. Get some sleep.* He closed his eyes and somehow managed to drift off.

Two hours later, Tommy was woken by the sound of the cell door unlocking and being opened.

'Come on, fella. Up you get. Here's a cup of coffee. Sorry, we're out of sugar.' The officer handed Tommy the cup and he slurped the hot coffee, which burned the inside of his mouth.

'Thank you,' Tommy's voice was croaky from his dry mouth. He then took further slurps, hoping the caffeine would kick in sooner rather than later.

'Ok, get up and follow me. Bring your drink with you,' the officer ushered him towards the door, waving his fingers impatiently.

Tommy stood and followed the officer through a maze of echoing corridors, which strangely had the smell of an old school. They walked past the police desk and he was taken into a small interview room – Interview Room Two.

'Take a seat,' said the officer. Tommy sat down and looked around the room. The officer then asked, 'Do you require a solicitor?'

'Do I need one?' Tommy replied.

'It's up to you. If you have your own, you can contact them. If not, we can arrange the duty solicitor for you?'

'No thank you, it's ok.' Tommy struggled with the whole concept. *Why a solicitor?*

'Are you sure?' asked the officer.

'Yes, it's fine, thank you,' said Tommy, nervously placing his hands on the desk in front of him.

Interview conducted by PC- Butler
0815 – 19th January 2018

'Okay, so you understand you are being interviewed under caution where you are currently suspected of committing a criminal offence. You do not have to say anything, but it may harm your defence if you do not mention when questioned something which you later rely on in court. Anything you do say may be given as evidence. Do you understand?'

Tommy felt very sheepish. His charismatic personality had vanished overnight, and he had become a mere shell of himself. He could almost feel himself shrinking into the hard, plastic chair in which he was sitting. He gave a nod in response to the question.

'Tommy, I need you to say you understand?'

'I understand,' he said softly with his head down, looking at his knees in shame.

'Can you tell me what you were doing at twenty-one minutes past eleven last night outside of the Millennium Centre of Cardiff Bay where you tried to avoid arrest by retreating down Lloyd George Avenue?' The officer was friendly and somewhat sympathetic. He showed that he felt this incident was fairly humorous.

'Honestly, I have no idea,' said Tommy. 'All I remember is, I was watching TV and then I was outside naked being chased by you. I think I sleep walked?' Tommy sat back, releasing a large sigh, holding up his surrendering hands.

'Have you ever experienced anything like that before, waking up in different places? Did you take anything last night, drugs, prescription medication, anything?'

'No, I didn't take anything. I don't do drugs or drink much, and I've never woken up in strange places. This is a first, and God, I hope it's the last! I'm really sorry. I honestly have no other explanation. I've never been in trouble with the police before. I feel my life's becoming a mess.' His eyes began to fill with tears and his voice wobbled.

'Would you like a glass of water, Tommy?'

'No thank you.'

'When you say your life is a mess, what do you mean? What else has happened for you to come to that conclusion?' asked the officer.

'Well, my girlfriend has left me over a horrible argument. Some things were said, I went out, and when I got back she was gone.'

'Okay, was there any violence involved in the argument?'

'What? No, of course not,' Tommy tried to maintain his composure in an attempt to avoid the look of a liar. 'It was just a silly argument that got out of hand, and I said something really nasty and personal.' Shame was written all over Tommy's face.

PC Butler knew he was hiding something. 'What was it you said?'

'Do I need to tell you?' Tommy felt slightly uncomfortable with this question and certainly didn't want to go into detail.

'Not at all, so tell me what else has happened?'

'I met this other girl straight away, the same day in fact-' Tommy explained. PC Butler tried to hide a grin. 'And I feel an element of guilt for moving on so quickly. I feel like I'm cheating, but I'm not. I've never cheated on anyone in my life. This is completely out of character for me and now this; being arrested for indecent exposure.' Tommy slams his fists on the table.

'Tommy, calm down. What's your girlfriend's name?'

'Taylor Wells.'

'What's her date of birth?'

'Err, I'm not sure. 17th January, but I don't know the year. She's 23 though.'

'I can work that out,' said the officer. 'So, going back to last night, you think you sleep walked naked from your home address to where we spotted you, which is a good twenty-minute walk, right?'

'That's about right, yeah, I think.' Tommy nodded as he replied.

'So, you walked around naked outside. It's about two degrees out there and you didn't wake up. Is that what you are saying?'

'I guess so, yeah, but I don't know. It's the only explanation I have.' Tommy started to become agitated. His left knee was shuddering under the desk, causing the table to shake with it.

'Ok, so let's take it from the top. You woke up Friday morning, what happened?'

Tommy took PC Butler through the details of his day. He included as much detail as he could remember. When he had finished going through his movements, he asked, 'Am I in trouble?'

The copper sat back, 'I'll be honest with you, I am going to charge you for indecent exposure. I have to, if I'm honest, and you will be going to court. You will be charged under the Sexual Offences Act, 2003.'

Tommy interrupted by standing up suddenly. 'Are you fucking serious! Will I go on the sex offenders' register?'

'Sit down, or I will handcuff you, and watch your language! You're in enough trouble as it is. You will have your chance to testify in court, and until then, you will -be released on bail until your court hearing, so don't go leaving the country.'

'This is ridiculous! I could lose my job over this! Can I go?' Frustrated, annoyed and disappointed were only some of the words to describe how Tommy felt at this time.

Eventually, arriving home in a taxi, Tommy made his way up to his apartment. The front door was wide open. Tommy questioned himself, *Did I leave this open?* He walked in slowly, trying to not make any noise.

Everything was where it should be. His clothes were piled on the lounge floor where he must have stripped off. He felt lucky he hadn't been robbed.

Tommy decided to run a bath to try and relax. He made it boiling hot. Whilst the bath was filling, Tommy found his phone. There was still nothing from Taylor, but there were messages from Emily.

"Tommy, please don't ignore me, get in touch. Em xxx"

Tommy decided he needed a friend and sent Emily a text back;

"Sorry hun, been a mad one. Got arrested last night, and I have no idea what happened. I'm a bit of a mess. Could do with some company? X"

Tommy felt this was a good move for him. Taylor was gone now. He felt lonely and didn't want to worry his family about this mess, so Emily was his shoulder to cry on and his support.

He stepped into the bath. The water was boiling and Tommy gradually sank down into it. A feeling of total -relaxation filled the body parts that the hot water covered, until it was only his head above the water. He closed his eyes and took deep breaths, wondering what else could possibly go wrong and how he would get out of this?

Tommy mapped out in his mind what he needed to do. The first thing was to sort out this charge he'd received, so first thing on Monday morning he needed to seek legal advice - he was sure there would be a way round all this. The next step was to see a doctor, explain what was happening, how stressed and anxious he was feeling and to discuss his sleep walking episode. If his doctor could confirm that he was under a great deal of stress, which could have caused him to sleep walk, this could support his case when or if he went to court. He then planned to work on getting things back on track at work and maybe do some extra hours to catch up. He felt a moment of clarity, once he'd rationally thought things through in his relaxing environment.

After about six minutes, Tommy was done in the bath. The heat caused him to feel faint, so he got out, dried himself off, wrapped a towel around his waist and poured himself a glass of Rosé to help him relax even further. Tommy's phone then went off. He checked it and saw that it was Emily, which gave him a little sparkle of happiness.

EW: "I can come over now, hun. You can tell me all about it? Xxx"

TM: "Yeah, come on over, Em. I'll pour you a glass. How long will you be? x"

EW: "I'll be round in 10 mins sexy"

Tommy jumped up, got dressed, brushed his teeth and sorted his hair. By the time he was ready, the buzzer was going from downstairs, which strangely caused him to jump.

'Come on up!' He held down the door release to unlock the door and waited for Emily to come up. Seconds later she was at his door. Tommy took one look at her, and all his problems vanished for forty seconds, but then he came back down to earth.

'Come in, excuse the mess,' Tommy said - a classic saying.

Emily giggled. 'There is no mess?' She was smiling, looking cute with her blonde hair tied back.

'It's just a saying! Would you like a drink? I've got Rosé?' Tommy asked

'Perfect, but only one - I'm driving,' she replied.

Tommy's face showed an element of disappointment at the thought of her not staying. 'Can I say, without sounding cheesy?' He didn't give her the chance to respond, he just said it anyway. 'I really like you a lot. You are hot and sexy, and amazing in bed.'

Emily grabbed his cheeks. 'Thank you for saying so. I feel the same about you. Now where's my drink?' She blew him a kiss. He returned her a smile and went into the kitchen.

They both sat next to each other on the sofa. Emily was totally relaxed and looked as though she had made herself at home, having tucked her feet sideways under her bum, causing her to slightly lean towards Tommy. He, of course, didn't mind.

'So, Tommy, what's been happening? Why were you arrested?' Emily asked.

Tommy felt comfortable with Emily, so he opened up to her easily. He told her what had happened with the indecent exposure incident. He felt like crying, like breaking down, but he held it together.

'Hun, who hasn't streaked naked in public?' Emily gave a cheeky look. 'Scary about being arrested for it though! What are you going to do?'

He explained his plan, and Emily nodded with agreement that it was a good way forward.

'I have a friend of a friend who's a solicitor. She might be able to help. I'll text you her number later.'

'Ok thanks. Now that the negative shit is out of the way, how's your day been, Em?' Tommy felt refreshed and his head was clear. Having Emily round was definitely a good decision.

'It's been a good day thanks. Went swimming this morning, met the girls for lunch, and I was just settling down to have a lazy afternoon when I got your text, so now I'm here.' Emily smiled, her white teeth looking perfect.

'Well, a better day than me!' Tommy exclaimed. 'So, Emily, how old are you?' He felt slightly embarrassed that he didn't know how old she was.

'You don't know my age?' She put her hands over her mouth. 'Hun, I'm 18.'

Tommy's eyes widened at how young she was compared to him.

'You know I'm thirty, don't you?' Tommy said.

'I know more about you than you think, Mister. What do you think Facebook's for? I probably stalk you on a daily basis!' Emily let out a giggle and placed her hand on her forehead as a sign of embarrassment.

'So, why me?' asked Tommy. 'Didn't take you long to jump in my bed?' He kept his tone light hearted, hoping she wasn't offended by his direct question. He wasn't even sure why he had asked it.

'I'm not a slag, hun! I've fancied you since the first day I saw you, so it wasn't exactly a one-night stand, was it?' Emily said, nudging his shoulder with hers. Tommy returned a nudge back and they giggled together.

They had been chatting into the evening and drinking wine. Tommy made some Nachos, and they put on a film. Later that night, there was a knock at the door. Tommy thought, *Strange, as no one ever comes around?* He peered through the peep hole in the door and saw it was the freak from the apartment above. He opened the door, 'Can I help you?'

'No, Tommy, but only you can help yourself,' he turned to walk away, but Tommy wasn't putting up with this.

'Hey, what's this shit all about?' Tommy was angry and felt slightly threatened. The freak stopped and turned back to face Tommy.

'It's about you.' He held up his finger, pointing directly at Tommy's left eye. It was shaking. Another inch and his finger would have been inside.

Tommy grabbed the freak's finger and pulled it back, making a loud click and causing the freak to wince in pain. Tommy still maintained a hold of his finger. 'Back the fuck away from me! Don't ever look at me, come to my door, or even try to talk to me! If you do, it won't be your finger I'm breaking!' He let go with a push. 'Now, fuck off!'

The freak caught his breath and held his finger. 'You will regret that! Say hi to Emily.' He turned and walked away before Tommy could respond.

Tommy shut the door and returned to the lounge with a very confused look on his face.

'What was all that commotion about?' Emily still had a smile on her face.

'Ah nothing, just this prick of a neighbour of mine. He's strange as hell! Don't worry, though.' Tommy sat back down next to her. 'So, where were we?' he asked.

'I know where we weren't,' Emily replied. She slowly leaned forward and gently kissed his lips. Tommy kissed her back. Taylor was a million miles from his mind at this point. He couldn't help but just enjoy the amazing company and thought to himself, *What a good way to end this day.*

The next morning, Tommy woke up first. He could feel Emily was still in the bed next to him, as they were back to back. He laid still and listened to her breathing, thinking to himself, *I really like this girl.*

He slowly turned and spooned her, trying to not touch her with his glory. However, she simultaneously pushed back against it and giggled. She rolled over and they gazed at each other.

'God, you are beautiful,' Tommy said, and they started to kiss passionately, unaware of their audience.

Taylor was sitting in the corner of the room. She had only come round to collect some more of her things, only to find Tommy in bed with the one girl she obsessed about, the girl she always thought he was cheating on her with. She sat there silently and just watched as they had hot, passionate sex right in front of her.

A few minutes later, they had finished. Tommy looked deep into Emily's eyes. 'Wow, you are amazing! The best ever! I mean it, no one has made me finish like that!'

'Glad to be of service, Mister,' Emily replied, smiling. 'I'm going to want seconds later. I need a happy ending too!'

'Right, I need a piss.' Tommy rolled off the bed and started to walk towards the bathroom.

'Get me some tissue, please!' asked Emily.

He suddenly stopped and saw a figure slumped over the chair in the corner of the room. 'Ah shit!' He jumped in pure shock and disbelief.

Seconds later, Emily screamed and started crying. 'Is she dead?'

'She is.' Tommy was kneeling beside Taylor with his fingers pressed against her neck. 'Shit, shit, shit, what the fuck! Why did you do this, Taylor? Why?' His cry was agonising and heartfelt.

Tommy pulled Taylor to the floor and attempted mouth to mouth. She was still warm. There was blood all over the floor. She had a Stanley knife gripped in her right hand and had slit the inside of her left forearm from wrist to elbow. She had cut through both her Ulnar artery and Radial artery, causing her to die within minutes.

Tommy sat up in bed with a sudden gasp, sweat was pouring off him, and Emily was laid next to him.

'You okay?' Emily asked.

'Fuck, I had the worst dream ever!'

'You were screaming in your sleep! It scared me, so I had to wake you up.' She rubbed Tommy's chest, which was rising and falling heavily as he tried to catch his breath.

'That's okay, glad you did. It seemed so real!' He leaned back against the headboard and let out a sigh of relief.

'What was it about?' Emily asked.

'Ah, just some scary shit, Em.' Tommy looked at her and smiled. 'I'll make us some coffee.' He got out of bed and returned ten minutes later with two coffees.

Emily was sitting up in bed, her platinum hair was roughed up from a long night of passion. Her face looked pure and fresh.

'God, you are beautiful,' Tommy said.

'Why, thank you, Mister. Not so bad yourself,' Emily replied and blew him a kiss.

Tommy had a strange and strong sense of Déjà vu.

5

It was a Monday morning and Tommy was on route to work. He had a Starbucks Americano next to him and he felt focused. The first thing he planned to do when he got into work was call the number for the solicitor Emily gave him and begin reviewing options for his indecent exposure charge. He had decided not to tell his company yet and to wait and see what he would be advised to do. In his heart of hearts, he felt things were going to be okay.

He was on the M4 motorway heading east towards London. He'd just passed J18 when he started to get a severe white cold, excruciating headache. His hands started to tremble, his eyes rolled back in his head and he passed out for two seconds. He opened his eyes to find a lorry about six yards in front of him, but he calmly moved his car into the outside lane, avoiding a collision - he was back in that trance-like state once again.

Tommy's eyes were fixed on the road, his face was emotionless, and he slowly pressed the gas, causing his car to pick up speed fairly quickly. The BMWs 2.5 Turbo Diesel engine was a powerful engine, and it didn't take long before Tommy was exceeding 120 mph. He weaved around any cars that were in his way, still showing no emotion and fixing his stare straight ahead of him.

Seconds later, the car was powering along at 135 mph. Other road users started to flash their lights at him, but his foot stayed flat to the floor. The speed dial crept up further... 143 mph. The engine roared and cars started to move out of his way as he proceeded down the M4 at staggering speed.

It was a cold winter's morning, so the conditions were precarious. Tommy wasn't only putting himself in danger but many other innocent road users.

Then all of a sudden, he snapped out of the trance. He screamed in fear at the realisation of what he was doing and gently pressed the brake pedal, bringing his car down to an acceptable speed.

He panicked, fear filled his veins, and he felt terrified. There was yet again a concerning black spot in his memory, and he couldn't account for the last six minutes. The ends of his fingers were tingly, and his mouth was extremely dry. He continued with his journey to Swindon filled with anxiety and eager to get out of the car before it happened again.

Tommy walked into his place of work, acknowledging the receptionist and security. He walked through the secure doors and made his way to his allocated desk for the day. He always liked visiting the Swindon office. The people were always friendly, and he liked the atmosphere.

He located his desk, pulled out his laptop and logged on. Whilst his machine was loading, he made his way to one of the break rooms to fetch a Black Americano – the only way he could start his day.

In the break room was one of Tommy's work colleagues, James; a tall, slim man, about 55 years old, very smart and very well spoken, but he always had a light dusting on his shoulders.

'Good morning, Tommy. How are you today?' James asked in his deep, posh voice.

'Very well thanks, James. Living the dream as they say! How are you?' asked Tommy.

'I am well thanking you. So how long-'

Tommy's headache came back again. The pain was even worse than before. He gripped at his temples with both hands, falling down on one knee, squeezing his eyes tightly shut.

'Good grief, Tommy! Are you ok?' James asked.

Tommy didn't respond, so James ran off to get some help and returned two minutes later with a first aider. They found Tommy in a daze, staring out through one of the floor-to-ceiling windows.

'Tommy, I've got Gillian here with me to help you.' James then stepped forward a little closer. 'Tommy, are you ok?'

There was no response from Tommy, he just stood looking out of the window, with no acknowledgement of his co-workers.

'Are you ok, Tommy?' James became intensely concerned, so he placed a hand gently on Tommy's shoulder, then gave a quick, confused glance back over to Gillian, who was still standing in the doorway.

Tommy still didn't move.

'Tommy, would you like me to call someone?' asked Gillian from the doorway, in an attempt to take over from James. Her voice was soft and sweet in the hope that this may help. Tommy then started to move slowly, turning around.

Both James and Gillian stared in disbelief, speechless at what they were witnessing. Tommy just stood there with no emotion, not even little movements. He just stood there like a statue, staring straight ahead.

Gillian couldn't bear the sight anymore and briskly walked off, feeling physically sick and needing to get some more help.

James looked Tommy up and down. 'Look Tommy, have you taken anything? Any drugs? Have you been drinking?'

Tommy didn't reply, he just stayed still like a statue.

'Tommy, listen to me!' James's voice became more authoritative. 'I'm going to walk out of the room, close the door and not let anyone in until you are ready, okay?' James, becoming increasingly concerned, did exactly that, not expecting a reply.

As James stood outside of the room, Gillian returned with one of the Directors of the company and a security officer.

'He's in there,' Gillian said, pointing to the closed door, which James was standing in front of.

'Something isn't right, gents. I've known Tommy for nine years, and this is not him.' James held out his left hand and placed it on the security officer's chest to stop him from entering the room. 'Don't go in there, not yet. Just give him a little time-'

'No!' interrupted the Director, who was a large man in his fifties. 'I want him out of this building this instant!'

The security officer went to enter the room, and James pushed harder into the security officers chest. 'I can't let you go in there, not yet,' said James. 'This is a health and wellbeing issue, not a security issue.'

The officer eased off and looked back at the Director for answers.

'Let me talk to him,' interrupted Gillian.

'That's not a good idea at all, considering the circumstances,' said James, taking control of the situation. Further concerns were growing, as a small crowd of colleagues began to form around the area.

'Well, I've already been in there, so it's nothing new. Allow me, please. I want to help him,' said Gillian.

James stepped to one side and allowed Gillian entry. She slowly closed the door behind her.

'Tommy, are you ok?' she asked.

'Yeah, fine thanks,' Tommy replied as he was making his coffee.

Gillian was taken aback. *Strange?*

'B,but, a minute ago you were standing there... you know?' Gillian nodded towards his crotch area with a look of confusion on her face.

'I was standing there doing what?' Tommy clearly had no idea what she was talking about.

Then James, the security officer and the Director walked in after hearing their voices.

'What in the holy fuck do you think you are playing at Tommy?' shouted the Director.

'I have no idea what you are talking about?' Tommy said, holding up both hands, surrendering to whatever it was he had done. Then fear struck his gut like a bolt of lightning. They could all see the look of fear as the blood drained from Tommy's face – he looked aghast. 'Really, I have no idea what you are talking about?'

'Cut the crap, Tommy! You had your dick out in front of your work colleagues! I need you to leave, and I will be in touch.' The Director was firm and straight to the point, taking no prisoners.

'What?' The cogs started to turn in Tommy's head. He whispered to himself, 'It happened again'. He covered his face and squatted on the floor in total embarrassment and panic. 'I need help! Please help me!' Tommy looked up at the three of them staring down at him. Tears were rolling down his face.

'What happened again?' said the Director. 'You got your dick out and wanted to wave it around! You are disgusting, LEAVE!' he shouted, anger enraged his face.

The drive home for Tommy was long and drawn out. It felt as though every mile took an hour – a never ending journey. Piece by piece his life was falling apart. First he had hit out at Taylor, then he had been arrested, and now he was almost certain he would lose his job. *What else could possibly go wrong?* he thought to himself. The car radio was off. He needed the silence as confusion eroded his mind.

Tommy arrived home two hours later. Stress overpowered him. He felt physically sick, tired, and worn out, with the concept of losing his job tormenting him. He loved his job. It was his lifeline and his livelihood. He had worked his way up from the bottom for years, and for what? For it all to be taken away from him, and he had no memory of what had even happened. It was the same as the indecent exposure incident down at The Bay. *What the fuck is going on?* he thought to himself. Tommy couldn't help the feeling that someone or something was out to get him.

He got out of his car, looking up at the freak's apartment. Once again, he was there looking down on Tommy, smiling. Tommy waved at him in an over friendly, sarcastic manner with aggression behind it, showing his frustration - this dick head was the least of his worries.

As Tommy was walking up the stairs towards his apartment, he could hear footsteps coming down from above. A few seconds later, he was greeted by the freak. He looked different; he looked fresh and was wearing a shirt for what Tommy assumed was the first -time in his life. He actually looked fairly handsome. *Still a freak though*, Tommy thought.

'Good day at work?' asked the freak in his usual high-pitched voice.

'What? Why are you asking me that? Why are you even talking to me? Move!'

The freak just stood there staring. 'I said, good day at work?' the freak asked, only this time in a robotic tone.

'Look mate, jog on! I'm not in the mood for this. Please move?'

'Get sacked, did you?' the freak gave a long smile.

Tommy flipped and grabbed him by the throat, pushing him up against the wall. 'What the fuck do you know?' Tommy was enraged. He stared the freak in the eyes without blinking.

The freak absorbed the grab and took it in his stride. He held his own for a skinny guy, compared to Tommy, who gripped like a gorilla.

'What do you know?' Tommy seethed through his teeth with spit following. Tommy's eyes were black with anger. For the first time in his life he had the look of a killer.

Moments later, Tommy released his grip. The freak's neck was dark red with finger marks, and his face was slightly purple.

The freak didn't move a muscle but asked, 'Well, did you get the sack?'

Tommy lost it completely. He threw a punch straight into his mouth, which the freak couldn't take. He buckled, falling back, banging the back of his head on -the wall, then flopping to the floor. Tommy saw red. He raised his foot. He wanted to stamp all over his head, but somehow managed to compose himself before he got into even more trouble.

'I own you, Tommy,' said the freak from the floor.

Tommy leaned in, pushing his face up close to the freak's. 'You own nothing! Keep this up and I will fucking kill you, understand? I will kill you!' Tommy's words were so direct, it was clear he meant every word.

He stepped past the freak with a kick of his heal to the side of his head and proceeded to his apartment.

The next day, Tommy had no work to attend. He hadn't heard anything, but he knew the letter from HR would be falling onto his door mat soon. However, he wasn't going to sit around the apartment all day sulking. He was going to get busy, get focused and have a major gym session until he could barely move. That was the only medicine he needed right now.

The gym was busy, considering it was only ten in the morning. He scanned the place to look for Emily, but couldn't see her. He felt slight disappointment.

Tommy pulled out his phone and dropped Emily a quick text, then logged into the IPEA. He completed a full-body scan of all his muscles and organs. They were all recovered, but his stress hormone levels were high, and his testosterone levels were low. He was also fatigued. The IPEA gave a notification to get rest and nutrients, but Tommy ignored it and continued to train anyway, purely for his own mental health. Half an hour later, Emily walked in. Tommy spotted her, then thought to himself, *God, she's got it bad.*

Emily spotted Tommy, gave him a wave and gently jogged over to him. Her top was tight, and for a split second his problems went away again.

'You look stunning,' Tommy said, literally looking her up and down with wide eyes.

Emily gave him a long kiss on the lips, then pulled away, sucking his bottom lip, followed by a sexy smile.

'So do you, hun! How come you're not in work?' she asked.

Tommy was not going to fess up to what had happened yesterday, so he just told her he had the week off.

'Me too!' Emily replied, making it clear how excited she was at the potential for them both to spend loads of time together - probably what Tommy needed right now, a sexy distraction. 'Tommy, can I ask you something?' her voice was soft.

'Of course?' he smiled.

'Well, how do you see us?' There was an awkwardness in the air.

'With my eyes,' Tommy laughed, instantly breaking the awkward atmosphere. Emily raised her eyebrows. 'Seriously though, Em, I really like you. I love your company, and you are so sexy, it hurts my eyes!'

Emily smiled at him and kissed him again. This time she sneaked in a little tongue, and he grabbed her arse.

'Right,' Tommy said, 'I need to crack on and finish this workout. Shall we meet after?'

'Yeah, I'll go and do some cardio and let you finish. Give me a shout when you're done.'

After an hour, Tommy's gym session had finished. The IPEA told him that there was a slight increase in his test levels, that his stress levels had reduced and his endorphins where at peak – exactly what he needed. He felt good but hungry, so he walked over to the cafe area and ordered the exact amount of chicken and rice that the IPEA calculated his body needed. He walked over to the table and scoffed it all in about a minute - Garfield style.

'Easy tiger!' said a sweet voice as Emily sat down next to him. 'So, what shall we do for the rest of the day?'

Tommy gulped a pint of water and breathlessly replied, explaining that he had shit to sort out, but that they could go out tonight and hit the town.

Emily was slightly disappointed that she wouldn't have him to herself all afternoon but was happy with a night out together. They kissed and went off to do their own thing for the afternoon.

Tommy went outside and got into his car. Another headache enraged his mind. The pain was like there was acid flowing through his brain and the feeling grew stronger and stronger. This time he didn't pass out, he just sat at the wheel of his car, his eyes locked straight ahead. He started the engine and slowly drove out of the car park onto the main road and headed towards the city centre.

Twenty minutes later, he parked up in an NCP right near town, got out and walked towards Queen Street.

Tommy always thought that Cardiff was a beautiful city. It felt clean and fresh with the skyline increasing year by year as developers took hold of dated buildings. The city centre was always busy with people shopping, working, grabbing a bite to eat, and just generally milling around. The weather was ice cold, and Tommy was still in his gym vest and shorts without a care in the world.

As he walked down Queen Street, he passed shops, a KFC, then arrived at a Merry-Go-Round where there were kids playing and their parents were standing at the side taking photos. Tommy walked past. To his right, there was a closed-down shop, and in the doorway were two homeless people huddled together, trying to stay warm.

'Got any change, sir?' one of them asked as Tommy passed, but he didn't acknowledge them. 'Have a good day anyway,' said the homeless person in response to Tommy's ignorance. The homeless were always pretty polite. They always said 'please' and 'thank you' and didn't hassle passers-by too much.

On his left, about one hundred yards down the street, there was a bank, and immediately to his right was a hardware store. Tommy walked in, went up on the escalator and walked through the first floor. His movements were almost robotic, he was almost invisible by the way he moved around the floor almost silently.

At an aisle displaying garden wear, Tommy found a red beanie hat, and he put it on his head with the tags still hanging down. Then he stopped at the kitchen hardware section and examined the knives. He took an 8-inch kitchen knife, removed the security tag from the packaging and placed it down the back of his shorts. He then picked up a tea towel and kept it in his hand. He turned and walked back across the floor, went down on the escalator and back out onto Queen Street. He had been so brazen, no one had even noticed the items he had lifted.

Now Tommy was wandering around Queen Street with an 8-inch blade down the back of his shorts. He found a McDonalds, walked in and went straight into a disabled toilet. He locked the door, took out the knife and removed the packaging, putting it into the sanitary bin that was available. There was a large mirror in the wash area, and Tommy didn't even look at himself, which was completely out of character, as he'd usually jump at any opportunity to check his abs were still there. He placed the knife into the band of the front of his shorts, pulled down his vest and exited the toilet, heading back out onto the high street.

It was about four minutes later when Tommy stopped outside the bank he had passed not so long ago. He hung around for five minutes, and then walked straight in, whilst simultaneously wrapping the tea towel around his face and tying it off at the back of his head. He walked up to a middle-aged woman, grabbed her and put the blade to her neck. The poor woman froze on the spot, feeling the cold blade pressed firmly against her skin. Tears instantly ran down her cheeks and she was shaking in fear. Another woman screamed, and a young man, who was about 20 years old, stood scared stiff to his right, his eyes frozen on Tommy and watching his movements, getting ready to run. Everyone else in the bank cowered away quickly and quietly, hoping to not become involved.

'Nobody fucking move, or this woman will bleed out in less than a minute. You!' Tommy gestured with his head to a young guy behind the cash desk, which had protective glazing. Tommy's voice was unusually deep, very assertive and robotic. 'Get as much money as you can in a bag and place it over there.' Again, he used his head to point towards a plain wall area on route to the exit door.

The guy moved very quickly and filled two carrier bags with as much cash as possible, walked out through the secure door, placed the bags where Tommy had instructed and very quickly moved back into his safe zone. In the blink of an eye, Tommy let go of the woman, grabbed the cash and was out the door, running faster than he had ever run before. It all happened so quickly, it was like a well-planned military operation, and Tommy was in and out within a few minutes.

People in the street moved out of the way of this crazed knifeman as he sprinted around and through people, heading towards his car. There were police sirens in the background, loud and clear, but Tommy wasn't fazed. He had no thoughts, no feelings and wasn't even out of breath. He was like a machine storming down the street. The knife was discarded down a drain after he had wiped it with his vest. He ran across a road and under a railway bridge towards the car park.

The tea towel and hat were discarded as Tommy entered the carpark and shoved them behind one of the ticket machines. He found his car, got in and drove off normally, but still in his trance.

As he drove out of the city, police cars were going in the opposite direction, presumably looking for the knife wielding bank robber. As always when Tommy was in this strange state of consciousness, he looked ahead whilst his body drove the car. He eventually stopped at a lay-by approximately six miles out of the city, got out of the car with the bags of cash and placed them in a bush behind a bin, then casually drove off.

The next thing Tommy knew, he was laid out on his sofa, as though he had just woken from a nap. He sat up, his mouth was dry and had that horrible sticky stuff that accumulates when you're really thirsty. His legs and arms were aching, and there was a slight burning sensation in his chest. He walked over to the fridge and grabbed himself a cold bottle of water, guzzling it down like he'd been denied water for two and a half days and was on the brink of dying of thirst.

After a nice long shower, Tommy sorted himself out with some dinner, sat on the sofa and flicked through the channels. Nothing was on that he fancied watching, so he then spent the next hour searching through Netflix - he was bored. A while later, his phone went off. It was Emily.

'Hey, my sexy man! What time are we off out?' She asked in a bubbly tone.

Tommy had completely forgotten they were supposed to be going out, but he just wasn't feeling too great and was pretty tired.

'Sorry Em, I'm not feeling it. I'm feeling a little unwell. I just need to chill out and have a night in.' He actually couldn't remember agreeing to going out.

'That's okay, hun. Not a problem.' Emily hung up and Tommy threw down his phone, flopping back onto the sofa.

An hour later, Tommy was woken. He must have dosed off again. The front door buzzer was sounding as loud as a fog horn. He reluctantly got up and answered.

'Hey, sexy man! It's only me,' said Emily, her tone was excitable.

'Thought I said we weren't going out?' Tommy said, slightly confused.

'You did, hun. You wanted a night in, so I've got us some nibbles!' Emily's tone had dropped instantly, wondering whether she had misunderstood - which she had.

'No, I meant on my own,' Tommy paused. 'Come up anyway.' He pressed the door release button, and moments later Emily walked in with a deflated look on her face.

'Sorry hun, I got it wrong. I thought you meant a night in together... here take this.' She handed him the bag of nibbles, kissed his cheek and went to leave.

'Em, wait! You're here now, and I'm glad you came over. In fact, I'm chuffed! Come in, it's lush to see you. I'm so sorry. I've been sleeping most of the afternoon. I'm not quite with it.'

The frown on Emily's forehead did a quick U-turn, followed by a large sexy smile. 'Yay,' she bounced, showing her age a little, but Tommy didn't care. She was good company.

Emily then jumped and threw her arms around him then wrapped her legs around his waist, starting to kiss him passionately. She pulled away with a smile. 'So much for not feeling well!'

They continued to kiss each other, then suddenly Tommy pulled away. His head was starting to hurt. The pain was worse than before, and he collapsed in a heap on the floor. Emily panicked, fumbled for her phone and called 999 almost immediately.

After a few minutes, Tommy still hadn't come round, and it took the emergency services a further twenty-five minutes to get to the apartment.

When they arrived, Tommy was conscious but very weak and unable to speak properly. His words slurred as he attempted to talk. The paramedics assessed Tommy and decided to take him to hospital, as there were concerns over a possible stroke.

He was taken to A&E at Heath hospital in Cardiff to be assessed. Due to the nature of his symptoms, he was then taken through to the PET/CT department where a CT scan of his brain was completed.

Whilst waiting for the results of the scan, Tommy and Emily stayed in the A&E department. Tommy was laying on a bed with an oxygen mask around his mouth, with Emily sitting on a chair beside him stroking his arm. He turned and talked to her through the mask.

'You don't have to stay with me, Em. I'll be ok. I'm sure you have better things to be getting on with than sitting here with me?' Tommy was looking her in the eye, and her big blue eyes returned a look of adoration.

'Don't be silly! I care about you more than you realise.' She stood and kissed his forehead. 'Plus, I need you to get better.' She kissed him again.

'What do you mean?' Tommy asked, holding the mask as he spoke.

'What I mean is, I need you in my life. I have feelings for you Tommy.' Emily's hand reached and grabbed his hand, squeezing tightly.

Tommy squeezed back. 'I need you too.'

She smiled at him. Then the doctor returned with the scan results.

'So, Tommy, everything looks as it should on your scan,' said the doctor, 'but I am concerned about these headaches. They shouldn't be as bad as you are describing them. Can I ask, have you taken any drugs or alcohol over the last 48 hours?'

'No,' Tommy replied. 'I do have the IPEA implant from Medi Corps.'

'Ok, and how long ago was that?' asked the doctor.

'It was a while ago now. Isn't it on my records? That wouldn't cause this though, would it?' Tommy became concerned about this advanced medical implant inside him.

'I wouldn't have thought so. However, I do want to rule it out, so you will need to be kept in overnight for further tests.'

Tommy sighed, 'Ok, but can she stay with me?' he asked, pointing at Emily.

'Are you a relative?' asked the doctor.

'She's my partner,' replied Tommy before Emily had a chance to respond, and of course that put a huge smile on Emily's face.

'I'm afraid not,' said the doctor. 'You'll be moved onto a ward shortly. Try and get some rest.' The doctor smiled and left.

'I don't care what they say, I'm staying.' Emily was sulking with her arms crossed.

'You look so sexy when you're angry,' said Tommy.

'I'm not angry, just annoyed. I want to stay... wankers!'

'Look, you can stay at mine tonight, and I'll be back tomorrow, ok?' Tommy handed Emily his keys from his pocket.

'You sure?' she asked.

'Of course, make yourself at home.'

Emily loved this. To her it felt like he was asking her to move in – of course, he wasn't.

'Yay, ok, thanks hun!' Emily kissed him on the forehead, and they said their goodbyes.

6

Emily walked into Tommy's apartment. The feeling was a little strange, like there was something missing. She wandered around just looking at pictures on the wall. There was one in particular of Tommy and Taylor, which angered her. She gave a sneer, a look of pure hatred, and spat at the picture, then wiped it off with her sleeve.

She opened the fridge to make herself a snack and stuck the kettle on. She sat on the sofa munching on a sandwich with the tele on in the background, then she grabbed her phone to text Tommy.

"Hey hun, just settling down keeping the place warm for you. Hope you're ok. I miss you ☺ xxx"

As soon as Emily put her phone down, there was a knock at the door, causing her to jump. She wasn't sure whether to answer or not, so she decided to leave it, ignoring whoever was knocking. A few seconds later, there was a knock again, this time louder with three short bursts. This caused her to feel a little frightened and somewhat uncomfortable about answering the door in someone else's house, so she sat still and prayed the person knocking would just go away. They didn't. This time there were four louder bangs. Emily got off the sofa, reluctantly walked to the door and peered through the spy hole.

She could see a suited man holding a bunch of flowers. His attire gave her a little relief, along with the fact that he was holding a bunch of flowers. She decided to open the door.

A well dressed, relatively handsome man stood in front of her. 'Hi?' Emily said, nervously.

'Hello, home alone?' the man asked in a deep voice.

'At the moment, but Tommy will be back shortly. Why?' Emily's voice broke with nerves as she spoke.

'I'm a friend of Tommy's. Can I come in?' The man gave a strange and unwelcoming smile. 'I got you these,' he said, holding out the bunch of flowers, pushing them towards her.

Emily took a step back. 'Please leave or I'll-'

'I'm a friend,' the man interrupted with aggression embedded within his tone. She felt a wave of fear coming from the pit of her stomach. *This isn't right.*

'I'm going to close the door now, ok?' Emily said, but as she was closing the door, the man's foot got in the way.

'What are you doing?' Emily asked, her heart pounding ten to the dozen. She felt sweat beading on her forehead and her mouth became dry. 'Stop it, you're scaring me, please!' She pushed against the door, but he forced it open and pushed his way in.

Emily screamed, 'Fuck off, leave me alone!' then ran through the apartment into the kitchen and grabbed the first thing she could find that could cause significant damage - a large glass bowl.

The man followed her into the kitchen, still holding the flowers in his hand. 'What are you running for? I just want to talk to you!'

'Please just go, you shouldn't be in here!' Tears wet Emily's pretty cheeks. She was terrified that the man had forced his way into the apartment. 'I'll phone the police!' Then the realisation that she had left her phone on the sofa hit her.

'Why would you call the police?' asked the man. 'I just need to talk to you.' His voice was calm but creepy, and Emily still felt threatened. 'You're so hot!' The man took a step closer.

'Don't come any closer! I'll throw this in your fucking face!' Emily held the glass bowl above her head ready to hurl it at the man. Her eyes were black with fear, but she tried to hide it with aggression. Her breathing came in short bursts, causing her to feel breathless and the tips of her fingers tingled.

The man then retreated, leaving the apartment. Emily watched him walk out of the kitchen. He was casual, calm and slow. She waited for the sound of the door closing, and when she heard it shut, she let out a sigh of relief. She put the bowl down and went to the front door to ensure it was locked, putting the chain across and securing the door further. She turned, placed her back against the door and slid down onto her bum, her whole body shaking, *what did he want?*

Tommy was sound asleep in the hospital bed but awoke with a sudden start. Something wasn't right. He had a gut feeling, wrenching and turning in his stomach. It felt as though his stomach was full of flies trying to bite their way out. He couldn't shake this feeling. It was intense, like a fire burning through fuel. There was a sense of fear for Emily. She was in danger or was going to be in some sort of trouble. It was as though there was a force pressing him to get home. He tried to shake it off and think nothing of it, but relaxation was driven away with the intensity of the feeling, which kept growing stronger inside him. He decided he had to leave the hospital, and he pressed the button to get the nurse's attention.

After waiting for a considerable amount of time, and with no appearance from the nurse, Tommy slowly took the IV line from his hand. There was a little pain along with warm blood tricking like a tap from the vein. He pressed on it hard to stop the bleeding, which didn't take long, and then grabbed some medical tape from the side. As he was leaving, the ward nurse stopped him, quizzing him about what he was doing.

'I've got to go, it's urgent. I can't stay here!' Tommy tried to pass, but she blocked his way.

'Tommy, you need to go back to your bed.' The nurse was somewhat insistent.

'No!' he paused and looked her in the eye. 'I don't have to do anything!' Tommy appeared angry with a deep, persistent look in his eyes, so the nurse stepped to one side to allow him to pass.

He had no car and no money on him, just his feet to get him home. There were about seven miles between himself and Emily. He started off with a light jog, which quickly turned into a run with an intensifying feeling of dread.

It was cold. Tommy was only wearing shorts and a t-shirt, but he didn't let the cold bother him. He just held his focus on getting home to make sure Emily was okay. His wandering mind generated all kinds of scenarios. He tried to dismiss each one, but all they did was fuel him to get home.

Four miles on, Tommy began to tire. He dug deep and pushed himself. He pushed through the pain in his legs. The cold air didn't help, as his chest burned. The streets were empty with the odd car driving by. Some of the drivers glanced at Tommy, probably wondering what the fuck he was doing running at two in the morning in shorts and t-shirt at this time of year.

After 30 minutes, Tommy was almost home. He had a mile left, and he upped his pace to a sprint. Tears rolled down his cheeks from the cold air stinging his eyes. His chest was on fire and he felt as though he had needles shooting through his shins.

He continued to focus, pushing and pushing, driven on by determination.

He could then see his apartment block, so he kept pushing further. He was flat out! Usain Bolt would have had trouble catching him at the rate he was going - it's amazing what the body can do when someone you care about is in trouble.

Tommy got to the front door, but realised he had no keys - Emily had them. He was gasping for breath as his diaphragm flexed. He looked up at the apartment, scanning for any movement – there was nothing. He hit the buzzer, holding it down hard so the buzzer sounded endlessly.

After five minutes, Tommy knew that something had to be wrong. That buzzer was loud enough to wake the dead. There was no way Emily could sleep through it. He banged on the main door in the hope that another tenant in the building would hear and open the door for him.

Ten minutes passed, and Tommy's attempts to gain entry had failed. He was gasping for breath more and more, and his mouth and throat were so dry, it felt like he'd been eating chalk. He banged on a window on the ground floor, causing a light to come on. *Thank God,* Tommy thought as old Mr Richards pulled his curtains aside, peering out to see that it was Tommy and then coming to let him in.

'Thank you so much! I'm so sorry!' Tommy exclaimed and legged it upstairs to his apartment, unintentionally pushing past Mr Richards.

The door to Tommy's apartment was shut and locked. He banged on it hard, causing a white pain in his wrist. He continued over and over, but there was nothing.

He shouted, 'Emily, it's me, Tommy! Open the fucking door!'

Tommy then heard the door unlock and open, and he pushed his way in. Emily was shaken up. She looked like she had seen a ghost.

'What's up? What's happened?' Tommy was frantic.

Emily threw her arms around him. 'There was a man. He pushed his way-.'

Tommy interrupted her. 'Did he hurt you? I'll fucking kill the prick! Tell me he didn't hurt you?'

Emily shushed him by placing a finger on his lips to try and calm him. 'No, he didn't touch me. He was intimidating, so I threatened to smash a bowl over his head, and he left! I was so scared, I didn't know what to do, and when I heard the buzzer going again, I thought it was him.' Tears ran down her face. She was clearly distraught by the whole episode.

'I knew something was wrong,' Tommy said. 'I could just feel it.' His voice turned to a whisper, 'I fucking knew it!'

'How come you're home?' Emily asked, pulling back and looking at him.

'I just had this feeling something was wrong. It was so strange. I've never felt it before. I just had to get back here, so I discharged myself and legged it home.'

There was blood that had seeped through the tape on Tommy's hand, and it was all over his one side from where he had been running.

'Bloody hell, hun! What have you done?' Emily was shocked at the amount of dried blood on him.

'Had to pull the IV out and get home to you! You are ok, yeah?' Tommy threw his arms around her.

There was a moment of silence whilst they absorbed one another. Tommy closed the door, locked it and they went into the bedroom.

'I'm so glad I came home, Em. So glad!' Tommy stripped off his bloodied clothes to take a shower. He gave Emily a kiss and went for a wash.

'Wait,' Emily said. Tommy turned. 'Can I come with you?' she asked. 'I don't want to be on my own.'

Tommy nodded, and she followed him into the bathroom.

They were both chatting. Their tension began to ease in the company of one another. As they both reached a state of calm, they heard the front door close. Tommy burst out of the shower, knocking Emily over, and checking the entire apartment frantically. There was no one there.

'Oh my shit!' screamed Emily. She started shaking profusely, breathlessness taking over her. 'He was in here the whole time, Tommy! The whole time! Oh my fucking hell, I have to go! Please take me out of here!'

Tommy hastily packed up an over-night bag with essentials, and they quickly fled the apartment, heading off to find a hotel.

They drove to the city centre, found a Premier Inn and checked themselves in. The room was basic, but clean and quiet.

'We should call the police,' suggested Tommy.

'Leave it for now, hun. I just want to try to relax and clear my head. It's half three in the morning! Let's just cuddle up and sleep in tomorrow. Things won't seem as bad in the morning.'

Tommy couldn't refuse the puppy dog eyes, even though everything inside him wanted to call the police. He decided to leave it, so they could both rest, especially as he hadn't been feeling well. They cuddled up, both exhausted, and fell asleep fairly quickly, considering the events of the night.

Emily was the first to come to life. It was midday. She decided to leave Tommy sleeping and nipped out into town to grab some food. The air was crisp and cold, but the sun was shining, providing patches of a little warmth. She looked up to the sky and took a long, deep breath, feeling fresh with a clear head. She then proceeded to find a coffee house, which didn't take too long.

'Two Americanos, no milk, ooh and I'll have two of those blueberry muffins as well, please.'

'To take away, Miss?' asked the Barista.

'Yes please.' There was a large smile on Emily's face, even though last night had made her feel uncomfortable and scared. She had never gone through anything like that, and to date it was the worst thing that had ever happened to her. However, she had Tommy where she needed him.

She made her purchase and was casually walking back to the hotel, when she spotted the man from last night standing still, staring at her, about two hundred yards ahead. He was wearing the same clothes he had been in the night before and was still holding the bunch of flowers.

Emily's heart pounded in her chest and heat filled her stomach. She closed her eyes and prayed the man would disappear - funnily enough, he was gone when she opened them ten seconds later.

Her mouth was dry. 'What the fuck?' Emily whispered. 'What's he playing at?'

She got back to the hotel room to find Tommy was gone. His phone was missing, but the rest of his things, including his wallet, were scattered around as though he had rushed out. Emily assumed he'd gone to look for her, so she decided to stay put, rather than risk missing each other in a game of cat and mouse. She tried to call Tommy numerous times but failed to connect.

After an hour, Tommy still hadn't returned, so Emily went down to the lobby to see if he was around, but he was nowhere to be seen. At the desk, she asked if Mr McGregor had left a note or anything, but their response was that he had already checked out. She stood and stared, feeling utterly confused.

'Well, did he say where he was going? All his stuff is still in the room,' Emily probed.

'No, Miss. He didn't say a word, just handed us the key.'

'No, this isn't right. He wouldn't have checked out without me!' Worry was written all over Emily's face.

She scanned her surroundings. Through the front windows she could make out that man again. He was standing staring into the hotel lobby, still holding the bunch of flowers.

'Call the police, there's a man after me!' Emily was frantic and her hands were shaking.

It was clear to the receptionist that Emily was in distress, and she escorted her through to the back office. As Emily walked, she anxiously glanced back and "he" was gone.

'Can I get you a glass of water, Miss? Or is there anyone I can call for you?' The receptionist's voice was full of concern.

'No thank you, it's okay. I thought I saw someone. I'm just being silly and over-reacting.' Emily tried to imply that she was a typical blonde. 'Thought I saw a crazy ex, that's all,' she said, followed by a giggle.

'Okay, Miss. As long as you are sure. I can ask one of our security officers to escort you through to the front and make sure there is no one there?'

'That's very kind of you, but I'll be okay, really,' Emily smiled. 'Can I just collect my things from the room, is that okay?'

'Of course, Miss. Not a problem.'

Emily gathered both of their belongings from the hotel room, packing up the over-night bag, then left the hotel. She flagged down a taxi as she stepped out towards the curb. She was miffed at the thought of Tommy leaving her like that. *So strange,* she thought to herself.

Back at the apartment block, there were two police cars parked outside the front. Emily hurried inside. There were two uniformed police officers in the apartment and a lady looking very official with a black and white police lanyard around her neck.

'You are?' asked the lady, dressed in a dark red blouse, black suit trousers and heels. Her black hair was tied back. She looked a little tired in the face, as though she'd had a tough life. From first impressions, she was not someone Emily would like to confront – bitch was written all over her weathered face.

'I'm Emily. This is my boyfriend's place.'

The two uniformed officers were searching the apartment, collecting belongings and placing them in large clear bags, then sealing them.

'What are you doing?' Emily asked.

'I'm DI Valentina. Can you confirm your boyfriend's name please?'

'Er, yeah sure, it's er-'

'Look, cut the I-don't-know or I-can't-think-of-a-fake-name bullshit! Just tell me. You don't want to incriminate yourself, do you?'

'Tommy, his name is Tommy McGregor.'

'And... where is Tommy now?'

'I actually don't know.' Emily's face looked sad, but DI Valentina wasn't taking any prisoners. She had little empathy for any suspected criminals or anyone who she could sense was being dishonest. Valentina was a good judge of character.

'Have a think, when did you see him last?' asked the DI.

'This morning. Can I sit down, please?' Emily pointed towards the lounge.

'You may.'

They walked into the lounge and sat down. Emily watched the uniformed officers as they proceeded to search the place, causing one hell of a mess.

'This morning. We were in the Premier Inn. I got up and left to get some coffee, and when I got back, he was gone!'

'What time?'

Emily was taken aback. She felt as though she was being interrogated – she was. 'It was around midday,' she replied.

'Midday when you saw him last, or when you got back?'

'When I saw him last. What's this all about?' Emily asked.

The DI ignored her question, giving a strong indication that she should be the one doing the asking and Emily should just be answering. 'Then what happened?'

'I sat in the room for about an hour, then went down to reception, where they said he had already checked out,' Emily explained.

'What time did he check out?'

'I don't know, sorry.' Emily was already becoming increasingly exhausted by the interrogation.

'DI,' said one of the uniformed officers. She turned and acknowledged him. 'We have everything we need,' he informed her.

'Great!' the DI replied, turning back to Emily. 'If you see Tommy or hear from him, you call this number immediately.' She handed Emily a business card.

'Ok, no problem,' Emily agreed.

They all left promptly, leaving Emily alone in the apartment that had been turned upside down. She went to close the front door and noticed it had been considerably damaged.

'Hope you're gonna pay for this damage!' she shouted down the stairs suddenly feeling brave, but there was no reply.

She made her way to the bedroom, laid on the bed and scanned the room. There was so much of Taylor still there. A picture of Tommy and Taylor was on the side next to the TV. They looked happy. Emily stood and walked over, looking at the picture. 'You horrible, evil bitch!' she said out loud, looking at Taylor, then punched the picture, cracking the glass.

Still feeling angry at the sight of Taylor and Tommy happy together, Emily went through the apartment and started to remove any pictures of the two of them, placing each one into a black bin liner she found under the sink. The last one she came to, she held out in front of her and shouted, 'This is only the beginning, bitch!' She placed it in the bin liner with the others and left the apartment with the bag of pictures.

Emily arrived home, she sat in her car outside her house and logged onto her laptop. She was using an instant message service on the Dark Net to message someone by the name of – Scientist83.

Emily: *"I've made good progress."*
Scientist83: *"Excellent news! Well done you!"*
Emily: *"What happens next?"*
Scientist83: *"Keep doing what you are doing. Now the bait has been taken, this is going to get messy."*
Emily: *"Will do. When will it all kick off?"*
Scientist83: *"Not sure yet. I'll let you know, or I might decide to surprise you."*
Emily: *"I like surprises, but not that kind."*
Scientist83: *"Suck it up. It has to be convincing."*
Emily: *"Ok, I'm nervous."*
Scientist83: *"Don't be, just think about the long game."*
Emily: *"I'll try. Oh and tell that idiot to stop harassing me. He's freaking me out and I don't like it... or him."*
Scientist83: ***IS NOW OFFLINE***

She closed down the laptop, leaving the pictures in her boot she then went into her house, there was no one home, she suddenly felt on edge... what's gonna happen?

7

It was dark and freezing cold, with the sound of the wind blowing through trees, as Tommy laid on a forest floor. His entire body ached, his mouth felt sticky and he had no idea where he was. He only had on a pair of shorts, a hoody and nothing on his feet. He felt exposed, perplexed and scared stiff about what was happening to him. His mind was numb with no memory of how he got to where he was. The last thing he remembered was being in the hotel with Emily.

'Emilllllllllllllly!!!' Tommy shouted at the top of his lungs.

There was nothing but the wind in the trees and the sound of his own breathing. He could also hear the sound of a fox screaming in the distance causing fear to flood his veins. His warm breath formed clouds in front of him when he exhaled as it hit the freezing air. He scanned the area, but there was nothing apart from a planation of trees and detritus. The sky looked clear through the trees with the stars on display, and he felt thankful that it wasn't raining.

Tommy decided he was going to walk in a random direction. He planned to continue walking in a straight line to ensure he didn't go around in circles, and he hoped that this would eventually lead him to a main road or path.

Just as he began to set off, he noticed his mobile phone on the forest ground, almost hidden by the rotting debris. He picked it up, giving it a wipe - there was blood on it. He checked himself over - not a scratch, so it wasn't his blood. Tommy's mind spun like a merry-go-round, completely confused at the loss of his memory once again. *What is happening to my life?*

He used to have it good; a gorgeous girlfriend a nice home and good job; yet now he was stuck in the middle of nowhere, stranded, freezing cold, without even any shoes on his feet, and with someone else's blood on his phone.

Tommy checked through his phone for any indication of what had happened. There was nothing of importance. He did notice that it was 02:15 – there were a few text alerts notifying of missed calls from Emily, he tried to call but there was no signal.

He then chose a direction and kept walking, hoping it would lead his out of the forest or to a path or even he might find someone to help him.

The trek was long and his feet were in agony from the cold and the rough debris on the ground that chewed into the soles of his feet. His teeth chattered uncontrollably with a high pitch sound.

After what felt like hours, Tommy checked his phone. Only thirty minutes had passed – this was a struggle. The battery on his phone was running low, so as there was no signal to use the maps or make calls he dimmed the screen and switched on airplane mode in an attempt to preserve as much battery as possible until he needed to use it. He dropped his phone from his shivering hands, then he picked it up and continued to walk very slowly, feeling frozen and having very little energy.

As he walked, he tried to take his mind off his throbbing feet by trying to piece together his last movements: *Someone had tormented or stalked Emily, so we left the apartment and checked into the Premier Inn, cuddled up in bed and fell asleep. I recall waking up to take a piss, and that was it?* Nothing made sense. Nothing explained the blood on his phone and why he was stranded in the middle of nowhere.

Hours had passed, and the sun had partially risen in the clear sky, turning it a beautiful orange and red. Tommy stopped, closed his eyes and listened.

'I,I,I c,c,can hear cars!' he said out loud, but his excitement quickly fell flat with the coldness that was eating his body from the outside in. Severe lethargy was getting the better of him. He knew he didn't have long before hypothermia would set in fast. However, he continued on his way - his survival instincts kicked in. He had to walk on the outsides of his feet to avoid the agonising pain from walking normally, which almost resulted in him twisting his ankle a few times.

Tommy stumbled upon a road a few hundred yards in front. A few cars sped past, and he could smell the exhaust fumes, which he found strangely satisfying. He then realised where he was.

'Bbbbrrecon ffffucking Bbbbeacons.' Tommy's voice was wobbly from shivering, and there was an element of slurring as he spoke. He was becoming increasingly disorientated.

When he reached the roadside, he could barely stand, although the shivering had slowed. He tried to flag down the first car – nothing. Second – nothing. Third – nothing.

'Someone please stop!' Tommy begged, as weakness was now overtaking him. His mind became even more confused and his legs buckled at the knees. His breathing was short, and the condensation from his mouth was now at a minimum, as his core temperature was dropping. His mind went blank, his vision became blurry, and then hypothermia got the better of him.

When Tommy awoke, he could feel warmth. There was the smell of an open fire, and the sound of flames crackling and popping as they ate through firewood. He felt comfortable and was laying on something soft. He then opened his eyes and could see wooden beams running along the ceiling as he scanned the room. He was in the centre of a large four poster bed with a fireplace directly opposite, which was providing the luxurious warmth.

'Hello?' Tommy's voice was weak and husky with a slight slur.

Moments later an old man walked in. 'Hello, chap. How are you feeling?' The man had a prominent Welsh accent.

'Like I've died, come back to life and died again,' Tommy said. 'Where am I and who are you, if you don't mind me asking?' He shuffled his body, so that he could see the man more clearly, which caused pain to shoot through his spine.

'My name is Alwyn, chap. I found you on the side of the road. I'll be honest, I thought you were dead at first, but when I checked you over, I knew what was wrong. I used to be a doctor, I did.'

'Thank you, Alwyn. Thank you for helping me, but I've got to go.' As Tommy tried to move, his entire body ached, and another electrical shock of pain shot through his spine and down to his feet. 'Ah, FUCK... sorry!'

'Chap, I don't think you'll be going anywhere for a while. You're Tommy McGregor, are you not?'

'Yes, how did you know that?' Tommy asked.

'You're on the news. You're a wanted man, you are.'

'What for?' Tommy asked. *Why on earth would I be a wanted man? I've not done anything!* This question repeated in his mind several times, but he never came to any conclusion.

'You robbed a bank at knife point two days ago!' Alwyn didn't seem to be threatened by Tommy. Tommy was unwell, so he wasn't planning on turning him in until he was better. Alwyn felt this was his duty as an old-fashioned man of medicine, ignoring the fact that Tommy had committed a serious crime.

'Well, can you take me to the station then, as I definitely haven't done anything. I have nothing to hide!' Tommy exclaimed.

'Don't go anywhere,' instructed Alwyn, and he walked out of the room.

Moments later, Alwyn returned with a very old-looking 14-inch tube tele. 'Let me set this up. The morning news will be on, and you can see.'

'Okay.' Tommy laid his head back down on his pillow whilst Alwyn worked out how to set up the tele. Once it was set up, Alwyn flicked through the channels until he got to the news channel. 'I didn't even know these TV's would still work?'

'It works, it does, you see,' Alwyn announced.

They both waited, and after twenty minutes, there it was; a CCTV image showing the world Tommy's knife-wielding actions in the bank. He had a red hat on and a tea towel wrapped around his face, but Tommy knew it was him. The grainy images then showed Tommy's face in full view without the tea towel, followed by a shot of him driving his car. The reporter provided a running commentary as the videos played. Tommy's most recent Facebook profile picture was shown and then the reporter went on to explain how Tommy was a dangerous man, and if seen, not to approach him, but to call the police immediately.

BBC Wales Today – 26th January 2018.
Latest Headline at: 10:43:
HSBC – Armed Robbery Tommy McGregor, 30.

HSBC has been robbed at knife point. The CCTV images show Tommy McGregor, 30, holding a 43-year-old mother of 3 at knife point. South Wales Police are on the search for McGregor. If seen, please do not approach him, as he could be armed and is considered dangerous – Anyone who has any information should contact South Wales Police incident room at once on – 02020 101101.

Tommy threw his hands to his face and let out a scream. 'I don't remember, Alwyn, I really don't! I swear to God, I'm telling you the truth! I need to call the police. This must be a prank or a misunderstanding. There has to be some sort of logic behind it.' Tommy sobbed, 'I wish I could see my mum'. Tears rolled down his cheeks, and Alwyn tried to comfort him.

'Listen, Tommy, I do need to hand you in, but I'll wait until you're feeling better.' Alwyn smiled at Tommy. 'I can see you're not a bad person, but you need to sort whatever that is.' He pointed at the screen. 'Can I get you a drink?'

'Thank you, Alwyn. I would love a coffee, and have you seen my phone?'

'I'll be back shortly. Your telephone is on the side over there.' He handed it to Tommy.

'Thank you, Alwyn. I mean it... thank you.'

Tommy logged into the IPEA on his phone to find that his body was experiencing numerous issues; low blood pressure, low oxygen levels, and soft tissue and nerve damage to his feet. His body temperature was reading 35 degrees Celsius, so was still on the cold side, but was getting there. The history showed it had dropped down to a minimum of 28 degrees Celsius. Tommy felt lucky to still be alive.

The battery symbol on his phone began to flash, notifying him that there was only 15% remaining. He switched off his phone and awaited Alwyn's return with his coffee.

Tommy took his time in recovery, trying to piece together the recent events that had led him to where he was now. He couldn't explain the loss of time. The robbery had been two days ago, so how long had he been out in the forest? He worked out that he couldn't have been out there for too long, as the temperature was at -1 degree Celsius, therefore he would have died laying there for any length of time. Therefore, the robbery must have happened before the hotel stay, and from the hotel he had ended up in the forest a night later. Now he was here with Alwyn. *So, how did I get to the forest and why is there blood on my phone, or better still, who's blood is it?* Tommy was baffled, he couldn't remember a thing and needed answers.

Alwyn walked in. 'Here you go, chap.' He handed Tommy his coffee. 'This will warm you up.'

'Thank you. You don't happen to have a phone charger, do you?' asked Tommy.

'In fact, I do.' Alwyn left the room. Tommy could hear some fumbling around, then Alwyn returned with the base to his portable house phone. 'Will this do, chap?'

Tommy smiled at him. 'Thank you, Alwyn, but no, for my mobile phone?'

'Oh, I see, then no I don't. I don't bother with them things. Now, get some rest and sleep. The body recovers best this way, it does.'

'Your Welsh accent is strong, Alwyn. You been here long?' Tommy asked.

'My whole life I lived in this house, I have. Now, rest. I will leave you be, but shout if you need me.' Alwyn closed the door and left Tommy to rest up.

The following day, Tommy was woken by Alwyn shaking him. 'Get up, Tommy! Get up right now!'

Tommy awoke and could easily see Alwyn was in distress.

'I need you to go! Put on these clothes and leave, now!' Alwyn's voice was full of aggression and a hint of worry. It was like he was possessed.

'Okay, but why?' Tommy felt scared and confused.

'You are a monster! Get out of my house!' Alwyn picked up a broom handle and started to wave it around, trying to hit Tommy with it.

'What?' Tommy was fending off the broom as he spoke. 'Why? Look, calm down! I will go. Just tell me what's happened?'

Alwyn had a tight grip on the handle; so tight his knuckles were white. 'What was your lady friend's name?'

'Emily...... Taylor?'

'Emily, that's her-' Alwyn broke down. He couldn't finish his sentence. There was something about an old man crying that upset Tommy.

'Emily what, Alwyn? Come on, tell me?' Worry and fear flashed through Tommy's mind, scared of what could have happened. 'Tell me, Alwyn?'

Tommy stood and Alwyn held out his hands, as though he was cowering from Tommy, like Tommy really was the monster he was calling him.

'It's on the news! Please, just leave.' It was clear Alwyn had become scared of Tommy. His eyes were filled with sorrow, and his hands were clasped together in prayer.

Tommy looked at Alwyn, confused by his behaviour, and left without any answers.

8

The previous night 24th January 2018

Emily lived with her mum in a place called Cathays in the centre of the city. When she arrived home from Tommy's, her mum wasn't home, which unnerved her no end, so she went around the house and turned on all the lights to try to give her comfort and a sense of security.

I'll have a nice long soak, Emily thought and ran herself a bath. She lit some candles, put on some music and soaked her cares away, which relaxed her almost immediately as she slowly sank herself down into the hot soapy water.

Emily felt glad to be home; she felt safe. At that point, she decided it was time to distance herself from Tommy. Her fulfilment was complete – especially now. She flicked through her phone and blocked his number, then instantly deleted it. A weight lifted, she felt glad this was over. It was all too much, and things were getting difficult for her.

The sound of the front door slamming shut caused Emily to jump. Her nerves came to life from being momentarily dormant.

'Emily, you in? Why is the house lit up like a bloody Christmas tree?' Her mum, Nicola, was always going on about wasting energy. She worked as a director for an environmental organisation and led by example. She was a strong, wealthy woman with a high moral standing.

Emily ran down the stairs with soap bubbles still on her shoulders and a large, fluffy towel wrapped around her. 'Sorry mum, I've had a strange few days.'

Her mum kissed Emily's forehead and told her to get into comfies, then she could tell her all about it.

Emily got changed, dried her hair and opened the window to cool down from the heat of the hairdryer. She suddenly froze, taking in a gasp of air. She could see a figure standing looking up at her from the other side of the road, but she couldn't make out who it was. The fear caused a knot to harden in her throat, making it hard to breathe. There was an ominous silence in the air. She felt herself mentally leave her body momentarily, speculating on the reasons why that figure would be there looking up at her, terrified of the thoughts of this person, their capabilities and motives – anything and everything went through her paranoid mind.

She slammed the window shut and pulled the curtains so aggressively that one of the curtains came off the rail. She ignored it and quickly walked down into the kitchen where her mum was pouring a glass of wine.

'Mum, there's a strange man outside.' Tremors ruled Emily's hands as she spoke through a heart-wrenching cry.

'Who is it darling? Do you know him?' Nicola pulled Emily towards her and gave her a squeeze.

'No, I don't know him!'

'Well, you're safe here, love. Shall I call the police?' Nicola asked.

'No, it's okay. It's probably nothing and just me freaking out.'

Nicola rushed to the front door, forced it open and stepped outside. The street was silent, apart from the sound of a dog barking in the distance. She slammed the front door shut and returned to Emily.

'Has he gone, Mum?' Emily asked.

Nicola explained that there was no one there. She suggested that they get out the chocolate and put on a girlie film along with a mother-daughter cuddle.

Ever since Emily's dad had left Nicola for another woman when Emily was a baby, Nicola had always been protective over Emily. In her eyes, Emily was the model daughter and Emily portrayed the facade very well - but inside, Emily had a little demon of her own.

The lights were off, and they giggled to each other as Magic Mike XXL started. They shared a large bar of chocolate between them and sipped red wine. They were relaxed together and enjoyed the film, still giggling at certain scenes, even though they'd seen the film fifteen times before.

They talked about boys and men from their past and shared funny stories. Emily's mum told her about this perv in work who always had her coffee placed on her desk every morning, exactly how she liked it.

Emily fell asleep quickly that night. She felt peaceful after spending a nice evening with her mum, even though she wondered when the inevitable was going to happen, thinking about Scientist83.

Around midnight, Emily awoke. She needed to pee but didn't want to get out of bed. She tried to fight the urge, to the point where she was clenching her thighs together. She had no choice but to get up, unless she was going to wet the bed. When she returned from the toilet, she let out a blood-curdling scream. Her mum hurriedly entered her room.

'What is it, love? What's happened?'

'Tttttthat man, he was in here! I,I,I saw him!' Fear took hold, causing Emily to struggle to get her words out.

'You were dreaming, my sweetheart! There's no one here, I promise. Go back to sleep.' Nicola kissed Emily's cheek and went back to bed.

Her eyes wide open and fixed on the ceiling, Emily lay in bed frozen, too scared to move or to allow her eyes to wander around her room. She knew someone was there. She had the feeling someone was watching over her. Fear saturated her body and her mouth was dry. Someone was definitely there watching her, and her joints were seized as the fear grew. She couldn't move; she didn't want to move.

'Please, leave me alone,' Emily whispered. 'I can't handle it! Just go! Let's forget all about it.'

A floorboard creaked, causing a large gulp in her dry, tight throat that felt like thorns scraping her tight dry throat. There was another creak, this time closer. Emily could sense someone standing next to her bed as she stared directly upwards. There was a smell of the outdoors that diffused off this person's clothes, along with a brief feeling of coldness. Emily lay stiff, just waiting in the still silence for the next move, trying to anticipate what would happen next and when it was going to happen. She knew this person was in here for a reason. It was just a matter of time until that reason was revealed.

A large heavy hand was suddenly pressed over her mouth. Still frozen in fear, absolutely terrified, Emily had no fight in her and she lay still, too afraid to look into her attacker's eyes. She could just make out a black figure in her peripheral vision.

Emily then couldn't help but look straight at the figure. She gasped. It was Tommy. She didn't know whether to feel relief or fear. She was confused.

'Please go!' Emily kept her begging voice to a whisper.

Tommy just stood staring downwards, his eyes were black and his gaze was distant, as though he was physically there but mentally someplace else. His breathing was deep and slow and his eyes hardly moved.

'Please, please, please!' she begged, however there was nothing but silence.

Emily was terrified. She knew Tommy but could see it wasn't him. It was as though he was under a spell, in a hypnotic-like state, that caused her even further anxiety. His body appeared stiff, and he didn't look as though he was in control. There was nothing there behind his eyes.

Tommy then moved. He knelt down slowly beside her bed and gradually dragged the blanket off her body.

'Tommy, no!' Emily tried to pull the blanket back, but Tommy easily overpowered her and pulled the blanket off and out of her reach.

His other hand raised from behind his back. He held a Stanley knife with the razor-sharp blade out at the ready. He placed it on the pillow next to Emily's face and slowly moved his index finger to his lips, as if to order her into silence - still his eyes hardly moved.

The knife was a symbol of death that Tommy was using to control her. He slowly pulled off her pyjama bottoms, leaving her bottom half completely exposed, then he ran his hand along the inside of her leg. Goose bumps appeared under her skin. Emily felt violated and dirty, knowing he was getting off from touching her naked body. There was a feeling of complete exposure and vulnerability. *How fucking dare he,* she thought. Her impulse reaction caused her legs to close.

She then felt Tommy's hands firmly grabbing her breasts, pinching her nipples, and running his hands over her from head to toe. She felt physically sick and horrified as her anticipation built, scared of what was going to happen next.

The blade was then held to her neck and Tommy applied a little pressure. Emily was petrified, scared he was going to rape her. She couldn't help but think that she'd rather he killed her.

Tommy then stood and walked out of her room, quietly closing the door. Emily waited; she listened for movement, for any sign of activity outside of her door, but it was silent.

The thought of what could have happened to her suddenly hit her like a brick to the face. Emotion took over, and she burst into tears, trying to be as quiet as possible.

Once she managed to calm herself, she got out of bed, her hands jittering from the adrenaline, and peered through the window, watching the street until she saw Tommy leave her house and walk off as though nothing had happened. *Thank God that's over,* she thought to herself.

Emily got back into bed. Adrenaline flowed through her veins, which kept her awake for hours. She felt dirty and disgusting, having had his hands touch her body without her consent. Eventually, she fell asleep.

It was dark and freezing cold, with the sound of the wind blowing through trees, as Tommy lay on a forest floor. His entire body ached, his mouth felt sticky, and he had no idea where he was. He only had on a pair of shorts, a hoody and nothing on his feet. He felt exposed, perplexed and scared stiff about what was happening to him. His mind was numb with no memory of how he got to where he was. The last thing he remembered was being in the hotel with Emily...

The next morning, Emily woke up naturally. She checked her phone to see the time was 1015. She had a text notification but wasn't interested in who it was from or what it said.

All of a sudden, the memory from last night came rushing back. It caused a surge in adrenaline, followed by a sickly, gut-wrenching feeling that churned inside her stomach as though it was full of flies.

Emily sat on her bed, face in her hands and cried. 'I can't believe it, I can't believe this has happened.' She felt angry, and mixed emotions controlled her body momentarily.

After about twenty minutes of ranting, Emily decided to move herself and to check on her mum. She turned the door handle to her mum's bedroom slowly. She could feel the presence of death, and the smell of fresh blood tormented her senses as she opened the door. Her heart pounded inside her chest and her eyes filled with tears. She knew this was going to be goodbye, and there was her mum.

Nicola's throat had been slit as she slept in her bed. The room felt warm and humid, and the air was thick with a putrid smell. There was so much blood, it had soaked through the mattress and into the carpet. Her eyes were still open, with the look of fear frozen on her face, as though it was the last emotion she had felt as she died. One of her hands was holding her slashed throat with the other resting at her side, firmly gripping the Stanley blade.

Emily screamed with a piercing screech and flopped to the floor in an agonised, emotional state. She couldn't believe this had happened. Her mum was dead, stone-cold dead, and Emily knew exactly who had done this. She felt an element of guilt about bringing this man into her life.

She then stood and looked down out her mum's fearful face. 'This shouldn't have happened to you, Mum. I'm sorry.'

Emily collected her phone and made the 999 call. She was hysterical on the phone. The operator had to try and calm Emily down to understand exactly what had happened. The woman acted quickly, then Emily hung up the phone and made her way downstairs, placing herself on the bottom step. She gazed at the front door in shock as she waited for the police to arrive. It was then she decided to unlock her phone and read the text message she had received —

Scientist83: "Job done, lay low."

9

It's freezing in the Brecon Beacons at this time of year. Tommy was grateful that Alwyn had given him warm clothes, proper shoes and gloves to wear, but still had no understanding as to why Alwyn had freaked out. Tommy believed the whole robbing a bank scenario must have been some sort of mix-up. There was no possible way it was even in his nature to carry out such a crime - his mind was baffled.

Alwyn's comments about Emily concerned him greatly. He cared for Emily a lot, so Alwyn mentioning her name whilst he was freaking out worried Tommy. He didn't know what to do. His phone was dead, and being stuck in the middle of nowhere with no place to go made him feel isolated.

Hours of trekking had passed. Considering the time of year and knowing that the sun dropped early, Tommy assumed it was about four o'clock. The freezing cold countryside was once again becoming a challenge for him, especially now the sky was becoming dark with the chill in the air increasing. His clothing would never suffice in these conditions.

The sun was descending quickly. Tommy needed to find shelter. He knew that by staying out in the open the cold would kill him this time. His survival instinct kicked in.

In the distance, the hills shone with an orange hazy glow, indicating a possible built-up area. Keeping off the country lanes, Tommy made his way towards the light, through fields and wooded areas. The frozen ground crunched beneath his feet. The gloves he was wearing were deemed useless and his face was taking the brunt of the cold wind. The shoes were too small, crushing his feet as he dragged them with a limp, falling and tripping as he struggled on the uneven terrain.

As time progressed, Tommy's face burned even more as the ice-cold wind picked up, blasting him head on. Self-pity was at the forefront of his mind and giving up became a serious option, bearing in mind that the news had planted his face nationally. However, he was getting close, the orange glow becoming more apparent the closer he got, boosting his morale slightly with the knowledge that there would be shelter.

Tommy came to rows of houses where chimneys puffed smoke from cosy open fires. He could see a church with a fuel station next to it lit up like Vegas. His morale increased further, diminishing the pitiful feeling in his mind that had been holding him back.

There was a large stone wall that separated Tommy from the church yard. His lack of energy made him weak as he struggled to climb the stone wall. After a number of attempts, he finally succeeded, but the pain in his cold joints caused him to wince as he landed on a grassy patch. He laid on his back, looking up at the sky, taking a moment to recuperate a little. The longer he was there, the harder it was to get back on his feet.

The yard was black, and there was no sign of movement in the church. With no energy and with the cold eating away at him, this would have to be his home for the night. He managed to get to his feet with a struggle and slowly made his way around the perimeter of the church, looking for a way in. The church was completely locked down, and it felt somewhat unethical to smash a church window, but if there was a God, and this was a matter of life or death, *the Big Man would understand.*

Tommy found a single-pane stained glass window. It had a complex design of varying colours with a cross in the centre. The window was at the back of the church, out of sight from the main road. Tommy hesitated at first, then with a quick jab from his elbow, the glass smashed into large jagged pieces, the sound echoing inside the church. He crouched down and paused, just in case someone had heard. He waited for a few minutes before making his way through the broken window, landing on his side – the drop was further than he had anticipated.

The church was dark and cold. It had an old wooden smell with a hint of damp. The building gave Tommy an uneasy feeling. A trickle of blood ran down his arm where he must have snagged it on the broken glass on his way in, but it wasn't severe enough to cause him too much concern.

As he walked around the church, his footsteps echoed, even though he tried to tread quietly. His feet were in agony and it proved somewhat difficult to not make any noise. He found a few stone steps leading to a room at the back of the church where they might keep spare kneelers, rugs etc. in the hope that it would take him to a warmer area of the church, a place where he could hide and feel and element of safety.

Luckily for Tommy, he found just that. There was a small room right at the back, which smelt strange and was dusty, but it was out of the way. He checked to see where his exit routes were in case he needed to make a run for it. He then found some dusty old church kneelers, which were textured with the embroidery of two keys crossing over each other. In the corner of the room was a rolled-up rug, which he unfurled and laid over the cold stone floor, and on a hanger next to it was a large purple robe. He made a form of bed, using the large robe as a blanket, and laid his head down for the night - not ideal or the comfiest of beds, but five-star compared to the alternative.

As Tommy laid there, slowly zoning into sleep, he could hear strange noises. The church creaked and the wind blew the roof tiles, making a clicking sound that echoed throughout the church. A *"coo roo-c'too-coo"* could he heard through the wooden panels in the ceiling as pigeons called and marked their territory.

His mind turned to thoughts of Taylor and how good his life had actually been. He missed Taylor's pretty face and would literally do anything to be able to turn back time and go back to that happy place in his life.

He thought about his job and how strange and surreal that incident had been. He had no memory of such actions, but knowing himself as a person, he knew he would never sanely do anything like that. His life was drastically changing.

Tommy thought about the news Alwyn had shown him of the robbery. He knew he had been the perpetrator; it was clear and obvious, but having no memory of the events was hard - hard to accept that he had done all those things. He felt scared for what was yet to come. As his mind spun webs of thoughts and fears, the confusion caused a feeling of nausea, but eventually his mind finally gave up the storm, and he fell asleep.

Back in the city, DI Valentina was investigating the bank robbery with her team. After the news release, the company Tommy worked for had come forward, giving details on what had happened back in the office – a picture was beginning to form with a trend of abnormal behaviour. Tommy's reported activities were pinned on a map as Valentina explained to her team what had happened and when. A photo of Tommy was on display next to the map.

Valentina explained that a search on Tommy's mobile phone movements had been completed, and that the connection had dropped at the A470 at Treforest. It was assumed that Tommy was en-route into the Valleys, which would be like smelling a fart in a windstorm - there was no way of sniffing him out, especially with the lack of CCTV.

The team were briefed to rely more on local knowledge, working from area to area, with another news release at six o'clock. Valentina had a gut feeling that McGregor was somewhere within the Brecons and was arranging for a PST to be authorised.

Hours later, the green light was given, and a fleet of wagons was dispatched with over one hundred officers on the search. The diesel engines roared as the convoy headed north bound on the A470. Valentina was in her unmarked car with DC Roberts riding shotgun.

Their first stop would be Nant Ddu, as there had been a report giving Tommy's description near this location.

An hour and a half later, the search was underway. The PST employed a systematic high-level offensive operation to track down Tommy McGregor, with well-trained police dogs that had been given a sample of Tommy's scent from clothing found in his apartment - it was only a matter of time until they found him.

The sound of a lorry passing by woke Tommy from his sleep. His back was in bits from the hard floor, but he was relieved that he had survived his first night sleeping rough. He stretched out, giving off a long loud yawn, then quickly silenced himself in case he wasn't alone. He had to reduce the risk of anyone seeing him until he'd worked out a plan.

A rumble came from his bowels, followed by an agonising pain. There was a sudden desperation to relieve himself and he didn't have much time before defecation. He searched the church and found an old toilet down in a cellar. It was dark, and the light didn't work, but Tommy had no choice but to go for it anyway.

There it was; the first snippet of pleasure Tommy had felt in a while, but that soon evaporated with the realisation that there was nothing to wipe himself with. It was a case of splashing a little toilet water and hoping he removed it all.

Tommy heard something. He pulled up his pants and slowly made his way up from the cellar. He tiptoed silently but painfully up some concrete steps to investigate. When he reached the top, he stopped and listened, breathing slowly to intensify his hearing. He could hear voices, but the echo of the church distorted the words, so he couldn't make out what was being said.

He decided he was just going to have to run for it. He worked out his route and off he went back through the broken window, legging it, whilst trying to ignore the pain in his feet. This was now a matter of prison time or freedom, and he moved fast.

The air was freezing and burned his chest as he gasped to fill his lungs with oxygen. He had run through two fields and was sitting behind a hedge that separated one field from the next. He needed a plan. This wasn't something he could sustain, living out in the middle of nowhere, especially at this time of year. If he couldn't find shelter for the next night, he was certain the cold would kill him.

After thirty minutes, Tommy had pieced together a rough plan, and he began to move again. First he needed to find some food and to work out a way to get some charge on his phone, so he could use Google Maps to figure out an appropriate route back to the city, where he would hide in hostels, disguising himself as sleeping rough and blending into the community. Once the storm had settled, Tommy then planned to relocate to another city, change his identity and move on.

Valentina was, however, an extremely experienced and competent detective. She was ruthless and determined, and she wouldn't stop until Tommy was where she believed he should be – behind bars.

Five miles away, the PST were on the right track, with the police dogs having picked up what they believed to be Tommy's scent. Tommy was oblivious, with no idea that the police were anywhere near, and he thought he was safe for the time being.

An hour later, Valentina received a call. There had been a break-in at Libanus Church, and a patrol was quickly dispatched. Valentina instructed one of her team to send over a 4x4 to take her to the church. Twenty minutes later she was there.

Blood was found on the smashed glass where Tommy had gained entry into the church, which was sent off to the lab to ensure it was a DNA match. However, Valentina knew this blood was Tommy McGregor's. Her vast experience and sixth sense told her so, and she always trusted her gut feeling. A flutter of excitement built up inside her as they were getting closer, but Tommy was still non-the-wiser about how close they were.

Tommy's trek through fields was tiresome, especially considering the current state of his health; recovering from hypothermia and barely able to walk due to his feet being in an awful condition. He came to a country road, which would eventually lead him to a fuel station in the distance. He needed food and water. He had to get into the shop, take whatever he could and be gone before anyone noticed. *If only it was that easy*, he thought to himself.

It took Tommy twenty minutes to reach the fuel station, and when he got there, he made his way round to the back of the building in an attempt to stay out of sight. He hunched his back slightly and stayed close to the walls to minimise his exposure. As he was walking, he was looking behind him, keeping an eye on who was around, when he bumped into a scruffy looking guy.

The man was short, unshaven and looked as though he'd had a tough life.

'Watch it, bud,' the guy said in a Welsh accent, which was strong and mumbled, so Tommy found it hard to fully understand what he was saying.

'Sorry,' said Tommy. He was sheepish and closed off. He felt awkward and didn't want to engage in any type of conversation, refusing to look this guy in the eye.

'You ok, bud? Look like death, no offence.' The scruffy guy pulled a fag from his tatty stone-coloured jeans and sparked up, taking an almighty drag, then inhaling further again with a long deep gasp. This guy was not wasting any of this fag.

'Yeah, good,' said Tommy. Feeling on edge, he was constantly looking around, slowly moving away in the hope that this guy would get the hint. Tommy didn't want the small talk.

'Well, bud, you don't look it. You been sleeping rough, yeah?'

'Yeah, something like that.' Again, Tommy was moving away inch by inch.

'Want some food?' the guy asked, causing Tommy's eyes to light up.

'Yeah, please!'

'Wha you fancy? Pasty, pie, rolls?'

'Anything, literally anything, please, thank you,' Tommy said gratefully.

The guy walked through the back door to the shop, and Tommy peered in, finding himself in the store room to the fuel station. There were crates of bottles and cans, and boxes of crisps, but he also noticed a mobile power bank. To Tommy, this was more important than food. He crept in slowly, taking carful steps, edging towards the power bank. He managed to grab it, then slipped back out the door and off into the distance, dragging his feet as he went. Tommy then heard someone shout.

'Oi, bud!! Don't you want your food, or what?' the scruffy guy shouted as he walked back out the door, waving packages of food in his hands.

Tommy stopped, then turned, pausing for a moment before walking back. The food was too appealing to Tommy at this stage. He reached out to grab a pasty and a bottle from the guy.

'Wait,' the guy hesitated, looking at Tommy intensely. 'You! It's fucking you! You're that killer!'

The guy reached out to grab at Tommy, but Tommy had already turned away, evading his grasp. The sudden movement caused him to feel slightly dizzy, but he dug deep and set off again over a fence that marked the rear boundaries to the fuel station and back into a field.

The guy made chase. 'Brynn, Brynn!' he shouted to whoever else was in the shop.

He was gaining on Tommy fast. Tommy ran with a limp from the agonising pain in his feet, which slowed him tremendously. Just as Tommy took a glance back, the guy tackled him to the ground, causing them both to fall into a freezing cold stream. Neither of them felt the pain of slamming onto the rocky bed of the stream.

They rolled around, trying to take control of each other. The water in the stream was ice-cold, which Tommy ignored, as his only concern was to break away from this guy and get out as soon as possible. Tommy was weak and tired, but he managed to roll over, so he was on top. He forced an elbow into the guy's face and saw thick blood trickle and gradually dilute in the stream.

Tommy relaxed, but the guy wasn't done. He managed to grab a stone and smashed it into the side of Tommy's head. Tommy dropped like a sack of potatoes, blood spilling from the side of his face. He felt woozy. The guy stood and took a step back, thinking it was over. Tommy managed to get back to his feet, so the guy came in for another strike, but this time his swing was weak, and he overstretched, missing Tommy.

Tommy managed a counter-strike, powerfully forcing his knee up into the guy's face. He wasn't messing around; the guy winced and fell face down into the stream, and water ran past his flopping body. Tommy turned the guy over to stop him from drowning and then quickly fled. He wasn't going to hang around.

Soaked through to his skin, Tommy had a bloodied face with mild concussion, but somehow he didn't forget the pasty that had been dropped on the muddy bank.

These events were reported to the police by Brynn from the shop, who went out looking for the guy after he'd heard his call. Valentina intercepted the radio and informed the control room she was on route to the fuel station, telling them to set up a code nine – a road block within a nine-mile perimeter of the fuel station.

Sirens from an ambulance could be heard in the distance, which Tommy assumed was heading towards the guy he had left unconscious.

Tommy found a waterfall at the top of a stream some two miles away. He could still hear the sirens, and part of him prayed that the guy was ok. He had felt he had no choice. Suddenly, a light bulb switched on in his head, *Fuck, the police know where I am!*

He scrambled away in panic and headed towards some hills that he could see in the distance. He decided he'd need to spend the night there. His feet were causing him tremendous pain, but he had to keep pushing through. There was no way he wanted to get caught.

The fields were boggy with a thin frost laid over the top that crunched as he stepped. Tommy needed to keep to the edge in order to stay out of view as much as possible, but this meant that the terrain wasn't the best, as this was where a lot of moisture and debris had accumulated.

The boggy ground became increasingly worse with each step, squelching as he trod. One of his shoes got sucked off his foot by some thick, boggy mud that stunk of rotting cow shit and piss. He had to go and retrieve the shoe, as continuing barefoot was in no way an option. Putting the shoe back on was agonising, as it was already two sizes too small, so forcing it onto a wet foot caused it to be even tougher and more painful.

Tommy finally made it to the bottom of the hills. He came across a large fallen tree that was rotten but good for cover whilst he caught his breath. He leaned against the tree, facing out into the fields in the direction he had come from, so he could at least keep an eye out for any movement.

Whilst resting, he took out his mobile and connected the stolen power bank to put some charge into his phone, so he could access Google Maps and plan a route out of this situation. Both phone and power bank were wet through, but surprisingly still worked. Whilst his phone was charging, he buried the packaging from the power bank, in an attempt to leave as little trail as possible. Little did he know there were dogs on his scent.

Once Tommy's phone had charged sufficiently, he turned it on and waited. It took some time to boot up, but once it had finished loading, he was inundated with text messages from his worried family. He had several missed calls from his work, which to Tommy was now irrelevant. He checked Google Maps and could then see his location. He was at the bottom of Pen y Fan, the famous Brecon Beacon mountains. There was a main road close by, the A470, which was the main artery back to the city, so he needed to avoid that. He decided he was going to follow that route off-road instead, but he needed to rest and regain some energy first.

Out of curiosity, he checked the online news, and low and behold, he was the main headline. He read through the article twice, and his brain hurt from having zero memory of any of his actions. Anxiety hit his chest, as though a brick had been thrown at him, when he learned that there was a hunt for a murderer.

There was a statement from a Detective Valentina, who strongly urged the public to not make contact with Tommy McGregor, as he was a danger, and she assured the public that her team were close to his arrest. Heat rose inside him, and mixed emotions of fear, anxiety, hurt and loss flowed through his body.

All of a sudden, Tommy had one of his headaches. It was extreme and caused him to cry out. His face went purple, his vision was completely white, and there was a constant ringing and pounding in his ear drums. He dropped to the floor in absolute agony, the pain causing him to throw up. Then suddenly he came around, and he felt fine, completely normal, or as normal as things could get for him right now.

He shrugged it off for the time being and continued to read articles about the police hunt. There was a section about the PST and the use of police dogs, which made Tommy think, *They'll be using my scent.*

This of course caused major concerns for Tommy, so he decided it would be a good idea to smother himself in cow dung. He made his way over to a large field with cows, climbed through a fence and searched for the dung he needed, which didn't take long at all. Without hesitation, and in complete desperation, he proceeded to cover himself. The dung was in his hair, all over his clothes, on his hands and even on his face. It stunk, causing Tommy to throw up a few times, until he moderately got used to the smell.

Tommy went back to the large fallen tree and made up camp for the night using fern leaves and grass from the fields. It was

115

going to be a very long and freezing cold night, which was made even more unpleasant with the cow dung smeared all over his body.

The sun was beginning to set. It projected beautiful colours through the sky, and Tommy imagined that was what heaven would look like. Part of him thought he would most probably be in that special place sooner rather than later, with no idea if he would last the night.

It was freezing cold and the temperature was noticeably dropping rapidly. Tommy gazed out into the distance. The sun was gone by this point and the moon lit up the area. The wind started to pick up, so he had to reposition himself to try and stay out of it as much as possible. That's when he noticed the lights in the distance.

These lights were clearly high-powered torches, and Tommy made the immediate assumption that it was the police hunting him down. The cold made it difficult for Tommy to start moving. He had no energy, his entire body was sore, and his feet were rapidly deteriorating.

The PST were getting close. The dogs were still on the scent and were moving in the right direction. Valentina had called it a day for herself and had checked into a nearby hotel as soon as a relief team had turned up. She had instructed them to call her the moment there was any news. The team continued, and the dogs were intelligently pursuing the trail and were amazingly still on point. Tommy may have masked his scent, but the trail left behind was still there, and Tommy staying where he was proved to be a failing decision.

After another hour, the team were incredibly close. The dogs had stopped and were circling an area. One of the dog handlers cautiously approached the area, and Tommy stood up from behind the fallen tree. He was still, there was no emotion on his face and he was in a strange state.

'Don't move, Tommy McGregor! Call the DI!' the officer said, turning to an officer that was standing behind him. The moment the officer's eyes left Tommy, Tommy was gone. The PST could see Tommy's figure in full sprint down through the field, heading towards a road. They all made chase, with the dogs in hot pursuit.

10

Tommy made it to the main road. He was still in his trance and there was nothing that was going to stop him. He ran like he had never run before, his painful feet pounding the tarmac as his over-tight shoes crushed him, without even a flinch. His breath was steady, as though running was no effort - there was no thought process in his mind.

He came to a layby where there was a man parked with a motorbike, the engine idling. The motorcyclist was wearing black leathers and a black helmet, and he had his back to Tommy. Without any hesitation, Tommy crept up behind and smashed the man over the side of the helmet with a large rock, which instantly knocked him off his bike, causing him to fall to the floor. Tommy quickly removed his helmet, while the man held out his hands as a form of defence. Tommy stared at the motorcyclist, then dropped the rock onto the poor guy's head, the sound of his skull crushing from the impact.

Seconds later, Tommy was off down the road, the engine roaring between his legs, leaving the lifeless guy in the layby - he had literally been in the wrong place at the wrong time.

Never having ridden a motorbike before, Tommy was a natural whilst in his trance-like state. It was as though he subconsciously knew how to ride a powerful motorbike. The bike roared as Tommy sped down the road, travelling at over 100mph. He was heading towards the city, still with no thought in his mind whatsoever.

After thirty minutes, Tommy stopped outside a house, got off the bike leaving the engine running, and walked up to the front door. With the black helmet on and the visor down, he rapped loudly on the door with the knocker - whoever was on the other side of this door would most probably have been concerned. The door opened slowly and a middle-aged woman peered her head round with caution. She observed at Tommy standing in front of her. He removed his helmet but did not say a word. He just stood there staring straight ahead with no emotion.

'You can't be here, Tommy. You need to leave now, or I will call the police! You have some front turning up after what you did to Taylor!' She was angry, but Tommy didn't even blink and walked straight past Taylor's mum into her house, knocking her to the floor.

'Tommy, stop! I'm calling the police!!' Her hands shook as she fumbled with her phone in an attempt to dial 999.

'What emergency service, please?' said the operator on the phone.

Taylor's mum was frozen in fear as Tommy stood in front of her with a large shiny kitchen knife. Taylor had heard the commotion and was running down the stairs. She also froze on the spot at the sight of Tommy standing aggressively, ready to kill.

'Hello, what emergency service would you like?' repeated the operator.

Taylor's mum stood there silently, and Tommy lunged forward, plunging the knife straight into her face. She fell to the floor, holding the wound as blood poured between her fingers. She didn't scream, as the shock of what had just happened took over. Tommy then stabbed her in the chest with a hard thud, removed the blade, then drove it in again. Taylor screamed, and Tommy simultaneously turned to Taylor, leaving her mum on the floor gasping for breath and choking on her own blood as it filled her mouth.

Tommy threw Taylor onto the floor next to her mum. He stood over them both, staring down with a black evil in his eyes. Taylor covered her face, scared stiff of Tommy's next move. He knelt down with both knees on Taylor's chest, crushing her. Taylor gasped for breath as his full weight pressed down hard. He took the knife and started to carve a word into her forehead. Taylor screamed, but her chest was constricted by Tommy's weight. He then stuck the knife in her right shoulder, stood up and casually stepped over them both. Taylor laid on the floor covered in blood, breathing erratically. Her mother was laying next to her, motionless, lifeless. It was clear she was dead.

The motorbike engine roared, then echoed down the street as Tommy sped off at full throttle. He weaved through the traffic. Other road users sat on their horns and flashed their lights, but he continued through the city at a dangerously high speed.

Tommy stopped outside his apartment. He stepped off the bike and just let it fall to the floor. He made his way up to his front door and kicked it open with tremendous force. He walked in, went into the lounge, got undressed and laid down on his sofa, closing his eyes.

Tommy came round about ten minutes later, feeling like he had a hangover. His feet were now so sore, he couldn't even put any weight on them. His arms ached, his lungs were burning, and his legs were completely numb. He tried to move, but the pain was too much. He looked down at himself and saw that he was covered in blood.

He tried to sit up. 'What the fuck?' He was confused and had no idea how he had got to where he was.

The last thing he remembered was being by the fallen tree, and now waking up in his apartment was freaking him out. Panic and fear flowed through his veins. He had no explanation for anything. *Was everything just a bad dream?* he thought to himself. Even if it was, he had no idea how he came to have blood all over him.

There were footsteps on the laminate floor leading from the front door to the lounge area. In walked Anderson, whom Tommy had nicknamed "The Freak" looking smug and somewhat pleased with himself.

'What the fuck are you doing in here?' shouted Tommy.

'What do you mean, what? You're a psychopathic murderer and I'm handing you in!' Anderson pulled out his phone, dialling 999.

'Police please.' There was a pause whilst Anderson was transferred through to the police department.

Tommy tried to get up but couldn't. His body had given up and so had his mind. He was finally defeated, and he just rested his head.

'Yes, I have an individual under a section 24a citizen's arrest.' There was a pause. 'I have Tommy McGregor.' Anderson then gave the address. 'No, I'm not in any danger. He's not going anywhere.'

Anderson hung up the phone and placed it back in his pocket. He folded his arms. 'I don't think they'll be long, considering this is such a high-profile case.'

'What are you doing?' asked Tommy, his voice pleading.

'Like I said, I'm turning you in, and my guess is, you'll most probably never be released.' Anderson looked terrifyingly self-satisfied to Tommy.

Minutes later, the sound of police cars could be heard, and it was obvious they were approaching fast.

'I have no memory of anything,' Tommy said with sadness in his voice.

'Well,' Anderson paused, staring into Tommy's eyes, 'you wouldn't would you-'

Before he could finish, police stormed the apartment. Anderson held his hands innocently in the air. Tommy was immediately dragged off the sofa and aggressively thrown to the floor; the pain was intense and caused him to yelp as they put handcuffs on him and read him his rights.

'You do not have to say anything, but it may harm your defence if you do not mention when questioned something which you later rely on in court. Anything you do say may be given in evidence. Do you understand?'

Tommy had nothing to say and was escorted to the police van, dragging his feet. On his way out, he looked back at Anderson, who waved with a smile. He saw armed police. *Who do they think I am?* Tommy thought to himself. *How has my life gone so wrong so fast?* His mind then went numb. All he wanted was the world to swallow him up and for him never to return.

At the police station, Tommy was checked in once again. This time, he knew he wasn't going home for some time. He was practically carried into his cell. It was clear he was in need of serious medical attention, but no one even acknowledged this. *Must be how they treat real criminals.*

One of the officers turned to Tommy. 'Valentina will be here in the morning, and she can't wait to meet you!' He then shut the door on Tommy.

As soon as the door shut, Tommy couldn't hold back the emotion no longer and he sobbed. He wished he was dead and started to think of ways to make that happen. His whole life had been turned upside down, and he had lost absolutely everything.

He wanted to see his parents and to explain to them that he wasn't the person the media were making him out to be; that he wasn't the one shaming the family and the people around him; that it wasn't him. Sadly, he felt he was the only person who knew this.

The cell was cold, grey and plain with a few markings on the walls, and a shitty thin blue blanket was all he had to give him comfort. He was in so much pain, it agonised him. There were stabbing pains in his stomach, most probably from hunger. He wished he had his phone, so he could go through the IPEA to see how bad his condition was.

A thought then occurred to him this was when everything had started to happen. It had all begun not long after he'd had that procedure. He wondered if there was a link, but his mind didn't have the capacity to even comprehend such ideas at that moment. He knew this was it now, his life was over, and when given the first opportunity, he would end it.

The next morning, Tommy was woken by the sound of the cell door opening. An attractive woman walked in and sat on a chair, which an officer had brought in for her, next to where Tommy laid. She explained who she was.

'My name is Anita Fowler, and I'm your brief. I'm the one who is going to try to protect you as much as possible, but the only way I can do that is if you are completely open and honest with me and don't hold anything back. If you lie, I can't defend you. If you tell me the truth, we will look at different defence options and ways around this situation. Do you understand?'

Tommy didn't even smile. His current situation was dire, and the pain from his rotting feet was killing him.

'Yes, I'll be honest, but you won't believe me. No one will.' Tommy's voice was weak and he felt nauseous.

'Well, you need to trust me and give me the opportunity to defend you. Have a think about everything. How are you feeling?' Anita asked with some concern.

'I'm in so much pain.' Tommy pulled the blanket back. He managed to sit up and remove his socks, causing him agony as thick, dead skin peeled away from his flesh. He let out a loud cry.

'Oh my God!' said Anita. 'You need to go to hospital.'

Tommy's feet were so swollen, his little toe was hidden on one foot, and his big toe on his other foot was black with the nail missing. The skin covering both feet was green with puss oozing out from the areas where the skin had peeled away - the smell was rancid.

'How has no one picked this up?' Anita asked, and Tommy just shrugged.

She left the room with a seriously concerned look on her face. In no time at all, Tommy was transferred to Heath Hospital and was kept there under 24/7 police guard.

Unfortunately for Tommy, he was not in a good way. The infection was causing him so much pain, the doctor had to prescribe him morphine. He was given Erythromycin via a drip, and his big toe had to be amputated. This not only had a physical effect on Tommy, but also left an emotional scar.

The fact that he'd had the IPEA procedure helped the team identify everything that was wrong with Tommy within minutes. All they had to do was download the report and then provide the necessary treatment. A copy of the report was also provided to Valentina, as this could be used as fundamental evidence.

The two police guards watching over Tommy never said a word to him. They didn't ask if he was okay or offer to provide any assistance. Why would they? He could sense the hatred oozing out of their pores. In their eyes, Tommy was a cold-blooded killer, but the medical team on the other hand treated Tommy as they would have treated anyone else.

DI Valentina attempted to pay Tommy a visit. She wanted answers, and as far as she was concerned, this monster shouldn't be given the time of day. However, the doctor looking after him wouldn't allow this to proceed until Tommy's condition had significantly improved.

After a month had gone by, Tommy was finally discharged from hospital. His physical state had improved after weeks of rest, medical care, physio and some counselling. He was told that he would have died if he hadn't received medical treatment within a couple of days, so he had been lucky that he was arrested when he was – which of course Tommy didn't agree with. He would have happily died, rather than face the hell he was about to endure.

The presence of the press outside the hospital was alarming for Tommy. He was classed as a high-profile criminal, and the police were forced to protect him from a mob that protested they wanted him dead. Tommy didn't take this too well. It was only a matter of months earlier that he had been living a decent life. Now he was being pushed into the back of a secure, unmarked police van with a blanket covering his face on a journey to life imprisonment, where the outside world would become a distant memory. The worst thing for Tommy was dealing with the fact that he felt innocent. He didn't care what evidence was out there, he believed that he had not committed those crimes.

Back at the station, Valentina didn't waste any time. Tommy was in that interview room so fast, his head spun. As he walked in, Anita was sitting at the desk with a detective opposite.

'You look much better, Tommy,' said Anita. 'Do you remember what we talked about?'

Tommy nodded and sat next to her. Valentina sat opposite Tommy. She was eager and ready to probe and prod Tommy's brain until she got a confession.

Valentina started with the basics. *Where were you at this time? What do you remember? etc.* However, Tommy genuinely didn't remember anything at all and proceeded to explain this. Valentina showed the CCTV footage of Tommy in the bank, of which he had no memory. She explained all about Nicola Wakefield and how she had been murdered in her bed. Tommy again had no recollection of any of this and had no understanding of his link with her death.

The biggest shock to Tommy was the murder of Taylor's mum, Sharon Gillingham. *Why would he kill her? For what reason?* This upset Tommy greatly and he became distressed. He'd always got on well with Sharon; she was a lovely woman, and he'd apparently killed her in cold blood.

Valentina read out the statement written by Taylor herself, who was currently in hospital with serious facial and shoulder injuries. Tommy couldn't comprehend all of this information and broke down. He lost control, slamming his fists on the desk in front of him.

'Fuck you all! I didn't do all this, I swear to God as my only witness!' Tommy shouted.

'Sit down, McGregor, or you will be restrained!' threatened Valentina.

'No, I want to go! You can't keep me here!'

'We can, and we will. We have up to ninety-six hours to charge you, and we'll be putting all the evidence to the CPS by close of play today. In my experience, this will go to trial, so sit your arse down.'

There was a polite interruption from Anita. 'I think my client needs a break,' she looked Valentina straight in the eye, serious and direct, showing that she knew Tommy had rights.

'Ok, we are suspending the interview at sixteen thirty-two hours at the request of Miss Fowler.'

The cell was still cold. Tommy sat up against the wall with the blanket wrapped around his shoulders, holding a cup of coffee between his hands. Again, the allegations rotted his brain. Having no memory of the events created great frustration and confusion, and he knew prison was inevitable.

After a two-hour rest, he was escorted back to the interview room. The same people were in attendance. Valentina looked pleased with herself, as though ready to give Tommy some bad news.

'So, Tommy, the CPS has approved your case with the evidence that has been submitted, and you will go to trial. Due to the nature of your crimes, you will be remanded in custody during your trial and until the outcome of your case has been confirmed. Do you have any questions?'

'No, no questions.' The life that once existed inside of Tommy evaporated out of him. His soul changed. He was an innocent man going on a murder trial and he knew it was going to be hell. He hated the fact that he'd been labelled as a murderer. It was something he never ever thought possible. He found himself with his back to the wall. There was nothing he could do to prove he hadn't done those things. Suicide became his next train of thought.

11

Anderson parked up in a lay-by just on the outskirts of Cardiff, locating the bin near where Tommy had dumped the money from the robbery, which had been hidden deep in the shrubbery. Anderson was surprised it was still there after all this time, but the money was damp with a few notes half eaten by slugs and insects. He hadn't been able to take any chances until the police had charged Tommy, which gave him the comfort that this wouldn't get traced back to him.

He counted the money in the back seat of his car and was amazed to see £32,000 in cash there in front of him. He felt this was now his money; he had earned it. He smelt it and absorbed its scent, then packed the money into a large leather holdall and tossed the carrier bags out of the window, driving off back to his apartment.

It was late afternoon on a Tuesday, two days after Tommy had been charged. The roads were heavy, and it took Anderson some time to get back. He drove a blue Vauxhall Corsa. It was an old banger that was falling apart with irritating rattles and squeaks, which caused Anderson to punch the dashboard hundreds of times – cars were of no interest to him whatsoever. His mind was greatly invested in something much more appealing.

The rented apartment he lived in on his own was immaculate. There was not a single thing out of place, with no clutter clogging it up. Anderson liked to keep things minimal, so that he had complete focus on his project, which to date, was proving to be successful.

He'd spend an average of ten hours a day in one room. It had a large bench desk that ran from one side of the room to the other. Above the desk were three large wall-mounted screens with only a single keyboard and a mouse in the centre.

In front of the desk was a large black leather chair, which was badly worn and looked well-used. Anderson took a seat, double tapped a button on the keyboard, and the screens lit up the room. He was examining the displays, taking in the information, when there was a knock at the door. He paused for a while before going to answer it.

'You disgust me!' exclaimed Emily as she pushed her way in.

'What do you mean?' Anderson asked.

'The way you groped me when you were in my house! You scared me! Lucky I don't have you taken out for doing that!' Emily walked into his room and sat on the black leather chair, crossing her legs.

'I'm sorry, I'm an opportunist!' Anderson replied with his hands held out, as if that was a decent answer with a twist of cockiness.

'You're a pervert and you disgust me! I threw up because of that and the thought of you doing you know what.' She looked down towards his crotch area.

'Anyway,' replied Anderson, 'I take it you're here because you have something for me?'

'Touch me like that again and you'll be sorry, and yes I have the money. All I need is your account details, and you'll receive your fifty thousand,' said Emily.

'What, why only fifty thousand? What about the one hundred K you promised?' Anderson was shocked at the large reduction.

'I deducted fifty K for your disgusting groping stunt whilst controlling Tommy's mind. I hated you doing that! Take it or leave it, I don't give a shit!'

Anderson held out both hands to calm her. 'Remember who came to who, yeah. You contacted me on the Dark Net to kill someone, don't forget that! How much did you get?'

'Two hundred and fifty grand. My mother had good life insurance. Well, I've not had the full whack yet, but it's coming,' Emily declared.

Smug cow, Anderson thought to himself. 'Whatever, here're my details.' He handed over a card, and Emily logged into her bank account, completing the transfer.

'So, what now?' asked Anderson.

'You know the plan. We've been through it a thousand times. Lay low for the time being. Keep your nose clean and get ready for the next phase.' Emily pointed at the computer equipment. 'This stuff is all that links us to Tommy and his crimes, so do whatever it is you geeks do to cover your tracks.'

'It's all in hand. There is no trace, so chill! Thanks for the money. I will see you soon. Any chance of a quick hug?'

'No chance! Shouldn't have pulled that pervy stunt! I will be in touch okay!' Emily's voice was stern, but she smiled, as if to indicate that it was okay.

As Emily walked down the stairs, she saw Tommy's front door was open and decided to enter to see what was happening. Taylor was standing there and Emily couldn't help but smirk at the sight of her.

'What are you doing here?' asked Taylor. She looked gaunt and drained, and her face was an absolute mess. It was clear she was having a tough time. Emily's frown took over her face. She had pure hatred towards Taylor.

'Saw the door was open and thought I'd have a look. You look a mess!'

'Just go away!' replied Taylor.

Emily smiled; she couldn't help herself. She then pointed her finger straight into Taylor's face. 'You know what, you fucking skank, you deserve everything you get!'

'What do you mean? Why does any of this have anything to do with me?' Taylor asked.

'Because you ruined my life!'

Taylor was taken aback by the extreme accusation. 'How?'

'My dad left my mum because of you! It turned our whole family upside down!' Emily exclaimed.

'What are you talking about?' Taylor was already defeated. She had no energy and no fight left inside her. She just wanted to collect her things and go home.

'Look in the mirror, you fucking bitch!' Emily went for Taylor, grabbed the back of her head and forced her to look into a large mirror on the wall. 'What do you see? What do you fucking see?' Her words seethed through her teeth.

'M,m,my ugly face,' cried Taylor as she tried hard to turn her head away, but Emily overpowered her.

'What else?' Being physically stronger, Emily forced Taylor's face closer, so that this time she was almost touching the mirror. There was the temptation to completely push her face through the glass.

'M.I.C.K, carved on my face!' Taylor continued, crying. She was horrified by the image that stared back at her. 'Let me go!' She tried to fight.

'No, and who was Mick, you slut?!' Emily's words seethed through her teeth again with a hiss of pure hatred and anger.

'Please, leave me alone.' Taylor was still trying to fight back with no success.

'Awww, please leave me alone,' Emily mocked in a baby voice. 'He was my dad, my dad!' She placed her hands on her chest and tears began to roll down her face, 'and you took him from us! We had everything, and you deserve everything you get! It's Tommy I feel sorry for. He's the innocent one, but we needed him!'

'W,what do you mean?' Taylor was confused by Emily's words.

'Nothing, now go and rot in your pitiful life.' Emily pushed Taylor's forehead with the palm of her hand, causing her to fall to the ground with a wince. 'Oh, and by the way, Tommy's great in bed! Said I was the best he'd ever had.' Emily just had to get that last dig in, but Taylor couldn't care less.

Emily walked out of the apartment, feeling satisfied that she had finally managed to speak out to Taylor after all those years, but also feeling emotional. She had finally sought revenge for her dad walking out on her and her mother, then killing himself. She'd also held her mum responsible for all of this. It was her mum, Nicola, who had put her work first, had turned her back on Emily's dad and hadn't given him the attention that he desired, causing him to go off with Taylor. She'd always hated her mum for that, and having her murdered hadn't been that difficult, due to the amount of resentment she had built up over time. Now she was entitled to a lot of money, so it was a win-win situation as far as she was concerned.

Tommy's cell was 13ft by 10ft with a sorry-looking steel-frame bunk bed against the wall, a message board full of graffiti, and a filthy toilet in the corner which leaked, leaving a vile smell of urine that burned anyone's eyes who entered the area. Cell E2-7 wasn't exactly luxurious accommodation - it was built for a murderer like Tommy McGregor. He was in one of forty-five cells in the first night centre of the prison's induction unit. This was where men who had been sent down by the courts began weeks and months on remand, awaiting trial or for their sentences for crimes ranging from murder and rape to owing fines.

Being on remand was almost the same as being in prison as a convicted criminal as far as Tommy was concerned. He might have been allowed to wear his own clothes and have access to his own money, but all that did was make him a target in the prison world. He had a cell to himself, which was appreciated, however, with no one to talk to for hours and hours on end, his mind fed on the negative thoughts that taunted him.

Tommy dreamt up various scenarios of killing himself. He thought about hanging himself, but he was too scared. He considered getting hold of antifreeze and downing a pint of the stuff, but he couldn't get access to any. He also thought about slitting his wrists, which again he was too scared to do. However, that didn't stop the avalanche of thoughts - the longer it went on, the more intense it got.

As a mere shell of himself, Tommy became grey and withdrawn. The HMP system didn't help him in the slightest, and this was purely down to Tommy actually being innocent in his own mind. He didn't remember the crimes. He had been there but only as a physical entity. However, no one believed him. With the evidence stacked up against him - eye witnesses, CCTV evidence and DNA - a life sentence was inevitable.

Tommy's breathing increased dramatically as the lights went out at 10pm. The noise level from the other prisoners always increased at this time, as they wanted to be heard, shouting anything and everything. There were loud bangs from mugs being knocked against the cell doors and screaming and shouting until a guard came round to shut them up. Eventually things quietened down, and this was Tommy's moment.

The sheets were easy to stretch as they were pretty much made of plastic. Tommy tied them round a rail on the top bunk. He moved slowly with a sense of calm in an attempt to keep the noise levels down to a minimum. The sheet was in place creating a loop for tying the noose. By using his body weight, the knot would become so tight, it would need to be cut off when they found him – hopefully dead.

He then took off his jogger bottoms and detached the waistband. It separated fairly easily with little noise. This was the tool that would be taking his life. Once this was attached to the sheet, his noose was ready and he was ready. He sat on the edge of the top bunk with the waistband around his neck. All he needed to do was slip off the edge and that would be it, his troubles would be over and the world for those who knew him would feel like a better place.

1, 2, 3 Tommy counted in his head, but he just couldn't bring himself to do it. He wanted to, but his body just wouldn't allow it. By now, the whole centre was silent. The odd snore could be heard, but that was about it. He thought about his old life, the one he had loved, and how he'd had everything he ever dreamed of. His mum and dad had been proud of him. He'd had a beautiful but nutty girlfriend, who was by far the sexiest woman on the planet as far as he was concerned. He'd also had a good job and a nice home. The Tommy from back then still had plenty of ambition left in him. Now, that spark, that zest for life, had died. He wasn't Tommy McGregor anymore; he was a murderer, a cold-blooded killer in a world that didn't need him.

Millimetre by millimetre, Tommy edged forwards. Each sharp breath was assumed his last. What was seconds felt like hours. He moved again, his backside on the very edge. One more movement and it would all be over. He focused hard on what he was doing and his reasons. Fear filled him. He was scared to die. He was scared of the pain he might feel, but he reassured himself that it would only be for a moment, and then nothing; no pain, no hurt, no more of this mess of a human life. He then slipped off the edge of the bed.

12

'Who is this guy we are meeting?' asked Emily furiously. 'These types of people aren't to be fucked around with and they're certainly not people I want to engage with!'

Anderson became frustrated. 'Em, listen right, if we are going to arrange this, we need to have the right people to do it for us. So, unfortunately, it takes a special kind of person for what needs to be done.' He placed a hand on her shoulder as a means of comfort, followed by an inappropriate wink.

'For fuck sake,' Emily said feeling enraged. 'Can't I just leave you to deal with it?'

'No Em, if this goes wrong, that will make me the ultimate suspect. We started this together and we finish it together. So, unless you are in it with me, you can fuck off!' Anderson literally turned and walked away. Of course, all this was just an act - reverse psychology.

'Anderson, get back here!' Emily surrendered. 'Okay, I'll come with you... God sake!'

He knew this would get under her skin. She was so paranoid about the police finding everything out. They only had two options; either to have Tommy killed in prison or have him escape. Having him killed was by far the easiest and quickest choice.

'So, the guy we are meeting goes by the name of Joey,' Anderson explained. 'Don't ask his last name - I don't know it. Thinking about it, Joey is most probably a fake name anyway.'

'Okay, so what does he do?' Emily asked.

'What do you think he does, Em? We are meeting him here for one reason and one reason only, and you know why that is, so work it out.'

Emily just stared at him without an answer.

They were sitting in a Costa Coffee in the city centre. It was the place where Joey had arranged for them to meet him. They had no idea what he looked like, what he'd be wearing, or anything. The instructions were simply to be there by 11.25am and no later. They were there on time, of course. They were feeling slightly wary, their stomachs knotted, with no idea how the conversation was going to go – both were completely out of their depth.

Emily kept checking her watch. An hour had passed and still this guy hadn't turned up.

'This is stupid! He's got five more minutes, then I'm going!' Emily said.

'Look, just sit tight. He will be here. He's probably just vetting us first, checking the area to make sure there's no undercover police an' that. Just chill!'

Emily rolled her eyes back at Anderson. She knew he was right, but the anxious anticipation was getting to her.

Another hour later, a scruffy chap walked in. He was short at about five foot four. He wore his baseball cap turned backwards, a denim shirt and black jeans. He clocked the two of them almost straight away, making stern eye contact, looking at Anderson first, then over at Emily. His eyes were noticeably bright blue. He then looked away, walked over to the counter, and ordered himself a coffee.

After collecting his coffee, he walked over and sat on the table next to Anderson and Emily. He started to speak without even looking at them.

'Don't look at me, just listen.' He was well spoken and his pronunciation was clear – his voice did not match his attire.

Emily looked at Anderson and couldn't help but snigger, finding it hard to take this man seriously.

'All I need from you is a name and location, so I can carry out what is required,' the man said. 'I'll write down a figure and a contact number on my napkin. When I leave, look at my napkin. If you're ok to proceed with the required amount, which is non-negotiable, I want you to dial the contact number and say "yes", followed by the name of who you need dealing with and their location, nothing else.'

Again, Anderson and Emily looked at each other. Anderson then replied, 'Okay!'

Once Joey had left, they quickly grabbed the napkin. He was asking for twelve grand for the job.

'Less than what I thought it would be,' said Emily.

'Hmm, yeah me too. Seems dodgy, and as if he's a hitman?'

They both laughed, not taking this seriously at all. Anderson dialled the number. It was answered after three rings without a word.

'Yeah, it's errm, ah yes, Tommy McGregor, Swansea Prison.' He then hung up. 'That's it, Em. It's been sorted. Now, all we have to do is wait.'

'Okay, but something doesn't feel right.' Emily had a bad feeling.

They both left the coffee shop and walked down Queen Street together.

'So, what shall we do now, Em?' asked Anderson.

'I'm going back home. I feel so tired. Need some sleep.'

'Can I come?' Anderson couldn't help but hold a cheeky smile on his face, already knowing the answer.

Emily looked him up and down, as if to say, *as if.* 'No chance! We do business together, and that's it! I'm not mixing the two together, and once all this is over, you and I won't ever be meeting again.'

'Why, we've been through a lot together. Thought we were friends?'

'Because I don't like you! You're a vile pervert and you disgust me. You might have an amazing brain,' Emily looked him up and down again, 'but that's it!'

She pushed passed him and walked off down the street. Emily's insolence left Anderson feeling pissed off. He had done a lot for Emily; everything she had asked him to do, he had done. Those words from Emily hit a nerve with him, cut him a little. *Who the fuck does she think she is?* he thought to himself.

When Anderson arrived back at his apartment, he had made up his mind, and that was to change the plan. It was Emily who wanted Tommy dead, not him. He called the number on the napkin from the coffee shop. This time it was answered instantly.

'I want to abort the request, please. Sorry to mess you around.' Anderson then hung up.

Later that night, Anderson awoke with a start, as a hand gripped tightly around his throat. He could hardly breathe. He couldn't even swallow, the grip was so intense. The blood pressure in his head increased so much that he could feel the blood vessels on his temples expand. He tried to fight off whoever was doing it, but their strength was too much.

Seconds before Anderson was about to pass out, they released their grip. Anderson took a life-saving gasp for breath, so deep it sounded like a fog horn.

'Do you think this is a game?' asked the person, in a deep male voice with a posh twang.

Anderson was still gasping for his breath. He tried to reply, but there wasn't enough air in his lungs.

'I'll ask you again. Do you think this is a game?'

'Wwwwhat? No!' Anderson managed to get his words out this time, shaking his head at the same time.

The assailant then shone a bright light into Anderson's face, making him feel extremely vulnerable, exposed and scared of whoever this person was. They were completely invisible, as Anderson was blinded by the sudden light.

'So, why do you FUCK about?' There was absolute emphasis on the word *fuck*.

Anderson realised who this was. 'I'm not, I'm sorry! I don't want him dead. It's Emily.'

'You will still pay me the money, okay! If not, I will kill you and the girl, got me?' His words pierced like a needle.

He then turned the light off but didn't leave the room. Anderson moved out of his bed, then felt a heavy blow straight to his face that knocked him back.

'I'm not done with you yet!' exclaimed the attacker. 'I saw you both laughing at me. I might not look like a killer, but I can ensure you, I am, and I could make you disappear like that.' He clicked his fingers.

'I know, I'm sorry for what we did.' Anderson wiped the warm blood from the cut on his face. 'Can you turn the light on, please?'

'No lights. Now listen, I want that money by noon tomorrow. There will be a black taxi outside this block at 11.30 tomorrow morning. You will get in, the driver will drive you to a location, you will pay him ALL the money and then leave.'

Joey then left the room without a sound, not quite sure whether Anderson was completely clear on the instructions.

Anderson wanted to follow him to make sure he left but decided to sit tight and wait a few minutes, just in case – he didn't want another blow.

'Yes?' Emily's voice sounded irritated by Anderson's call in the middle of the night.

'Emily, it's me, Anderson. We have a problem. We need to pay the twelve K by noon tomorrow!'

'Why tomorrow? I thought we were to pay him after the job?' Emily asked.

Anderson paused whilst thinking, not wanting to fess up to the unexpected incident.

'He's changed his mind and wants the money first.'

There was a huff from Emily. 'Why?'

Anderson paused again, thinking quickly on his feet. 'Because Tommy's in prison!' There was slight exaggeration in his tone.

'Fuck sake!'

Anderson was slowly starting to dislike Emily. Her attitude had changed. She used to be such a lovely girl, but now she walked around with a massive chip on her shoulder, like the world owed her a favour.

Becoming increasingly pissed off with her, he gave her some attitude back. 'It is what it is! I don't have the cash, so you need to come up with it!'

Emily then hung up the phone, leaving Anderson in limbo. *What does hanging up mean? I'll bring it over or fuck off?* he questioned.

He couldn't get back to sleep. It was now 4.00am, so he decided to log into the system he used on Tommy. The system worked by sending out a signal that attached itself to any mobile phone network, and would bounce around the entire network within a selected postcode area until it found a host – *an individual with the IPEA implant.* The system could also find a particular host with a search of the IMEI number specific to that chosen person. The implant had constant communication with the user's mobile phone, therefore the phone acted as a conduit into the individual's brain, with a direct feed back to the system. This then allowed Anderson to take control of the individual, giving him ultimate control.

Anderson had designed this system. He was once employed at Medi Corps, working on the initial start-up for the project Sovereignty, which was the project name for the IPEA. He had been sacked due to gross misconduct for hacking into the company's personnel system in order to obtain an employee's home address. He had then turned up at her home with a bunch of flowers. This had freaked out that particular member of staff, and she had reported him for harassment. Medi Corps had taken a zero-tolerance stance, and had ultimately sacked Anderson, despite all the knowledge he had.

So, Anderson sat in his room, allowing the system to search for anyone with the IPEA implant, and it didn't take long to find a host. He did this sometimes for pure amusement. He called it his *real GTA*. He would find a host and toy with them. It gave him the feeling of power and ultimate control.

The next morning, the black taxi was outside, as Joey had stated. Anderson didn't have the money and he panicked. He gave Emily another call.

'A taxi is here to pick me up! It's the driver - I need to pay him!'

'What taxi?' Emily asked.

'Joey told me I had to get in a taxi and pay the driver all the money.'

'So, do it!' Emily was blunt with an I-don't-care attitude.

'I don't have the money, do I?!'

'Not my problem!' Emily hung up, leaving Anderson feeling completely helpless.

He did have the money, but he didn't want to part with his cash. However, he now felt that he had no option.

The taxi smelt fresh and clean, like how you'd expect a brand new car to smell.

'Morning mate,' said Anderson, but there was silence. 'Excuse me, please?'

Again, there was no answer. The driver didn't even look in the rear-view mirror. He drove around for a little while and then parked up in a disused industrial estate. This was when the exchange was meant to happen.

Without a word, the driver got out of the car, walked to the rear door and opened it. Anderson sat in the back like a rabbit in headlights. The driver stood over him. He was old, around 70ish, and very broad with a tired and tough leathery face.

'Get out!' the driver ordered in a German accent.

The driver stood tall with a mean look on his face as Anderson climbed out of the car. Anderson was intimidated. The driver then leaned forward, and in the blink of an eye pulled out a taser, pressing it against Anderson's neck, causing him to furiously convulse until he passed out.

Anderson awoke some time later. The roof above him was made of corrugated tile with the odd Perspex tile allowing a little sunlight through. He laid on a hard, cold surface, and the air smelt dusty and old. It took seconds for Anderson to realise he was tied to a table, with his arms and legs immobilised. He could only move his head. He tried to look around, but his body ached from the stun-gun. His view was limited, but he noticed he had pissed himself.

Suddenly, someone spoke. 'Not so much of a joke now, am I?'

Anderson tensed up. 'Nnno, I'm sorry!'

'Sorry ain't gonna cut it, fella. I told you what would happen. I would have been more lenient if you and your girlfriend hadn't laughed at me, but cancelling wasn't an option, so do you have the money?' Joey looked over to his driver, who nodded, indicating he had searched Anderson and had retrieved the money.

Anderson became distressed. 'We didn't mean anything by it, I promise.'

'Too late, fella.' He then stood in Anderson's view. He was suited, his hair was combed over to the side and he was clean shaven. 'I have to deal with wannabes all the fucking time. You and your girlfriend are the FIRST to ever fucking disrespect me. Who the fuck do you think you are?'

'I'm sorry, I'm really sorry! I will never do it again!' Tears streamed down his cheeks and around his head as he laid on the table unable to move. Death stared him in the eyes.

'Haha! I know that fella. Ooh and what do I have here?' Joey waved a white bottle of liquid in Anderson's face.

'I, I, don't know?' said Anderson with a stutter.

'Sulphuric acid, and this shit can cause extreme pain and life-long side effects.' He removed the cap and held the bottle above Anderson's face.

'No, please,' Anderson pleaded and begged, 'please don't do that, please, I'll do anything!'

'Too late!' Joey poured the liquid all over Anderson's face, causing him to scream.

'Ahh stop, please stop, it's burning!!'

Joey couldn't help but laugh, then clicked his fingers. 'Calm down, it's only water! Let this be a lesson to you, little man. Never ever judge a book by its cover.'

Anderson came to the realisation that it was indeed only water, and his face was fine.

'It's amazing how something can have such a psychological effect,' said Joey smugly.

'What's going on?' asked Anderson, still catching his breath.

'Let this be a lesson to you, son,' said the driver, leaning down into Anderson's face, then setting him free from the restraints.

'I'm sorry.' Anderson stood cautiously. 'Where am I?'

'Find your own way back!' Joey and the driver turned and walked out, leaving Anderson alone in the warehouse, still shaken from the threat.

13

The grey cloud that once hovered over Tommy had blackened since he failed at suicide, pushing him into a deeper, darker place. His mind was in turmoil and he was on a set path to self-destruction. Word got out about Tommy's state of mind. The other inmates knew that he was weak and vulnerable, which some used to their own advantage. They took his food at meal times, taunted him, did what they could to push him over the edge. The stakes were high for the one who managed to get him to finally perish in his depression and leave the prison in a body bag. They pushed him hard.

Tommy would just take it and wouldn't even fight back or show any sign of emotion. He didn't want to show them that they affected him. All he cared about was trying to take his own life again, but being under constant watch twenty-four seven made it almost impossible – suicide watch was a bastard.

To Tommy he was in hell physically and emotionally. His life had been turned upside down, swallowed up and shat out. To the world he felt like scum, having been charged for murder; murders he felt he hadn't committed. The concept of it boiled his brain. He had no comprehension – it was like confusion on steroids. He'd spent hours, days, even weeks trying to piece things together, and it hurt like hell. The pain of what had happened fried his very soul to the devil.

Tommy wanted to talk, but he couldn't speak out to the psychologist provided by HMP. Having a cell to himself was becoming increasingly difficult. His mind was being eaten from the inside out by the negative thoughts and energy. His heart craved communication, but his body would not allow the words to come out. Being left alone was the worst thing for him. He needed a friend; just someone to listen to him when he could finally find the strength to voice his thoughts.

There was no distraction. Watching TV or reading was impossible. His mind would not allow him to focus, to take himself away from the darkness just for a little while by losing himself in a book or a film. The HMP services were becoming increasingly worried and concerned. Even the experts didn't know how to deal with Tommy's state of mind.

Tommy felt as though his parents had disowned him. No one ever came to see him apart from Valentina. To Tommy it was like he had evaporated from the outside world.

One night, he laid awake in his cell. He stared up at the metal slats that supported the mattress on the bunk above, and once again the darkness took hold of his thoughts, like heroin to an addict. His mind surfed the dark waves of hell. His subconscious became a thick darkness, taking him away from the prison cell for a moment.

He looked back at himself as a little boy when he had lived on the farm with his parents. He could see himself laying in bed, tossing and turning, trying to sleep. His mum had come to check up on him, and as the handle on the door to his bedroom moved, he had turned and pretended to sleep. She sat on the end of his bed and started talking to him. 'No matter what you do with your life, I will always be there for you. I love you with all my heart, and so does your daddy. We will always protect you, listen to you and try to understand. You can always talk to us, my angel, always.' She had kissed his cheek and left the room. Tommy didn't know why he had pretended to be asleep. Maybe he thought he'd get into trouble if he was still awake. He would never know.

The words from his mum had been fake, unreal, lies, deep lies - *where is my mum now?* He then had an image of himself hanging, his neck stretched, a bone had pierced through the side of his skin, dark dried blood created a line down his neck and had soaked into his t-shirt. His eyes were open, bloodshot and strained. His lips were dark purple, ready to burst. There was a light above him, flickering as a moth flicked off the bulb. He hovered towards himself, looking into his own bloodshot eyes. His dead mouth started to twitch, turning into a smile. *'Do it Tommy; it only hurts for a second.'* With a start, Tommy jumped from his bunk with a terrorised scream, and the guards ran in.

'It was a dream, McGregor! Get back in your pit!' shouted the guard.

These thoughts and dreams became a nightly occurrence. They hurt and tormented Tommy. They were somehow a reminder of how he couldn't even rely on his own family. The one person who he thought he would have stood by him his whole life had let him down - his mother. She wouldn't visit, even though he had put in various requests. Neither his mother or father ever came or even tried to make contact.

That night, the black mist in Tommy's mind came back as he drifted off to sleep. He was hurt by old memories. At that point, he wished he had no memories, wished to forget everything – he needed something to get rid of the black agonising thoughts.

The next morning, he was awoken on doctor's orders - a lovely dose of Diazepam, 2.5mg twice a day to keep him drowsy, weak and pretty much not with it. It only masked the issues Tommy was facing, but it was better than the terrors that swam through his mind and pounced at any given time.

On that particular day, Tommy was going to get the best form of medication he needed, besides Diazepam; exactly what he needed to survive in that shithole prison. Although he didn't know it at the time, things were going to change.

Breakfast was served in the mess hall. Tommy would always walk into the large room with his head down, absolutely avoiding eye contact with anyone. The room was loud and noisy, and it caused him claustrophobia and internal panic – Tommy managed to hold it in, but only just. Other inmates were either bantering one another or looking to pick a fight just to let off a bit of steam. Tommy was always the favourite amongst them all, due to his emotionless state. They trusted that he wouldn't grass on them, plus if he killed himself, someone would benefit.

The brown scrambled eggs were thrown onto Tommy's tray by the kitchen staff, with a bit splashing onto his trousers as he moved down the line. The inmate behind was taunting him at the same time. He was a big fat, bald bastard who went by the name of Killroy - maybe because his name was Roy and he had killed someone. The beans then followed with a side order of cold toast.

'I'm gonna fuck you, McGregor! I'm gonna fuck you hard, baby,' said Killroy from behind.

The words cut into Tommy on the inside, causing adrenaline to burst into his bloodstream, but on the outside, he just looked like he always did – the lights were on, but no one was home.

'I'm coming to your cell tonight. I'm gonna get you so good, you'll never want pussy again.'

Tommy took the verbal abuse. He didn't rise to it and he didn't say a word, but the adrenaline was taking hold of him. His hands started to shake. Tommy's ignorance and lack of response didn't go in his favour at all. Killroy wanted a rise out of him, wanted him to snap so they could brawl in front of everyone. Killroy wanted to show off and wanted to show other inmates the damage he could do. He wanted to be the one to push Tommy into that body bag.

Because Tommy didn't snap, the punishment came. Killroy decided to ditch the verbal bullshit and take it a step further by giving him a pelvic thrust from behind, connecting with Tommy's arse. Tommy was enraged with the force, which caused him to go flying. The sloppy breakfast on his tray spilt everywhere and humiliation kicked in, blending with the anger and adrenaline.

'Back off!' shouted Tommy.

The whole mess hall erupted with a roar of cheers. Finally, someone had got a rise out of Tommy McGregor, the Walking Dead. Most inmates were standing to watch the show as guards forced their way through the crowd. Killroy then planted an elbow into Tommy's eye socket, busting it open instantly. Blood poured down Tommy's face. Seconds later came another right jab in the same spot, opening the cut further. The inmates cheered even more.

The guards were getting closer, pushing and shoving to get through, but before they got there, Killroy stamped on Tommy's face, fracturing his eye socket. He felt his nose break as the cartilage twisted under the force. Blood poured over his face, filling his eyes, so that he couldn't see. Tommy gave up, taking more blows to the face. The pain faded as his mind dulled towards unconsciousness. He thought he was dying and gave Killroy a little smile out of the side of his bloody mouth.

Killroy was taken down by the guards as Tommy flopped unconscious on the cold mess hall floor. A first responder came to his aid.

The Princess of Wales was a nice clean hospital. Tommy was on a bed in the corridor waiting for a brain scan to see if there had been any serious damage. Once again, his mind fixated on the black mist taking hold of his thoughts, *I wish he'd killed me. I wish I was dead. Maybe if I wind him up enough he'd kill me next time?* He imagined the scenarios in his mind, fantasising how he would die and how empty his funeral would be. He was floating above his open casket. He could see his own face, half of which was caved in, and an eye was missing with the optic nerve spreading down over his temple. He then snapped out of his thoughts.

'Looks like you've had a nasty injury!' explained the operator of the CT scan, who was dressed all in green, was around mid-forties and probably lived a happy life with his wife and kids; something Tommy knew he would never have, but something he wished he had.

'I don't want to talk about it.'

'Suit yourself.' The operator then proceeded to explain what he needed Tommy to do.

After the scan, Tommy was taken to a private room where he had two uniformed officers by his side the whole time watching him. He was handcuffed to the bed; not that he was in any fit state to try and do a runner, and why would he now?

Hours later, a consultant came to see Tommy and confirmed he had a broken eye socket and a broken nose. He also explained that he would need twelve stiches in his face and that he would need to be kept in overnight due to his concussion and possibly another night, depending on how he progressed throughout the first night.

A few days later, Tommy was on the road to recovery and was put straight back into the system. Nothing had changed, apart from a metamorphic thought process. After the event, Tommy had decided to take his fate into his own hands. He was going to stand and fight. He was going to get himself out of prison and start to rebuild his life. He wanted a family, a wife and kids, and a normal nine to five job, but first he needed respect.

Every man stared at Tommy as he went down the line collecting his processed breakfast. They stared at his scarred face and looked intensely for any sign of emotion, but Tommy wasn't going to give anything away. He only thought to himself, *Look at you all - a bunch of low-life wankers!*

There were murmurs and whispers as Tommy sat next to an old inmate, who shuffled along, creating a significant gap between them. Then Killroy caught Tommy's eye. He was sitting with other inmates, with his back to Tommy. Then the man in front of Killroy gave a nod as a gesture to look behind. Killroy took the hint and looked round.

Tommy gave Killroy a smile. It was a silent message; a message that said, *You tried, but you won't break me.* This was the first time Tommy had smiled properly in months.

The sound of Killroy's fists hitting the bench caused jumps and gasps from the inmates, followed by light chatter and a feeling of excitement – another show to keep them entertained. Tommy didn't flinch, and the room went quiet. Guards started to move quickly to stop another incident from happening. Tommy felt somewhat protected and he smiled again, looking Killroy in the eye as he continued to eat his food, giving the impression he had no cares in the world – *Bring it on! You didn't kill me. You made me stronger, fool!*

When the lights went out at night, Tommy used that time to make a shank - a weapon. He wasn't going to let Killroy get away with it again. Sweets were easy to get hold of in prison, so he'd arranged to get a stick of rock. The rock was about eight inches long and perfect for what he needed. He took the time to rub the rock against the concrete wall of his cell. He could only get so much done at a time, but the result would be worth it.

A week later, his shank was ready. Who would have thought a simple stick of rock could be shaped into an ice pick, sharp enough to pierce through human flesh. Now, he had to sit tight and bide his time, pick his moment and shank Killroy. He wanted to kill him and to send out a message that he wasn't going to be doomed in that place. Tommy wasn't going to get caught, he knew it, and would earn the respect he needed to survive his remaining time in prison. No one would grass. No one grassed in that place – that was the culture. If you did, then you might as well have been the person on the end of a shank.

The shank was well hidden in a hole in the wall just the right size for it under Tommy's bed. Weeks were spent with Tommy observing Killroy's movements. He spotted a routine; cell doors were opened for two hours per day, when the inmates could roam in their enclosure, mingle with one another, go outside for a fag, play pool or just chat shit.

As soon as the cell doors were opened, Killroy always made a beeline for the smoking area. He'd chain smoke three fags and then go for a shower. He would be on his own most of the time, and this would be Tommy's moment.

The day had finally arrived, Tommy watched Killroy go about his daily routine. As soon as he went to the smoking area, Tommy went into the shower room, the shank hidden in a safe place – lodged uncomfortably. He went into a toilet cubicle, stood on the toilet, squatted and passed the stick of rock into his hand, wiping it with some toilet paper. He then waited silently, still standing on the toilet seat. A cocktail of nerves, adrenaline and fear flowed through his bloodstream, filling every cell in his body, gearing him up to knowingly, *for the first time*, take another life.

On cue, Tommy heard someone walk into the shower room and turn on the shower. The water hissed through the shower head and splashed onto the red tiled floor. He could hear grunting from the enjoyment of the hot water massaging the bastard's body. Tommy was able to identify the man as Killroy, as he had a slight tick that caused him to grunt every few minutes. This tick had driven the other inmates crazy, but no one had the bottle to say or do anything about it.

Tommy stripped completely naked, his bath towel hung around his neck, with the shank in his right hand, hidden underneath the towel. Killroy was washing himself. His back, thick with black matted wet hair, was to the entrance of the large open shower room. He was on his own as planned.

Tommy slowly crept towards Killroy, the sound of the powerful shower disguising any sound Tommy made. He got closer. He could smell the scent from the shower gel and feel the steam from the shower, and the splashes from Killroy's back wet Tommy's face. He was at arms-reach now, and just close enough.

He took the shank and planted it straight into the side of Killroy's neck. This took Killroy's breath, and he fell to his knees. Tommy withdrew the weapon. Blood poured and diluted in the water as it flowed across the shower floor into the drain. Tommy had hit the jackpot - straight into his carotid artery. Ten seconds later, Killroy was on the ground and was dead within minutes.

A sense of excitement, fulfilment and complete gratification filled Tommy - he felt totally exhilarated. Within seconds he had gone back to his cell, smiling and looking forward to the outcome of this attack.

The stick of rock went down a treat with Tommy. It took great effort to eat, but it was gone within the hour. It was the only safe way he could think of getting rid of the evidence without a trace. With no evidence, Tommy knew he'd get away with it. When Killroy's body was found, all hell broke loose, with every cell locked down, searched and every inmate interrogated. Tommy maintained his black cloud facade – the lights were on, but no one was home.

That night, Tommy slept better than he had done in a very long time. There was no black mist haunting and controlling his mind – *a mental release.*

14

'This had better be good,' said Valentina, checking the time and seeing that it was 3.00am.

'We have a breakthrough, Valentina. I need you down at the lab ASAP!' exclaimed Professor Conroy, a well-established professor for the local university, specialising in Neuroscience.

Valentina walked into the medical lab in the city centre. She had roughed-up bed hair and was wearing sweatpants, a hoodie and trainers - not her usual look.

'What is it?' she demanded of the well-respected professor.

The professor was a polite gentleman in his 60s, who always dressed smart in jeans and a tweed sports jacket. He looked like a typical professor, but he was not a man to be underestimated.

'It's Tommy's brain activity. There are peculiar anomalies never before heard of. Please,' the professor held out his hand, 'take a seat.' He then pulled out a brown leather chair on the other side of his large oak writing desk with green leather lining.

'Thanks, okay so what is it?' Valentina's voice buzzed with anxiety.

'Using a download from Mr McGregor's IPEA implant, I've been able to study Mr McGregor's brain activity and the chemical movement in his brain during each incident. Here look,' the professor turned his laptop round and pointed at a line graph. 'His brain activity is what we would class as normal or as expected during normal behaviour. Then thirty minutes before he commits the indecent exposure incident earlier this year,' he paused, 'two brain chemicals interacted that would normally lead to the development of psychotic disorders, such as schizophrenia. The results here suggest abnormal levels of the neurotransmitter glutamate, which may lead to changes in the levels of another neurotransmitter, dopamine, causing the transition into psychosis. However, in Mr McGregor's case, a third synthetic chemical binds with the glutamate and dopamine, putting Tommy's brain into an unconscious state. Are you with me on this?'

'I am,' Valentina replied, giving an unconvincing smile, confusion written all over her face.

'Good,' he smiled. 'So, I've found that during this unconscious state, the disruption to the connectivity in the brain and greater modularity created an environment that is inhospitable to the kind of efficient information transfer that is required for consciousness.'

'Okay, now you've lost me?' Valentina admitted defeat, combing her hair with a hand.

'Okay, Mr McGregor's brain can only transfer local information, only within the brain, a bit like an island. He has no control over his body; he can't consciously think, see or hear. Then it gets tricky-'

'Sorry to interrupt. So, you're telling me, Tommy had no control over his body when these acts were carried out?'

'Correct, but wait, don't get ahead of yourself,' the professor paused. 'The third chemical is synthetic,' he paused again and elaborated. 'Not real.'

'Thanks, Professor, I know what synthetic means.' Valentina was slightly insulted, but she let it go.

'I've never seen anything like this before. It's come from an external source; not something that Mr McGregor's brain could produce – that would be impossible. How it got there...I do not know, yet.' There was a slight pause whilst Valentina registered the information. 'To me, and please feel free to have a second opinion, but this information suggests a third party is using Mr McGregor as a host. Someone has been taking complete control over his body, so he has no idea what is happening.'

Valentina used her fingers to comb back her matted bed hair once again. She was frustrated by the information she had received and it was a little too early in the morning for it all to sink in properly. 'Okay, so how does this work?'

'That I don't know, Detective. I apologise,' said the professor.

'Professor Conroy, you must be one of the most intelligent men on this planet. Do not apologise!'

'That's very kind of you to say so, Detective, but I can assure you, even this is beyond me. Can I suggest you have a discussion with Medi Corps. They created the IPEA. I think, but could be wrong, the IPEA is the conduit into Mr McGregor's brain.'

'Okay, well my brain is well and truly fried!' Valentina admitted.

'Mine too, Detective, mine too!' Professor Conroy gave a smile.

'If I can get Medi Corps in for a meeting, would you sit in on it with me? I'll need you to explain this. I'd get lost in the introductions!'

'Of course, please have my secretary schedule me in when you have arranged the meeting,' said the professor.

'Professor, thank you so much for your time. Your help on this case has been invaluable.'

Professor Conroy stood politely and shook her hand with a gentle grip. 'It's a pleasure, Detective Valentina, as always.'

They both exchanged pleasant smiles, then Valentina left the lab moments later.

It was now 5.00am, and the dregs from the night clubs could be seen staggering home, pissed. Valentina called up Detective Constable Roberts. Roberts had been in the police force for twenty plus years and had supported Valentina for six of them. He was her trusted right-hand man.

'Roberts, sorry to wake you, but as soon as you can, I need you to make contact with the CEO of Medi Corps. It's the McGregor case. We've had a development we can't ignore.'

'No problem, DI. What's changed?' Roberts' voice was broken with a yawn.

'It's a long story. I'll fill you in with the details later, once you've woken up. Set up a meeting with him as soon as you can. I don't care where he is, we must see him!' Valentina used a direct tone, hoping he would grasp the urgency. Roberts was good at taking direction; he never took her abrupt approach to heart.

The shower was hot, making goose bumps appear on Valentina's body at first and giving her an intense need to pee, as her body quickly adjusted to the sudden change in temperature. She washed her hair and freshened up, getting herself ready for the day. Although tired from the 3.00am start, Valentina never slept in, never switched off. Her life revolved around the force. Even though she was nearing her fortieth birthday, she had no urge to meet and marry anyone. Valentina feared that type of commitment and had built a life for herself on her own. She was not ashamed to admit that she was too selfish to have children – and fair play, not many can admit that.

A self-confessed coffee snob, Valentina loved the aroma that filled her house when she filtered fresh coffee through her coffee machine. She loved the rich taste and polished off pints of the stuff on a daily basis. She believed it kept her focused, kept her mind in gear, got her blood moving and made her feel energetic – she would never start a day without it.

Down at the station, Roberts was waiting for Valentina. They had an 11.00am meeting scheduled with the CEO of Medi Corps, Mr Russell Davidson MBE. Davidson was a high profile individual, however he kept himself to himself. He didn't believe in social media and was known to say that it was the route of all evil. Since his company produced products and services that made use of social media, he would admit the hypocrisy, but would state, 'In business you produce what sells'.

Roberts greeted Valentina with a kiss on the cheek as she walked into her office. He was itching to know what had happened, and judging by her tone, he knew it would be big.

'Are you going to leave me hanging for much longer DI?' Roberts asked, handing her a cup of black Americano without sugar.

She savoured the coffee with an expression of pure joy, a bit like an addict sucking on a crack pipe. 'You'll need to sit down for this one. It'll take me a while to explain. My brain has been spinning ever since I got the info.'

Roberts parked his backside, and Valentina told him everything in as much detail as she could remember from her discussion with Professor Conroy.

'Fuck... I think I get it, sort of?' said Roberts, shocked at the evolutionary shift in the McGregor case. 'So, what now?'

'We need to ensure we have all the evidence to build a strong case and support this finding,' said Valentina. 'I was aggressive in taking down McGregor, and I will be just as aggressive if we can prove his innocence. You know me, I'd never let anyone innocent go in the clink.'

'True. Wait,' Roberts held out both hands, frowning as the cogs in his mind turned, registering what was being said. 'Someone else was controlling Tommy's body? Nah, can't be true! I don't believe it!'

'Professor Conroy, that's all I'm saying.'

'He's never been wrong, DI, but I just don't get it.' Roberts quizzed what he had just been told. 'You normally see this stuff in a movie, not in real life.' Roberts was sceptical. The crimes committed had been gruesome and horrific. People had been murdered and lives had been ruined by this man – Tommy McGregor.

Medi Corps HQ was an enormous, very modern building with outstanding architecture. It was clear how much money this company was turning over and what must have been invested into their HQ.

The front entrance had a large water feature, with crystal clear water flowing from the top of a chrome globe, trickling into an oval base. There was ambient classical background music playing; not too loud so you couldn't hold a conversation, but not too quiet that you couldn't hear it. It was a nice touch, which gave an instant feeling that this place delivered.

Inside, the walls were white, and the ceilings were at least twenty feet high, with daylight LED lighting illuminating the large space. Voices in conversation could be heard in the background with a large screen placed centrally on a wall, displaying marketing features on new products and services delivered by Medi Corps.

The front desk was large, with the front panel coming up to chest height. Four smartly dressed receptionists stood behind the desk. Valentina and Roberts approached the closest receptionist.

'Good morning, how can I help you?' The receptionist's smile filled her face with pearly whites so bright, it was obvious they weren't natural.

'I'm Detective Inspector Valentina, and this is my Detective Constable, Roberts. We have an appointment with Mr Davidson.' They both flashed their warrant badges to prove their identities.

'Yes, of course. Mr Davidson has been expecting you. Please take a seat. I will let him know you are here.' The receptionist gestured for them to take a seat in a nearby seating area.

'It's okay, we can wait here,' replied Valentina, giving off a type of alpha female, just-because-you're-pretty-you-can't-tell-me-what-to-do attitude.

Roberts couldn't help but give a little snigger. Valentina looked at him and raised her brow, as if to say "what?" He returned a smile.

'As you wish, Officer,' said the receptionist. Roberts shifted on his feet awkwardly. Calling the DI an officer wasn't something Valentina would take lightly.

'I'm a detective inspector, not an officer.' The claws were out, but the receptionist was quickly saved by Mr Davidson greeting them both with a hard and firm handshake.

'It's a pleasure to meet you both. Please, come with me,' said Mr Davidson.

Spare me, Valentina thought. They followed Mr Davidson through a maze of corridors whilst listening to his Cuban heels strike the floor tiles as he walked. He was a well-dressed man in a sharp grey pinstripe suit with a blue shirt and a white tie that matched his hair colour. He pulled it off well. The corridor led them to a glass lift that took them to the top floor, which opened out onto his office.

Mr Davidson's office was as expected... large. A huge saltwater fish tank took over almost the length of one wall, with an array of beautiful colours that swam around, and live coral that carpeted the bed of the tank. The trickle of water from the pump provided a sense of calm.

'Please sit,' offered Mr Davidson. 'Can I get you anything? Sparkling water, tea, coffee?'

'Coffee please, black no sugar,' Valentina requested.

'Just a water is fine, thank you,' replied Roberts.

Mr Davidson picked up his phone to place the order.

Valentina didn't give Mr Davidson a chance to kick off the conversation and dived straight in herself. 'We have a high-profile case and have received some very important information from a respected source regarding one of your products.'

Mr Davidson looked concerned. 'Before you go on, are you here to interrogate me? If you are, I'll need an advisor with me.'

This raised a red flag for Valentina immediately – *Why would he instantly assume adversity?*

'No, Mr Davidson, we are here for clarity, and we are hoping you can provide this for us?'

'Okay, I'll do my best.'

There was a knock at the door. Mr Davidson granted access and a host entered with the order of drinks.

'Thank you,' said Valentina.

'So, where were we? You needed clarification on what exactly?' asked Mr Davidson.

Valentina grew more suspicious by Mr Davidson's attitude. He was defensive from the outset.

'Mr Davidson, this case involves a client of yours who has had the IPEA installed. Our source believes this implant in your client has created a back door into this individual's brain.'

Mr Davidson shook his head. 'What exactly do you mean by a back door into their brain?' He took this light heartedly. His words rolled off his tongue with no seriousness at all.

Valentina became frustrated, which was obvious by her retaliation. 'We believe, Mr Davidson, that this back door has allowed someone to take control of another human. They have used their body to commit horrendous crimes.' She pressed her index finger into the desk with frustration.

'Impossible! Who do you think you are, coming in here with your witchcraft bullshit?!' He was completely dismissive of the "story" and his light heartedness turned to anger.

Roberts then piped up, 'We believe this is a matter of fact! Do you think we'd waste our valuable time coming here if we weren't one hundred percent sure? Think about it, Mr Davidson. If this gets leaked to the press, you'll have the authorities all over this establishment. So, I strongly suggest you take this seriously.'

Valentina looked over at Roberts, giving him a discreet wink and a smile – *well said you!*

'With the greatest respect to you both, what you are suggesting is ludicrous,' Mr Davidson declared. 'If this got leaked to the press, then you'd be a laughing stock. No one in their right mind would believe this nonsense! If you don't mind, I have work to do.' He stood tall and guarded.

'Mr Davidson, we have not come here to pick holes in your products. We need clarification that you can support this evidence. If not, then we will need to investigate further. I don't think you realise how serious this is,' Valentina warned.

'Okay, so what crimes have been committed? What has this so called "Avatar" done to bring you to my door?' Mr Davidson asked pointedly.

'We can't divulge that information yet. If you can support us, together with whoever else you need to involve, you'll need to sign an NDA, then you and your "advisers" can meet with our source and we can go from there?'

'I can't help you.' Mr Davidson announced, shaking his head.

'Can't or won't?' shouted Roberts, angry at the lack of cooperation from such a highly respected man.

'I won't help. Go and write a book about it instead. I'm sure this ridiculous concept would do well as a fictional story. Take your *Black Matter* rubbish and leave.' It was clear Mr Davidson wasn't prepared to assist with the case.

'Well, Mr Davidson, we are talking about murder, so we will be in contact with you, and would like for you to reconsider and to cooperate with us in ensuring the right people are taken off the streets.' Valentina smiled self-righteously, then both left the building.

'He'll come round,' said Valentina.

'How do you know?' asked Roberts.

'Trust me, he will.' She gave a confident smile, and they got back into their car.

Before they even reached the station, there was a call from Mr Davidson. 'DI Valentina, it's Russel Davidson from Medi Corps. I've had a think about our previous conversation.'

'I'm all ears, go on?' she replied.

'I'd like for my technical adviser and myself to meet with your source, if that is still an option?'

'Of course it's still an option! When will you be available?' Valentina turned and gave Roberts a sly wink. He smiled in return.

'I will be free to assist your team anytime; anything to help with the case,' said Mr Davidson.

'Great, I will come back to you. Can I ask you one question, Mr Davidson?'

'Of course?'

'Why the sudden change of heart?'

'I've had a good think. I'm always defensive when my company or my employees have potential exposure. A lot of the work we do is highly confidential, and some things can be taken the wrong way. On top of that, you mentioned murder, and I feel we have a duty to assist in such crimes.'

'I appreciate your honesty. I will be in touch.' Valentina hung up the phone before Mr Davidson could say anything else, and she turned to Roberts, who was driving. 'See, one nil to Valentina!' she exclaimed, licking her finger and pressing the air whilst making a hissing sound through her teeth.

Valentina and Roberts arrived back at the station and made the arrangements with both Professor Conroy and Mr Davidson. They were due to meet the next working day, not wanting to waste any time.

The next day came around quickly. It was agreed that they would all meet at Professor Conroy's lab at the University. Valentina and Roberts were already there when Davidson arrived with his adviser. They met in the main reception.

'Good morning,' said Mr Davidson. 'This is Tammy Bezuidenhout. She has been my adviser for the last fifteen years. She's the brains behind the IPEA.'

'Pleased to meet you,' Tammy said as she shook hands with Valentina with gentle calmness.

There was something refreshing about Tammy. She was well dressed, wearing a long black pencil skirt, a black long-sleeved top with a yellow belt and yellow shoes. Her hair was long and dark, tied right back into a ponytail, and her eyes were a stunning brown, which complemented her facial features well.

'Likewise, Ms Bezui-'

'It's Bezuidenhout, but please just call me Tammy. Most people can't pronounce my name.'

Valentina didn't appreciate the interruption. She felt more than capable of pronouncing her name, but she smiled anyway. 'This is my Detective Constable, Roberts.'

Roberts took Tammy's soft hand to shake. She had kind eyes. Mr Davidson looked somewhat awkward, probably following his previous behaviour.

They all followed Valentina through the university and went through the introductions with Professor Conroy.

'Please all take a seat, but help yourselves to any refreshments,' Professor Conroy offered, pointing at a trolley with fresh fruit, tea, coffee and bottled water.

Valentina kicked off the meeting by again going through a quick introduction of all present and handing out an NDA for all to sign regarding the confidentiality of the meeting. She then stood. 'We have a man charged with the murder of two women - Nicola Wakefield and Sharon Gillingham. The same man has also been charged with GBH to Taylor Gillingham.'

Davidson nodded. It was clear he recognised the names from the news and knew who had been charged.

'My trusted professor here,' Valentina held out her hand towards Professor Conroy, who nodded with her, 'has explored the IPEA download from Tommy McGregor's implant and has made the following discovery – over to you, Professor.' Valentina sat down as Professor Conroy was simultaneously standing and turning on a screen.

'Can I ask you all to pay attention to this screen.' The professor clicked on the mouse on his laptop and a series of graphs and data filled the screen. 'What we have here is Mr McGregor's brain activity.' The professor pointed at the same graphs he had shown to Valentina. 'The brain activity here is normal, but when you look here, there are two chemical reactions and another unknown synthetic reaction. Thirty minutes after this reaction, he commits an indecent exposure act.'

Valentina then handed out the report detailing this particular incident.

'Can I interrupt, please?' asked Tammy, holding a hand in the air.

'Of course, please,' replied the professor.

'I can see by the data that the two chemicals were Dopamine and Glutamate. The third, that you correctly call synthetic, were Circuitoids. These were developed electronically with research from stem cells and can communicate with neurons. These Circuitoids exhibit spontaneous rhythmic activity of the kind known to repetitive movement.'

Valentina interrupted. 'Can we please try and keep this in simple terms. I've understood what you have said so far, but please appreciate that we are not all medical scientists in this room.' She then stood and poured herself a cup of coffee.

'Sorry Tammy, please.' Professor Conroy gave Valentina a respectful smile across the table.

'I understand, sorry. I just wanted to clarify that the synthetic brain function is a known entity, more so in the technological world than biological.'

'Thank you, Tammy. That is helpful information,' said the professor, followed by Davidson rudely interrupting.

'So, what has this got to do with my IPEA?' Frustration took hold of Mr Davidson's face. He was clearly a man with a short fuse.

'I was getting to that, Mr Davidson. So...these Circuitoids, which the lovely Tammy has clarified for us, are being manipulated by a third party, who have been taking control of Mr McGregor's brain. At the times when these Circuitoids are active, Mr McGregor's brain is in an unconscious state, so theoretically speaking, he has no idea whatsoever what he's actually doing. We have asked you to join us today to provide clarity on how this interception takes place?'

Tammy absorbed the information on the screen and asked, 'Can I have some time to go through the download from his implant, please?'

'Of course,' said Professor Conroy. 'Here, take a seat.'

'No, I mean I will need to take it away. Can you transfer the files to a USB for me, please?'

'You can, but the USB will need to be encrypted,' Valentina then interrupted.

'Not a problem,' said Davidson as he pulled a USB stick from his bag. 'This has an encryption on it.'

'Well, that's fine then. We will need to have it returned after use,' said Valentina. 'How long do you think this will take?'

'Depends on how far we need to dig. These reports are highly comprehensive. It will take some time.'

'Can we meet again tomorrow to go through your findings?' asked Roberts.

'I'm going to need a couple of weeks,' Tammy explained.

'We don't have weeks. We need this done as soon as possible.'

'That is as soon as possible,' Tammy clarified. 'The IPEA talks to extremely large groups of neurons, with millions, if not trillions, of connections that take place, and it processes these, resulting in the report. We will be in touch once we have evaluated everything, and due to the nature of your case, it's not something I'm prepared to rush.'

'That's fair enough,' said Roberts.

They all shook hands, and Davidson and Tammy left the room to navigate their own way through the maze of the university.

'What do we all think?' Valentina was in high spirits.

'Very interesting about the Circuitoids. I think this will be a needle in a haystack, if you want my honest opinion. Even if they can prove Mr McGregor was being controlled by someone else, it's going to be almost impossible to find out who.' Professor Conroy didn't share Valentina's enthusiastic optimism.

'DI, we just need to do our job as we know it; carry out the detective work our way and let the academics investigate in their way. I think a bit of cold calling to those closest to Tommy would be a good start.'

'That's why you work for me, Roberts. Thinking for me,' Valentina smiled then turned to Professor Conroy. 'Thank you so much once again for your time.'

'Always a pleasure!' The professor gave a respectful smile.

En route back to the station, Roberts' brain was in deep thought as he was searching through McGregor's Facebook profile. Valentina always admired Roberts' resting bitch face. She'd never seen anyone look so pissed off when they were really not.

'Share your thoughts, Roberts?'

'DI, I'm going to pay Emily Wakefield a visit. Looks like her and Tommy had a thing leading up to and during the murders.'

'Good thinking. I'll leave you to that one, but please do me a favour. When you pay her a visit, make sure you're in uniform.'

Roberts knew what Valentina meant by this; uniformed police always gave off an air of authority.

'I need to visit McGregor and get a steer on his events once more,' said Valentina.

'Good thinking, boss.'

Swansea prison looked like the typical 1800s prison with large front gates about thirty feet tall and high stone walls towering at about forty feet. It had been some time since Valentina had been to this place. The last time had been eight years ago on a child murder case. The place instantly gave her the creeps, causing a cold shiver to take over her nerves, cascading down her spine from her head to her fingertips for a few seconds.

The visitors' centre was outside of the main walls. Valentina presented herself at the reception desk. There was a little to-ing and fro-ing with the front desk, as it was outside of visiting times, but with the dropping of a few names of those in high places, it didn't take long for them to agree for Valentina to speak with Tommy McGregor.

Valentina was given an interview room, with the insistence of HMP services that there was to be a guard present, which firstly Valentina didn't feel was necessary, and secondly, she wanted to have a private one-to-one conversation with Tommy. The room was cold, and the walls were bare, with a heavily stained carpet, but it would do.

After a forty-five-minute wait, Tommy was brought into the interview room. He was in a pair of jeans and a light grey hoodie, which looked like a prison-issue hoodie but was actually his own. She guessed it was his way of attempting to blend in.

'Tommy, how are you?' Valentina asked with a friendly tone.

'So, so.' It was clear his spirit had been sucked out of him. He had large dark circles under his eyes and a nasty cut above and around his right eye.

'What happened there?'

'Nuffin.' Tommy's head was hanging down, his hair was scruffy, and he was unshaven, his beard curling at the ends with a slight hint of ginger.

'Tommy, I've come to see you today to go through your version of events from when you were arrested for indecent exposure. Can you do that for me?'

'Why?' Tommy asked, still looking down and not making any eye contact.

Valentina glanced over at the guard in the room and gave him a side nod to leave. The guard reluctantly left the room.

'Look Tommy, between me and you, there has been new evidence that supports your case. I can't go through it in detail, but I can tell you that it is looking promising for you.'

'Please don't do that!' Tommy said, his voice wobbling and his blue eyes filling with water. He was on the verge of crying but trying to hold it back.

'Do what Tommy?'

'Give me any hope. I'm out of hope. I've given up on life and have accepted the inevitable.' Tears rolled down his pale cheeks. 'I wish I was dead.'

'Look at me, Tommy,' said Valentina firmly.

He shook his head.

'Fucking look at me, now!' Valentina's voice was raised, and she glanced at the door to make sure no one had heard her elevated tone. Tommy then looked up at her with his bloodshot eyes.

'I no longer think you did these awful crimes. If you think I would come all the way here to fuck with your head, then you're very much mistaken. I was gunning for you at the beginning, and I was pleased to have caught you, but now things have changed, and I have a duty of care to ensure an innocent man doesn't spend the rest of his life behind bars.'

Tommy shook his head and put his palms together. 'I didn't do any of it. I swear on my mother's life!'

'I know you didn't, and now we need to prove it. Tell me what you can remember from when you were arrested for walking the streets naked,' Valentina entreated.

'I've been going through everything over and over in my head. That day, all I remember is laying on the sofa,' Tommy paused and took a breath. 'The next thing I recall, I was naked down Cardiff Bay, freezing cold with two policemen running towards me. I just ran back towards my flat as fast as I could. People were staring at me. I was so confused. Thought I had sleep walked.' He then paused again.

'What happened next, Tommy?'

'I was thrown to the ground, handcuffed and put into the back of the van.'

'Think, Tommy, do you remember anything else? It doesn't matter how small the detail is?'

'There was one thing.' He folded his arms across his chest. 'My neighbour, we called him the freak-'

'We?'

'Me and my girlfriend at the time, Taylor. Oh God, Taylor.' Tommy burst into tears, the image of her face haunting him. The black mist started to shadow his mind.

'It's okay, Tommy. Talk to me.'

'He was there in the crowed of people watching me. I felt humiliated, and he had this look on his face, like he was enjoying it, you know? Getting a fix out of it.'

'What's his name?' asked Valentina.

'I don't know. He was always staring at us weirdly. He'd intercept my post at times, hand it to me and walk off without saying anything. Why?' He looked up at Valentina. 'Do you think he has something to do with it?'

'Tommy, I have no idea who's behind all this. All I know is that you, as Tommy McGregor, didn't do it.'

The door to the room opened then.

'Time's up folks,' said the guard, using a thumb to point at the door as a clear-off gesture.

'One more minute, please?' demanded Valentina.

'Sorry, time's up. Got to leave now. Come on.'

They both stood, and Valentina gave Tommy a gentle nod.

'Thank you,' he whispered, and Valentina returned a soft smile.

Roberts hadn't worn his uniform in months and felt proud to wear it once again. Being CID, there weren't many opportunities to wear it, and it felt good. He walked up the path to Emily's house and knocked on the door, peering through the front window to see if there were any signs of life. He waited for a few more moments and knocked again, this time harder. Moments later the door opened.

'Emily Wakefield?'

'Yes, that's me. What can I do for you?' Emily asked, then put one foot out the door and looked up and down the street.

Roberts looked at her, appreciating her beauty, then quickly snapped back into police officer mode.

'I'm Detective Constable Roberts. Do you have a moment for a chat? It's about Tommy McGregor?'

'Errm, yeah okay. Can we do this inside?'

'Of course,' he followed her into the lounge.

'Please, take a seat. Can I get you a drink?'

'No, I'm fine, thank you.' Roberts removed his hat. 'Can I ask, when was the last time you saw Tommy McGregor?'

'The night he murdered my mother,' Emily replied.

Shit, thought Roberts, *that was an insensitive start.*

'Sorry, Miss Wakefield, what I meant was, before that night?'

'I don't remember. Why?' Emily looked nervous and Roberts picked up on this straight away. She started to rub her hands on her legs.

'We're just going through some formalities. So, you don't remember at all?'

'No, nothing!' Emily replied.

Roberts then skipped that question to catch her off guard. 'You were an item, weren't you?'

'Not really an item. We had a little thing, but it was nothing really. I hardly know him to be honest.'

'Didn't you check into the Premier Inn on the seventeenth of January this year?' Roberts asked.

Her pupils widened, and she had a look of fear in her eyes.

'We did, yeah, I think.' Emily's tone was blunt.

'Okay, so why did you check into a hotel ten minutes from Tommy's apartment?'

'We just did.' Her nervousness was now even more obvious.

'*We just did*, that's not an answer. What made you both decide to check into that particular hotel?'

'You know... for fun.' Emily then gave Roberts an awkward smile.

'When you could have just stayed at Tommy's for fun? What time did you check in?'

'Sorry, am I being questioned here for a particular reason? Have I done something?' Emily asked.

Roberts decided it was now time to cut the discussion short. He'd now planted the necessary seeds in Emily's head.

'Not at all. I was just enquiring. I'll leave you to it.' Roberts then stood and simply let himself out without another word.

Emily stayed put. *Shit, what was that all about?* she thought to herself and started to pace the lounge in a mild panic, worried in case they had sussed her already.

15

It was a pleasant day and the sun was gleefully shining with a beautiful clear blue sky. Down in Cardiff Bay, Asda was busy as usual. It was one of the large Wallmart Asdas that sold literally anything and everything. Emily walked aisle by aisle choosing bits and bobs for the week, carefully checking the nutrition information to ensure she was eating the right stuff. She enjoyed cooking and was going to rustle up some nice healthy meals to see her through the rest of the week. She felt ready to get back into the gym and start training again.

She reached the confectionary aisle and felt as though she wanted to satisfy her sweet tooth. *Just a little treat*, she thought to herself. *It won't hurt to have a little sugar? Yeah, it'll be fine - I'll just work harder in the gym,* she convinced herself.

Emily left the trolley and focused on the display of colours and sweet smells, which made her crave the sugar even more. It was a complete sweet tease. She picked up a bag of Cadbury's buttons, that she would nibble on throughout the week, working out how many per day she would allow herself. When she returned to her trolley, there was a large bunch of flowers resting on the top of her already chosen goods.

'Eh?' she said, looking around. No one else was down the aisle, and she certainly hadn't put them there herself. She peered around the corner into the main long aisle, but there was no one that she knew nor anyone acting suspiciously that stood out. She removed the bunch of flowers and shoved them between some shelves, damaging the flowers with petals falling to the floor, then she walked off, creeped out by the gesture.

The tills were busy, and conversation was loud, with music playing in the background, but a little too quietly. Emily couldn't work out what song was playing. Looking for the shortest queue, as we all do, her eyes clocked each item in her trolley calculating each item's price, so she knew how much it would all cost before the amount was revealed at the till.

She waited. There was an old lady in the queue in front with her trolley full to the brim. Emily huffed, *bet this is gonna take ages. I always manage to pick the slowest queue,* she thought to herself. Whilst waiting, she cast her eyes across the supermarket, scanning to see if there was anyone she knew. The flowers had been creepy, and she was hoping it was just some kids or perhaps someone she knew pulling a silly prank. However, she couldn't see anyone she knew.

Finally, after a gruelling twenty minutes at the till, Emily approached her car. There was something on it. The closer she got, the clearer she could see – it was the flowers. She upped her pace with her heart beating in her chest. Horror incensed her when she saw that it was the same bunch of flowers from in her trolley. She looked around the carpark. Again, there was no one that stood out.

'Who's doing this?' she shouted, causing people to look at her.

Emily grabbed the flowers and threw them to the ground in a temper, frustrated that someone was purposely trying to creep her out. She hurriedly loaded all the shopping into her boot and drove off in a panic, leaving the trolley still with the pound coin in it.

When she arrived home, there was someone at her front door dressed in a smart suit. At first, she thought it was CID wanting to chat with her again, but when the person turned around holding a bunch of flowers, she freaked out.

'You!' she pointed. It was the same man that had stalked her at Tommy's flat. 'What do you want?' Emily didn't know whether to run or to confront this man before it all got out of hand.

'I'm just a friend. I only want to talk,' he said.

The flowers he was holding were the same ones again, this time even more battered than before.

'I don't want to talk! Please, leave me alone!'

The man didn't move, but just stood in the doorway.

'What's wrong with you?' Emily began to tremble as the fear increased, filling her veins with adrenaline.

'Nothing's wrong with me. I just like you.' He smiled at her, creeping her out even more. Then he shifted forwards, causing Emily to drop the bags she was holding.

'I'm calling the police!' She fiddled with her phone in a panic, but was shaking so profusely, she couldn't unlock it. The man then stepped a little closer and pulled a small bottle from his pocket. 'What's that? What are you doing? Get away from me, you fucking freak!' Emily froze on the spot in fear and her eyes widened as everything moved in slow motion.

'Just a little lesson for you!' The man undid the lid to the bottle and sprayed the contents into her face.

Emily screamed to high heaven. It burned like boiling water. The pain was long but slow and never ending. She screamed more and more, holding her face. The substance continued to burn through her skin. She fell to her knees and vomited. Her skin was melting into her hands, and the pain was so severe, she lost her balance and face planted the concrete floor. She laid there defeated.

Her neighbour ran out to help her. He could see what had happened and ran back into his house, coming back moments later with a washing up bowl full of cold water. Placing the bowl on the ground close to her, he helped to gently splash water on her face, as the substance boiled and ate her skin like a starving stray dog. The neighbour pulled out his phone and dialled 999.

'Which emergency service, please?' the operator asked calmly.

'Ambulance,' the neighbour responded urgently.

'One moment,' said the operator, who then put him through to the ambulance service.

'Please help, I need an ambulance as soon as possible. I'm with my neighbour, Emily Wakefield, and it looks as though she's been attacked.'

'What's the address please?' asked the ambulance service operator.

'49 Cosmeston Street in Cathays, Cardiff, CF24.'

'Is the victim still conscious?'

'Yes,' the neighbour answered impatiently, glancing nervously at Emily.

'What is the extent of her injuries?'

'It looks as though she's had acid thrown in her face. Quick, hurry.'

'Do you know what type of acid?'

'No idea, but it's bad. I've given her cold water, but it's not helping,' replied the neighbour.

'Keep applying the cold water. Get others to help you. Don't stop until the ambulance arrives. Can I take your name please, sir?'

'Jon Harrington. Hurry!'

'Please try and stay calm. Keep talking to the casualty. The ambulance is on its way,' said the operator reassuringly.

Within minutes, Jon could hear the sirens in the distance. By this time, more neighbours were helping with the water and trying to comfort Emily. He stayed on the phone to the operator and was given further instructions on how to assist, communicating this to the other helpers. Emily laid on the ground, kicking her legs in pain as the acid continued to eat away at the flesh on her face.

The ambulance turned into Cosmeston Street. Jon stood and flagged it towards them. He asked everyone to step away to allow the paramedics to treat Emily. By this point, Emily's breathing had noticeably increased. The onlookers were in shock at the sight; some were crying, and others were just looking away, feeling helpless and upset by the whole incident. Soon after the ambulance had arrived, two marked police cars also arrived.

In Cardiff Central Police station word spread quickly about the acid attack, and Valentina received a call to let her know that Emily Wakefield was the victim, with the investigation falling into her lap. She called Roberts almost immediately after.

'I've heard, boss. I'm on my way to Heath Hospital as we speak. I need to find out if this is connected to the McGregor case,' said Roberts, not giving Valentina a chance to say a word.

'Slow down! They're not going to let you see her,' said Valentina.

'I know, but the officers at the scene can give me all the info they have as a starting point.'

'Good thinking,' replied Valentina. 'I've got Martinson looking at the CCTV within a two-mile perimeter of Emily's home address. Keep me in the loop with your findings.'

'Will do, boss.' Roberts hung up and continued towards the hospital.

BBC Wales Today - Saturday 24ᵗʰ February 2018
Latest Headline at 12:32:
Horrific Acid Attack: Took place in Cathays, Cardiff this morning. Emily Wakefield, 18, gym enthusiast, was targeted outside her home. South Wales Police are appealing for witnesses and anyone who might know anything about the attack to come forward.The BBC has learned from a South Wales Police spokesperson that they are investigating this incident in great detail and will be taking this attack extremely seriously. Anyone who has any information should contact South Wales Police incident room at once on 02920 101101.

The blackness took over Emily's mind. Her hearing was a little fuzzy and her body felt cold. The burning sensation in her face had reduced, but it was still at a nine out of ten on the pain scale compared to the original one hundred out of ten. Her legs still felt jumpy. She was restless but tired, with no way she could get comfortable.

'Is there anyone there? I can't see,' said Emily, her voice soft but broken.

She felt someone touch her arm, and she turned her head, but her vision was still black. The pain throbbed, taunting her and reminding her of what had happened.

'Just rest, sweetheart. My name is Jenny. I'm your duty nurse. You're in Heath Hospital, the place you need to be right now, but you'll need to be transferred to the Welsh Centre for Burns at Morriston Hospital, Swansea.'

'But, why can't I see? I want to see!'

'You have a facial dressing applied sweetheart,' Jenny replied. 'Try to rest. You've been given some morphine for the pain. A consultant will be with you shortly to go through things in more detail. Can I get you anything?'

'No, thank you.' Emily rested the back of her head on the pillow and let the morphine do its job.

The intensive care unit was behind secure doors. All Roberts had to do was flash his warrant card and entry was granted. However, he was suddenly approached by the ward sister.

'Can I help you?' Her eyes looked strong with a protective instinct.

'I'm DC Roberts from South Wales Police. I'm here to see how Emily Wakefield is doing. I understand she's been brought in following an acid attack.'

'She's stable, but I can't allow you to see her.' The ward sister folded her arms in an authoritative manner, like a bouncer at a night club entrance.

'It'll only take a minute.' Roberts knew this nurse had Emily's wellbeing at heart, and so did he.

'You CID are all the same. Come on, Roberts! Think of her welfare first for a change!'

Roberts was taken back by her attitude. He felt the need to defend his reasons for being there.

'Yes, our part in her wellbeing is finding the scumbag who did this to her, am I right?' Roberts countered.

'Yes, completely, but not yet. Give her time, please!' Her eyes widened as she said the words.

Roberts backed off but asked, 'Are there any officers still here from the scene?'

'I believe so. They are with the ambulance crew going through some details. If you go back through those doors, take a second left, then a right, they're in a family room down that corridor.' The nurse then stood and waited for Roberts to leave.

Eventually Roberts found the room. The place was like a maze. He knocked on the door.

'Come in,' said a voice.

There were two paramedics and a uniformed officer sitting in the room. The officer was taking a statement from the paramedics. Roberts flashed his warrant card.

'DC Roberts. Just wondered if I could have a quick chat?'

'PC Daniels. I'll just finish this statement, and I'll be with you.'

'No problem,' replied Roberts and took a seat on a faux leather chair with a slight tear in it showing the yellow sponge inside which he couldn't help fiddle with whilst he was waiting.

Seven minutes passed, and PC Daniels finished with the paramedics. The paramedics got up to leave, and Roberts simultaneously stood up out of respect, followed by a hand shake with each.

'Daniels, Emily is connected with another case, and I have reason to believe there may be a link with the attack. What can you tell me?' Roberts asked.

'Her neighbour was the person to call 999, as he was first at the scene. His name is Jon Harrington. Lives at number 47 Cosmeston Street.'

'Okay, what information did he have?'

'I've not interviewed him, but my colleague has. They are still at the scene.'

'Do you know anything else?' asked Roberts.

'It was sulphuric acid that was used to harm Emily. Her burns are so severe, it's going to shift her entire life, poor girl.

'That's awful! What an horrific and horrendous thing to do to someone!'

'I agree! Do you need anything else?' asked Daniels.

'Any other information you have would be appreciated.'

'That's all I have at the moment. Why have they got you lot involved anyway?'

'Like I said, there could be a link to another case. I'll leave you to it,' stated Roberts. He then left the hospital and gave Valentina a call.

Valentina's phone had barely rung, when she answered it straight away. 'Roberts, what do you have for me? Is there a link?'

'Not much from the hospital. I'm en route to the scene. Emily's neighbour who found Emily may have some info to give me,' Roberts responded.

'Okay, how's Emily?'

'I didn't see her. They wouldn't let me in.'

'Thought as much,' said Valentina. 'They always give us detectives attitude at that place. Carry on with the neighbour and then report back to our office. Something else has come up with McGregor.' She ended the call before he had a chance to ask what.

Cosmeston street was taped off at both ends. There were Sky and BBC media vans blocking the road with their cameras pointing towards number 49. Roberts was allowed through the tape as he made his way up the road on foot. Crime scene investigators were in their chemical suits, collecting evidence from the area. Roberts approached number 47. The door was open with a tall bearded man filling the doorway.

'I'm looking for Jon Harrington?' said Roberts.

'That is me, and you are?'

'Detective Constable Roberts. Do you have a minute?'

'Of course, come in. Would you like a drink?'

'No, thank you.'

They both took a seat at a large table in the kitchen. The place smelt of stale cooking fat and cat poop. There was a litter tray five feet from where Roberts was sitting. He looked at it, then awkwardly looked at Jon.

'Sorry, I was meant to change that. I'll do it now.'

'It's okay, leave it. Can you go through what happened to Emily, please?' asked Roberts.

'That poor girl! First her mum and now this! Do you think it's related?'

'I can't discuss that with you. Please can you take me through the series of events?'

'I was sitting on my sofa with my cat on my lap when I heard screaming,' Jon explained. 'I jumped up and looked out the window. All I saw was a man walking past my window dressed in a grey suit. There was more screaming, so I went out to look, and that's when I saw Emily, face down on the floor. It was clear something had been thrown in her face. I thought it was boiling water at first, so I ran back in here, filled the washing up bowl, then used the water to sooth her face. It was when she moved her hands away, I saw the extent of her injuries, so I dialled 999.'

'Thank you, then what happened?' asked Roberts.

'Well, the operator gave me guidance on what to do, and other neighbours also helped until the ambulance arrived.'

'Tell me more about this man in a suit?'

'I only saw him briefly. He had dark hair, that's all I remember.'

'Did you see anyone else?' asked Roberts. 'Has there been anyone hanging around that looked suspicious over the last few weeks?'

'Not that I've noticed. I normally keep myself to myself, sir,' Jon explained.

'Okay, that's great, thank you.' Roberts stood, shook Jon's hand, then left the house, making his way back to the station to meet with Valentina.

Not long after Emily had been moved, Anderson managed to locate her whereabouts. He could taste the strong smell of disinfectant as he entered the Welsh Centre for Burns and Plastic Surgery. It was situated within Morriston Hospital in Swansea. The place was huge, and it took Anderson some time to find his way round. He found out the ward Emily was on after some investigatory work and was given directions by a porter -Tempest Burns ITU.

The unit was of moderate size and fairly modern compared to other parts of the hospital. Anderson entered the ward and explained who he had come to see. The nurse pointed him in the direction. *That was easy!* he thought, expecting to be challenged.

He looked around the ward. There were only ten beds and he couldn't see Emily at first. Then he recognised her unkempt platinum hair that she once obsessed about. She was sleeping and her face was covered in a thick white dressing. That beautiful, pretty girl that he appreciated immensely (for her looks anyway) was now disfigured. Empathy engulfed his heart as he stared down at her whilst she slept. There was a book on the side next to her. It looked brand new and untouched – *Black Matter.*

Part of Emily's head had been shaved. Anderson knew that would hit her hard. He sat down in the chair beside her bed and picked up her book, *Black Matter.* He started to read whilst waiting for her to wake up.

Six paragraphs in, Emily began to stir, and she awoke with a groan.

'Emily, how do you feel?' Anderson asked.

Emily seemed dreadfully unwell. She was weak, and it was clear that she was having difficulty simply trying to move.

'I wish I was dead,' she exclaimed, as tears filled her visible eye. Her voice was croaky, as though phlegm was sitting in the back of her throat.

Anderson bypassed her "wish I was dead" comment. 'What are the doctors saying?'

'I have blood poisoning. Sepsis, I think they call it.' Her speech was slow. It was an effort for her to talk, but Anderson kept pushing.

'What's happened to your eye?' he asked, as he looked at a disfigured eye ball through the facial dressing.

'I've lost it. I swallowed some of the acid too, and it has burned all the inside of my mouth and throat.' Emily's eye lids closed from the lethargy. She was feeling drowsy and slowly drifted back off to sleep.

Anderson sat for a little while longer, watching her rest. *Her life is ruined*, he thought to himself. A nurse walked in to check Emily's blood pressure and stats.

'Nurse, will Emily be okay? You know, will she get through this? She looks really unwell!'

'It's hard to say. You are?'

'I'm her brother, Anderson.'

'She never mentioned about her brother,' the nurse stated. 'I know both her parents have passed though. Well, she needs to be moved back into intensive care. The consultant will be round soon to advise me when she's going.'

'Right, okay, she's going to make it...right?'

'We've just got to stay positive. Are there any other relatives? Can you make contact with them, please?'

'Of course,' Anderson replied, standing to leave and feeling partially uncomfortable with his lie.

'Oh, before you go, Emily mentioned a Tommy. Do you know him?' asked the nurse.

'I do, but he won't be here, I can assure you of that.'

'Oh, okay, strange! She's mentioned him a few times now.'

'He killed her mum. Well...our mum,' Anderson corrected himself, then left promptly before he dug a deeper hole of lies. The nurse was left feeling somewhat confused.

16

Tammy's office at Medi Corps was busy one. She had been working intensely for over a week, going through all the data from the download that was extracted from Tommy's implant. Tammy was able to trace the Circuitoids back to an IMEI number for a mobile phone that strangely differed from Tommy's own IMEI. Concerned, she picked up the phone and called Davidson.

'Tammy?' he answered abruptly, as though he didn't appreciate being disturbed.

'Russell, I've made a discovery. The Circuitoids have come from a ghost mobile phone. Professor Conroy's judgement was correct.'

'Doesn't the IPEA communicate with a mobile phone anyway? That's how it works!' exclaimed Davidson.

'That's correct, via Bluetooth, which is the only connectivity we built into the system. These Circuitoids have attached themselves to the signal generated by the Bluetooth, but their source is from a different IMEI number to Tommy's, hence my comment referencing a ghost phone,' Tammy explained.

'Okay, I don't understand. Isn't the application encrypted so third parties can't gain access? That was part of the agreement with the Medicines and Healthcare Products Regulatory Agency. If this gets out that the system can be hacked-'

Tammy interrupted. 'Listen to me. It is encrypted. We can prove we have an encryption in place. What I'm saying is, within the application, Circuitoids don't actually exist; they are not part of the system. That would be too complex and wouldn't work with the IPEA the way we designed it to. They are also not part of any mobile phone application. The construction of these Circuitoids is way beyond my comprehension, so someone with extraordinary knowledge has put this together. I doubt even the whiz kids at Google could come up with it. They must have been generated from somewhere else and have used Tommy's phone to gain access to his brain via the Bluetooth signal.'

'So, where have they come from?' Davidson huffed, signalling frustration.

'The report doesn't give me that information. I'll need Tommy's phone. I can then trace the Circuitoids via the IMEI number, but I think a ghost signal has been created from another phone.'

'A ghost signal?'

'A ghost signal is created the same way as a mobile phone network, which then uses a legitimate mobile network as a host. It's never been done until now and would be completely illegal. The technology needed isn't something you could go into PC World and buy.'

'Thank you, Tammy. I'll get on the phone to that detective to ask if we can have Tommy's phone.' Davidson ended the call and instantly phoned Valentina.

'DI Valentina.' She also sounded distracted as she answered the call.

'It's Russell Davidson from Medi Corps. We have discovered something that may interest you!'

'What is it?' asked Valentina.

'We need to investigate Tommy's phone.'

'Why?'

'The information is sensitive. It can't be discussed over the phone,' explained Davidson.

'Well, if you want his phone, you'll need to come to Cardiff Bay Police Station, and we can discuss it further. It's not normally a legitimate process to hand evidence over just like that.'

'Detective, this could be a huge breakthrough in medical science and in the case you are working on. Your professor,' Davidson paused, trying to think of his name, 'Conroy; his assumptions are proving to be correct, and we can help. Can you please very kindly send the phone via a same day courier, so we can look into it further. Tammy believes she may be able to trace where this came from.'

'You can be polite when you want to be. Okay.' Valentina processed a thought. 'I'll have it sent to you within the next two hours. Once you have more information, please let us know ASAP, and we will come and meet with you.'

'Will do! Thank you, Detective.' Davidson hung up.

'That bastard seems to love it when he can pull the strings,' Valentina muttered to herself whilst looking at her phone.

The phone arrived at Medi Corps an hour later and was delivered to Tammy's office once it had been scanned. Medi Corps had a strict postal policy. All mail had to be scanned and run through an X-ray machine to ensure that there was nothing nasty – not everyone agreed with the products produced by the company.

As soon as Tammy was in possession of Tommy's mobile, she turned it on, only to find it was PIN protected, and Valentina hadn't given her the PIN. She used a trick that could bypass the

PIN, which was illegal, but she felt confident Valentina wouldn't follow through once she found out the full scale of what was happening.

She connected the phone to the system, where more data was extracted and re-coded into simpler terms. There it was; an IMEI number:

IMEI: 2.0.000098Z-3243458324-T.

The number didn't match the original format, which threw Tammy off balance, confusion taking hold for a moment. She ran a trace on the number, which came up as unidentified, an unknown network.

'Shit,' she cursed to herself as concern flowed through her. The investigation was proving to be tougher than expected and highly illegal. Tammy continued to explore the data and realised that the IMEI number had been scrambled into a different number, assumed to make it untraceable. She called Davidson to provide him with an update.

'Please tell me you have some positive information for me?' Davidson's mouth was full of food as he spoke, a pet hate of Tammy's. *If you're eating, don't answer the phone,* she thought.

'Yes and no, Russell. The IMEI number traced from the Circuitoids isn't a valid number. It's not recognisable.'

'So, where does that leave us?'

'Well, I've managed to identify that it's been scrambled once it connects to Tommy's phone to make it untraceable.'

'Okay?' It was obvious Davidson was frustrated. Tammy echoed that feeling.

'I've managed to unscramble the number, but when I put a trace on it, I need authorisation to access the data,' Tammy explained.

'So, who do you need to authorise it?'

'I don't know, the police I assume. I need to do some more digging. I'll see what I can find out.'

Davidson just hung up the phone without another word, causing Tammy agitation. She was working hard on this, and it felt like she was receiving no appreciation.

It was now quarter past one in the morning. Tammy found herself still sitting in her office, five empty cups of coffee cluttering her desk along with a half-eaten salmon and soft cheese bagel. Mozart filled what would otherwise be a silent room, playing in the background to help her concentrate.

'Got it!' she exclaimed, tapping her desk with a sense of accomplishment. She had managed to override the authorisation request and had traced the IMEI number back to a device in a specific area. The trace wasn't pinpoint accurate but was accurate within at least a few hundred yards. Anticipation increased the endorphins in her brain as she became excited at her finding. She was really on to something. Tammy picked up her phone to call Davidson but realised the time; there was no way in hell she could call him at that time of the morning. Her adrenaline was pumping and there was no way she would be able to go home to bed, so she made the decision to follow the trace herself to see if she could spot anything of significance.

The M4 was clear and the drive from Bristol to Cardiff only took Tammy forty minutes. She played Mozart in the car to keep her brain ticking, hoping her mind would conjure up some solution to enable her to pinpoint the location where the signal was coming from.

The trace of the IMEI number directed Tammy to Lloyd George Avenue down at Cardiff Bay. There was a ridiculous number of apartment blocks and buildings – it would be like hunting for a needle in a haystack, and she had no idea where to start. It was raining hard and the wind had increased, causing adverse conditions, so she parked up outside a Vista store in a small street just off Lloyd George Avenue. She loaded her laptop and put out a trace of the IMEI number - the signal was live! It was connected to something or someone, but she couldn't work out the code as to where the signal was coming from, as it was scrambled. She punched the steering wheel, frustrated that she didn't have the software on her laptop to decode it.

Tammy's heart pounded and heat filled her veins with mixed feelings. She didn't know if she felt excited or nervous at the prospect of her findings. It was raining even harder, the sound of the rain hitting the roof of her car, sounding like the beating of drums. She looked up from her laptop and could see something in front of her car. She switched on the wipers to reveal a dark figure standing in front of her. Sudden panic caused her to jump as she gasped for breath.

There was a man dressed in a grey suit, a white shirt and red tie. He was soaked through to the bone as rain water ran down his face and off his hair, causing drips to form on his chin. He stared at her. He was so still with no reaction to the coldness that he must surely have been feeling, looking like one of those street performers that pretend to be statues.

Fear struck Tammy again with an intense hot feeling in her stomach, as she slowly closed her laptop and placed it under her seat, keeping her eyes fixed on the figure in front of her. With minimal movement, she put the car into reverse, still keeping her wide eyes on the man. As she glanced in her rear-view mirror, she hit the gas. The wheels screeched, as though in a drag race, as she pulled away, reversing straight out onto the main road without even looking. A car swerved, just missing her, sounding his horn as he drove past, but she stayed focused on the man.

In the blink of an eye, the man started sprinting quickly towards her. Tammy's fight or flight mode kicked in, and with a trembling hand, she put the car into first gear. Failing to engage the first time, she tried again with the sound of the gears crunching. Her panic increasing, she screamed, losing her breath. With another attempt, the car was finally in first gear, and she sped off down the road, shark tailing as she tried to maintain control, then steadying the car.

The man continued to chase her, but shrank into the distance, unable to keep up as she sped off up the road. Tammy took deep breaths and managed to take control of her breathing, getting away as fast as she could and heading home. She felt overwhelmed with regret for going out to nose around, playing detective.

Later that day, Tammy was feeling overpowered by exhaustion and was still shaken up. She went straight to see Davidson to discuss what had happened. Even though they had a close working relationship, she still felt the need to knock on his office door before gaining entry.

'Come in.' He was sounding more approachable this morning.

'Russell, something happened last night. I managed to find the trace and the location of the device that hacked Tommy McGregor.' Tammy tried to hold it together, reluctant to let her anxiousness become apparent.

'Okay, that's good news! Why do you look so... What's the word-,'

'Rough?' she interrupted.

'Not rough, just not yourself. Has something happened?' Davidson enquired.

'Well, I followed the trace into Cardiff at about 2.00am this morning,' she began.

Mr Davidson noticed a tremble in her voice and grew concerned. 'That's illegal, Tammy. What were you thinking? What happened? Are you okay?' He stood, feeling concerned for her wellbeing.

'There was a man,' she said, pausing whilst thinking of how to elaborate. 'It was raining hard, and he was strangely dressed in a suit. I've got it all here.' She held up a dash cam. 'It's a little distorted from the rain.'

Davidson took the dash cam, fiddled with it for a brief moment, then watched the footage.

'You should never have gone, Tammy. I'm not happy about this. Anything could have happened to you. Your job is to be a technical director for me, not running around trying to be a detective.'

'I know, I'm sorry. I just got carried away. I just wanted to help,' Tammy tried to explain.

'Well, we need to report this to the detective. This man needs to be checked out. That's not normal behaviour. I'll arrange a meeting. What's your calendar looking like today?' asked Davidson.

'It's clear today,' she replied.

'Well, go home and get some rest. I'll call you if I need you. See you tomorrow.' He waved his hand towards her.

'Thanks Russell.' Tammy turned to walk away, when Davidson spoke again.

'Tammy, please don't ever do anything like that again, do you understand? I might be a hard-faced bastard, but I do care!'

'I know you do, and I won't,' Tammy said. 'I'm sorry! See you tomorrow, Russell.' She left Davidson's office, leaving him feeling miffed over her actions.

There was a missed call from Davidson on Valentina's phone. She returned the call from her office. Roberts was present.

'Mr Davidson, DI Valentina here. Sorry I missed your call. What do you have for me?'

'Morning! Tammy has made good progress with the data retrieval from Tommy McGregor's mobile phone. I'll need you to meet with me to go through everything in detail. It's a matter of urgency.'

Valentina covered her phone with her hand and mouthed to Roberts, 'They have something'. He returned a smile and gave a thumbs up.

'We can do that. We'll come to you. When are you available?' Valentina enquired.

'I'll keep my afternoon clear if you can make it?'

'We'll be there after lunch,' Valentina stated.

'Thank you, see you then.' Davidson ended the call.

'What was it, boss?' asked Roberts with eagerness.

'They have something. He was actually polite for a change. Must be important; he's keeping his afternoon clear to go through the details.'

Roberts nodded a smile, then continued to work on his computer, scrolling through details about the acid attack on Emily. He found the extent of her injuries upsetting. Even though he was professional, he could still appreciate a pretty looking woman and understood what effect this would have on her.

Davidson showed an element of disquietude as the detectives arrived. Valentina was an expert in human characteristics and body language. 'Take a seat both,' Davidson said as he ushered them into his office.

'So, what do you have, Mr Davidson?'

'Please, just call me Russell. Well, this needs to be an off-the-record conversation.'

Both Valentina and Roberts looked at each other puzzled.

'I can't guarantee that, I'm afraid,' said Valentina, causing Davidson to fidget in his chair.

'I need that, or I can't share with you what I know.'

Valentina felt pleased to see this powerful, arrogant man, who she had disliked from the outset, becoming a little vulnerable.

'Come on, Russell. Let's just talk it through and we'll be the judge,' interjected Roberts before Valentina could say anything.

'It's Tammy,' said Davidson, followed by silence. 'Let's just say, she's gone a little above and beyond her call of duty.'

'What do you mean?' Valentina asked, giving him an inquisitive look. Davidson then placed the dash cam from Tammy's car on his desk. 'What's on there?' she asked.

'It's footage from Tammy's car. She traced the hack back to Cardiff and decided to take a trip to investigate.'

'She traced it?' Valentina enquired. 'No wonder you wanted to keep this off the record. Hacking a mobile phone network is a serious offence!'

'She's a little shaken. Take a look.' Davidson pushed the cam towards them both, looking intrigued as they played the footage.

Roberts immediately put a potential link between the description of Emily's attacker and the man on the cam.

'What is it we are actually looking at here?' asked Valentina. 'And please don't leave anything out.'

'Tammy has all the technical details. I've sent her home for the day, but she'll be back tomorrow. In a nutshell, she decoded a scrambled IMEI number. That's the number that-'

'I know what an IMEI number is,' Valentina interrupted abruptly, feeling that her intelligence had been mildly insulted.

'Sorry. She managed to trace it, as I've explained. She foolishly took a trip to the location. The signal then became live. It was being used by someone, and that's when she saw this man in front of her,' Davidson explained.

'I'll need to speak with Tammy and get all the details. Is that all you know?'

'It is. What will happen to Tammy?' Davidson looked concerned.

'Let me get all the information, and we'll go from there. Can you also send me that video from the dash cam, please? We'll need to investigate it further.'

'Of course. Well, I have nothing else for you. Thank you for coming.' They all shook hands, and Davidson looked worried as they left the building.

Roberts turned to Valentina in the car. 'What are you thinking, boss?'

'Well, the man in the video matches the description of Emily's attacker. Also, I want to know how on earth Tammy managed to hack the mobile network and trace an IMEI number?'

'She's clearly a very intelligent woman to be able to manage that, boss.'

'Yeah, and a stupid one for trying to play cops and robbers. Could have got herself killed! Although, we don't know if that man is linked with the hacking of Tommy's implant. He could have just been a drunken opportunist seeing a pretty woman in a fancy car.'

'Very true, I'm going to have the CCTV checked in that area to see what his movements were and run a facial recognition to see if he comes up on the database,' said Roberts.

'Excellent,' Valentina smiled. She felt as though they were making progress, and she had a positive feeling in her gut that they were on the right track.

The footage on the CCTV was grainy due to the adverse weather conditions, as Roberts sat in the control room directing the operative on where he wanted to look and at what time. They both flinched at the near miss of the rear of Tammy's car as she reversed onto Lloyd George Avenue.

'Wow, he's got some pace on him,' said the operative to Roberts.

'He certainly has, fella. Play it back again but go from zero two twenty hours this time. I want to see where he comes from.'

The operative played back the footage from that time as requested, and a little movement from the bottom left corner of the screen was just visible.

'He's coming from the direction of those flats,' said Roberts.

'That's Aprillia House, Detective,' the operative advised.

'Is there a camera looking from the south of that area?' Roberts asked.

The operative searched around. They could just make out the man coming into shot from the rear of Aprillia House.

'My gut says he came from there,' Roberts said pointing at the screen. 'Do me a favour and burn all this to a disk for me. I need to go through it with the DI.'

'Will do.' The operative made the disk and handed it over to Roberts.

'Thanks, fella. Could you ask your team to look out for this individual? If you see him again, call me straight away.'

Back in the detective's office, Valentina was having a cheeky fag out of the office window, even though smoking was prohibited in the building. She felt that she needed it, but was careful to ensure the smoke stayed outside.

Roberts walked in.

'Smoking again, boss?'

'Yeah, but you didn't see me!'

'Makes no odds to me. I got this!' Roberts held up the CD.

'What is it?' asked Valentina.

'The CCTV footage from Lloyd George Avenue. I think we could be onto something here.' Roberts loaded the disk into his laptop and played the video, giving Valentina a running commentary.

'Get down to Aprillia House and do a door-to-door, but stay discrete,' Valentina ordered. 'Your face has been on the news recently from the acid attack, so I don't want you drawing any attention to yourself and blowing this case.'

'Will do, boss.' Roberts left the office, and Valentina sparked up another fag the moment the door shut.

In an Umbro t-shirt, blue jeans and a pair of Nike Air Max, along with a snap back cap, Roberts approached Aprillia House, pressing the first buzzer. There was no answer. He pressed the next buzzer, and again there was nothing. 'God's sake,' he said to himself, trying the last buzzer.

'Hello?' said a woman's voice enquiringly.

'Afternoon, I'm Detective Roberts from South Wales Police. Can you let me in, please?'

He heard the door click open and he pushed through it, making his way up the stairs to the top floor where the flat was number 47.

Roberts gently tapped on the door and a middle-aged woman answered in a pink dressing gown, folding her arms across herself. Roberts flashed his warrant card.

'You don't look like a policeman,' the woman said, half closing the door, suspicious of Roberts.

'I'm CID, madam. I have reason to be in this attire. I don't want to come in. I just need to ask you one or two questions?'

'Just me?' the woman looked puzzled.

'No, we are going door to door. Can you tell me, do you live alone?' asked Roberts.

'No, I have Crystal living with me.' She gave him a smile from the corner of her mouth.

'Is Crystal home?'

'Yes, she never goes out. I'll get her for you.' Roberts waited, and within seconds the lady returned holding a grey-brown cat. 'This is Crystal,' she smiled again.

'Sorry Madam, do you live with any other persons?'

'No, just me and Crystal.'

Roberts knew the person he was looking for wasn't going to be in number 47.

'That's great, thank you for your time.' He smiled and walked away with the sound of the door closing behind him and then locking. He then proceeded to knock on each door within the block, which consisted of only twelve apartments. He had no luck, as most people were out, presumably at work or doing whatever they did.

As Roberts was driving out of the area, he spotted a man driving past in the opposite direction towards the apartments. The man was wearing a white shirt. A gut feeling triggered inside him, trying to tell him something, so he decided to hang fire in his unmarked car. He watched in his mirrors as the car parked up. A man got out, opened his boot and retrieved a work bag of some sort.

Roberts watched intently as the man went into the block that he himself had just left. He instinctively got out of his car and went back. Luckily the door hadn't shut properly, and he was able to gain access without bothering anyone. He quickly went to each apartment where there had been no answer previously and listened for the sound of any movement. It was flat 42 that caught his attention. No one had been home before, and now there was a stinking black bag outside the door. He placed his ear close to the door and could hear movement, so he tapped gently.

'Who is it?' asked a male voice from behind the door.

'I'm Detective Roberts from South Wales Police. Do you have a second to chat, please?'

'Hold your ID up to my peep hole.'

Roberts did exactly as the man asked, and the door was opened. The man was wearing pyjama bottoms and a black vest. In return, the man looked Roberts up and down, giving him a similar look that the lady from number 47 had done.

'What do you want?' The man seemed to be agitated by Roberts' presence.

'I'm just making a few enquiries, sir.'

'Wearing that?' the man said with a slight chuckle.

'I have a reason to be wearing this, thank you. Can you tell me, do you live alone, sir?'

'That's none of your business. Why are you asking?'

Roberts knew this guy was going to be difficult. It was always the ones who had either been in trouble with the law before or had something to hide that gave the attitude.

'Like I said, I'm making a few enquiries. Can you tell me your name, please?'

'No, not until I know what all this is about,' replied the man insolently. 'I know my rights. I don't have to tell you anything.'

Stay calm! Roberts thought.

'True, you don't have to tell me anything. That's correct. However, we are investigating a serious crime within the area, and we are hoping with the cooperation of neighbours such as yourself, we might be able to get to the bottom of it.'

The man took a step back. 'Okay,' he said, 'what crime?'

'I can't tell you that, but if you could kindly tell me your name and where you were between the hours of 1.30am to 2.30am this morning, that would be helpful?'

'Andy Styles. I was in here asleep.'

'Did you hear anything? Did anything from outside wake you at all?'

'No, nothing.' Andy pulled his chin towards his neck and frowned.

'Mr Styles, what is it you do for a living?'

'I'm an accountant.'

'Okay, thank you. That's all for now,' said Roberts.

'That's it?' Confusion set on Andy's face.

'Yes sir, I'm just making enquiries to see if anyone heard anything in the early hours of this morning.'

Andy held out his hand to shake, and Roberts noticed there was a white dressing covering his hand.

'What happened there, if you don't mind me asking?' Roberts asked.

'This?' Andy said, holding the bandage with his other hand. 'I just burnt it making a coffee; spilled boiling water over it, because I was trying to text at the same time. You know how it is? I tried to run it under the cold tap, but it didn't help.'

'I see, thank you Mr Styles.' Roberts walked off deep in thought.

After two rings, Valentina answered.

'Roberts?'

'Boss, I think we have our suspect, but we don't have enough evidence on him. It's just my gut feeling.'

'Explain?' demanded Valentina.

'I checked all the apartments within Aprillia House. Only a handful of people were home, but as I was leaving, I saw an individual matching the appearance of the guy from Tammy's dash cam and the description of Emily's attacker. I then followed him into the apartment and asked a few standard Qs.' Roberts took a breath. 'He told me his name is Andy Styles. Ring any bells?'

'No, nothing. You?'

'Not to me. However, there was one thing, boss.'

'Go on?'

'His right hand was heavily bandaged. I challenged him on it, making general convo, and he explained that he did it when making a hot drink. He gave a lot of detail though, considering it was just a case of spilling boiling water on his hand,' Roberts rationalised.

'That's always a red flag for me. When they provide a lot of detail for something minor, liar springs to mind!'

'I agree, boss. Do you think we have enough to pull him in?'

'I do, if he matches the description and has a burnt hand, presuming he burnt it whilst throwing acid in Emily's face, then bring him in.'

'Will do, boss.' Roberts turned his car round for a second time and made his way back to Andy Styles to make the arrest – even after twenty plus years on the force, he still got the adrenaline buzz from it.

17

Every breakfast, lunch and dinner was the same bullshit for Tommy McGregor. A man named Makka wouldn't leave him alone with his constant taunts – it had become a routine. Tommy could take it as it came and made sure he gave a little back when he was feeling brave.

Makka was one of Killroy's chums. They all knew it was Tommy who had killed Killroy, but no one could prove it. The rest of the inmates sat back and just watched the show, some scared that Tommy would kill them too. Makka, however, didn't fear anyone. 'Try and kill me,' he'd say, or, 'I invite you to stick a knife in me'. Clearly, Makka was in the right place behind bars. No one sane would be walking around saying that.

It was morning, and Tommy collected his breakfast as usual. It was the same food every morning; eggs on toast, prison standard. He sat down, and the neighbouring inmates moved away, creating a gap between them in anticipation of an outburst. Tommy was sitting minding his own business, not looking at anyone, sipping his black coffee. He had zoned out and was lost in his own mind.

All of a sudden, something firm hit the top of his head hard as a dinner tray struck him. The impact was loud, sounding worse than the actual blow felt, but it pushed him off the bench at the dinner table. The fall hurt more, as he banged the back of his head on the hard floor.

A few sniggers could be heard from the other inmates, then silence fell in anticipation of what was going to happen next. Tommy brazenly got up off the floor, rubbed the top of his head sarcastically, and blew a kiss to Makka. He then sat back down to finish his food. *Wanker!* he thought.

The same thing happened again, but this time Tommy didn't fall; he just absorbed the impact. This time, it hurt like hell, but he wasn't going to show it, and he tried to continue eating.

SMACK! Lights flashed across Tommy's eyes. Another blow came, this time harder, causing the tray used as a weapon to break in half, with one piece flying across the room, just missing another onlooker. This one hurt, and he became slightly dizzy. However, Tommy was getting tough, and he held his own, fighting the pain and ignoring as much as his body would allow. *Pain is in the mind*, he told himself.

Frustration increased inside Makka. He couldn't handle not getting a reaction from Tommy. It angered him and he felt humiliated. It was Tommy's way of making a fool out of him and making him look stupid. He upped his antics to the next level. He grabbed Tommy by the back of his collar, throwing him to the ground.

Tommy banged his head again. He felt it split open, and this was followed by a prison-issue trainer stamping down hard on his face. Tommy couldn't take this. The pain of his nose dislodging once again made him weak and he screamed out in pain.

Within seconds, Tommy found a little strength, with no idea of where it had come from. He managed to stand with a wobble, steadying himself against the table. Blood poured from his nose, and he had a strong taste of metal in his mouth. Guards came forward to assist him, and Makka was escorted out after the guards had put him on the ground and restrained him.

Once again, Tommy had ended up back in the medical centre being treated for his injuries; two black eyes and blue tape across the bridge of his nose. Tommy looked an absolute state.

Still with a cell to himself, he sat on the top bunk and read a book, which had now become his favourite pastime. He would read for hours on end. It was his escapism from the harsh realities of his way of life. Tommy knew deep down there would be light at the end of the tunnel for him one day. He finally had hope. Valentina had given him hope.

The following day, a guard presented himself outside Tommy's cell.

'McGregor, there's a detective here to see you. Up!'

Tommy didn't say anything, but just climbed off the bunk, waiting for the guard to open the door to his cell. He was marched through the prison, through various security doors and across a yard to the visitors' unit, where he was greeted by Valentina.

'Tommy, how are you today?' Valentina asked.

He still looked grey and even more roughed up than before, with black eyes being the primary focus on his face.

'Okay,' he replied, refusing to make any eye contact.

'What happened to your face?'

'Fell over.'

Valentina was not stupid. She knew he'd been fighting or had been caught up in something, but she didn't push him, allowing him comfort.

'Shall we?' Valentina asked, pointing to the worn down, scruffy interview room.

Just a nod was all Tommy was able to muster. He was dubious about her intentions.

The room smelt of damp, as thought it had been cleaned with a dirty mop. Tommy slouched in his chair, oozing discomfort.

'Come on, Tommy! Sit up, please,' suggested Valentina.

He responded by shifting to an upright position in his chair.

He's acting like a kid! Valentina thought to herself. She wanted to shake him.

'More promises today?' Tommy's tone was sarcastic; a defence mechanism, not wanting to open up.

'Look, I wouldn't come here to give you false promises, Tommy. I'm here to let you know that we now have strong evidence that supports your case.'

'So, what is this evidence?' Tommy asked intrigued.

'That, I'm afraid, I can't tell you.'

'You said that last time. Can't you give me anything? Nothing makes sense at all. I can't explain anything that happened to you, so I don't see how anything would make sense to you either, this is all so confusing?' he mumbled.

'Trust me, Tommy. Things are going to change for you soon enough. You need to keep your nose clean whilst in here, okay?' Valentina advised.

'Don't make out I'm some sort of troublemaker! The idiots come to me. I'm the one who has to take the shit from them!' Tommy paused for a second. 'I mind my own.'

'Look!' Valentina snapped with a tone of tough love, 'Stay out of trouble! The cleaner you are in here, the more support it will give your case. If there are numerous reports of you fighting - sorry, I mean violence, then it could go against you.'

Tommy placed both palms flat on the table.

'What if what you're saying is true, and I've gone through all this, and I'm proven innocent? Where does that leave me?' He then sat back, waiting for the answer.

'You become a free man, get your life back! Isn't that what you want?'

'What, free to walk the streets? Once tarnished as a murderer, that shit sticks! No one will want to know me, let alone employ me! My life is fucked either way!'

Valentina retorted abruptly to his negative response.

'Look Tommy, I'm trying to help you. I could walk away from this if I wanted to and leave your sorry arse to rot. You won't get the chance to have your life back then. You'll never leave these walls until you die.' She gritted her teeth and leaned forward over the desk towards him. 'Do you understand what I'm saying?' Her face was angry.

This gave Tommy a little clarity, with the realisation that he'd offended her efforts to help – *Under what motive though?* He decided to take a different angle, back-tracking a little.

'Sorry DI, what I meant was, would I be compensated for all this; the fact that my entire life has been chewed up and spat out? I was happy once, until all this started. I even tried to kill myself!' He pulled down his collar, revealing the marks around his neck that were still fairly apparent.

'I heard, Tommy,' said Valentina sympathetically. 'You need to stay strong. Also, to answer your question, yes, there would be a form of compensation.'

Tommy, still not fully trusting Valentina, despite her efforts, couldn't help but think, *There must be more behind this?*

Valentina looked at him intensely.

'Tommy, let me work on getting you out. Just stay out of trouble, okay?' She stood and left the room without even a goodbye, offended with his I-don't-trust-you attitude.

Back in her car, Valentina sat for a moment before starting the engine. *Why challenge freedom?* She questioned Tommy's actions. *Something's not right. And to bring up money! Yeah, okay, that's understandable to a certain extent, but surely freedom is far more precious than any amount of money?*

'Yes boss?' Roberts answered Valentina's call promptly.

'How did the arrest go?' asked Valentina.

'He fought like hell. I'm glad I had a uniform officer supporting me. The little prick bit my arm, and I had to go for a tetanus.' Roberts could hear Valentina smiling, trying not to laugh. 'I know you're laughing, boss! It bloody hurt! He was lucky there was a crowd, as I would have got a cheeky foot in otherwise!'

Valentina managed to compose herself before responding.

'Okay, so what do we have on him so far?'

'Not enough to charge him, boss. But, I have a gut feeling he's the one we are looking for. We only have ten hours left before we have to release him though.'

'Okay, it's a long shot, but we need to get Emily to identify him,' said Valentina.

'She's still in hospital. I doubt that they would allow her to come down to the station for that, not in her condition.'

'Still worth asking. What about her neighbour, what was his name again?' Valentina searched her memory.

'Ah, yes, Jon Harrington. I'll see what I can do. It'd be a good idea to have Mr Harrington ID Styles. We might have enough to charge Styles then.'

'Well done! I'm going to be offline for a bit, so drop me a text and I'll call you later.' Valentina sounded a little off balance.

'All okay, boss?' Roberts sensed something was not quite right.

'Of course, just a few chores.' She quickly hung up, avoiding any other questions.

Roberts had arranged a video identification, where moving images of Styles and eight other men of a similar appearance were shown to Harrington.

Harrington was very cooperative with Roberts and his team. He was keen to help find Emily's attacker. He'd known her for some time and felt emotionally involved. He sat at the screen and watched it with great concentration. Roberts watched

Harrington closely. He looked like a gambler on the roulette wheel, waiting for the outcome and praying for a win!

It took a few viewings before Harrington raised his hand to signal he was now finished. Roberts was on top of Harrington almost immediately, eager to hear the verdict.

'None,' said Harrington.

'Are you sure?' Roberts asked. It was important that Harrington was 100% on his decision. 'Okay, thank you for your time, Mr Harrington. PC Butler here will take you through to sign out. I will be in touch with you shortly. Do you still have my card?'

'I do. It's on my fridge. I hope you get to the bottom of this, I really hope you do!'

They shook hands firmly. Roberts could see in Harrington's eyes that this incident with Emily had hit him hard.

'She was a lovely girl, you know,' Harrington said.

'She still is, Mr Harrington.' They released hands, and PC Butler escorted Harrington out to the reception area, signing him out, then he was on his way.

Roberts shut the office door and sat gazing, almost day dreaming, as his computer loaded up. Whilst waiting, he sorted himself out with a cup of strong coffee – much needed.

Valentina allowed the rain to fall on her. She had no raincoat or umbrella. She just stood there looking down. The graveyard of Western Cemetery was deserted. Crows could be heard in the trees, and there was a squirrel in the distance minding his own business. Valentina's eyes filled with tears as she read the headstone of her mother's grave.

'I lost you twenty years ago today. My life has never been the same without you in it. Thank you for watching over me and protecting me when I have needed you. Thank you for listening to my prayers. I hope you are still as happy as I remember you -

always laughing and joking. You were such a good mum to me, and not a day goes by where I don't think about you. You are and always will be my beautiful mother.'

Twenty-five minutes had gone by, and the silence was broken by her mobile. She checked the screen, and seeing that it was Roberts, she didn't hesitate to answer.

'Roberts?' Valentina's voice sounded broken, but Roberts looked past that.

'Couldn't get the ID on him, boss.' His voice sounded deflated.

'If it's him, we'll get him another way. If it's not, at least we won't have another McGregor case to deal with,' Valentina offered.

'I know, boss. I just think Harrington didn't see enough of him on the day to get a positive ID.'

'Well, I'll be back shortly.' She hung up, kissed her hand and placed it on her mum's grave. 'I love you, Mum.'

18

Breathlessness took over Tammy as she stood outside Davidson's office, hesitating before knocking, in anticipation of the outcome of the conversation she was about to have with him. After a minute or so of looking conspicuous by the way she was hanging around, hopping from foot to foot, like a child outside the headmaster's office, she eventually knocked on the door.

'Who is it?' Davidson's tone was abrupt, making it clear that this wasn't a good time, but it was important and she had to tell him.

'It's Tammy, Russell,' she said as she slowly opened the door in a sheepish manner, poking her head through.

'Tammy, what is it? I'm up against it at the moment with the new launch. You of all people should know that.'

'Sorry, Russell. It's just that I've got some more information on Tommy McGregor.'

'Don't tell me you're still messing around with that? We've got too much on Tammy. I pay you to work for me, not the South Wales Police. If you want to be a detective, then please feel free to make your way over the Severn Bridge. I've not got time for this.' He waved her off, as though she was a peasant working for a king.

'But, sir,' Tammy said, diverting from first-name terms, 'you're going to want to hear this.'

'Tammy, I'm not going to tell you again! Do the job I pay you for! Now leave! We have the launch, and I need you onboard and your head in the game.'

'Okay sir,' Tammy backed down, again avoiding using his first name - but he didn't notice.

The information she had could potentially damage the entire company's reputation, let alone the launch.

Back in Valentina's office, the silence was broken by the sound of her phone ringing.

'DI, you need to get here fast! I'll text you the address,' explained a frantic Roberts.

'What is it?'

'Please, just get here, boss!' Roberts hung up the phone, and Valentina grabbed her keys and bag, heading towards her car whilst waiting for the text message with the address.

Valentina was on scene within twenty minutes. The press were hovering around like gulls waiting for scraps. The apartment block was secured, with Scenes of Crime Operatives already present. Access to the block was strictly for authorised personnel only. Valentina was required to put on a form of protective wear and sign in before attending the scene.

BBC Wales Today Friday 9th March 2018
Latest Headline at 10:45: Presumed Murder down the Bay: An unidentified man has been found dead in his apartment on Lloyd George Avenue this morning.
The BBC has learned from a South Wales Police spokesperson that they are asking for witnesses to please come forward. Anyone who has

any information should contact the South Wales Police incident room at once on 02920 101101.

'So, Roberts, what do we have?' Valentina asked as he greeted her outside the door to the apartment.

'It's not pretty, boss. It's Andy Styles. As soon as I received the call for this area, I knew it would be him. Bit of a coincidence if you ask me. We have him pulled in for an ID parade, he gets released, and the next thing we know he's dead.'

'Assumed murdered?' Valentina asked.

'Oh, he's been murdered alright,' replied Roberts. 'We're trying to keep it low profile and away from the media for obvious reasons, boss.'

'Good luck with that! The vultures are already pecking around for info. So, let's see what's happened to Mr Andy Styles.'

'Here, boss.' Roberts held out a small tub of Vicks Vaporub. 'You'll need this.'

'Christ,' she replied, dipping her index finger into the tub, then smearing a clump under her nose, causing her eyes to burn from the fumes.

There were two SOCO members working in the apartment, going through the area and looking for anything that could provide any clues as to what had happened.

'Can you guys give me a minute, please?' asked Valentina, and they both left.

There was a shower curtain across the bath. Smears of blood decorated the white floor tiles, proving that there had been a form of struggle. There was a sink in the corner, full to the brim with dark red blood. A black shadow rested in the centre of the red fluid. *There's something in there*? Valentina thought to herself, but parked that notion for the moment, pulling across the blood-stained shower curtain.

The scene before her eyes was instantly ingrained into her mind for eternity. She looked away for a moment to process the sight, whilst screwing up her face.

'God, Roberts! You could have warned me!' Valentina gasped.

'Sorry, boss! Didn't think it'd bother you too much, considering the amount of dead bods you've seen.'

'Well, this isn't just a dead body is it? He's been mutilated. Whoever did this is sending a strong message.'

'What do you mean?' asked Roberts.

'To me, this is a strange style of killing. Why cut his head off?'

'Very valid point. Don't know. There's more.' Roberts walked over to the sink and placed his gloved hand in, pulling out a mass of flesh.'

'Is that what I think it is?' Valentina enquired.

'It is.' He placed the mass back into the sink.

'So, not only have they beheaded Mr Styles, they've also cut out his tongue and removed his genitals.' She took a moment, looking around the room. 'Any sign of a break in?'

'No boss, nothing.'

'And... what about witnesses?' she asked.

'There's a lady from apartment forty-seven. She heard some commotion, opened her door to listen out, then it went quiet, so she assumed it was nothing.'

'Okay, I want to see her,' Valentina insisted. 'Also, get control on the CCTV. Anything unusual, let me know.'

They both left the bathroom and SOCO entered immediately afterwards to continue with their work.

Tammy sat at her desk, feeling worried, and double checking her findings to make sure they were accurate. They were. On the back of the McGregor case, she'd found a glitch with the IPEA implant; a back door into the user's brain via their mobile phone. Mr McGregor wasn't the only person who could be hacked; this applied to anyone who'd had the implant installed since the last upgraded version in February 2017, affecting tens of thousands of people.

If this gets out, Medi Corps will have a company-destroying lawsuit on their hands, along with manslaughter charges, she thought to herself. The thought of prison scared her. She was accountable for the security aspect of the company's products, and Davidson would take whoever he could down with him.

It then crossed her mind that there was no way to repair the glitch, apart from removing the implant. However, doing so would cause significant damage to the user's brain or could even kill them. Medi Corps were backed into a corner, and the CEO had no idea. Tammy had to be the one to break the news to Davidson, but she knew this was ultimately her error, and losing her job was a certainty.

'Yes!' shouted Davidson from his desk. Tammy just walked straight in, accepting the consequences.

'What is it now, Tammy?'

'It's the 2017 IPEA implant, sir!'

'What? And stop calling me sir. It doesn't suit you!'

'Well, there's a glitch,' Tammy began.

He stared at her impatiently, waiting for her to open up. Her mouth was open with no words coming out. 'Well, come on! What?'

'The glitch basically allows the user's brain to be hacked via their mobile phone. It's the encryption.' Tammy took a deep breath.

'Which part are we talking about? Internal or external?'

She placed her chin to her neck in shame, then whispered, 'Internal, Russell.'

He slammed his fists onto his desk, simultaneously causing a mug of coffee to topple over onto all of his papers.

'It was your job to ensure the implant was encrypted to Government standards! Do you know the ramifications of this?'

'Unfortunately, I'm fully aware of the ramifications.' Tammy took a seat in preparation for the inevitable.

They both sat in silence. Davidson sat quietly, the cogs in his powerful mind turning as he tried to invent a way out. Tammy waited for the verdict, with her palms sweating profusely as anxiety progressed through her body.

After what felt like hours, but was in fact only a matter of minutes, Davidson spoke.

'Who else knows about this?'

Tammy shook her head,

'No one. I've not told anyone.'

'Good, let's keep it that way. How easy was it for you to find the glitch?' Davidson asked.

'It wasn't easy at all. You'd need to understand the blueprint and its coding first, let alone the firmware installed within the implant, which was designed by Medi Corps. There would be no other company in the world that uses or would understand the technology we use. We far exceed any authority or government company.'

Davidson frowned.

'So, what you're saying is, there's no way anyone could find out about this?'

'It would be impossible, unless you worked for Medi Corps in the NeuroTech Department, which only consists of four of us and an assistant,' Tammy explained.

'Do any of your team know about this?'

'No one.'

'That's reassuring. But, how did Tommy McGregor get hacked?'

'By mistake, Russell. Whoever hacked Tommy wouldn't have seen the glitch. It was literally a matter of luck.'

'Okay, let's keep this under wraps. Delete whatever it is you have stored regarding this. Update the implant going forward to avoid this happening to our new customers and carry on as normal.'

Tammy looked confused. *This isn't right.*

'Russell, I'm going to be honest, is that the correct course of action? I mean morally?'

Davidson stood, his face going purple and his eyes bulging from their sockets as his blood pressure rose.

'Have you gone mad? If this gets out, you and I are looking at prison, PRISON!' he shouted.

'I appreciate that, but covering it up is wrong.'

'Tammy, if you value your livelihood, you will forget your findings and forget this conversation! It never happened – UNDERSTAND!' Davidson wasn't a person to upset.

Tammy had balls to stand up against him like that. She held back the tears as her morals took control, telling her that this was all wrong.

'People have died because of this, because of our product, because of my failure.' She left quickly, not allowing him enough time to answer her.

Davidson stood tall, his chest puffed out in anger. There was no way he would be going to prison - he would make sure of that.

Tammy, feeling backed into a corner, was ready to hand in her notice to leave the company. With her errors causing tragic consequences, she morally couldn't stay employed with Medi Corps. She sat at her computer and began typing away.

"It is with regret...."

There was an interrupting knock on her office door.

'Come in!' Tammy shouted in a broken voice. 'Russell,' she sighed. 'What can I do for you?' she asked, looking at him as he stood tall in the doorway of her office.

He didn't look right. Something was wrong.

At the murder scene, Valentina was still working with SOCO, hoping to find a trace or any clue that could be linked to the murder of Andy Styles. Time was pressing on, and her impatience was increasing by the minute.

'Roberts?'

'Boss?' Roberts turned to talk, breaking a current conversation with a uniformed officer.

'Where are we with control on the CCTV in the area?'

'We have two characters that are looking suspicious during the hours of twenty-three-twenty-one and zero zero thirty-two,' Roberts explained.

'Do you have an ID on them?' Valentina asked.

'Not yet, boss. I'm going to make my way to control in a bit to view the footage myself. I'll update you later.'

'Okay, but, before you go, the lady at forty-seven said she heard the disturbance at around midnight. Uniform is with her now taking a formal statement.' Valentina turned and continued with SOCO on their investigation. Normally, this would be considered rude, however, when Valentina was in work mode, she could come across this way, and Roberts didn't take offence.

One of the two leads from the CCTV footage had been confirmed as Andy Styles. The other appeared to be another male of similar height. Their movements could be traced back to the city centre, where it was assumed they had been on a night out in the clubs and bars, judging by the clothes they were wearing. After hours of studying the CCTV of the city centre, it was clear that the majority of their time had been spent in the Walkabout bar. Roberts needed to review the CCTV in that place, as Styles was seen entering the bar by himself at 2101 hours on the night he was murdered.

It was now late afternoon and the bar was already open with loud music blaring. Roberts could feel the base from the speakers through his body, causing his internal organs to mirror the beat. The floor was sticky, and the place stunk of cheap, stale lager. There was a young girl behind the bar. Opposite, there was a staircase that led down to another area. Roberts hadn't realised the sheer size of the place before.

'Excuse me, miss. Is the manager around? I need to have a chat.' Roberts flashed his warrant card, so she was obliged to assist immediately.

The girl wandered off, leaving the bar unattended, to locate management. Moments later the manager arrived. Dressed in a smart black suit with a white shirt, he could only be described as tall, dark and handsome.

The manager smiled. 'Yes, officer, what can I do for you?'

'Pardon?' asked Roberts. The music was far too loud for them to hold an important conversation.

The manager then walked off, waving Roberts to follow.

'That's better,' said Roberts, his ears still ringing from the music.

They entered an office in the basement of the building. There were no windows, with only artificial light filling the room, and the brick walls were painted black. The office had a damp smell to it. Roberts sat opposite the manager at his desk.

'What can I do for you, officer?' asked the manager.

'I'm detective constable Roberts.' He leaned forwards to shake hands.

'Kevin,' the manager replied. 'So, what brings you to my establishment?' His voice was rugged to match the sharp designer stubble on his face.

Roberts squinted, *Establishment? It's just a bar*, he thought to himself.

'Just making a few enquires on an urgent matter. The CCTV in this place; is it up and running?'

Kevin sat back and placed a foot across his knee, showing a nice pair of Gucci's.

They're fake, Roberts thought.

'Yeah, it's working. It has to work, to be honest. It's a God-send, considering the amount of trouble we get in here. Is there anything you're looking for in particular?'

'I'm looking for an individual; Andy Styles. Have you heard of him?'

'Doesn't ring any bells to me,' Kevin said.

'Can you take me through your CCTV footage of the main entrance door from around nine PM last night, please?'

Kevin stood and turned on a large screen situated on a wall behind them. It displayed thumbnails for all the cameras throughout the "establishment". Roberts then stood to take a closer look. Kevin enlarged the thumbnail of the camera on the main entrance from last night and slowly played back the footage. It showed Styles entering the bar, holding his mobile phone with the screen lit up.

'You got anything showing where he went when inside?' asked Roberts.

'Give me a sec.'

Kevin then clicked on various thumbnails to find the correct cameras. Finally, they found the one. It showed Styles at the bar, ordering himself a drink, then taking a seat across the floor, sitting himself next to another man. They start to chat, and throughout the night they only leave that table to either collect a drink or to take a comfort break. They look friendly towards one another; it was obvious they knew each other.

The CCTV footage confirms that the second man seen walking towards Styles' apartment was the man he was talking to in the bar.

'Do you know this guy?' asked Roberts.

'Yeah, I know him, a little too well I'm afraid. He's a bit of a troublemaker if you ask me. He was barred for six months last year for exposing himself in the toilets.'

'In the ladies, yeah?'

Kevin shook his head.

'No, the gents. Caused one hell of a scene.'

'So, why only bar him for six months?'

'He sent us a letter of apology, promising to never behave like that again. He explained that he had just been having a laugh!' said Kevin.

'Do you still have that letter?'

'No, wouldn't have kept it.'

'Did you inform the authorities of his behaviour?' asked Roberts.

'No, we try and resolve things locally,' Kevin winked, 'if you know what I mean.'

Roberts ignored and completely bypassed this statement, not wanting to get involved with anything else that went on in the bar at that moment. He put it to the back of his mind. 'What's his name?'

'Charlie Wright.'

'His age?'

'About mid-forties, I think. What's all this in connection with?' Kevin asked as Roberts scribbled down all the information.

'Can you burn this CCTV footage to a disk for me, please?' Roberts requested.

Kevin looked frustrated by the way in which Roberts had avoided answering his question.

'Yeah, okay. You going to tell me what this is all about?' He then inserted a disk into the DVR and began to upload the footage to the disk.

'No, sorry.'

Kevin handed Roberts the disk, and in return, Roberts handed over his card.

'Contact me if you have any more information on either of these two, please?'

Kevin nodded and then escorted Roberts out of the bar.

Tammy had never been wary of Davidson – until now. This was the first time she'd felt this way in all the years she'd known and worked for him. He was currently making her feel uneasy. He stood bold in the doorway to her office, looking somewhat upset.

'Russell, look, I'm going to have to –'

He cut her off abruptly.

'Tammy, I'm sorry for how I reacted, I really am. I should never have been that way with you, and I am truly sorry. I know you're a good person. Please don't do anything rash tonight. Sleep on it, okay?'

Tammy smiled with relief, expecting... well, she didn't even know what to expect, especially not an apology.

'Thank you, Russell, and it's okay. We just need to talk it though rationally tomorrow. Is that okay?'

'Yes, that's fine. See you tomorrow.' Davidson smiled and walked out of her office.

Tammy felt comfortable with how things had been left. *At least I'll be able to sleep tonight*, she thought.

When Tammy arrived at work the following day, Davidson was already hovering around waiting for her. Before she had even put down her bag, he was trying to converse with her. She didn't like this one bit and felt like her space was being invaded.

'Tammy, I was hoping we could have that chat, you know, about your findings?' Davidson sounded rushed, eager to get things sorted. His eyes were wide, his pupils even wider, presumably from the amount of coffee he'd probably been drinking.

'Of course, you're the boss.' She raised her eye brows, and he took a seat while Tammy sat at her desk opposite.

'Tammy, tell me, what are your thoughts?'

'About what now, Russell? About my job? Or playing detective? Or about my mistake?'

Davidson looked sheepish. Her tone was direct, and he didn't like it, but he had to stay calm.

'Both really, which ever you want to talk about first?'

'Well, I would like to talk about work. I think I'm going to hand in my notice, and, yes, I will be going to Valentina about the mistake I've made.'

He looked at her intently.

'Look, Tammy, we've known each other for a very long time. Can you please reconsider your position? I'll increase your salary!'

'This isn't about money, you old fool. This is about my integrity to our customers, and the lives that have been lost, and the ones still at risk.' Tammy was stern, and Russell could see she wasn't going to budge - he knew her well enough.

'Okay, well,' he focused, trying to stay calm, 'don't work your notice. You can leave now, and I'll pay you your notice period of three months... I'll add in a twenty percent bonus as well.'

Tammy gave an I-don't-care smile. Initially, she didn't offer any words, but just grabbed her bag to leave.

'Russell, if I were you, I would get to the bottom of this as soon as possible.' She walked out of the door, with the sound of her heels echoing down the corridor.

In Tammy's heart of hearts, she knew she was doing the right thing. She couldn't continue to work for a company, well, a boss like Russell, who only cared about his own skin. She hadn't created the IPEA to allow people to murder, to rape, or to commit other vile crimes. She had created it to help increase lifespan and wellbeing. Therefore, this completely went against her beliefs.

Once she arrived back home, she felt relieved. She had no mortgage to pay on her luxury apartment. With three month's pay and twenty percent bonus she could live comfortably for at least the next two to three years. However, amongst all that was the niggling notion of what had happened as a result of her error and the potential for more crimes and deaths. It lingered uneasily within her soul.

19

Scientist83: "How much does she know?"
Anderson: "Everything."
Scientist83: "She's got to go!"
Anderson: "I can't do that - the acid was hard enough."
Scientist83: "You're in too deep now."
Anderson: "I can't."
Scientist83: "See you soon."
Scientiest83: **IS NOW OFFLINE**

Anderson sat back in his chair, knowing full well what Scientist83 meant by "see you soon". He knew he had to do what was being asked of him. He took a deep breath, grabbed his keys and got into his car.

Morriston Hospital felt like the devil's playground to Anderson, with Scientist83 being the devil. He walked up the corridor, wearing the same clothes he had worn the last time he had visited Emily. He walked into the ward, but this time there was a different nurse on duty.

'Can I help you?' she asked.

'I'm here to see Emily, my sister.'

'And you are?'

'Her brother, obviously.' Anderson gave a sarcastic grin.

'I meant your name?' the nurse asked, red faced from his arrogance.

'Anderson.'

'She's through there,' the nurse offered, pointing towards a private room.

The room was clean and had a fresh smell. An aircon unit was running, keeping the room nice and cool. Emily now had some of her dressings removed from her face, causing Anderson to look away in the first instance. She was sound asleep. From what he could see, both eyelids were severely deformed, with one side of her face still heavily bandaged. Tubes ran through a mask helping her to breathe. There was a gentle rushing sound as the air flowed into her lungs.

The nurse followed him in.

'She's struggling, Anderson. She inhaled a lot of that acid, which has caused her lungs to deteriorate.'

'She's going to make it, right?' Anderson asked, putting on a facade of concern.

'It's hard to say. I'm sorry, but that's all I can say at this stage. Her consultant will be round at two to check on her.'

'That's three hours away! Is there any way he could come now whilst I'm here?' Anderson enquired.

'I'm afraid not.' The nurse left the room with a sympathetic smile.

Once the coast was clear, Anderson closed the door and walked over to Emily, who was laying lifeless, as though she was in a deep and peaceful sleep.

The door suddenly burst open. It was the nurse.

'Please keep this door open,' she insisted, nodding with a sign of seriousness.

Anderson turned to look at Emily again, and thoughts raced through his mind. *What an absolute waste. You were so beautiful. I'm so sorry I did this to you. I'll be sending you to a better place soon.*

The clear, corrugated breathing tube that was assisting her breathing stretched from the ventilator into the mask, which directed the tube into her airways. Anderson looked over his shoulder. The nurse was no longer standing in the doorway. He leaned forwards to put a kink into the breathing tube. Just before he grabbed it, he heard footsteps from behind.

'Good morning. I'm DC Roberts.' He flashed his warrant card. 'And you are?'

'Anderson, Emily's brother.'

Roberts looked puzzled and evidently suspicious.

'I wasn't aware she had a brother. She was an only child?'

'Well, half-brother, what do they call it...? Oh, yeah, a love child.'

Roberts squinted. With years of experience, he knew Anderson was lying, and he could sense something wasn't right here. The lies oozed from Anderson with evilness.

'What's happened to poor Emily is horrendous, don't you agree?' Roberts probed.

'Completely, have you caught him?' Anderson knew full well that they had not caught anyone.

'Strange, you used the word him?' replied Roberts.

'Well, I'm just assuming it was a male. A female wouldn't do something like this.'

'What makes you say that?' Roberts folded his arms. 'Tell me, Anderson, what do you know about what's happened to Emily?'

Anderson became a little flustered with all the questions.

'Errrm, she had acid thrown in her face!'

'Clearly.' Roberts raised his eyebrow.

'Right, I've got to go.' Anderson became hasty, giving Roberts a slight nudge on his way past with his shoulder.

Roberts grabbed his arm, looking directly into his eyes.

'I'm watching you, Anderson.' He then let go, allowing him to leave, knowing full well he'd be seeing him again soon.

Minutes later, the nurse came back, returning to check on Emily's stats.

'What do you know about that Anderson guy?' Roberts asked with an inquisitive look on his face.

'He says he's her brother, but he seems a little creepy. I don't trust him.' The nurse looked at Roberts cautiously, thinking she'd said too much. 'Sorry, am I allowed to say that?'

'It's a free country, and I agree with you. Can you do me a little favour? Next time he shows up, if he does, call me on this number.' He handed her his card.

'Of course.' The nurse smiled and continued to check on Emily. 'Is there anything else I can help you with?'

'To be honest, I'm the detective investigating this case. I just wanted to pop in and see how Emily's doing?'

'Not good. It's her lungs, you see. She breathed in a lot of the acid as it was splashed into her face.'

Roberts returned a look of empathy.

'So sad! A girl full of life, just lost her mother, and now this.'

'I know, what's the world coming to?'

'You tell me! Look, I've got to head off. Like I said, if that Anderson returns, call me.'

Back in his car, Roberts called up Valentina. She didn't answer the first time, so he dialled again straight after. This time she answered.

'Boss, what do you have on that Anderson character?'

'The guy who lives above Tommy?'

'That's the one.'

'Not much to be honest. Why?'

'I've seen him hovering around Emily at the hospital. It's the second time he's been there, and he says he's her half-brother or something,' Roberts explained.

'Can't be! I've done a full check on Emily. There is no half-brother. Her dad died a few years back – suicide. Killed himself in prison.' There was the sound of Valentina sucking on the end of a cigarette, then blowing out the smoke. 'Her mother, as you know, was murdered, and there are no grandparents left. She has no one.'

'That's sad. I've got a gut feeling about this Anderson. I'm going to run a few more checks on him, maybe even show up at his place.'

'Okay,' said Valentina, ending the call.

Anderson: *"I tried, but a detective showed up."*
Scientist83: *"What did he say?"*
Anderson: *"Just asked a few pointed questions, but I left before he went in too heavy."*
Scientist83: *"Do you think he suspects anything with you?"*
Anderson: *"Not at all!"*
Scientist83: *"Suggest you move all your kit."*
Anderson: *"Why?"*
Scientist: *"Because if they search your home, they will seize the lot."*
Scientist83: *IS NOW OFFLINE*

Anderson began to pace the room, thinking about this detective Roberts. If he was actually on to him, it would raise a lot of issues, not just for Anderson but for Roberts himself. He knew Scientist83 wouldn't stand for anything.

Two years ago, back in August 2016, Anderson, being a dark person, had trolled the Dark Net, looking at new ways to hack UK banks in order to steal a lot of money. He wanted to have enough to go and live abroad with no worries. This was when he had come across Scientist83, who had made contact via a chat room. At the time, Anderson had been profiling hacking software he had developed; this wasn't just basic stuff.

Scientist83: "How intelligent is your system?"
Anderson: "Similar to Nmap. Why?"
Scientist83: "Nmap traces IP addresses. Can you trace mobile IMEI numbers?"
Anderson: "Possibly. Why?"
Scientist83: "If you can build me software that can track and hack IMEI numbers, I'll pay you handsomely."
Anderson: "How much are we talking about?"
Scientist83: "That's negotiable. Build and prove, then we'll discuss a price."
Anderson: "Ok, what is it you're trying to do?"
Scientist83: "I need to be able to track and hack a mobile phone device."
Anderson: "What for?"
Scientist83: "That's my business. Want the job or not?"
Anderson: "I do. Just need to understand what it is you want to achieve?"
Scientist83: "Have you heard of IPEA?"
Anderson: "I have."
Scientist83: "I want to hack that via a mobile phone."
Anderson: "Ok, what for?"
Scientist83: "That I can't tell you. Contact me when you have the software, then follow my instructions. I will then pay you."
Anderson: "I need to have an idea of price?"
Scientist83: "At least six zeros."
Anderson: "How do I know you will pay?"

Scientist83: "It's a trust game. You build this for me, and I'll pay you. I'll be in touch. Keep this page open all the time."
Scientist83: **IS NOW OFFLINE**

Attracted by the proposed amount of money, Anderson had started work, stretching his abilities. By December 2017, he had achieved what had been asked of him - he had developed the illegal software Scientist83 had requested.

Anderson had made contact with Scientist83 again, who had given Anderson various complex tasks to carry out in return, in order to prove the effectiveness of his software. He called it *Black Matter*.

Over the past year, they had stayed in touch via the Dark Net. Once *Black Matter* was ready, Scientist83 had set Anderson to work creating a destructive trail of murder and attacks that would hit the media. This was the proof Scientist83 had needed before payment to Anderson could be made. He needed to ensure that it was completely untraceable, and if Anderson was able to get away with these horrendous crimes, which had to be high profile, then he knew he could use the software for what he needed without getting caught.

Part of Anderson regretted ever starting this project, but the promised reward was too attractive. He so desperately wanted to leave the country. Despite regret, he was now in too deep to even consider backing out. If he tried, he'd be dead.

A heavy weight pressed down on Anderson as he paced his room, stressing about killing Emily. He didn't want to, but he had no choice. Foolishly, he had let Emily in on the work, and she knew everything about what he'd been doing. Her knowledge was dangerous to him. If Emily was to spill the beans on Anderson, then Scientist83 would be sure to make him disappear.

Emily and Anderson had also met via the Dark Net. She had needed someone to hurt Taylor, to seek revenge for losing her dad, without it coming back to her. However, she had got caught up and had seen financial opportunities by having her mum murdered. She had become greedily carried away, offering Anderson a stake in her inheritance, but had now become the victim of an acid attack – karma's a bitch!

Anderson used *Black Matter* to search IMEI numbers. He needed Emily gone and just couldn't do it himself, especially as CID were now onto him. He located someone within the hospital with the IPEA implant and got to work.

A 21-year-old Welsh nurse, Emma Jones, crouched down in agony on the floor of Morriston Hospital suffering from an intense headache. The pain was like nothing she'd ever felt before. It hurt like hell. Hospital staff went to help, but strangely, all of a sudden, she was fine. She got up from the floor, her blonde hair matted from the commotion, and she didn't say a word as she walked off. A member of staff watched as Emma disappeared down the corridor , shrugging off the incident, not thinking too much into it. Why would they?

Emma walked the footslog through the maze of corridors. She looked lost at times, but being in uniform and recognised as a member of staff, no one batted an eyelid. Eventually, arriving at the Welsh Centre of Burns, she walked in, passed the reception desk, went up the stairs and entered Tempest Burns ITU, where Emily was still recovering from her injuries.

The ventilator pumped the flowing air and oxygen into Emily's lungs, keeping her alive, despite the heavily scarred lung tissue. Emma looked down at Emily, who looked peaceful and at rest.

Emma showed no emotion in her zombie-like trance. Using her hand, she put a kink into the ventilator tube, which didn't take long. Emily's chest rose and fell aggressively as her body begged for the oxygen. Emma held the tube tight, watching the monitors as they emitted an alarm.

Another nurse ran in and fought with Emma, trying to pull her away from the tubes, but her grip was too firm, as she held on tight. Emma then let go, once it was clear that Emily had passed on.

More hospital staff entered the room and began resuscitation, but it was too late. Emily had died. They looked around, and Emma had already left the building.

She was found sitting on a bench in the hospital grounds, staring ahead of herself. She had a confused expression on her face and was clearly troubled.

Emma was a charming, caring, wonderful nurse and had worked so hard to land her dream job. She was one of those people who served her patients' needs wholeheartedly and provided outstanding care, so that when her patients were discharged, they left the hospital thinking, *she's in the right job*! For such an incident to have happened was shocking to anyone who knew her.

Roberts sat opposite Miss Emma Jones with a uniformed officer beside him, and Miss Jones's lawyer sitting next to her. Roberts had volunteered for this case due to previous and other ongoing cases, which he believed might have a direct link.

The outcome of the primary interview with Miss Jones was very similar to that of the McGregor case. They'd both had strong headaches followed by no memory, and that was it. There was no recall of the actual incident. Roberts's gut feeling came fighting back, but this time with a hint of venom. *These are linked, I know it.*

'Are you sure you're ok to take this on as well?' asked Valentina over the phone.

'Yes, boss. I'm telling you, it's that Anderson guy. I don't know how, but it's him.'

'What have the CPS come back with on Jones?'

'Still waiting, boss, but with the evidence stacked up against her, she'll be remanded for sure.'

'Let's pay Anderson a visit, just as a general enquiry.'

'Good plan, boss. Meet you outside?'

'Give me an hour, I'll be there,' Valentina stated.

The detectives met outside the block of flats. From the outside, Tommy's flat looked lifeless, however, so did the flat above, which was Anderson's. They had a member of uniform with them, who gave them access through the communal door. Roberts insisted that he would knock and that he wanted to take control of the questioning. Valentina agreed, happy to allow him the pleasure.

Anderson took some time to answer the door, and when he finally did, he recognised Roberts instantly.

'Yes?' said Anderson in his usual high-pitched voice, wearing his usual scruffy clothing.

'Anderson, would you mind if we came in for a chat?' Roberts asked.

'Why would I mind?' he said over-confidently, standing aside and allowing them to pass.

'You don't have much, do you?' asked Roberts casting his eyes through the apartment.

'I lead a simple life, thank you.'

'Mind if we sit?'

'Do what you want. I gather you will anyway.'

At these words, Valentina raised her eyebrows and couldn't hold back, even though she had promised to let Roberts lead the enquiry.

'I suggest you drop the attitude!' Valentina's tone was sharp.

Anderson showed no emotion to her, coming across as somewhat cocky; an attitude Valentina hated.

Roberts then continued. 'How close were you to Emily?'

'We were okay. We bickered now and then, but pretty much the norm.' Anderson placed his hands in his pockets, and the uniformed officer moved forwards, reacting swiftly. Anderson retracted his hands quickly, realising that was a wrong move.

'Keep your hands where we can see them, fella,' said the uniformed officer.

'What is this? I can't even relax in my own home!'

'Like he said, just keep them where we can see them, okay!' Roberts was eyeballing Anderson, who was returning the gaze.

'Can you tell us why you felt the need to lie about being a sibling of Emily Wakefield,' asked Valentina, with Roberts giving her a look.

'Why would I lie?'

'That's what I've just asked! Why did you? You see, we did a check on you, and you don't seem to have any immediate family, let alone any sisters!'

'Well, your checks are wrong,' Anderson exclaimed.

'I doubt that. Do you know an Emma Jones?' asked Roberts, taking back control.

'Nope,' Anderson shook his head.

'Do you mind if I take a quick look around?' asked the uniformed officer.

'Fill ya boots!'

It only took five minutes, then the uniformed officer returned, giving a slight shake of the head to Valentina. She then nodded to Roberts as a gesture to leave.

They stood outside discussing the situation. Roberts looks up towards Anderson's flat, noticing the blinds twitching.

'We have nothing on him at this stage. The CCTV confirms that he wasn't at the hospital at the time Emily was murdered. I think your hunch might be wrong.' Valentina got into the car.

'Look, I'm not trying to piss on your chips here, but we didn't ask the right questions. We literally have nothing on Anderson. He didn't kill Emily.' Valentina watched Roberts, waiting for his response.

Roberts paused for a second, knowing that his gut feeling had never let him down before.

'I'll prove you wrong, boss.'

'Well, detective, I hope you do.' She gave him a wink, then pulled away.

20

Hours had passed by as Tammy stared at her laptop screen, heavily engrossed with going through all the data downloaded from Tommy's implant. It was 10.00pm, and tiredness was kicking in fast, her eyes straining from looking at the screen for so long. Her phone started ringing, making her jump and breaking the silence, pulling her from her deep thoughts. She answered the phone with caution, as it was from a "Private Number".

'Hello, Tammy speaking.'

'Tammy, it's DI Valentina. I need your urgent assistance.'

'Okay, what seems to be the problem?'

'Not over the phone. Can you meet me at the university, same place as before?' Valentina asked.

'Erm, yeah, when?'

'Now?'

'Sorry, Detective, it's a little late. I'm really tired and need sleep.'

'If it wasn't urgent, I wouldn't be calling you.'

There was a slight pause whilst Tammy thought this through, then she reluctantly agreed.

'Okay, I'll make my way down there. Give me an hour or so.'

Tammy hung up with frustration. She was frustrated with herself for being a "yes" person and always feeling obliged to help others. She hadn't wanted to give Valentina the chance to say anything else.

It was now 11:30pm, and the roads were dead. Tammy couldn't park in the university carpark, as it was locked, so she parked on the roadside some hundred yards away and walked to the university. There was a chill in the air, with a light wind that blew through the trees. Tammy felt overwhelmed with uneasiness, as she could hear someone walking behind her. She upped her pace, but so did the individual behind her. Her heart rate began to increase the quicker she moved. She found herself running, and her heart was pounding in her chest.

Tammy began to panic as the person gained on her, getting closer and closer. She fumbled for her car keys to use as a weapon, placing a key between her knuckles. She turned suddenly, taking a deep breath as a jogger in a hi-vis vest wearing over-ear headphones jogged past. He nodded politely, and she felt embarrassed. All this was playing with her mind.

The entrance to the university was locked. Tammy peered through the glazed doors of the main entrance and could see a security guard sitting at a desk, his face lit up from whatever was on the screen in front of him, and the rest of the area was in darkness. She tapped gently on the glass, catching his attention. He looked up, slightly startled at her silhouette pressed against the glass. He walked over to the door and started talking through the glass.

'What do you want, madam?' Tammy could only just make out what he was saying.

'I'm here to see DI Valentina and Professor Conroy.' She tried to pronounce her words as clearly as possible, making over-exaggerated movements with her lips.

'What?'

'I'm here to see-,' Tammy stopped. 'God's sake!' She felt frustrated, and decided to use her mobile to call Valentina in order to let her know she was outside. She used her other hand to wave the guard away.

A few minutes later, artificial white LED lighting lit up the reception area, which caused Tammy to squint as her eyes tried to adjust to the sudden brightness through the glass door. Valentina walked through with Professor Conroy in tow. They opened the door, greeting Tammy with smiles.

'Thank you so much for coming like this. It's very much appreciated,' said Valentina.

'It's okay. So what can I help you with?' Tammy asked.

'Follow us, Tammy. We'll go through in detail.'

This time, they didn't go to Professor Conroy's lab. Instead they headed towards the morgue. The corridors were long, and the tubed lighting above was on a PIR system, automatically lighting up the corridors as they progressed towards the morgue. Tammy had never been in a morgue, nor had she ever seen a dead body. Anxiety clung to every cell of her being the closer they got.

As they walked into the morgue, the room lit up. It was smaller than she had originally imagined. There only appeared to be three autopsy tables. Moments later, a man walked out of a hidden room. He looked young with a kind face. His hair was combed to the side and he had redness around his eyes, as though he had been rubbing them, or possibly sleeping.

'This is our diener, Malcom Mathews.' Conroy introduced them.

'Pleased to meet you,' Malcom replied, following with a polite nod.

'Mr Mathews, please can you present your findings,' Professor Conroy requested.

Malcolm walked off and returned with a small steel tray. He placed the tray on a table and, with a gloved hand, held up a small electronic device surrounded by a strange looking matter. It looked like flesh but artificial.

'Does anyone recognise this?' asked Professor Conroy.

Tammy raised her hand, and all three looked at her.

'No need to raise your hand.' They all smiled.

'Sorry, yes, that is the IPEA implant,' Tammy explained. They all looked round at one another. 'I designed it myself. It works with the Smart Injection along with the IPEA application. Sorry, I thought this was common knowledge?'

'It is; yes. However, Mr Mathews has found an abnormality within the area of the brain where it was installed,' explained Conroy.

'Okay, how do you mean? This was thoroughly trialled and tested. There was no evidence of any anomalies?'

'There is no damage. However, over time, additional nerve cells have formed around the implant,' replied Conroy.

'Okay?' Tammy looked confused. She was puzzled – this was news to her.

'These cells are abnormal cells,' Conroy explained.

'What? Are you referring to c-.' Tammy was cut short by Conroy.

'No, not that type of cell.' He smiled at her. 'More like enhanced brain cells that also communicate with the nervous system.'

'Okay, this is strange. So, what does this mean?' asked Tammy.

'At this moment in time, we are not sure. However, with your expertise relating to the design of the implant, you may be able to help us discover what this is?'

'Okay, I will try.' Tammy looked unconfident, worried that her skills may not stretch to what they were asking. 'How do you want to do this?'

'We'll provide an intricate report of the findings. If you could look through these and come back with what your findings or thoughts are?'

'Err… yes, of course, I will try. Can I ask what that matter is surrounding the implant?' Tammy enquired.

'That is the cell formation that has grown on the implant.'

'Good, is she okay to take the implant as well?' asked Valentina. 'We need a full data log of everything that has happened to Andy Styles.'

'I'll need his mobile phone as well,' suggested Tammy.

'We can provide that,' said Valentina. 'That is back at the station.'

They continued to bounce information around for the next hour, but Tammy was starting to feel even more tired. Valentina picked up on this and suggested they call it a night. Tammy was handed a small sealed bag containing the implant and a USB stick containing all the information that the professors had found. Valentina then walked Tammy back to her car alone.

'Tammy, we fully appreciate the time you're putting into this. I know you've left Medi Corps,' said Valentina.

'How do you know that?' Tammy was shocked that she knew this information.

'Mr Davidson called me earlier today asking me not to involve you with anything, stating that you had resigned due to work pressures.'

'Okay, that's not true. Well, I have quit my job, but not because of work pressure-.'

Valentina interrupted.

'I'm not bothered why you resigned, I just need your help. If I'm honest, I'm not particularly interested in what you find for the professors. I'm interested in whether you can find out who intercepted Andy's brain. Conroy only agreed to this if you would assist in their research.'

'Okay, I'll do my best, but I can't promise anything.'

Valentina took hold of Tammy's shoulder.

'We really need to get to the bottom of this. There are other lives at stake. You will be compensated, but it is strictly confidential. I would appreciate it if your efforts were focussed on the case in question and not their research.' She then looked Tammy directly in the eyes. 'Just tell them your tests came up inconclusive.'

'I understand,' replied Tammy, getting into her car and driving off.

Tammy awoke the next morning with her mind clear, and her focus on downloading all the information from the implant, then waiting for Andy's mobile phone to be delivered via a same day courier. The information she downloaded was very detailed and complex, and it would take days to convert the codes.

By mid-morning the phone had arrived, and upon turning it on, it seemed to activate the implant. *This shouldn't happen?* Tammy thought. She then discovered that the cells that had formed around the implant seemed to keep the implant active. This enabled Tammy to actively use the app on the phone to communicate with the implant.

She became excited about this finding, but she tried to maintain focus until she was one hundred percent certain that this could trace back to the source that had been manipulating Andy's brain.

Two days passed, and Tammy had slept for only three hours tops, having drunk over a gallon of coffee to keep her going. She had the trace to an IMEI number, which again was scrambled, but she eventually managed to reverse the connection back to the source, providing an exact location. She didn't waste any time and called Valentina straight away.

'Valentina,' the detective answered.

'It's Tammy. I've had a breakthrough, but we need to meet as soon as possible. I don't know how much time we have.'

'I'll come to you,' said Valentina. 'Text me your address.'

Tammy sent the text straight after their call. Two hours later, Valentina arrived with Roberts.

'Nice place you have here! Medi Corps must have been paying you well,' exclaimed Valentina.

'Thank you,' Tammy replied, feeling slightly embarrassed, being the humble person, she was. 'Drink anyone?' she offered.

'Just coffee, please; black, no sugar,' said Valentina.

'Same,' replied Roberts, not wanting to seem fussy.

'So, what do you have?' asked Valentina. 'All I need is an address or a name, that's it. None of the technical jargon; I get enough of that from Conroy!'

Tammy smiled.

'Here's the address. I don't have a name.' She handed a piece of paper over.

Valentina examined the address and showed Roberts. He smiled and nodded. It seemed as though they knew who the source was.

'If this proves to be genuine and we can put solid evidence to the CPS, you'll be changing lives.' Valentina smiled at Tammy, trying not to crack her own moody face.

Tammy returned the smile.

'What about the professors?' she asked.

'Just tell them the findings were inconclusive, like I said.'

'But I have found something they might be interested in!'

'Tammy, you have done an outstanding job, but trust me, leave this be. If it gets out you have assisted with this, Davidson could sue you.'

'True! Seems a shame.'

'Trust me, leave it there. No one will know how we came to this.'

Valentina and Roberts were like two children at Christmas. They called for backup and headed to the address to make the arrest.

They pulled up at the address, and uniformed officers let them in to the apartment block via the communal door. They all accumulated outside the apartment, battering ram at the ready. An officer knocked first, and they all waited patiently. There was no answer, so they barged their way in.

After a search of the apartment, it was clear there was no one home. The place was still lived in, but there was nothing of immediate concern.

'Must be on a VPN,' said Roberts.

Valentina called Tammy for clarity.

'Tammy, Valentina. Are you sure this is the address?'

'Yes, I'm one hundred percent certain. I would never have given it to you if I wasn't,' Tammy replied.

'There's nothing here!'

'The signal is still active.'

'Could they be using a VPN?' asked Valentina.

'They are, yes, but I managed to override it. That is the address where the source is.'

'Argh, okay, thank you. I'll call you later.' Valentina hung up and turned to Roberts.

'She's one hundred percent.'

Roberts looked confused.

'There's nothing here, boss.'

'We've got something!' shouted a uniformed officer from another room. They both hurried into the room where the officer was standing. They could see a plug socket. The cable was going directly to the floor below through the floor boards.

'Let's go!' shouted Valentina.

They all gathered outside the apartment below and knocked on the door, then waited.

'Do it!' shouted Valentina.

'Wait, we don't have authorisation for this address.'

'Do it!' she shouted again, and they proceeded to force their way into the apartment.

21

Anderson jerked his laptop across the desk in his hotel room. The last thing he wanted to do was kill anyone in the police force. Too many people are dying from this; it wasn't the plan, he thought to himself. However, as instructed by Scientist83, he had no choice, and he knew full well that if he declined the request, he'd be dead before the sun came up in the morning. This he had to do himself, without the use of Black Matter, now that his system had been compromised.

He ran a bath in an attempt to relax, to clear his mind and to refocus on the task in hand. The bath helped, but only for a moment, with a glass of whisky taking the edge off his troubles. He really didn't want to kill the two detectives who had discovered his setup.

Anderson: "I can't do it."
Scientist83: "You don't have a choice!"
Anderson: "There must be another way?"
Scientist83: "You have until midnight tomorrow."
Scientist83: **IS NOW OFFLINE**

He rubbed the belly of his beautiful wife, then kissed it, talking to the baby.

'Daddy's going to love you so much.' Roberts then looked up to his wife, Annette, giving her a loving kiss.

'I love you, beautiful.'

She smiled,

'I love you too.'

Roberts left the house ready for the day ahead of him. He got into his car and made his way to the station to meet with Valentina.

En route, he noticed a tatty F Reg, Ford Escort that had been behind him for some time. From memory, he recognised the vehicle from his street. Strange, he thought to himself. He continued on his usual route, checking his mirror constantly to find that the tatty car was lurking a few cars back. It could have been nothing, but as a matter of caution, he decided to take an alternate random route in order to work out what the driver of this car was up to.

Roberts made a right turn at the bottom of Cathedral Road, where normally he would have gone left. He made his way down Cowbridge Road, and the tatty car was still a few cars back. He then made his way down Wellington and turned onto Leckwith, parking up in the football stadium. The tatty car followed and stopped outside a pub called the Sand Martin.

A hooded individual just sat there, staring in his rear-view mirror at Roberts. Roberts got out of his own car, collected his taser and slowly walked towards the tatty heap of junk. The engine grumbled and choked, showing the car's battered age, then it roared off, wheel spinning from the car park, leaving the smell of burnt rubber. The driver then jumped the red lights, heading towards the A4232. Roberts got the reg number, reciting it a few times to make sure he'd remember it.

When Roberts arrived at the station, he explained to Valentina what had happened and ran a check on the battered vehicle – "Put to Scrap" back in 2010.

'It's probably someone you've pissed off trying to mess with your head. I wouldn't worry about it,' said Valentina.

'But what if it's connected with the McGregor case? Everything we're working on at the moment links back to that!'

'Roberts, if you're worried about some idiot following you around, then you're in the wrong job. It happens!' Valentina fobbed off his concerns, but he couldn't settle.

He ran a check of previous owners and came up with a dozen names, none of which caused any significant concern. He tried to let it drop for the moment and focussed on his work.

'Boss, what's next now for Anderson?'

'I've run a check on his mobile phone and bank cards. Nothing's been used since a few hours before we showed up. It's as though he was expecting us. We have control reviewing CCTV in the area, but there's nothing so far.'

'I hate these blimmin' cat and mouse games,' Roberts exclaimed, showing frustration.

'What's up? It doesn't normally bother you!'

'Nothing, sorry. Annette's not been feeling too great lately.'

Towards the end of the day, they had come to a brick wall with their search for Anderson; a needle in a haystack was the term Valentina often used. They had to sit tight and wait for him to surface again. With eyes and ears on the street, they hoped it wouldn't take too long.

Roberts retired early for the day, keen to get home to his eight-month-pregnant Annette. As she hadn't been feeling too well recently, he wanted to spend a bit more time at home and to be there for her. Valentina was supportive.

Roberts took a different route home. This time, he went the long way up the A4232, and then down the M4, which added another 35 minutes to his journey. He still had an inkling in the back of his mind that he was being followed.

A few streets from his home, he strangely noticed the tatty white car again. A cold shiver went down his spine as he drove past. He pulled over to check it out.

The car was filthy. The windows were desperately in need of a good clean. Roberts had no idea how someone could be driving that thing. He used his sleeve to wipe part of the driver's side window and peered in. The car was just a disgrace; full of food packages and bottles, and an abundance of used fag ends stumped out in the centre console. He dreaded to think what it smelt like in there.

All of a sudden, the vehicle unlocked. There was a sharp pain in the back of Roberts's head, and then he was out cold.

With a sudden gasp that whistled as the air travelled up his nose, Roberts awoke. The pain in his head was intense. He tried to rub it, but he couldn't, and he quickly learned that his hands were tied. He was sitting on a chair, and he tried to move, but whatever was holding him in place was strong and tight. His mouth had an object lodged in it, with tape across.

The room was dim with the smell of dust in the air. Roberts looked around as best he could. From what he could see, it looked to be a room in a house. The wallpaper was dated with brown and orange circles, like a scene from the nineteen seventies, with parts hanging off. The ceiling was of crumbling aertex with a bulb just hanging from its wire. The carpet was a mustard colour with a large dark red stain in the centre – blood, was his initial thought.

Roberts could hear a noise. It was the sound of a locking mechanism, then the door he was facing opened. A broad figure stood, almost filling the doorway, wearing a plain white mask over his face with only holes to see and breathe through. The figure walked over to Roberts and pulled out a blade, pressing it firmly against Roberts's neck. The person holding the knife trembled, either from fear or from being full of cocaine.

Roberts tried to speak, but he couldn't, and only a muffled sound came from within him.

The figure then pulled the knife away.

'Roberts, you need to back off!' The voice was deep, almost fake, but he recognised it but couldn't work out where from. 'You see, we've been watching you work, and that work needs to stop. Understand?'

Roberts returned a shake of his head.

'Well, Roberts, the thing is, if you carry on with these investigations, then that unborn child of yours will never open its eyes. You catching my drift?' There was a snigger. Whoever was doing this was enjoying taunting him.

Roberts's eyes widened with fear and immediately filled with tears, not for himself, but for his wife and baby. He tensed to try and break free, but there was no give.

'Nod if you agree!' the figure demanded.

Of course, there was nothing more important than his wife and baby, so he nodded.

'Ahh, that's a good boy! We're getting somewhere.' The figure then took the knife and jabbed it into Roberts's thigh, causing Roberts to squirm like a trapped rat.

Trying to fight the pain, Roberts screamed, though no real sound could be heard. The figure then removed the knife slowly from his leg, causing even more agony, then pressed it against his neck again.

'I want to kill you. I'd enjoy killing you.' Even though there was a mask, Roberts could sense a smile, an enjoyment of this torture.

The masked figure then left the room, locking the door behind him.

Roberts could feel the warm blood soaking his trousers, and a drip could be heard as it trickled from the hem to the floor. He felt weak, with no idea how much blood he was losing and no idea if he would be left in this room to die and rot. He tried to move again, but still nothing.

Fear for his family filled his heart. Flashbacks of Annette's face lit up the room. She was smiling and happy. All he'd ever wanted was to make her happy. He cried and his body trembled. He tried to scream, but all it did was waste his energy.

Roberts closed his eyes and took his thoughts home. He then thought about the last holiday Annette and himself had been on in the south of Spain. The sun had been warm and radiant, just like his wife. The food and wine was superb. They had spent most of their time walking, laughing and making love. It had been a happy, fruitful time. These cheery thoughts were quickly diminished by the sound of the door opening once again.

'I'm back!' the figure announced, wearing the same outfit as before. He was holding a camera. 'People would pay good money to see this,' he cackled.

Roberts was pale from the loss of blood in his system. The figure danced around the room. It was exaggerated enjoyment, almost passive aggressive. He waved the knife around, then walked behind Roberts.

Suddenly, the figure slashed open Roberts's throat, spilling and spraying blood across the room, with a hissing sound. Within seconds Roberts was dead.

BBC Wales Today | Monday 19th March 2018
Latest Headline at 12:00 hours: Detective Constable – Missing.
A spokesperson from South Wales Police has informed BBC Wales of the details of missing Anthony Roberts. Married father-to-be went missing on Saturday 17th March.
Anyone who has any information should contact the South Wales Police incident room at once on 02920 101101.

Scientist83: "Looks like I had to do the job for you."
Anderson: "Was that you? Did you kill him?"
Scientist83: "No comment."
Anderson: "What's next?"
Scientist83: "You know the plan."
Scientist83: **IS NOW OFFLINE**

22

There was outrage at Cardiff Bay Police station. One of their own had gone missing, and it was their duty to have Roberts returned safely. Little did they know, he was already dead.

Valentina's phone rang, and she answered quickly with aggression. 'Valentina!'

'It's PC Galloway. We've found Roberts's car.'

'Where?'

'Milestone Close, not far from his house.'

'On my way,' said Valentina.

Valentina used the blues on her unmarked car to get to the location urgently, mainly for her own sanity, as there was no real necessity for them to be used. She pulled up and addressed PC Galloway.

'Valentina,' she introduced herself. 'What do you have on the car?'

'Nothing out of the norm, I'm afraid, but-,' Valentina nodded with relief, 'there are a few spots of blood fifty yards over there on the pavement.' The constable pointed towards the blood and explained that forensics had already sent a sample off for a DNA profile.

Anxiety and tension increased as Valentina waited for the results. On a positive note, if the DNA came back as a match to Roberts, it would be a lead. However, it was a catch-twenty-two situation, because blood was never a positive sign. Valentina's gut feeling was that it was Roberts's blood.

Anderson was cold, shivering as he sat outside Bristol train station posing as a homeless person. He was dirty and had that rank smell of an unwashed human. He had found an abandoned blue sleeping bag, which was his only comfort, even though it stank of urine and God knows what else. He had a used Starbucks cup displayed prominently on the pavement in front of him, in anticipation of a kind gesture from the general public. He was shocked by people's kindness. If only they knew who he was.

He blended in well within the area. Sadly, there were many homeless people around who regularly approached him. There was one young man in particular, who had sores on his face and a scar stretching from the bottom of his left eye down to his jaw line. His two front teeth were missing, and his breath was noticeably pungent as he spoke.

'You new round 'ere?' the homeless man asked, his voice weak.

Anderson looked at him for a moment before speaking.

'I am, sadly,' he replied.

'There's a group of us not far from here. You can join us.' The man seemed harmless, but Anderson didn't want to interact too much with people, seeing as he needed to maintain a low profile.

'I'm okay, thank you. I won't be here long.'

'That's what they all say,' the man replied, turning as he spoke.

It started to rain later that day. Anderson stayed put, as there was shelter from the downpour. He sat under the entrance canopy to the train station. He was shivering, so he wrapped the dirty sleeping bag around himself further. At this stage, the smell didn't bother him too much.

A lady walked past, well dressed and pretty. She looked at Anderson, then did a double take.

Tammy recognised the homeless man by his eyes and the shape of his face. She was certain it was him - She pulled out her phone hurriedly.

'Valentina,' the detective answered her phone in no time.

'It's Tammy. How are you?'

'I'm okay, but I need to keep this line free. Is it urgent?'

'Yes, very! That man you were looking for, the one who lived above Tommy; I think I've just seen him.' There was a pause for a few seconds.

'Where?'

'Sat outside Bristol train station,' Tammy replied.

'Are you sure it's him?'

'I'm one hundred and ten percent certain it's him. I recognise him from the news release that went out. I took a screen shot of his picture and compared it.'

'Fantastic! Talk about being in the right place at the right time!' Valentina exclaimed.

'What do you want me to do?' Tammy asked.

'Nothing. Just keep an eye on him. Act normal, but do not under any circumstances approach him. I repeat do not approach or talk to him,' Valentina warned.

'Okay, I can do that. I'll hang back and act normal.'

'I mean it, Tammy! This man is seriously dangerous. Don't go near him, and make sure you call me if he starts moving. I'll send a unit ASAP.'

Instantly, Tammy felt on edge. *What have I got myself into?* she asked herself. She felt she had a duty of care. After all, she did feel partially responsible for the murders, due to her mistake on the encryption.

Tammy waited and hovered twenty yards from Anderson, pretending to scroll through her phone. It was intense as she kept looking over at him as discreetly as possible. He then clocked her beady eye watching him, and Tammy's heart skipped a beat, but he then looked away.

Look at him less, she thought to herself, trying not to be so obvious. When she looked up a minute or two later, Anderson was gone. She panicked and started to move quickly towards the area where he had been. There was a small dry patch on the pavement from where he had been sitting. She made a random guess as to which direction he had moved in and went on the hunt.

Tammy went down the next street, which became more residential. As she passed an alley, someone aggressively pulled her in. A hand was pressed firmly over her mouth, making it hard for her to breathe, so it was pointless trying to scream out. With the other hand, they pulled her body into theirs.

'Who the fuck are you?' he whispered angrily in her ear, whilst looking around, making sure no one had spotted them.

'N,no one! Get off me!' Tammy struggled.

Anderson wasn't that strong, and she managed to break free from his grip, instantly making a run for it. He made chase, his sleeping bag flung over his shoulder as he sprinted after her.

Tammy's heels were slowing her down, and Anderson was gaining fast. She headed back towards the train station, knowing it was a densely populated area. She looked behind her, and he was still on her tail, red faced and angry. Seconds later, a black car pulled up beside Anderson. Two men scrambled out, grabbing him, then putting him on the ground. There was a fumble, with Anderson putting up a feeble fight. The police had arrived.

Tammy sighed with relief when Valentina pulled up ten minutes later. She must have had her pedal to the metal.

Valentina marched towards Tammy.

'I told you to hold back and not to go near him!' she said angrily.

Wow, does this strong character of a woman care? Tammy thought as she smiled sheepishly.

'Stop smiling! He could have killed you and probably would have.'

'Sorry, but he started to move, so I followed.'

'That was foolish, but,' Valentina started back tracking, 'I am also grateful. Thank you, Tammy.' She gently shook her hand. 'Do you need any assistance or anything?'

'No, I'm fine, thank you.'

'Okay, well, let's grab some lunch in a few days,' Valentina suggested. 'My treat okay! I'll be in touch.'

Back at Cardiff Bay station, little courtesy was shown towards Anderson. He was the prime suspect in this whole case, and Valentina was relieved to have him in custody. They now only had twenty-four hours to charge him.

No time was wasted. Anderson was provided with the duty lawyer, and they went into the interrogation room, where Anderson was pushed for a confession.

'Can you explain why you were posing as a homeless person?' asked Valentina.

'I was hiding,' Anderson replied.

'From who?'

'You, him, everyone.' Anderson had a defeated look in his eyes.

Valentina picked up on this and used it to her advantage.

'Him?' she questioned.

'I can't say. I honestly don't know who he is.'

'What do you mean?' asked Valentina.

Anderson dipped his head, looking down at his feet. His left knee was shuddering. It was clear he was uncomfortable.

'I don't know who he is. He gives me orders, and I do what I'm asked!' Anderson was still not making eye contact.

'You're not making any sense! Start from the beginning. When did you meet him?' Valentina enquired.

'Online on the Dark Net. I was promoting a small service. I had no idea it would lead to this.'

'What service was that?'

'I can't say. It's illegal,' Anderson stated.

'Look, the more honest you are now, the more lenient the prosecution will be with you,' Valentina advised.

'But I've been breaking the law!'

Valentina leaned forwards, looking him straight in his eyes.

'Just fucking tell me!'

Anderson looked scared.

'It was just hacking software, that's all. Then I was approached by someone who asked me to build him software to hack mobile phones through the networks.' He took a breath. 'So, I did. Then I was able to hack into people's minds through their mobiles and make them do things.' He sat back and folded his arms. 'I'm sorry.'

'Did you have anything to do with DC Roberts?' Valentina asked.

Anderson looked up at her guiltily.

'I was instructed to, but he beat me to it.'

'He?' Valentina asked, trying hard to keep her anger at bay now, being emotionally attached to the case with the disappearance of Roberts.

'Yes, the person who's been instructing me to carry out the jobs. He told me to kill Roberts, but I couldn't. He then threatened to kill me, but instead killed Roberts himself. He needed me alive, despite his threats.'

'Where is he?' Valentina demanded.

'I have no idea!'

'Who is this he? Give me names, anything!'

'Scientist83.' Anderson turned white and threw up over the desk. The smell was putrid, causing Valentina to suspend the interview.

In her office, Valentina got on the phone to Tammy.

'Scientist83, does that mean anything to you?' she asked.

'No, what's this about?' replied Tammy.

'The McGregor case. We believe it's all linked. Anderson said-' Valentina stopped herself, then whispered, 'I shouldn't be telling you this.' She then picked up her voice. 'Anderson told us that someone by the name-tag Scientist83 had been tasking him to carry out various jobs via the Dark Net.'

'I don't know if I should get any more involved. I'm in way over my head, and the other day spooked me.'

'Tammy, I really need your help!'

'Don't you have a department within the force for this type of stuff?'

'I do, yes, but if I'm honest, they're not as good as you. I know you can track this down.' There was a long pause. 'Are you still there, Tammy?'

'Sorry, I am. Just thinking. I'm just not trained for this,' Tammy responded.

'Tammy, people have died! I wouldn't ask you if I didn't need you. I promise to not let you come to any harm.'

Again, there was a long pause followed by a sigh.

'Okay, I'll do it for you, but please don't use my name in any statements or in court. Is that okay?'

Tammy could hear the change from desperation to excitement in Valentina's voice.

'Thank you, Tammy. I really, really appreciate it!'

'Please, just don't make me regret helping you.'

'I won't!' The call ended, and Valentina sat back in her office chair, feeling an element of excitement. She had confidence in Tammy.

Tammy got to work straight away, hunting for Scientist83, trying to discover what connection this person had to Anderson, and so forth. The Dark Net wasn't a place most people would like to visit. Tammy knew all about it due to the capacity of her work, but she had never jumped into the dreaded online darkness. The Dark Net was a routed allocated IP space that didn't run any services. It was a place to access illegal sites and services.

She set up a virtual private network to protect her identity on the internet, then downloaded a Tor browser that would find the illegal sites, because Google just wouldn't cut it. Tammy was then able to explore the dark depths of the internet. There were things on there that were beyond her imagination; things that shocked her to the core.

However, it was still like searching for a needle in a haystack. She needed more information, so she made a call back to Valentina.

'Valentina!' The detective's voice was abrupt.

'It's me; Tammy. You okay?'

'Could be better! How can I help you, love?'

'I need more information. I'm on the Dark Net, but I've hit a brick wall.'

'Okay, what information do you need?' Valentina asked.

'The chat site Anderson was on, and if possible, his computer equipment. Any IP addresses link to him?'

There was a pause.

'This could get me into a lot of trouble, but I'm happy to cut corners in order to track down who is responsible.' The call ended with Valentina agreeing to ship the computer equipment over to Tammy, a dodgy but "worth the risk" scenario.

Forty-eight hours later, all of Anderson's computer equipment arrived at Tammy's home address. She was shocked that she actually had evidence for a murder case in her grasp. She was a little excited, as she felt like she had a purpose and was as keen as Valentina to find out who this perpetrator was.

It took Tammy a while to set up all the kit, but once sorted, she was able to bypass the encryption on Anderson's computer. She finally found Black Matter and explored the system.

'That clever, evil bastard,' she muttered to herself as she went through it all.

In the bottom corner of the screen on Anderson's computer, she finally found what she had been looking for – Onionchat, an encrypted Dark Net chat site.

Logging in was easy, as Anderson foolishly had auto login enabled. The page loaded to over twenty chat logs. The one that caught Tammy's eye was Scientist83. The chat log had been saved and had been going on for pages and pages. She converted the log to PDF and sent it to her printer. Reading through, it was clear that this Scientist83 was in control and was willing to pay Anderson for *Black Matter* once he had proved it worked, which it did. Tammy decided to make contact posing as Anderson.

Tammy: "Hello?"

There was a long pause of about thirty minutes, then Scientist83 came online.

Scientist83: "You're not following the rules."
Tammy: "What do you mean?"

Scientist83: *"You're not meant to contact me at all."*
Tammy: *"Sorry, I just wanted to chat."*
Scientist83: *"Chat?"*
Tammy: *"Yes, about my payment?"*
Sceintist83: *"Work isn't yet complete."*
Tammy: *"But I've proved the system is working."*
Scientist83: *"One more job. I need you to kill one more person for me."*
Tammy: *"Ok?"*
Scientist83: *"Tammy Bezuidenhout."*
Scientist83: ***IS NOW OFFLINE***

Tammy sat back, and her heart pounded in her chest as she saw her name appear on the screen.

'Why me?' she said out loud. Tears of fear rolled down her cheeks. She was confused as to why this person, Scientist83, wanted her dead. In a panic, without considering the time, she called Valentina.

'This had better be good!' Valentina opened the call.

'I need your help!' Tammy was hysterical, causing Valentina to jerk up in her bed.

'With what, Tammy?'

'They want me dead!' She was screaming down the phone and could hardly get her words out.

'Tammy, calm down! No one is going to hurt you. Take deep breaths.'

'I need you here, now! Come quick, please!'

'Tell me who is after you?' asked Valentina.

'Scientist83. I was posing as Anderson.'

'What have you done, Tammy?'

'I'm sorry! I was trying to help.'

'Get in your car and drive to a hotel. Call me from the reception phone when you get there. Do not use your mobile and make sure you leave it at home,' Valentina ordered.

'Okay....' Tammy replied, hanging up her phone with trembling hands.

23

The Radisson Blue Bristol was a plush four-star hotel. Tammy had dined in the restaurant a couple of times but had never stayed there. Wheeling her Cath Kidston holdall by her side, she approached the reception desk and checked in for three nights, optimistic that whatever was happening would be over by then.

Her suite was as expected; large glass wardrobes, separate lounge and study area, and a luxury bathroom area. Still, it wasn't as nice as her own home, but it would do. Tammy loved her home. She had worked hard for years to build it up to what it was now. Having a maniac forcing her to leave her home didn't sit right with her, giving her a constant nauseous feeling in the pit of her stomach.

In an attempt to relax, she ordered a bottle of red, made herself comfortable on the bed and flicked through the available channels on the wall-mounted TV. There was a film just starting; a comedy about two people who had a drunken one-night stand and the woman fell pregnant. The couple were complete polar opposites. Tammy found it comical and it helped her to switch off. She was able to put all the adversity she was experiencing in her life to sleep for the time being.

Towards the end of the film, her eyes became heavy, but she tried to fight the urge to go to sleep. Fear of sleeping put her in a vulnerable position, but eventually the fatigue got the better of her, causing her to dose off. She fell into a peaceful sleep.

After a few hours, Tammy awoke suddenly. The room was partially dark with a radiant blue glow coming from the TV screen where the movie had finished. There was a gentle tapping noise, causing the hairs on her arms to stand on end. She lost her breath as the thought crossed her mind that Scientist83 had found her. *You're paranoid*, she thought to herself, trying to provide a sense of self reassurance.

There was more tapping, only this time louder. This time, Tammy realised it was coming from the door to her room. There was someone outside the door. Was it Scientist83, room service? Combinations of scenarios played with her mind. She immediately jumped out of bed and threw on a pair of jeans and a jumper, followed by a pair of trainers she had packed. Fully dressed, she was ready to investigate the noise.

As she slowly tiptoed towards the door, the tapping increased in number from four to five. She looked through the viewing hole in the door, but there was no one there. She looked again, questioning whether her eyes were playing tricks on her following the bottle of red.

The tapping came again, causing her to jump back. Tammy, too scared to open the door, hovered on the safe side, unsure of what to do. She cast her eyes around the hotel room. There was a phone on the side under the TV. She walked over, picked up the receiver and listened. There was nothing; no dial tone. Frantically, Tammy pressed all the buttons in an attempt to bring the phone to life, but her attempts proved to be ineffective.

The tapping came again, and she rushed to the door, looking through the viewing hole, which once again revealed nothing.

'Who is it?' Tammy asked, her voice broken with fear. She waited, but there was no response. 'Who's there please?' she asked again.

'Me!' said the soft, sweet voice of a little girl.

Tammy opened the door quickly, as she loved children. She assumed that the child was lost and looking for the room of her parents.

In the doorway stood a cute blonde girl, dressed in a school uniform, about six or seven years old. Tears were streaming down her face as her eyes fixated on Tammy. Sorrow was apparent within the girl's big green eyes, and she blinked her eyelids, sending more tears rolling down her face.

'What's your name, little girl?' Tammy crouched down to the girl's eye level, attempting to diffuse any form of intimidation.

'Jeska,' the girl replied through a trembling bottom lip.

'What's wrong, Jeska?' asked Tammy, speaking softly whilst reaching out to wipe the child's eyes and to dry the stream of sorrow pouring from them.

'It's my daddy; he's gone!' Her sobs were heart-wrenching for Tammy.

'What room number are you looking for, sweetheart?'

'I don't know what you mean?' Jeska replied.

'The room number your dad is in? Do you know it?' Tammy asked gently.

'Daddy and mummy's room. I can't think of a number.' She stepped forwards, seeking comfort from Tammy, throwing her arms around her and squeezing as tightly as she could.

Tammy returned the comfort, but not as hard. 'Okay, shall I take you down to reception? They can help find your daddy for you.'

'Yes please,' Jeska replied, her voice sweet with an element of relief.

Tammy gently held Jeska's hand, pulling the door to her room closed, then they made their way down to the reception in the lift.

The doors opened to the main reception, but the place was deserted with no one around. The main doors were locked and the lights were out, apart from a few spotlights faintly illuminating the area.

Tammy searched the front desk, looking for a bell or something to notify a member of staff that they required assistance, but there wasn't anything. Tammy then crouched again, so that her eyes were level with Jeska's.

'I'm not sure what to do sweetheart. There's no one here.'

'I need my daddy! He's gone!' Her eyes darkened this time, giving out anger and annoyance aimed towards Tammy.

'Sweetheart, you can stay in my room until we find someone. I promise to look after you,' Tammy offered.

'No! I want my daddy, and he's gone! It's all your fault!'

'I'm trying to help you, my darling. I didn't make him go away. We will find him, don't you worry.'

'I want my daddy!' Jeska screamed, giving out an ear-piercing high pitched cry.

'He'll be here somewhere. We will find him. Try to calm down.'

'It's all your fault! He's dead, and it's you! You did it!'

Tammy froze in disbelief at the words this little angel was saying. Jeska's face was red with upset, and she tried to pull away from Tammy, but Tammy kept hold of her hand tightly, not wanting her to run off.

'You need to stay with me until we find someone. I promise, I didn't hurt anyone,' Tammy said.

'You did, you did, you did, you did!' Jeska repeated the same words over and over.

Tammy became frightened as a result of the words, concerned that this little girl was blaming her for her daddy's death.

'I promise you, it wasn't me. He's here, okay? Let's go back to my room, and I'll make you a hot chocolate?'

Jeska went silent, and her face paled as fear and upset caused the blood to drain from her. Tammy then stood from her crouched position and walked Jeska back towards the lifts. They both got in a lift, and Tammy pressed the button for floor twelve.

Tammy stood staring ahead, not wanting to say anything else in case she upset the girl further. She didn't want to cause her any more distress. "Floor Twelve" said a polite robotic female voice as they reached their floor. Tammy looked down and the girl was gone, nowhere to be seen. Frantically, she looked around the small area of the lift. The little girl had disappeared.

'Jeska!' Tammy called out with a whisper, not wanting to alarm the girl or anyone else. There was no response. She peered out of the lift doors just as they were closing again, and they instantly reopened with the obstruction of Tammy's top half.

'Jeska darling,' she called again. There was nothing. The place was deadly silent.

The lift lights began to flicker, causing Tammy to jump and step out without realising. The doors closed, then the lift left the floor. Tammy looked up at the blue floor counter. The lift was moving up. She pressed the lift call button rapidly, trying to bring it back and praying that Jeska would reappear when it returned.

Within a matter of minutes, the lift came back. There was a "ding" and the doors opened. Jeska stood there, the light above still flickering. Tammy reached into the lift and took hold of her hand, gently pulling her out.

'Where did you go?' Tammy was confused at what had just happened.

'I'm here! I want my daddy back!'

'Please don't run off, sweetheart. You scared me.'

'Good!' replied Jeska, her eyes black with hatred.

Tammy was confused at the words. Kids are hard work, she thought.

'I hate you, and so does my mummy!' Jeska shouted.

'I don't understand, sweetheart?'

'My daddy's dead because of you! The electronic thing he had in his head is your fault, and someone killed him!'

Tammy looked away completely aghast. Her hands began to tremble, and she felt herself leave her body for a moment at the realisation of Jeska's words. Streams of guilt flowed through her veins as her increased heart beat pumped it into every organ. She was speechless and horrified by the words that had come from this poor little girl. She looked down, and again, Jeska was gone.

Tammy was frozen on the spot. She didn't know what to think, what to do or where to go. She wanted to find Jeska but became scared. She didn't want to face up to the accusations, knowing they might be true. She was confused as to how this little girl would know such a thing.

Minutes passed, and Tammy was still standing in the lift lobby, waiting for something, but she didn't know what. She moved slowly, pressing her back against the wall, sliding down until she sat with her eyes fixed forward. The agony of Jeska's words had injected cortisol into her blood. Tears fell as a result, and she continued to stare ahead. She blinked from the sting of the tears, then closed her eyes.

There was the sound of ringing. Tammy stretched out her body as she awoke. She was in her hotel room, and the bed was warm and comfortable. She opened her eyes. The sun shining through the large windows caused her to squint then rub her sleepy eyes. She turned and reached out to lift the ringing hotel phone next to her bed.

'Morning Miss Bezuidenhout! I hope you slept well?' asked a polite female voice from the other end of the phone.

Tammy gathered her thoughts for a second before replying.

'I did, thank you. How can I help you?' she asked with a broken, sleepy voice.

'There is a visitor in reception for you.'

The words caused Tammy to dart up from her pillow. 'Who?' she asked with worry.

'A detective from South Wales Police.'

Thank God, thought Tammy.

'Are you okay to send her up to my room please?' The relief was evident in her voice.

'Of course, Miss Bezuidenhout. I'll send her up right away.'

'Thank you.' Tammy placed the phone back onto the receiver, checking the time to find that it was only 9.00am. She laid her head back down onto the soft, fresh pillow, gathering her thoughts.

There was a knock at the door with a one, two, three. Tammy climbed from her bed, wearing a pair of jogging bottoms and a kitten pyjama top. She quickly brushed her bed hair using her fingers and wiped the sleep from her eyes as she walked towards the door and opened it.

'You were meant to call me when you got here. I had to trace your debit card in order to find you. I was extremely worried about you! You okay?' asked Valentina as she walked into the hotel room. 'This is nice,' she exclaimed, looking around the room.

'I'm so sorry. My head's all over the place!'

'That's understandable. How are you feeling?' asked Valentina, concern written all over her face.

'I'm okay, thanks. Been having strange dreams though. This whole thing is affecting me more than I realised,' Tammy said, thinking about her dream about the little girl.

'That's understandable,' Valentina nodded.

'Can I make you a drink?' asked Tammy as she switched the kettle on.

'Sure, just a black coffee, please.'

'Have you got anything on Scientist83?' Tammy spoke fast in her worry-stricken state.

'Unfortunately, no, but we are working on it. We do have reason to believe that the instigator of this case works for Medi Corps.' Valentina took her coffee from Tammy's hand and sat on a sofa, with Tammy following suit.

'What makes you think that?' asked Tammy.

'Anderson,' Valentina collected her thoughts. 'He explained to us that Scientist83 mentioned some time ago that he works for a large well-known organisation. He didn't say the company name, but he did say that the company developed a life-changing medical product.'

Tammy shifted on the sofa. 'I see.' She looked puzzled.

'We have officers on their way down to Medi Corps to start an investigation,' Valentina informed.

'Okay, that's a little concerning. I know nearly everyone in that building, and for the life of me, I can't think of anyone with that kind of intent.'

'That's because you're a nice person, Tammy. But trust me when I say, a lot of people have a dark side. The world is full or sociopaths, psychopaths and not so PC... fucked up individuals.'

Tammy gave a little nervous smile. 'Is there anything you want me to do?'

'No, nothing. Stay here and relax. I'd recommend that you don't go outside.' Valentina gave her a look of sympathy.

'Hmm, that sounds like fun! Can I ask a favour?'

'Of course, considering everything you've done for me. I would say I owe you the world!'

Tammy smiled again. 'Don't be silly, I just need a tablet. If I give you my card, can you get me an iPad or something. I'll go out of my mind sitting here doing nothing, especially with all the dross they have on TV these days.'

Valentina glanced over with suspicion. 'What for?'

'Oh, just so I can download some books and films, nothing else.' Tammy looked away after her sentence.

Valentina picked up on the body language. 'You cannot start any more work on this case. I'll get you an iPad, but you have to promise me it's for entertainment purposes only.'

'Of course, I promise,' Tammy replied, doing a scouts honour sign with her hand.

Valentina gave her another look of suspicion but let it slide. 'Okay, give me your card. What's your PIN?'

'One, eight, four, six,' Tammy said, passing her debit card over.

On her way to the electrical store, Valentina walked past a cash machine. Something was playing on her mind. A gut feeling was nagging at her, urging her to just check the balance of Tammy's account. She loaded the debit card into the machine, keyed in the PIN and waited for the machine to load the relevant information.

Staring back at Valentina was a bank balance she never thought she would see in her life; a life-changing amount. Tammy never has to work again! How does she have so much money? Valentina thought, not realising that Tammy was actually a millionaire.

24

'Nice to see you again, Tommy. How are you feeling?' asked Valentina as Tommy sat his skinny body down onto the hard, plastic chair in interview room two at Swansea Prison's visitor centre.

'Been better! You here to give me some good news?' asked Tommy weakly. His skin was pale, his eyes were bloodshot, and he had sores around his mouth.

'Depends what you consider as good news.' Valentina leaned forwards, talking with a whisper. 'I'm going to be candid, Tommy. You look like absolute shit.'

She sat back in her chair, waiting for his response. He looked at her, his eyes filled with sorrow and sadness. Something wasn't right. This place was killing him. Prison can do that to an innocent man.

'I know.' Tommy turned his face away as his eyes begin to fill with tears. He fought them back, as he didn't want to cry in front of Valentina, but he lost his strength, and began to sob.

Valentina stood, walked around the desk and placed a hand on Tommy's shoulder as he hunched forwards, crying into his forearms resting on the table.

'I can't take it in here anymore! I want to die, but I can't even do that properly. This place is torture! You've got to get me out of here!' He raised his head and turned to Valentina. She felt a little on edge. 'Please, you've got to get me out of here.'

She gently rubbed his shoulder a little more, then moved back around and took her seat.

'Tommy, what's happened to you to make you like this?' Valentina asked.

'It's the others here. They do things to me; beat me, spit at me, and other stuff.' He was looking down as he spoke, his shame obvious.

'What other stuff?'

'You know, you see it all the time.' Tommy was still unable to look up.

'I don't know, Tommy. Can you please elaborate. Look at me.' His eyes slowly met with hers. 'If you tell me, I can help you. I can make it go away, but you have to be open with me.' Valentina gave him a nod of reassurance.

Tommy stood, his fists clenched, as though he was ready for a fight. Whatever thoughts were going through his mind, he was reliving them now. He grabbed the chair and launched it across the room. A guard rushed in to restrain Tommy, but Valentina intervened and placed her palm on Tommy's chest, which was heaving with his heavy breathing. Tommy slowly calmed down.

'Stand back, ma'am,' insisted the guard.

'No, I can handle it.' Valentina positioned herself as a barrier between the two.

'Ma'am, I need you to move, please. You are interfering with prison procedures. McGregor needs to be restrained and returned to his cell immediately.'

Valentina looked at the guard, then back at Tommy, who was seething through his teeth with his eyes looking through his brow.

'You're not going to do that again are you, Tommy?' Valentina looked him deep in the eyes, gesticulating as she spoke.

Tommy looked at the guard, slowly shaking his head, confirming Valentina's words. The guard admitted defeat.

'Then sit your arse down, McGregor. Act like that again, and I'll have to put you to the ground!'

Tommy moved to collect his thrown chair and sat back down without saying a word. Valentina then followed suit. Just as her backside touched the seat, the guard made a move for Tommy, tackling him straight to the floor, then tied his hands behind his back.

'Get up!' the guard bellowed as he pulled Tommy to his feet.

'I told you I had it sorted!' shouted Valentina. 'There was no need for that!'

'It's standard procedure. I had no choice.'

'I asked you not to,' Valentina stated.

'You can ask me till you're blue in the face, but procedure is procedure. If I didn't restrain him after that action and he then harmed you, who they gonna look at?'

Valentina knew the guard was right in what he was saying, but she couldn't help feeling somewhat protective over Tommy.

The guard pulled Tommy from the room, and Valentina called after them, 'Wait!' They both halted.

'Tommy, I'll be back in a few days, okay, and we'll talk some more. Keep your head strong and I'll see you soon.'

Tommy gave a little smile, which Valentina returned, then she looked to the floor. *I'm getting too emotionally involved here,* she thought to herself as she walked back to her car, but she couldn't help feeling that she had a duty towards Tommy with the information she had.

Back in his cell, Tommy was shaken up from the meeting. He sat on his bunk with his knees pulled tight to his chest, thinking, hating the world, hating his world and what it had become.

He felt a pain and an itch. He was sore from sitting, so he stood and moved towards the toilet in the corner. He dampened some toilet paper, then pulled his joggers down, placing the damp paper on his back passage to try and soothe the wound. It stung, so he removed the paper and looked at it. The toilet paper was soaked with dark blood. He took some more paper and pressed it hard against him to try and stop the bleeding. He needed medical assistance but was too ashamed to come forward about the damage caused by Killroy and his mates.

25

Valentina had been informed that she was not to be involved in the planned raid, following a tipoff about where Roberts was possibly being held. She was too close to Roberts to be within the vicinity, in case their worst fears were confirmed. It was Valentina's wellbeing that they had in mind, but, of course, Valentina herself had fought this. She wanted to be there, but the powers that be had ensured that Valentina got the message.

DI Alex Wright was to take over for this particular incident, with Valentina waiting on the end of a phone ready for the verdict; dead or alive, if found at all. For the team, tension was high as they prepared to raid the property where they believed Roberts was being held.

DI Wright was a highly experienced detective, with over thirty years of service under his belt. He was tall and trim with rugged features; a man not to be taken lightly. Wright stood tall facing his team, ready to give the briefing on what was about to go down. Valentina reluctantly took a back seat.

'WE' Wright pronounced with exaggeration, 'all know why we are here. One of our own has been taken.' His voice propelled across the room, hitting the back wall, while his eyes scanned over the thirty officers sat facing him. 'Detective Constable Roberts.' A portrait of Roberts was displayed on a screen behind Wright. He pointed at the portrait. 'It's our job to ensure we bring him back.' He paused, taking his time, making sure everyone was listening. 'There's an abandoned farmhouse, here.' He used the cursor on his screen to highlight the area. 'It's just off Leckwith Road. I'm sure you are all familiar with the area? Any questions before I continue?'

The officers looked around at one another. No questions.

'Good! So, Team Bravo will gather at this section,' he used the cursor again to point, 'with Team Alpha here. Standard house clearance procedures, ladies and gentlemen, and please remember our firearms protocol.' He looked around the room. 'I don't want the paperwork that would follow if someone decides to get trigger happy, seeking revenge for Roberts.' He stared intently at a few officers who were close to Roberts. 'You know who I'm talking about. Keep it a clean in-and-out operation. Just to prepare you all, we believe Roberts has been murdered, so bear that in mind when searching.' Wright continued with the brief.

Valentina sat at the back, her palms sweaty. She wanted to be involved but understood why she couldn't be. Hearing the brief relating to the possible murder of a colleague and friend was a hard pill to swallow. She promised herself she would allow herself time to grieve once this was over and they had caught whoever was responsible.

She fought the tears that teased the ducts in her eyes, trying to maintain her composure. Anger filled her veins like a virus, with sadness tagging along behind. Her thoughts went out to Roberts's poor wife and unborn child; the child he had always wanted, who would never get to kiss their daddy or see him smile and laugh. She squeezed her eyes tight, pushing away the thoughts, but it was impossible not to cry.

The ground around the farm was wet and boggy, but luckily the sky was clear with the sun trying to peer over the horizon, casting a morning glow across south Wales at 07.00am. The farm smelled fresh, but there was the scent of smoke in the air from a nearby fire, presumably from another farm.

Team Alpha got into position at the front of the farmhouse. From the outside, the house appeared to be empty. The front gate was closed and there was a black cat outside, purring and rubbing itself up against the gatepost. The front garden was overgrown, with the path barely visible from the weeds. The house was derelict, with smashed windows, fallen roof tiles and ivy climbing the walls in a rough attempt at decoration. There was a small square window in the centre of the wooden front door, and the green paint on the door was flaking.

Team Bravo gathered at the rear of the farmhouse. The back yard contained a fallen, rusty, corrugated garage and there was a deteriorating, clapped-out old Peugeot 106 sitting on bricks. The back of the house was built from red bricks. There were two windows at the top and two at the bottom, with an old wooden door in the centre, which had a cat flap built in at the bottom.

The teams were on standby, ready for the green light to enter the building. Anticipation built whilst they waited for their orders from Wright, who was crouching behind a hedge near the front gate with two armed police officers inches in front. He radioed over to the look-out patrols to ensure that there were no members of public nearby, then he gave the green light. 'Go, go, go!' he shouted over the radio.

Team Alpha stormed the front of the house. 'Armed police!' they shouted as the brittle door gave way with one kick from a police-issue boot.

Downstairs was searched within a matter of seconds.

'Kitchen clear!'

'Front room one clear!'

'Front room two clear!'

'All of ground floor clear!'

Then the dreaded confirmation could be heard over the radio. 'First floor front room one, confirm, we have a body.'

Whilst Wright investigated the front room on the first floor, the rest of the house was searched and the entire house and grounds were contained.

The room on the first floor was humid and muggy from the rotting body that had been found. Blue bottles were buzzing loudly as they hovered around the body. The smell was rank and putrid mixed with a hint of sickening sweetness. The body was sitting in a wooden chair, which was straining to take the dead weight, and the head of the body was bowed. A blood-soaked shirt clung to the corpse, and a large dark red patch circled the chair.

Wright knew straight away that it was Roberts. He looked up at the ceiling, closed his eyes and said a little prayer for Roberts's poor wife and unborn child, promising to find whoever had done this. He looked back over at Roberts, fought the emotion that was climbing up his insides, then turned and exited the room, unable to stand another second in there. It was time for CSI to do their job, whilst Wright handed back over to Valentina.

Wright stepped outside, pulled out his mobile and made a call to Valentina, as he promised he would as soon as he had any information.

'Valentina,' she answered with a tremble in her voice.

'It's me. You okay?' Wright didn't sound himself, and Valentina knew instantly what the verdict was.

'With the greatest respect, Wright, spare me any small talk,' Valentina demanded.

'I'm sorry, V. It's Roberts.' There was silence on the other end as Valentina took in the bad news. 'You still there, V?' Wright asked. He could almost hear her broken heart through the phone without her saying anything. There was no reply. 'V, please, just take a moment, and call me when you are ready.'

'Okay,' Valentina replied with a whisper as she ended the call, not wanting to talk, as she needed to process what had happened.

Valentina sat in her office at Cardiff Bay station, crying and holding a photo that Roberts had kept on his desk of himself and his wife. They looked so happy. The photo was filled with their white smiles, and their eyes were full of love for one another. They were only 17 when they had met and had been together ever since. Valentina felt the pain but realised that it was not a smidgen on what his family would be feeling.

Roberts had been a caring, kind man, who had devoted his life to the force and his family. His big heart had touched many lives during his career, with the number of lives he'd saved and the justice he'd given to many victims. He was a man who would never be forgotten and would always hold a place in Valentina's heart.

Valentina pulled out a cigarette and sparked up, not caring that she was within the office; something Roberts had hated but tolerated. 'I know you'd hate this,' she said and gave a little chuckle with a side of sadness.

Back at the crime scene, Wright's team were combing the entire house, with forensics taking sample after sample, and bags of evidence being loaded into the back of the van. It was confirmed that there had been a lot of traffic through the house, so the team prayed that there would be a lead.

The BBC and other media organisations swarmed the area outside the farmhouse, with officers marginally keeping them at bay. Wright was required to inform the public of their findings and reluctantly stepped forwards. Cameras flashed, and there was a large BBC camera only metres from his face. They all fell silent as they waited for the information. Knowing the news feed was live, Wright wasn't able to confirm the name of the victim, as Roberts's family were still unaware of their findings and needed to be informed first.

'It is with deep regret that I have to inform you that we have found the body of an officer of South Wales Police. The death is being treated as suspicious, and I ask that you respect the family of the concerned. I cannot confirm the name of the officer at present, but I can assure you all that South Wales Police will be pursuing this horrific crime through to the end, and we will leave no stone unturned.'

Wright paused to compose himself, not wanting to get carried away as his emotions began to take hold. Being live, he could not say the wrong thing.

'An official police statement will follow shortly. That is all for now.' He took in a shuddering breath as he turned his back to the cameras and the cacophony of journalists shouting questions. Wright ignored them and slowly walked off, placing himself in the back of one of the vans to gather his thoughts.

Valentina's phone rang, and she ignored it, not wanting to answer. However, the moment it stopped ringing, it started again. She looked at the display; it was Annette, Roberts's wife. *She's seen the news! She knows! Fuck, she knows! Why does it have to be me that has to break the news to her?* Valentina thought as her phone screen flashed, begging her to answer the call. *I can't! I can't be the one to tell you!* Her emotions pulled on her heart strings. She didn't want to answer. She didn't want to be the one to deliver the sad news. She ignored the calls, then received the notification of a voicemail.

"I know it's him! Please call me. The pain is killing me! I don't want to wait for Family Liaison. I want to hear it from you!"

The sound of Annette's voice and the heartbreak within her tone caused Valentina to break down. She took a moment to gather her composure, then returned the call.

'Annette, I'm so sorry I missed your calls.' Valentina couldn't camouflage her cries.

'It's my Daniel, isn't it?' Annette asked despairingly. Valentina had no words. 'Just fucking tell me!' screamed Annette.

'I'm so, so sorry! I'm sorry!'

Annette hung up with the confirmation she needed. Valentina buried her head into her arms on her desk, her breathing becoming uncontrollable. Suddenly, there was a knock at her office door.

'Not now!' Valentina shouted.

The door opened anyway. It was the chief constable. 'We need to chat,' he stated.

'Please, can you give me a minute?' Valentina raised her head from her arms. Her eyes were bloodshot, her face was mottled, and her hair clung to her damp cheeks.

The chief walked in and closed the door, taking a seat opposite Valentina at her desk. He was calm and collected, oozing sympathy. 'I know this is a difficult time, V-.'

Valentina cut him short. 'You're telling me! Please, I don't want to talk at the moment!'

'I'm still your commanding officer, V. I want to talk to you.'

She sat up in her chair with anger on her face, knowing he wouldn't be going anywhere. 'I'm sorry, I'm finding it hard to come to terms with all this.'

'I understand. That's why I'm taking you off the McGregor case. You're too emotionally involved now.'

Valentina slammed her fists down hard on the desk, but the chief didn't flinch. 'NO! I want to see it through to the end!

Please don't do this to me!' Tears trickled down her face as she spoke.

'I'm sorry, V. I need you to take some time off.' He nodded at her, making it clear that it was a command. 'Okay?'

'Please don't do this!'

'I'm sorry, V. It's my job to look after you. Go home. I don't want to see you around here for at least two weeks, and then we'll chat.' He was stern again, but with sympathy.

Valentina respected him and understood what he was doing, but she simply couldn't step down from the case. 'If you pull me off the case, then you can accept my resignation.' Anger pushed the words from her mouth.

'Just go home, V, please. I will not accept any form of resignation. You are too emotional. Come and see me in a couple of weeks, and we will talk then.'

Valentina stood. 'No, fuck you! I've just lost a dear friend! I want to seek justice for him, and if you pull me off the case, I'm done! I mean it!' She glared at him. She had never barked at him like that in her entire career.

'Easy now, V. I will let that one slide, given the circumstances. I mean it, go home. We will talk soon.'

Valentina walked past him, slowly placing her badge on her desk in front of him and walked out of the office. The chief sat for a moment, staring at her badge, then shook his head.

26

Tammy watched the news feed intently on the TV in her hotel room. Tears filled her eyes, as she knew full well that it was Roberts that had been found murdered. Sitting on the hotel bed in a white dressing gown, she sipped her morning coffee, and all she could think about was Valentina and how she must have been feeling.

There was a knock at the door, and she slid off the bed, going to look through the viewing hole before quickly opening the door.

'I was just thinking about you.' Tammy looked at Valentina's face, which was engulfed with sadness. She threw her arms around Valentina and whispered in her ear. 'I'm so sorry.'

Valentina squeezed Tammy with her trembling body. 'I didn't know where to go. I couldn't bear to be at home on my own.'

Tammy ran her hands down Valentina's back, gently rubbing her for comfort. 'Let it out,' she whispered in return. They then moved from the doorway and closed the door.

'Coffee?' asked Tammy.

'Please, with a drop of something stronger, if you have anything?'

Tammy smiled, collecting a whisky miniature from the minibar and pouring a small amount into Valentina's coffee.

'Why come here, if you don't mind me asking?' Tammy sat on the sofa next to Valentina.

'In my line of work, you don't make many friends. To be honest, you're the only person I wanted to see.'

Tammy was flattered, being in the same boat and not really having anyone. 'Well, I'm flattered DI.'

'Please, call me V. The small number of friends I do have all call me that.'

Tammy smiled. 'Well, I'm flattered.'

'I miss Roberts,' Valentina said solemnly. 'He was my only close friend, and now the Chief Constable has removed me from the case, so I've quit.'

Tammy raised her eyebrows in surprise. 'Really? Surely you can't mean that?'

'I do. I can't do this job anymore. It's too much!'

'Well, V, don't do anything rash. I'm sure it's just the emotion taking over.'

Valentina shook her head. 'No, I really can't.' She slurped her coffee, flinching at the shot of whisky as it tickled her throat, forgetting she'd asked for it. She then turned and looked at Tammy. 'It's me and you now.'

'What do you mean?' Tammy asked.

'We're going to work together and find out who's behind all this.' Valentina gave off an air of confidence, but Tammy was not so sure as she shifted on the sofa.

'Oh, I don't know,' said Tammy.

'I'll take full accountability. You will not be associated with this, you have my word.' Valentina took another sip of her coffee.

'I do trust you, V. I'm just not sure.'

'Tammy, I promise you, there will be no come back on you. I need your help. You can say no of course, but I need to seek justice for Roberts. Without you, the whole case will fold.'

'What do you need me to do?' asked Tammy sheepishly.

'Track down Scientist83, give me all the evidence, and I'll take it from there. I'll get you all the kit you need to achieve this and will support you throughout.' Valentina nodded as she spoke.

Tammy smiled. 'Okay, but I have one condition?'

'Go on?' Valentina was confident she'd be able to fulfil the deal.

'You stay with me until it's over. I mean, I can't be on my own. I'm a nervous wreck as it is!' Tammy stared into her coffee.

'I can do that! We'll work from here,' Valentina suggested. 'I'll nip home and get some basics. Write out a list of what you need, and I'll pick them up.'

Tammy was relieved that Valentina had agreed to stay with her. She was not trained for this and appreciated the company, feeling more comfortable knowing that Valentina would be with her.

Hours later, Valentina returned. She squared the bill with reception and upgraded the room to a suite, so that they could both have separate bedrooms. They moved rooms to the seventh floor and set up all the equipment to get started - no time like the present.

'Where do you want me to start?' asked Tammy.

'See if you can get him to communicate with you.'

They logged onto the Dark Net and, using Anderson's profile, they made contact with Scientist83.

Anderson: *"What's next?"*

The system showed Scientist83 as being offline. However, they waited patiently for his reply.

'What if he knows Anderson has been arrested?' asked Tammy, turning to Valentina.

'That won't be possible, don't worry.'

'What if he still wants me dead?' Tammy's eyes widened as her mind processed these thoughts.

'If he does, then we will deal with it. You are safe, I promise.' Valentina rubbed Tammy's back to provide reassurance.

'Okay.' Tammy took a deep breath, then noticed that Scientist83 had come online.

Scientist83: is now typing...

Tammy could feel a small amount of sweat starting to bead on her forehead. It felt like hours as they waited to see the message that he was typing.

Scientist83: "You know what!"

Anderson: "What? Payment?" Tammy used the fact that money was owed as the incentive to contact him.

Scientist83: "You will get your money once you've completed the last task, as I have requested!"

Anderson: "What task?"

They both knew what the task was, but they needed him to say it again, so it could be logged as evidence. Everything was being logged and captured. The wait was long as Scientist83 paused before replying. Anticipation built as they waited.

Scientist83 is now typing...

Again, it felt like hours passing them by as they waited for the words to come up on the screen. The sweat on Tammy's forehead became more apparent.

Scientist83: "Remove DI Valentina."
*Scientist83: **IS NOW OFFLINE***

They both looked at one another, and Tammy was the first to speak.

'It was me the other day, now he's switched to you?' Her voice was low.

'That's okay, let him try.' Valentina was not phased by her name coming up on the screen.

'Doesn't it bother you? asked Tammy.

'Not at all! He's either playing with us or genuinely wants me dead. Either way, I will be meeting this person face to face.'

'Aren't you scared?'

'I'm terrified, but I have to seek justice for Roberts. If the only way to find out who's behind this is by using me as bait, then so be it.' Valentina tried to look brave, but Tammy could see through the facade.

'So, what do we do now?' Tammy asked.

'Can you track him?'

'I'll try, but he's most probably on a VPN. There is one way, but it's going to be a tough one.'

'Which is?' asked Valentina.

'Through Anderson.'

'No chance. I'll never get near him in my current situation. There's got to be another way.'

'I'll try,' said Tammy, turning away and focusing on the screen. 'I need my own laptop. It's got my tracking software on it.' She looked at Valentina. 'You'll need to go to my place. Do you mind?'

'Not at all. Where will it be?' Valentina asked.

'In my office. Go through the front door, turn left through the kitchen, then head towards the back. The door is locked, but this is the key.' Tammy held out a bunch of keys. 'And this one is for the front door. The alarm code is one eight one eight.'

Valentina nodded and set off to find Tammy's laptop.

The alarm panel beeped as Valentina entered Tammy's home. She punched in the digits, disabling the alarm instantly, then followed Tammy's instructions. The place smelled empty, like that noticeable smell when you first get back from a holiday. Her footsteps echoed on the kitchen floor as she treaded through towards the back of the house.

There was a strange noise, and Valentina froze on the spot to listen. She heard it again, this time causing a cold shiver to cascade down her spine, as she had the feeling that someone was watching her. She began to move quickly through the house, found the office and fumbled with the key to unlock the door, not remembering which key it was.

Eventually, she found the right key, turned the lock and went into the plush office. Tammy's laptop was sitting there on her oak desk. *What a lovely place to work,* Valentina thought. Then another sound broke the silence, causing her to flinch. The knowledge that someone wanted her dead had quite rightly put her on edge. She started to move quickly again, locking the office door behind her and making her way back through the kitchen.

The hairs on her arms stood on end as a shadow crossed her peripheral vision. She gasped, turning her head in the direction, but there was nothing there. Moving again, she headed for the front door, feeling panic-stricken. She couldn't press the numbers to set the alarm and gave up, managing to lock the door behind her.

Back in her car, Valentina exhaled, taking a moment to regain her composure. She looked over at the house and could see a light on, although she couldn't remember having touched any lights. She argued with her conscience about whether to re-enter the house to investigate or to just leave it. Looking up at the house again, she noticed the light was now off. Her conscience won, and she decided she couldn't just leave it. The police officer in her urged her to check it out.

Valentina treaded carefully up the path towards the front door, inserted the key into the lock and re-entered Tammy's house. The feeling that someone was watching hit her instantly, and she shivered.

'Is there anyone there?' Valentina shouted. 'I am Detective Inspector Valentina from South Wales Police. If there is anyone here, please come forward.'

She listened for movement, but there was nothing. She spotted the stairs, that curved upwards to the first floor. Suddenly, the light flicked on and she jumped, but edged forwards cautiously.

'I repeat, this is South Wales Police!' Valentina took baby steps towards the stairs, looking up, then placing her foot on the first step, slowly making her way to the top. The stairs opened out onto a large landing area. The spot lights felt warm as they pointed downwards onto her face. She moved slowly across the landing. There was another noise from a room at the end of the corridor with the door slightly ajar.

'Who's there? Show yourself?' she demanded, the back of her neck tickled as her nerves were electrified with fear.

Valentina stepped into the room, and the light went on without her touching the switch, causing her to jump. There was a large bed in the centre of the room. She checked behind the door, but there was no one there. The noise could be heard again, and she worked out that it was coming from under the large bed.

On one knee, Valentina crouched down and peered underneath. Two eyes stared back at her, watching her with suspicion. Then a chocolate coloured cat slinked out from under the bed, purring against her.

Her body relaxed immediately, relieved it was only a cat. She looked up at the light and realised that the lights were all on a PIR system. More relief followed and Valentina stroked the cat, which returned the enjoyment with a purr.

Valentina casually left the house, setting the alarm and getting into her car. She turned over the engine and looked ahead, only to be confronted by a large, broad figure staring directly towards her with a black balaclava covering their face.

Valentina's fight or flight response kicked in, and she hit the gas. The car propelled forwards towards the figure, causing them to jump out of the path of her car seconds before impact. Then Valentina was gone.

Tammy jumped as Valentina burst into the hotel room, catching her breath.

'What's wrong?' asked Tammy.

'He was there,' Valentina replied with breathlessness.

Tammy's hairline shifted with surprise. 'Who?'

'I think it must have been Scientist83.' Valentina parked herself on the sofa, taking off her shoes.

'What happened?' Tammy looked shocked.

'For starters, you could have mentioned you had a cat! Scared the crap out of me!' By this point Valentina had caught her breath and was able to talk in a more relaxed manner.

'Sorry,' said Tammy, stretching her face. 'That's Whisper. He just does what he wants.'

'Anyway... I left the house, and there he was, standing in front of my car. I just floored it, and he jumped out of the way.' Valentina placed her palm on her forehead. 'I was terrified!'

'I bet you were! Similar thing happened to me not so long ago.' Tammy sat next to Valentina on the sofa.

'Yes, I do remember. He must be watching your house to know that I was there.' Valentina looked at Tammy, but Tammy avoided making eye contact. 'Did you get anywhere?'

'With the system? No, I tried to make contact with Scientist83 again, but he's not been online yet.'

'Okay, did you keep a record of your attempt?' asked Valentina.

'No, sorry, I forgot,' replied Tammy, placing her chin to her neck.

'If we are going to catch him and put him behind bars, it's imperative we log every single communication, okay?' Valentina's tone was stern, trying to get her point across.

'I know, sorry.' Tammy looked sheepish, and Valentina picked up on this.

'You okay?' Valentina asked.

Tammy still avoided eye contact. 'Yeah, of course.' She stood and collected her laptop, taking it over to the desk to begin working on the trace back to Scientist83. Valentina watched her. Tammy turned back and looked at Valentina, seeing that she was watching, and then looked away instantly. Valentina frowned. *Something's not right!* she thought to herself.

27

Cardiff Prison didn't differ too much from Swansea Prison. Anderson had been remanded, but there was a need for him to be transferred to Cardiff Prison due to conflict with the case, as Tommy McGregor was already being held in Swansea.

Anderson laid on his bunk, bored and regretful of ever starting all this nonsense. Nothing was worth incarceration. It was 11.00pm, the lights were out, and snores could be heard from the occupier of the top bunk. A guard passed Anderson's cell, gently tapping on the door to get his attention.

'Some Becks for you,' said the guard, handing him a small plastic cup of beer. Anderson smiled, and the guard looked shiftily from left to right. 'Courtesy of cell fifty-two.'

Anderson looked at the guard with suspicion. 'I don't know anyone in here?' he whispered back.

'Well, apparently you have some supporting fans. Quick take it! You didn't get it from me, okay?' The guard moved swiftly away from the cell.

Anderson sniffed the beer. *It's lager alright,* he thought to himself and swigged it back in one, instantly feeling the warmth in his stomach. He laid back on his bunk, thinking and letting his mind drift to another place.

From the age of twelve, Anderson had some horrific memories. His stepfather had been a horrible man, who was drunk most nights, and was often aggressive and abusive to Anderson's mother. One night, Anderson had been sitting playing on the rug, watching as his mother screamed in fear as she took blows from her husband in his drunken rage. His stepfather had been angry because she hadn't done something or other.

When the abuse had first started, it affected Anderson badly. By the age of twelve, he had become accustomed to it, as though it was the norm; something no twelve-year-old should ever have to witness, let alone become accustomed to.

It was 17th August 1997, a night that Anderson would never forget. He had laid in bed, listening to his Walkman, trying to drown out the sound of the screaming and shouting. A sickly feeling had grabbed hold of his tummy, like a fist, as he tried to take his mind to another place. His bedroom was dark and his eyes were closed when his bedroom door had burst open, the light in the hallway lighting up the room. His stepdad stepped in, and Anderson had watched him through a small gap in his eyelids as he had pretended to be asleep. His bedcovers were pulled from him, causing the cold to hit him as he shrivelled into a ball with his arms covering his face. He could hear his mum shouting something but couldn't hear the words. He'd felt a sudden pain in his back as his stepdad punched him.

'You little shit! When are you going to learn?' his stepdad had shouted. Anderson didn't move. He had tensed his body, absorbing the pain, trying not to yell out. 'I said, when are you going to learn?' his stepdad shouted again. Anderson had rolled off the mattress in fear and scrambled under his bed, trying to get away.

Suddenly, light filled the area as the single wooden bed frame had been thrown across the room. Anderson was now vulnerable and had scrambled to the corner of the room, cowering, terrified of his stepdad.

His stepdad had lurched forwards, planting a size twelve into Anderson's face. He'd screamed in pain and fear, terrified of this large man on a mission to assert control. Another blow had hit his little legs, and Anderson screamed again.

His stepdad had suddenly gulped, his empty eyes staring into Anderson's as he gasped for air, then his dead weight had fallen on top of him. Anderson had squirmed from the weight and had run to another corner of his bedroom. His mum was standing behind his stepdad trembling with fear.

Anderson had looked back at his stepdad laying lifeless on the floor as a large kitchen knife had stood on end, protruding from his back. Anderson screamed and his mum had rushed over to him, cradling him close.

'I'm so sorry, my sweetheart. I'm so, so sorry this has happened to you,' she'd whispered into his ear, kissing his face over and over, and brushing his hair.

Anderson had sobbed his little heart out. Police sirens could he heard and he'd looked up as blinking red and blue lights illuminated his bedroom wall.

'Police!' shouted the policemen as they burst into the bedroom, pulling his mum away from him.

'Mum!' Anderson had shouted, holding out his arms as she was pulled away from him.

'It's okay, my little prince. You'll be safe now,' she'd sobbed as she was moved out of his bedroom.

That was the last time Anderson had ever seen his mum. She had been arrested for the murder of his stepdad and subsequently committed suicide, not being able to cope with the guilt that Anderson had been hurt by a man she had brought into his life.

The soul of the lovely little boy inside Anderson had died that night. He hated the world, hated anyone who tried to be his mum or dad, causing problems throughout his childhood, his schooling years and his adult life. All he wanted to do was make enough money to leave the country, leave his horrendous memories behind and rebuild a form of life. That was why he had built Black Matter.

Anderson was looking down on himself, laying lifeless on his prison bunk. His body looked cold. The poison had peacefully killed him, set up by Scientist83. How he had done it, no one knew.

Anderson drifted away, his soul rising higher and higher, watching the world he had lived in get smaller and smaller. He started moving slowly through a tunnel, towards a soft glow of light ahead of him. He urged himself towards it, feeling pure peace; a feeling he'd never felt before. Anderson heard a voice calling his name; a voice he'd not heard for many years. A beautiful, indescribable smell filled his soul. He felt young again. There was no pain and no adversity. The light grew brighter as he moved closer towards it.

He found himself standing in a place, surrounded by beauty and visions he couldn't even contemplate. He knew he had left the old world behind.

There was a woman walking towards him. She was smiling, and happiness appeared to radiate from her. Anderson reached out, warmth connecting them both. He was twelve again, and love drew them closer.

'Mum!' he said as she grabbed his hand. They moved towards visions of different colours he'd never seen before. He felt peace at last, as they moved into a colourful haze, a new world, a new beginning.

The news of Anderson's murder spread fast, hitting the headlines worldwide. There were investigations to identify how the poison had got into his system, but detectives hit a brick wall quickly with no leads.

Valentina heard the news on the TV. She was shocked, but she knew who was responsible. She needed to work fast to at least get Tommy out before Scientist83 got to him as well.

28

Valentina was suspicious of Tammy, concerned she knew far more than she was letting on. She decided to continue working with Tammy, but was now watching her every move, not letting on about her suspicions.

'Try and set up a meeting with Scientist83. I want to meet him,' said Valentina, now not caring about the danger. All she wanted was to seek justice for Roberts and to give Tommy the freedom he deserved.

'I'll try,' replied Tammy, confused by Valentina's disregard for safety.

'Let's catch this mother fucker!' Valentina exclaimed.

Tammy's eyes widened and she fidgeted in her chair with a sense of uneasiness. 'How do you think I should approach this?' asked Tammy, hesitating to make contact with Scientist83.

'Send him a message informing him that you'll get Valentina for him.' Valentina paused taking a breath. 'Tell him you're going to set me up.' Valentina felt fearful at her own words, but she knew it was the only way.

'B,but what shall I say?' stuttered Tammy.

'What I just said.' Valentina propelled her assertiveness. She dictated to Tammy exactly what to type, telling her to pose as someone who had been working with Anderson on *Black Matter*.

XXwells79: "Hi, I have been working with Anderson. I'm his contingency in case anything happened to him."
Scientist83: "You are?"
XXwells79: "Aaron Wellington."

There was a long pause, and Valentina could feel the nervousness from Tammy as they waited for the response, both knowing how dangerous this was.

Scientist83 is now typing...
Scientist83: "How do I know you are who you say you are?'
Tammy looked back at Valentina, and she instructed Tammy to type exactly what she said word for word.

XXwells79: "I will meet you to give you the software and to show you how to use it at a location you choose and a time you choose. I just want to be done with this, so I can grieve for my friend.'
Scientist83: "Meet me?"

Adrenaline surged through Valentina as she thought to herself, *He took the bait.*

XXwells79: "Where?"
Scientist83: "I'll be in touch. Stay online."
*Scientist83: **IS NOW OFFLINE***

Tammy again looked back at Valentina. 'What are you thinking?' she asked.

'Well, to be honest, I didn't think that far ahead. I wasn't expecting him to take the bait so quickly. He must want this *Black Matter* desperately.' Valentina smiled out of the corner of her mouth. In the back of her mind she was thinking of how to conduct this meeting. She knew she couldn't do it alone.

'True,' said Tammy, limiting her words and creating more suspicion for Valentina. 'So, what now?'

'We wait. Keep an eye on that chat, and I'll make some calls.' Valentina smiled and walked out of the room before Tammy could say anything else.

Valentina stood outside the hotel and made a call to an old friend. He was an ex-Royal Marine and an ex-boyfriend. They had parted purely to further their careers and had always remained friends, staying in touch for the last fourteen years.

'Mike speaking,' he said, answering his phone, his voice deep and precise.

'It's me,' Valentina said.

'Hey V, how are you?' he enquired, letting go of his macho tone.

'Not so good. I need your help!'

'Go for it?' Mike replied.

'Not over the phone. Can you meet me?' Valentina asked.

'I'm in Plymouth. Where are you?'

'Cardiff. I'll come to you tomorrow. Say about ten in the morning?'

'Sure, where?' he asked.

'Church House Inn?' Valentina suggested, as this was a place they used to meet regularly.

'For you babe, I'll be there.' Mike had picked up on Valentina's urgency to meet and realised it must have been important.

'Thank you, Mike. I'll see you tomorrow.'

'It'll be hoofing to see you again!' He hung up.

Mixed feelings ran through Valentina as she cast her mind back to their hot and heavy sexual relationship from many moons ago.

Valentina walked back into the hotel room, and Tammy was watching TV.

'You not keeping an eye on the chat?' Valentina checked.

'I've set a notification, so as soon as he makes contact, we'll know,' Tammy explained.

'Good thinking. I'm going to bed. I've got to head out early tomorrow to meet an old friend.' Valentina walked off into her room.

'An old friend, ey?' said Tammy with a slight cheekiness, trying to hide her concern.

'It's not like that! Purely business.' Valentina closed the door, not wanting to divulge too much information.

The drive to Church House Inn in Devon was a long one. Valentina felt nervous. She'd not seen Mike in years and couldn't help but fret about the feelings that might arise when she saw him.

Valentina was early and ordered herself a black coffee. She wrung her palms together whilst waiting for his arrival, wondering how she was going to ask him to break the law, still knowing full well that he'd do it for her.

Mike walked in bang on time, like a typical Marine, looking buff and as handsome as the day she had met him. Valentina felt slightly intimidated and insecure, feeling that she'd aged during her career as a detective.

'Babe!' Mike shouted in his deep, direct voice. 'So good to see you!'

Valentina held out her hand to shake his, which he completely bypassed, instead going straight for a hug, lifting her off the floor. She felt flustered, feeling a slight flutter. It'd been a long time since a man had handled her like that.

'Good to see you too, Mike!' she replied.

He put her back down and planted his lips straight onto hers. Valentina's knees buckled slightly, but he didn't notice.

'Can I get you a coffee or anything?' she asked with nervousness in her voice.

'Nah, I'm good! Had a litre of oggin in the car. Bursting for a piss!' Mike explained and quickly walked off to the gent's.

On his return, he sat next to Valentina, his wandering hand placed firmly on her knee. Valentina liked it.

'So, babe, what is it I can do for you?' Mike came across as arrogant, but Valentina found it a turn on.

She curled the ends or her hair with her fingers. 'Well, it's complicated and strictly confidential.' She looked into his eyes, and he understood her seriousness, removing his hand from her leg.

Valentina then went on to explain the entire situation, knowing that she could trust Mike. He sat back for a second, thinking. *What's he thinking?* was the only thought that crossed Valentina's mind.

He looked her in the eye. 'I'll do it,' he said, 'but...' *There's always a but,* Valentina thought to herself. 'I need back-up. This sounds a little dodge, if you ask me!'

'It's completely off the record, and nothing will come back on you, I can assure you of that,' Valentina stated.

Mike smiled at her, then asked, 'Will I need any weapons?' There was slight excitement in his voice.

'I'll leave that for you to decide.' Valentina left Mike to make up his own mind, knowing full well that he would.

'Okay,' he said, winking, as if to say that he was on it. 'So, when will you need me?' he asked.

'I'm not sure. I'm waiting for him to set the date and time.' Valentina smiled with nervousness.

'Okay, I'm due to go out in four weeks, so as long as it's before then, not a problem.' Mike smiled. Valentina couldn't help but feel an urge towards him. 'So,' he said, 'that's business out of the way. How have you been? Any men in your life?'

'I've been good,' Valentina replied. 'Lonely, I must say, and certainly no men.'

Mike smiled again. 'So, you got any plans for the rest of the day?' he asked.

'No, none. Why?'

He returned a wink, and Valentina giggled like a girl in return. He smiled some more.

A satisfied woman, Valentina drove back to Cardiff. Mike had always been able to press the right buttons, and she had needed it. A little escapism never hurt anyone, and she smiled, tapping the steering wheel to the songs blasting from the car radio. Eventually, she arrived back at the hotel.

'How did your meeting go?' asked Tammy, not actually knowing why Valentina had arranged to meet Mike. The less she knew the better.

'Let's say... fulfilling.' Valentina smiled.

Tammy appeared shy. 'Good to hear! Been a while since I've been with a man,' Tammy replied.

Valentina bypassed her comment, not wanting to go into detail. 'Anything from Scientist83?'

'No, nothing. I've been so bored,' said Tammy. Valentina noticed a shift in her tone. She was talking differently and Valentina became concerned.

'Nothing?'

'No, nothing. Why do you question?' asked Tammy.

'Why do you question me questioning?' said Valentina, now pushing the boundaries. 'You seem... a little on edge?'

'Just anxiety about all this. If I'm honest, I feel a little scared,' said Tammy.

Valentina raised her brow. 'It'll be fine. Relax, this will be over soon.' She no longer trusted a word Tammy was saying.

'So, when you meet with Scientist83, will I be coming?' asked Tammy.

'Definitely not!' shouted Valentina. 'I will not be putting you in that situation. Once I've met with him, all this will be over, and you can have you life back.' She was now testing Tammy.

'What do you mean?' asked Tammy.

'Trust me, the less you know the better.'

Tammy stood and began pacing the room. She appeared agitated, and Valentina picked up on this straight away.

The sound of the chat notification caused both of their adrenal glands to become stimulated, putting them on edge. Tammy walked over to the PC, logging back on, with Valentina following closely behind.

Scientist83: "0600 hours, peak of Pen Y Fan."
*Scientist83: **IS NOW OFFLINE***

They both looked at each other and the hairs on Tammy's arms stood on end. Adrenaline surged through Valentina's veins.

'I've got to make a call,' said Valentina, leaving the room and quickly stepping outside.

'Mike, it's me,' she said.

'Hey babe!' he replied.

'Zero six-hundred, peak of Pen Y Fan,' she informed him.

'We'll be there.'

'What's your plan?' asked Valentina.

'We'll make our way up there in the early hours and wait.'

'Okay great. Wait for my signal, okay?'

'Will do babe. Stay safe. We've got your back.'

'Thanks Mike, this means so much to me.'

'Not a problem. Let's say, when this is all over, you and I rekindle our relationship from where we left off.'

Valentina paused, feeling excited but not wanting to seem too keen. 'Let's get this sorted first and we'll go from there?'

His tone flattened slightly. 'Okay babe, stay safe!' he replied and hung up.

Valentina gripped her phone with excitement, then reality struck her with the thought of Scientist83 and what could go wrong. From experience, these things never fully went to plan.

Valentina's alarm sounded at 03.00am. She was already awake, as she had not been able to sleep from the worry of what was about to happen. She got up and ready, then walked out of her room to make a coffee to find Tammy was already up.

'Let me come with you?' asked Tammy.

'I can't,' replied Valentina, rubbing her face and trying to eliminate her fatigue.

'I'll be in the background!' said Tammy.

'No chance, it's too risky! You've done your bit. It's now time for me to do mine. Stay here and try to relax. I'll be back before you know it.'

Tammy sighed, but she understood the risks.

It was dark and cold as Valentina stepped out of her car into the carpark at the bottom of Pen Y Fan. There were a few cars around but no one to be seen. She put on her hiking boots and a black Helly Hanson winter coat, then opened her boot. She pulled out a survival kit and a rucksack, donned a woollen hat and placed a scarf around her face. She was ready for the hike.

The wind was sharp, and the conditions were bitterly cold. Valentina's torch only lit up the first ten feet in front of her. Mist blurred her path of vision as she started her ascent. Her eyes watered from the cold air and she felt slight confusion as she tried to navigate her way up the stony path.

The first ten minutes were hard. Valentina struggled to catch her breath, but as her heart rate increased, she became more comfortable. The sound of the wind was loud as it battered her ears, with the occasional sound of the trickle of water from a nearby stream. The sky was clear with a cluster of stars above her head. She couldn't help but think that heaven must be up there, and then she thought of her mum watching over her.

'I love you, Mum,' Valentina said out loud. 'If this goes wrong, I'll be seeing you soon, but please watch over me and protect me. I'm scared.'

She pretended to hear her mum respond, which gave her comfort as the wind howled and whistled past her head. The cold bit at any exposed flesh, but she ignored it.

Valentina then spoke out loud, 'Roberts, my dear friend, I miss you. I think about you all the time. This is for you.' Emotion took hold and she cried for him, thinking about their working life together; happy times, near misses, times when he'd saved her life, times she'd saved his. 'Sorry I couldn't protect you,' she said. She felt warmth, unsure whether it was in her mind or not, but either way it gave her comfort.

Forty minutes later, Valentina reached the top. It was deserted, cold and windy, but the sky was still clear, and the weather had been on her side. She looked around and took in the view, peering at orange glows in the distance and working out which was Cardiff.

Valentina approached the stone head at the peak and took a seat. Unsure of her feelings, she waited for Scientist83. She was an hour early, but knew he'd be ahead of her. She sensed eyes on her, and she could feel Mike close. She trusted him and knew he was watching over her, giving her comfort. Valentina sat and waited.

Another forty minutes later, the sound of the gravel crunching underfoot startled her, breaking her relaxed state. A dark figure walked towards her, fully kitted out for the environment with a full-face balaclava. Valentina's body tensed at the sight, which caused her breathing to become heavy. She swigged water from her bottle as the figure approached. Her hairs stood on end. *This is it!* she thought as adrenaline took over her insides. She felt brave and ready, and she stood as the figure drew near.

There was a thud and a gasp of breath as the figure suddenly fell to the ground. Valentina froze.

'It's a hit!' shouted a voice and three more figures made themselves visible. Then she heard words that gave her immediate comfort.

'You okay, babe?' asked Mike, sounding calm and relaxed.

'You shot him?' she asked.

'We had to. He was going to kill you,' said Mike as he stepped into view.

'How did you know?' Valentina's voice was breathless.

'We've been watching him since he turned up three miles away.'

'But we now have a dead body?' she asked.

Mike placed a hand on her shoulder. 'We do, but it's better than yours,' he replied with a smile, with seemingly no remorse for killing a man.

The four of them walked over to Scientist83. He was slumped face down on the floor. The metallic smell of the blood pouring from his head was prominent.

'Would you like to have the honour?' asked Mike, holding out a hand as a gesture to remove the balaclava.

'No, you do it!' Valentina replied.

Mike walked over and ripped the balaclava off the body without concern. Valentina gasped at the person underneath.

'You know him?' asked Mike.

'Very much so,' she replied as she stared at the lifeless face of Russell Davidson.

29

Valentina returned to the hotel room. Her feet were sore from the hike, with blisters as big as her feet causing her issues. Her phone beeped notifying her of a text message, which she ignored as she wandered around looking for Tammy.

The computer equipment was gone, along with all Tammy's stuff. Valentina made her way down to reception, where she was informed that Tammy had left first thing that morning. That's when it hit Valentina; her suspicions had been right.

Valentina went back up to the room and collected all her things, not wanting to stay in the hotel a second longer. She checked out, to find that Tammy had already settled the entire bill, which she found strange. *Why would she do that?*

Valentina became overwhelmed by a there's-no-place-like-home feeling as she stepped over the threshold into her house. It was warm due to the fact that she'd left the heating on, and she decided to run herself a bath as she unpacked.

Her phone started to ring. It was the Chief Constable of South Wales Police.

'Valentina, do you know anything about this?' he asked.

'About what, sir?' Valentina replied.

'The body of Russell Davidson found at the top of Pen Y Fan?' His tone was somewhat light-hearted, urging her to deny any knowledge.

'No sir, what's happened?' Her ignorance was obvious.

'Come down to the station in the morning. I have some good news for you.'

'Will do, sir,' Valentina replied, hanging up, then stripping off to take a long hot soak in the bath.

The next morning, she was greeted by the chief constable at the station.

'Nice to see you where you belong,' he said. 'Follow me.' He walked her to his office. 'Take a seat,' he gestured.

Valentina sat, feeling slightly nervous at what he needed to tell her.

'Russell Davidson was found dead, assumed murdered, at the top of Pen Y Fan. I trust you don't know anything about it?'

Valentina shook her head. The chief knew the truth, but he didn't want to know. 'Okay, what happened?' she asked.

'He was shot in the head with a military issue 5.56 calibre bullet. We searched his home.'

'Okay?' Valentina said, shifting nervously in her chair.

'He's Scientist83, the man you've been looking for. We now have all the evidence we need to prove Tommy McGregor's innocence. Tommy's being released today. Thought you'd like to go and pick him up from the prison. We need to go through a few things with him first, and he's going to need your support.' The chief smiled at her.

'You mean I'm back?' Valentina asked eagerly.

'Indeed, you are.'

'Thank you, sir,' she said, smiling from ear to ear.

'But,' he said, holding up a finger.

'Yes?' she asked.

'The McGregor case is now over, and I don't want you looking into it anymore!'

Valentina smiled. 'You have my word!'

She stood and walked into her office. There was a display of balloons and a large cake with her face printed on the icing. She smiled, feeling overwhelmed, and picked up the photo of Roberts and his wife, kissing it with relief.

'It's over Roberts. We got him!' Valentina said with a smile, then placed the picture back in its rightful place. She then checked her phone, remembering the text she had received last night. It was from Mike.

"Hi babe, it's only me. I can't help it, and don't freak out, but I still have all my feelings for you. Please call me."

She grinned at the words, feeling there was a happy ending for everyone. She replied to the message.

"There's a few things I need to do, then I'll be in touch. Don't go anywhere!"

Her phone rang and she answered. 'Valentina.'

'McGregor is ready for collection.'

'No problem, I'll go and pick him up now.' She replaced the handset, collected her keys and made her way to Swansea Prison.

Tommy was standing there, looking a little glum, holding a carrier bag of all his belongings whilst waiting for Valentina. He lit a cigarette, dragging the smoke deep into his lungs, then exaggeratedly blowing it out. He looked up at the sky and saw the birds flying about above his head. It was only then that the sense of real freedom hit him. He could go anywhere and do anything he liked without anyone even telling him what time he had to go to bed.

Valentina pulled up outside the prison, parking opposite Tommy whilst simultaneously winding down the passenger side window.

'You getting in McGregor?' asked Valentina with a joyful tone in her voice.

Tommy looked over and smiled. 'Of course.' He opened the door and climbed in, placing the carrier bag between his feet.

'How are you feeling?' she asked.

Tommy stared out of the window at all the passers-by, thinking how life just goes on. 'Not too bad, thanks. Glad to be out of that shithole!' he exclaimed.

Valentina raised her brow. 'I'm not surprised, considering the hassle you've had.'

Tommy didn't look at Valentina as she continued to drive. 'So, who was it,' his head turned, 'behind all this? Who made me do all those things?' There was a sadness in his eyes.

'I'll explain all back at the station. I'm required to give you a de-brief to provide you with some clarity on all that has happened.' Valentina became more serious.

'Okay,' he replied and turned to look out of the window again. Driving through streets had never been so interesting.

At the station, Valentina took Tommy into her office, feeling it would be more appropriate than an interview room. Tommy sat in an armchair placed in the corner of the room.

'Can I get you a drink?' Valentina asked.

'A pint of beer will do me,' Tommy replied with a smile.

Valentina couldn't help but wish she could give him a stronger drink, but he'd need to wait until he got out of the station for that. 'I'll get you a coffee, then we'll make a start.'

She returned with two cups and took a seat on the chair next to him, where she began to explain all that had happened; Davidson, Tammy, and the tragic news about Roberts. Tommy shifted in his chair as he listened to the details, finding it difficult to take it all in.

'So, you're telling me the freak made me do all those things?' Anger boiled his blood. This man had ruined his life and many others on the back of it all.

'The freak as in Anderson?' Valentina asked. Tommy nodded. 'I'm afraid so, Tommy, but he's also passed away.'

Tommy couldn't help but deliver a little smile at the news of Anderson's death. At the same time, he thought that had been the easy way out, rather than going through the system being punished.

'What about any form of compensation, you know, for my false imprisonment?' Tommy asked, sitting back in the chair, looking into Valentina's eyes and waiting for her to respond.

'Yes, there will be a form of compensation. That won't be anything to do with me. However, I can put you in touch with the team who deal with that side of things.'

Valentina finished going through the fine details of the case, bringing Tommy up to speed with all that had happened.

With his mind processing all that information, some of which he wished he didn't know, Tommy didn't feel any better. He walked out of the station and made his way back to his apartment, which was only a twenty- minute walk.

The door to his apartment jarred on the first push, then opened. The place smelled fusty and damp, followed by a vulgar smell of something rotting. He moved around the flat, memories of his previous life hitting him straight in the face. The last time he had been there was with Emily, and now she was dead at the hands of Anderson.

Tommy noticed a broken picture turned upside down on the floor. He picked it up, with the broken glass falling from it. It was a picture of Tommy and Taylor; a happy memory they had once shared. A numb feeling came over him as he remembered the good times and also the horrendous times. He had an urge to visit Taylor to see how she was, and he hoped, with the breaking news of his false imprisonment, she may be able to forgive him.

He knocked on the door to Taylor's house. The last time he had been there, he had murdered her mother and disfigured Taylor's face, although he had no memory of any of it happening. The door opened cautiously and Taylor peered out. There was a pause as the two of them stared at one another, shocked at the sight standing in front of them.

Taylor looked prettier than ever. Her hair was cut differently, with a fringe covering her forehead, masking the horrendous scars Tommy had left there. Her eyes had a glint in them as they filled with tears.

'D,do you want to come in?' she asked with a stutter.

'I'm not sure,' Tommy replied, hopping from one foot to the other as awkwardness overpowered him.

'It's fine, please come in, just for a minute?' Taylor stepped aside, allowing him through.

They both sat in the front room, unsure of what to say to one another as a cloud of awkwardness hovered between them both.

'I'm so sorry-' Tommy started to say, but he was quickly interrupted by Taylor holding out her hand.

'Please, don't say that.' Taylor's eyes glazed over. 'I've seen the news, and DI Valentina has been round explaining everything. I really don't want to talk about it, is that okay?' A tear rolled down Taylor's cheek.

Tommy wanted to wipe the tear away but was too scared to get too close. He just watched the tear roll down her pretty face and drip down onto her neck.

'You been up to much then?' Tommy asked, a slight quiver in his tone.

Taylor shrugged, 'Not really. I've been back in work a few months now, and it's going well. Other than that, not much really. I just like to keep myself to myself these days.' Taylor then tucked her feet under her bum.

'I only just got out of prison today. I'm not sure what to do!' Tommy bowed his head. It was clear to Taylor, despite being proved not guilty, that his shame was still there.

After half an hour, Tommy felt he'd stayed a little too long, and he didn't want to push things with Taylor, as it must have been a shock already with him just turning up at her door.

'I'm going to go now,' he said, 'but please stay in touch.' He gave her a partial smile, but there was an element of sadness in it.

'Okay, yeah, of course. Come round any time. It's been nice to see you.'

Tommy stood and left quickly, holding back the intense emotion that was building up inside him. As soon as he stepped outside and the door closed, he burst into tears.

Tommy decided to clean his flat throughout, bought new bedding, and changed things around to make it look fresh, ready to start his new life. He picked up the carrier bag from the prison, took out his phone and threw the remainder of the items in the bin.

Tommy charged his phone, but hesitated to turn it on, as he was scared of what might have been on there. He held off, deciding to watch a film to lose himself for a couple of hours and take himself away from the reality of his life.

After the film, he found the courage to turn on his phone, switching it straight to flight mode to stop any unwanted messages coming through. He made a note of any numbers of old friends he wanted to keep, then removed the SIM card, destroying it. *A new life, a new number.*

The following day, Tommy made his way into town to get himself a new phone. Some passers-by gave him a look, and he wasn't sure if he was being paranoid or not.

Once he had bought his new phone, he then decided to get himself a haircut and some new clothes. He grabbed a coffee and sat thinking about what he was now going to do with his life. He had some money in savings, enough to keep him going for a little while, so there was no immediate pressure to find a job straight away. That was if anyone would employ him again.

Back at home, Tommy set up his new phone, downloading all his previous apps off the cloud. He sent Taylor a text straight away.

"Hey, hope you're ok? Just wondered if you'd like to meet tonight, maybe food?"

The silence in his apartment was broken by the buzzer sounding from the communal door. It caused Tommy to jump, and he hesitated to answer. He built up the courage and picked up the receiver.

'Hello?' Tommy's voice was quiet with scepticism.

'It's Mum! You going to let me up?'

He picked up on her blunt tone, and every muscle in his body tensed up, fear taking hold of him. Tommy had become a fragile man. He didn't say anything, but pressed the buzzer to release the door, allowing her up.

Tommy stood in the doorway as anxiety built inside him. His chest felt compressed and his palms sweaty, listening to her footsteps as she climbed the stairs. She came into view. Tommy didn't know what to feel.

'Hello Tommy,' his mum said. She looked withdrawn and cold towards him.

'Mum.' He moved aside as she walked into his apartment, walking straight past him into the lounge with the expectation for Tommy to follow. *Who does she think she is,* he thought to himself.

Tommy followed her into the lounge. She'd already made herself comfortable, while he remained standing, feeling uncomfortable.

'What brings you here?' Tommy asked.

She looked at him with raised eyebrows. 'Why do you think?'

Tommy was taken aback by her attitude. 'You tell me! I've not seen you since I was sent to prison!' Sadness was written all over his face.

'We need to talk. You've shamed us,' his mum paused, her face filled with anger, 'me and your father.'

'Can you leave, please?' Tommy asked, not wanting the third degree when she had no understanding of what had actually happened.

'I will be in a second. I've come round to let you know, we don't want any contact with you. You're dead to us.'

Tommy buckled at the knees from his mum's words, forcing him to take a seat. 'That's fine,' he replied. 'I've written you both off already.' He stood again and walked to the lounge door. 'I'm going to go into my bedroom. I want you to leave. No goodbyes, nothing.'

Tommy lingered in his room with the door shut, waiting for the sound of the front door to close. As it slammed shut, he burst into tears, feeling lonely. He had no one.

After a moment of heartache, he returned to the lounge and picked up his phone. There was a message from Taylor.

"Hello, I would really like that. Call me later and we can arrange."

Tommy felt a sense of happiness; something he'd not felt in a long time. He didn't reply straight away and thought about what he was going to say. He imagined how the dinner would go. *Is this the start of "us" again?* he thought to himself.

30

Tommy's palms were sweating as he waited for Taylor down at Cardiff Bay. He stood outside Nando's, pacing the footpath. *Will she turn up?*

He saw her in the distance walking towards him. She looked beautiful and radiant, lighting up the night sky. His feelings for her came racing back. *I love her,* he thought to himself. She drew closer, her smile wide, filling him with happiness and butterflies fluttering inside his tummy. Then the unexpected happened.

Taylor threw her arms around him, drawing him close and tight. There was a magnetism pulling them into each other.

She turned her head and whispered in his ear, 'I love you.'

Tommy felt overwhelmed. He pulled her closer, but it was not close enough. He felt her love for him transferring, pulling at his heart. 'I love you too,' he replied with a wobbly voice, fighting the urge to cry.

They separated, looking into one another's eyes. The passion was overwhelming for them both as they absorbed one another. They smiled and Tommy thought he had never felt so happy.

The pair sat opposite each other in the restaurant, constantly smiling. Food was placed in front of them, but they couldn't take their eyes from each other. The connection was intense;

something they'd never felt before. All this adversity had brought two soul mates closer together and nothing could come between them now.

The night progressed, and they laughed and cried as they slowly walked back to Tommy's apartment, which was once their home together. They both needed and wanted each other, feeling intense overwhelming urges that felt natural and meant to be.

They made love all night, like never before. The connection between them was like two planets colliding with an intense explosion.

The next morning, Taylor awoke first. She looked over to see Tommy sleeping soundly and she grinned, feeling happy. She decided to wake him, as she missed him while he slept.

'Good morning,' she said, her voice sweet and soft.

Tommy stirred and opened his eyes, looking deep into Taylor's. 'I love you,' he said.

'I love you too,' Taylor replied.

'This is only the beginning, babe,' he said, looking into her eyes.

'It is,' she said with a smile, 'but,' she paused, and Tommy looked worried, 'we can never talk about before. This is a new start, a new beginning.'

He smiled at her words and pulled her close. They kissed intensely, regardless of their morning breath. They then separated looking up at the ceiling, overwhelmed.

Tommy felt great. He hadn't expected this. He'd thought he was destined to be alone for the rest of his life, but now he had Taylor, and nothing could affect them. They could get through anything together.

Taylor served coffee in bed. They laughed together, finding light humour from some of Tommy's stories of prison. He then looked at her, closed his eyes, and it came over him suddenly...

one of his headaches took over his mind. The pain was intense. He screamed, not being able to take the pain. Taylor was scared, frozen, watching the agony as it took control of his body.

She stared at the screen, a smile stretched across her face as she took control. *The fool,* she thought to herself. *He downloaded the IPEA app on his new phone. Some people never learn.*

Tammy watched as she began the next phase of her plan, directing Tommy's actions, evilness flowing through her brain cells. She was clever. She had beaten the system. She'd got away with it, and every fool involved had fallen for her facade of kindness, as though butter wouldn't melt.

A sociopath should never be underestimated! thought Tammy, taking control of *Black Matter.*

Biography

GD Parker is the author of his debut novel, Black Matter. Book one of a three-part series that explores the depths of the unfolding high-tech world we now live in, making it a dangerous place.

The novel is available to purchase in e-book and paperback formats on the Amazon store.

Gareth was born in the UK in 1981. A family man spent much of his working life in South Wales working in a professional capacity. One day he made the decision write about an idea he dreamt about.

Still working full time for a large organisation, he enjoys reading all manner of books, and spending time with his world, his family.

If you would like to connect with Gareth Parker, he would be very happy to hear from you:
Instagram: @gp.parker_author
Twitter: @GDParker_Author
garethdparker81@outlook.com

Acknowledgements

I hope you all enjoy my debut novel "Black Matter" I dreamt this idea for a book and having mulled over the idea for almost a year before I decided to put pen to paper (as they say) I fully enjoyed the journey of writing this book, it's been a tremendous experience and I am so excited to have this published after so long.

There are a few people to thank. First and always, my beautiful wife, Beth. She's a constant source of love and encouragement which is invaluable as I took the step to reach into the depths of my mind to write my first novel. My two boys who I love and cherish with all my heart that bring me nothing but joy and happiness.

I would also like to say a special thank you to my editor, Vicky Swann, who has made me sound literate with her invaluable work as she guided me through and helped towards the first of three books.

34945802R00193

Printed in Poland
by Amazon Fulfillment
Poland Sp. z o.o., Wrocław